Praise for Jill Eileen Smith

"Smith excels at writing fiction that brings women in from the margins of biblical history and allows their achievements to shine."

Booklist

"Jill Eileen Smith is a master storyteller and really keeps the reader captivated."

Life Is Story

"Smith's stories are always exciting; she puts our imagination into full gear."

Interviews & Reviews

"That's one thing I love about Jill's books: she takes biblical people or stories I think I know and gives them layers that make them even more real."

Christian Fiction Book Reviews

"Jill Eileen Smith's writing is superb."

Urban Lit Magazine

"The author does a wonderful job capturing the time and place and helping us understand an ancient culture."

Evangelical Church Library Association

DAWN of GRACE

Books by Jill Eileen Smith

· THE WIVES OF KING DAVID ·

Michal

Abigail

Bathsheba

· WIVES OF THE PATRIARCHS ·

Sarai

Rebekah

Rachel

· DAUGHTERS OF THE PROMISED LAND ·

The Crimson Cord

The Prophetess

Redeeming Grace

A Passionate Hope

The Heart of a King

Star of Persia

Miriam's Song

The Prince and the Prodigal

Daughter of Eden

The Ark and the Dove

Dawn of Grace

When Life Doesn't Match Your Dreams

She Walked Before Us

DAWN
of GRACE

Mary Magdalene's Story

Jill Eileen Smith

Revell
a division of Baker Publishing Group
Grand Rapids, Michigan

Library of Congress Cataloging-in-Publication Data
Names: Smith, Jill Eileen, 1958– author.
Title: Dawn of Grace : Mary Magdalene's story / Jill Eileen Smith.
Description: Grand Rapids, Michigan : Revell, a division of Baker Publishing Group, 2025.
Identifiers: LCCN 2024018370 | ISBN 9780800744793 (paperback) | ISBN 9780800746841 (casebound) | ISBN 9781493448739 (ebook)
Subjects: CYAC: Mary Magdalene, Saint—Fiction. | LCGFT: Christian fiction. | Bible fiction. | Novels.
Classification: LCC PS3619.M58838 D39 2025 | DDC 813/.6—dc23/eng/20240429
LC record available at https://lccn.loc.gov/2024018370

25   26   27   28   29   30   31   7   6   5   4   3   2   1

To those who long to be healed and set free from physical, emotional, mental, or spiritual bondage. May you find hope in the gracious touch of Jesus our Messiah, who loves you more than you can begin to imagine.

PART ONE

The Twelve were with him, and also some women who had been cured of evil spirits and diseases: Mary (called Magdalene) from whom seven demons had come out; Joanna the wife of Chuza, the manager of Herod's household; Susanna; and many others.

Luke 8:1–3

Prologue

———— AD 21 ————

I t's this way, Mary. Come on!" Susanna shouted above the
noise of the wind whipping off the lake. Her long legs had
already carried her several paces ahead of me. I couldn't
keep up with her with the storm coming, no matter how hard
I tried.

"I'm hurrying!" I yelled, the wind whisking my words from
me. I placed a hand on my head to keep my scarf from flying
away, lifted my robe with the other hand, and ran harder. Why
had God made me so uncoordinated and spindle-legged at eight
years old when Susanna was able to do anything at the same
age? It wasn't fair.

"Why do we have to run?" I stopped, bracing against a sudden gust. The waves of the Sea of Galilee churned a short distance from us, and the wind forced me to catch my breath.

Susanna stopped and waited. I half ran to meet her.

"Why did we have to come today? I want to go back!" I
shivered at the dark sky. Thunder rumbled. I raced ahead to
the copse of trees and clung to one of the trunks.

"Stop worrying. It's just a little wind. Besides, if it's still there,
it will protect us." Susanna gave me one of her know-it-all looks.

"If what's still there? I don't like this, Susanna. What are you talking about?"

"Stay there while I look for it," she said around a mouthful of scarf the wind had shoved across her face.

I laughed at how she looked, but she didn't pay me any mind. She knelt in the dirt near the palm tree next to mine and began digging. The sprinkle of raindrops reached me through the trees, and I smelled the fresh earth mingling with the fishy scents of the sea. I loved watching the sea when it was calm. But I feared its unpredictable, violent waves. I wanted to go home.

"Here it is!" Susanna pulled a small object from the ground, brushed it off, and held it up. "It's a figure of one of the gods."

The gods? I stared at it, and my heart pounded. Abba's voice quoted the Torah in my mind. *"You shall have no other gods before Me."*

"You shouldn't have that," I whispered.

Susanna gave me a strange look. "Don't act so silly, Mary. It's only a carved stone. I found it at the water's edge near the rushes the other day and buried it until I found a place to keep it at home. Come on!"

I didn't move, despite my intense longing to run. "What if it's real?"

Susanna walked on, staring at the object. Had she heard me above the wind?

"Susanna!" I shouted.

She turned and looked at me. "What? Come on before we're soaked!"

"Put it back first," I insisted. "You know what the priests say." Little bumps crawled up my arms.

"We aren't going to worship it. No one is going to care if we have it." Susanna lifted her chin, her look determined.

"My abba will care, and he'll be angry. Your ima will too."

We both went to synagogue every week, and my abba was a respected member of the community. I would be in a lot of trouble if he found out I'd looked at an idol. But Susanna's abba was Greek, though her ima was Jewish. Susanna did a lot of things I thought wrong, but what could I say when her abba didn't care and her brother Marcus filled her mind with Gentile things?

"It's pretend, Mary. Like a doll. We can play with it," Susanna said, pulling me out of my thoughts. "Now come on!" She grabbed my arm and tugged.

I followed to escape the storm, running to keep up with her again. "I don't want to play with it," I shouted.

"You have to play with it. I've already named her Hedia," Susanna yelled back.

Rain came in a burst as though the clouds would no longer hold it. I held my scarf against my neck, and we both ran down Magdala's streets and ducked into one of the market stalls. The awning did little to keep out the rain, but it let us stop and breathe.

"You can't call it that. Hedia was my savta's name. I don't want you to use that name." I was angry and cold and cross. "Use *your* savta's name!"

"Fine! We'll call her Livia." Susanna crouched beneath the table, which held loaves of fresh bread, the smell making my stomach growl. I knelt beside her.

The streets were muddy now, and if we ran home, we would slip and fall and be covered in mud. The merchant did not pay attention to us as he spoke with a customer who also waited out the storm. He had at least pulled his awning over the tables to protect the bread. Storms like this might be long or short, so the merchants were prepared.

"What do you think of this storm, Livia?" Susanna whispered loudly.

"Shh . . . don't talk to her," I hissed. I gave Susanna a stern look.

"You worry too much, Mary." Susanna held the idol out to show me. I recoiled. "She can't hurt you. Touch her."

"No!"

"Are you scared?" Susanna was my friend, but sometimes she was so bossy and mean.

I looked away. "It's wrong."

"You *are* scared! Don't be silly, Mary."

Why was she taunting me? A flutter in my middle told me to ignore her and run out into the rain. Flee. But another part of me was curious. Would it hurt to *look* at it?

I didn't want to, but I couldn't help myself. I glanced at Susanna's open palm where the piece of stone lay. It was shaped like a grown woman with no clothes on. Was that all? A carving of a person? Who would want to worship such a thing?

"I told you." Susanna gave me a smug smile.

"We should go," I said, angry to think she'd gotten the better of me.

"It's still raining. No one will miss us yet. Let's talk to her."

"No." But I couldn't make myself leave.

Susanna ignored me and knelt, facing the idol she'd now placed in the dirt. "Oh, Livia, what can you tell us to make Mary smile?"

I tossed a look behind me, but the merchant was talking to the customer. Still . . . "Don't talk so loud," I hissed.

Susanna laughed. "Oh, Mary, you're such a baby! Marcus says idols are nothing but spirits are real. We aren't praying to her. We're pretending, remember? If a spirit like your savta or mine speaks to us, that's real. Why are you always so worried?"

I drew in a breath and looked at the piece of dirty stone. It didn't glisten or draw me to it in any way. Maybe it was a doll. I touched it, then pulled back. The cool stone was smooth beneath my fingers. Of course it wasn't real. Stone couldn't talk to me. Just because someone had shaped it into a woman didn't make it real.

A piece of the fear drained away, and I gave Susanna a small smile.

"There. That's better. Livia made you smile." Susanna laughed and tucked the idol into her pocket. The rain had slowed to a few sprinkles. "Time to go home. Next time maybe she can get my savta's spirit to talk to me. Marcus said we can."

"I don't think your brother should say those things."

I had been promised to Marcus since I was born, despite the fact that his father was a Gentile. I'd asked my abba why, but he would not explain it to me. I was too young, he said. His mother was Jewish, and what his father was didn't matter. But why?

I didn't understand my abba or his religious ways.

"I'm going home." I pulled away from Susanna and her idol.

Susanna grasped my hand before I took a step. The rain stopped and the merchant began to lift the coverings over the bread.

"Don't be scared, Mary." Susanna leaned next to my ear. "Marcus says it's all in fun. We aren't *really* talking to people who have died like our savtas. But don't you wish it was possible? At least, we can *pretend* they're talking to us. It makes missing them easier."

I did miss my ima, or rather what I imagined of her. She had died giving birth to me. My savta had raised me for a few years, but she had died last year, leaving me in the care of our housemaid, Darrah, and Abba, though I rarely spent time with him. I had no idea what it was like to live in a normal home like Susanna did. So why did she need to talk to her savta when she had her ima?

"Don't you?" Susanna asked again, pulling me out of my thoughts. "Miss your savta, I mean?"

"Sometimes. I guess so."

"So you won't mind pretending with me?" Susanna linked arms with me, and we stepped around the bigger puddles, making our way back to our homes.

"I guess not." Susanna would keep at it until she persuaded me.

"Maybe tomorrow?"

"Or the next day." My head was too full of strange new thoughts. Could people talk to those who had died? What would I ask Ima if she spoke to me?

We reached the street, where we parted.

"Promise to meet me tomorrow?" Susanna squeezed my hand.

"I'll try." I refused to give her more, and before she protested again, I ran until I reached the gate to my father's house. Until I was safe.

ONE

————— AD 26 —————

The Hebrew letter *aleph* formed in the clay beneath my stylus. I smiled, at last happy with the result. My father's scribe would be pleased. I studied the dappled light coming through the high windows in the small room where I worked. I dug my feet into the Persian rug. One more word and I would be done for the day. At least as far as I was concerned.

"Why do you need to learn to read, Mary?" Susanna often asked me. While she was busy learning to spin and weave and stitch patterns on cloth, I was stuck in a dismal room, stylus in hand, pressing Hebrew letters into clay.

"My abba wants me to learn how to take over for him one day when he goes the way of the earth." Though I said the words, I never allowed myself to dwell on them. I had already lost my ima and Savta Hedia. I was certain Abba resented and blamed me for Ima's death, but how could an infant cause someone to die? I never thought it fair to be blamed for such a thing.

Worse, my father never tried to make up for the loss of my mother. I needed a woman who loved me, and all I had was my servant Darrah—an old woman, in my opinion—who made sure I was fed and had clothes to wear but never gave me the affection I craved.

I held the stylus over the clay, carved the letters for "Shalom," and pouted. Why couldn't Abba love me? Whenever I tried to embrace him, he took hold of my shoulders and gently stepped back. If I tried to kiss him, he turned his head, refusing the greeting he accepted from others.

A knot formed in my middle as I thought about things I was not able to forget. I set the stylus on the table and pushed away. I didn't want to be here. I tiptoed to the door, opened it, checked the hall for servants, and, finding it empty, slipped out of the room.

I walked on silent feet down the stairs, aware of every sound. No one would miss me once I was gone, I reasoned. No one cared what I did, so why should I sit in that room all day?

I ran to the back door to avoid being noticed and entered the cook's herb garden. Scents of cumin, coriander, dill, and mint filled my nostrils. I loved the various gardens my father kept. My stomach rumbled, longing for a piece of Chana's dill bread, but I didn't want to risk being seen. So I hurried away from the house to the gates of the estate.

I slid past the iron bars meant to add a layer of protection to the grounds. I think they were meant more to keep me in than to keep people out, but maybe that was because Darrah allowed me so little freedom. My father didn't care.

I took the back streets to Susanna's house and entered her father's equally imposing gates and walls encompassing his estate. Our fathers were wealthy in comparison to everyone else, except for the religious leaders and Romans who lived nearby. I should count myself privileged, Darrah said often enough, but I didn't. I wanted a normal family, even a poor one where love was, rather than a wealthy one without it.

I sighed, passed through Susanna's gardens, and knocked on the back door.

Susanna exited quickly, grabbed my hand, and pulled me away from the cooking rooms to the far edge of the wall.

"Why are we running?" I asked when we finally stopped where the gardens ended and trees bordered the brick enclosure. The house was on a rise, but the wall ran along the creek that bordered their land.

"I have news." Susanna placed her hand on the bricks and caught her breath. "I'm glad you came."

"I couldn't stay in the learning room one more moment. Besides, if they check on me, they never ask where I've been. Only Darrah gets upset if she catches me, but she's a servant." I shrugged. "I don't have to listen to her."

"That's all going to change soon." Susanna's dark eyes gleamed. "I have a secret." She laughed.

I smacked her arm. "Tell me!"

She laughed again. "My father and Marcus are coming to your house tonight. They are going to ask your father to sign the ketubah and make their agreement official." She jumped up and held her hands to her heart. She loved knowing things before I did. "Isn't it wonderful? We'll be sisters!"

I stared at her. "I'm only thirteen. I can't marry yet." It was no secret between us that I was not a woman yet, but no doubt Marcus didn't know that because most young women my age were nubile. He would expect to be able to wed soon.

"You will no doubt be able to in a year. The wedding won't happen before then, and besides, you don't have a choice." Susanna lifted her chin.

"I can say no." Defiance rose within me. I crossed my arms over my flat chest.

"Mary. Your father promised you to Marcus when you were

born, and our fathers have been friends forever. He's not going to let you say no." She gave me the knowing smile I detested. "Besides, Marcus likes you. And he can't wait forever. He's nearly twenty!"

"Far too old for me," I insisted. But men often waited for marriage, while women married as soon as they were able to bear children.

"Be glad he isn't an old widower," Susanna said.

I hated when she was right. There were several old widowers in Magdala, and my father might have promised me to any one of them in my early childhood. Marcus was the right age to protect me and not make me a widow before any sons I had could care for me. On the other hand, he was Susanna's brother. I would never love him like *that*.

"Just be prepared because your father might ask you. Make sure you say yes." Susanna touched my arm. "The spirits told me this is a good thing, Mary. Trust me."

I pulled away from her and searched her face. I wrapped my arms about me, suddenly wary of the wild gleam in her dark eyes. "You shouldn't listen to them. Why did you ever let them in?"

Susanna's interest in idols and spirits had never waned. Not since the day she had introduced me to one when we were eight. The spirits made her unclean, according to the rabbi, but she hid her uncleanness well.

"You know why, Mary. They tell me things no one else knows. They are powerful. They protect me . . ." Her voice dropped off.

Susanna had been hurt by a friend of her father's when she was seven. I shuddered at the memory of her tears. The man had made her promise not to tell anyone, but she had told me. I'd never forgotten, and I was glad Barukh, my father's scribe, and the other men my father dealt with paid me little mind.

I didn't want what Susanna had, even if the spirits did make her feel she had some kind of power over her circumstances. I didn't want to have that need.

"Please tell me you'll say yes," Susanna pleaded, snatching my hand between both of hers and squeezing.

I yanked my hand back, but her grip held. "You're hurting me."

She released me. "I'm sorry. I just want you to agree."

I looked beyond her. I loved Susanna despite the spirits. And I liked Marcus. "I guess so," I said at last. "I don't suppose there is anyone else."

"And you have to marry."

I nodded. Most women married. The few who were unmarried had legitimate, lucrative businesses or were prostitutes. Though I didn't understand what that word meant, I understood Darrah, who had warned me it wasn't a good word or a good thing to be.

"I'll say yes," I said. Susanna stepped closer as if to hug me, but I moved back and held up a hand. "If they ask me. I have to go home."

She glanced at the sun's place in the sky. "You should wear your best robe."

I laughed, though it sounded strange to my ears. The realization that Susanna was stronger, truly stronger than I, and we would one day live under the same roof—unless she married first—unsettled me. "It's a betrothal, not a wedding. Besides, my father might not ask me to come into the room when they sign the ketubah."

"You should be there in case." Susanna motioned for me to follow her along the creek, past the gardens, and toward the gate. "Don't mess this up, Mary."

Her warning added to my wariness as I walked away, worried. How could I mess up something over which I had no control?

I did not hurry back to my father's property, despite Susanna's urging. I shook out my hand and rubbed it where it still ached from her hold. If Susanna could hurt me so easily for something so insignificant, what else could she do—might she do—to me if I didn't comply with her wishes?

I'd gone to visit her to have some fun. I didn't want to learn letters in Hebrew or talk about marriage or think about her spirits. I also didn't want to go home. What I really wanted, I didn't have. I wanted someone to love me. But I highly doubted Marcus was my answer to that longing.

I wandered about my father's gardens later in the afternoon. I had not returned to studying Hebrew, nor had I gone into the house. There was no place to go without Susanna. I didn't feel like walking along the Sea of Galilee alone, and I had no money to purchase anything at the shops in the market. I suppose it should have troubled me that I had no friends except Susanna, but none of my father's friends had daughters my age.

I sat on a bench beneath the shade of an almond tree and picked at the petals of a nearby poppy plant. The sun angled toward the west, creating shadows along the walk.

"Mary! Mary? Where are you?" Darrah called from inside the house.

I didn't want to answer her. I didn't want her to tell me about my father's plans for me this night.

"Mary!"

I stood but took my time, kicking stones along the path toward the house. I opened the back door, removed my sandals, dipped my feet into the water bowl meant for feet washing, then rubbed them on a towel. I moved toward the main area of the house.

"I'm here, Darrah," I called, catching a glimpse of her on the floor above me, no doubt about to check the room where I should have been.

She swung around and came down the stairs to meet me. She brushed stray strands of hair from my face. "Where have you been, child? I've been looking for you."

"I was in the garden. I'm here now. What do you want?" I didn't mean to sound irritated, but nothing had gone right this day. It hadn't helped that I'd awakened in an unhappy mood.

Darrah placed her hands on her hips and tsked. "Really, child, you need to listen better and do the things your father asks of you. He doesn't require much. You should work to please him."

I studied my feet. I almost asked why but held my tongue. "Is there something you need of me?" I looked up at her.

Darrah lowered her arms and touched my cheek in a kind gesture. "We need to get you fed and cleaned up. You are having visitors tonight."

"Who?" I wanted to confirm Susanna's words. I still hoped she was wrong.

"Doron is coming with his son Marcus. They are going to sign the ketubah for your hand in marriage to Marcus." Darrah gave me a rare smile. "He is a good man. You will be well cared for."

I nodded, but hearing it confirmed did nothing for me. "Why does my father want this so soon? Marcus is *old*!" I pouted, knowing Darrah would not appreciate my attitude.

She placed a hand on my shoulder. "Come. I've had Elazar warm the water for you. After you are washed and dressed, you can eat. I don't want you looking like you've rolled in the dirt when they come."

Why hadn't Darrah answered my question? I glared at her as I followed her into the small room off the cooking area where I bathed. It wasn't a mikvah but similar. My father had installed it for my ima, though we all used it.

I let Darrah help me, allowing her to wash my long dark hair. It had never been cut, so it fell to my waist, though most of the time I kept it tied up. It took hours to dry, but we had time.

When I was cleaned and dressed, I reclined on the cushions and ate the food Chana set before me. No one ate with me, as the servants ate at a different time and my father never joined me. I hated the loneliness. What would it be like to be married? Would I share meals with Marcus, or would he be like my father and keep me at a distance? Would he expect me to do things Susanna had learned, like weave and spin and stitch patterns on cloth?

A knock sounded on the great door in the center of the house, jolting me out of my thoughts. Voices I recognized drifted to me. So, Susanna and Darrah were right. The men spoke their greetings, but as their footsteps echoed on the tile floors and they entered the room where my father conducted business for his land holdings, I shuddered.

Darrah poked her head into the dining area, where I sat picking at a fresh date. "They're here."

"Yes." I avoided her gaze. "Do you think they will want me to join them?"

She moved into the room. "Maybe at some point. They will work out the conditions of the agreement for the ketubah. Barukh will write them down, and they will press their seals onto the goatskin. Then they might call you."

"So they won't ask me if I want this." I closed my eyes, wishing all of this would go away.

"Your father is going to Rome on business in a few months. He wants to secure your future before he goes." She came and knelt beside me. "I realize it's not what you want, child." She touched my chin, coaxing me to look at her.

A rush of emotion rose within me, and my eyes filled with tears. I blinked, embarrassed.

"Don't fear, Mary. I will be with you until the wedding, and I will stay on afterward if you want me to."

"I want you to," I said, surprised at how much I needed her. I didn't want to enter Marcus's home without her, even with Susanna and their mother there.

"Marcus may want me to stay here." Darrah looked beyond me and let her hand fall to her side. "But he will understand your need of me."

I would have to obey Marcus once we were wed. I had no idea if he would be kind to me or not. He'd acted like an older brother on the few occasions I'd been with him, but most of the time he left me alone with Susanna. Why did he want me to be his wife?

"Mary?" My father's voice came from across the house. "Come here."

I jumped up from the cushion and smoothed my robe, then looked at Darrah. "What do I do?"

"Whatever he asks of you." Darrah patted my shoulder. "Come along."

She walked with me to the room where the men sat on chairs in a circle. Barukh sat near the wall at a table, an ornately designed parchment spread before him.

"Mary." My father motioned me toward him. "Doron has come with Marcus because Marcus is ready to seal your betrothal. I have stipulated he must maintain you for five years. You will wed about a year from now."

I gave my father a quizzical look. "What do you mean?"

"If you should be unpleasing to Marcus, he may not divorce

you for five years." My father's brows drew down. "Make sure that you do not disappoint him, my daughter."

I swallowed. "I won't, Abba."

Rabbis taught that a man could divorce his wife if he didn't like the way she cooked his food. It seemed so wrong, even to my young heart. But no one disagreed with it, so I should have been grateful my father wanted me to be protected until I was old enough to take over his estate should something happen to him.

"And my estate will remain yours in the event of my death. It is your inheritance," he said, jolting me.

I couldn't speak, so I nodded my understanding. I didn't want my father to die. He was all I had.

"Are you ready to set your seal to the ketubah?" my father asked Doron.

"Yes." Doron and Marcus stood, then Doron and my father moved to the table, took their seals, and pressed them onto the parchment.

They hadn't asked me if I wanted this. I stole a glance at Marcus, who looked at me with interest. Why did he want someone so much younger than he was?

But my father was wealthy, as was his. Wealthy people married people of like means. I supposed Marcus didn't have many options in Magdala, though there were other cities nearby where he might have found a better bride.

I dared a look into his eyes.

He smiled at me. A warm, inviting smile.

I let out a breath I didn't realize I was holding. Marcus liked me well enough to live with me as his wife. So be it.

He stepped forward and placed a ring of gold with small rubies on my first finger. "Behold, by this ring you are consecrated to me as my wife according to the laws of Moses and Israel."

Then he draped a finely woven shawl over my head, the golden threads sparkling in the lamplight.

"Thank you," I said, feeling my cheeks heat at his gentle perusal. I could not hold his gaze, though I knew this giving of gifts, the mohar, was part of our custom. Marcus's gifts were a show of his father's wealth.

I glanced from the ring dazzling on my finger to the spark of delight in his eyes. I smiled. This would be a good marriage.

When my father dismissed me, I left the room with a lighter heart. In any case, I had a year to prepare. Until then, I didn't have to think about it again.

TWO

Six Months Later

M ary," Darrah called from the bottom of the stairs, drawing me out of my room. "Come down."

The sun's pink hues were not yet visible, and I was still in my nightclothes. Grumpy and aching from the cycle that told me I was at last a woman, I had no desire to rise from the bed. I squeezed my eyes shut, hoping she would stop calling, but footfalls soon sounded on the floor outside my room.

A knock on the door. "Mary, you must come. Your father is asking for you."

My father? Why call for me so early in the morning? Abba had rarely spoken to me or spent time with me in the six months since he had sealed the ketubah and my fate. I wondered if he was secretly anxious to be rid of me, but the thought hurt too much to dwell on.

"I'm coming!" I swung my legs over the side of the bed, splashed water over my face, and changed my clothes. I didn't have time to comb my tangled hair, but one look in the silver mirror told me I should. What if he had visitors with him at this hour? I glanced at the ring on my finger. What if Marcus wanted to wed sooner than the year we were supposed to wait?

I tugged the jeweled comb through my long locks, tied my hair back with a blue ribbon, and left the room.

"Hurry, child. Why didn't you ask me to help you?" Darrah shook her head at me, but her tone was kind. Still, I preferred to do things myself now that I was a woman.

My cheeks heated at the thought as I remembered the day I told Susanna. She had gushed over the news. "It's about time!" she said. "Marcus will be glad of it."

"You aren't going to tell him!" The idea mortified me.

"Why not? You're going to be his wife. Already are in name." She looked pointedly at my ring and laughed at my discomfort.

"No. Don't tell him!"

She'd been surprised by my forcefulness, but for some reason becoming a woman had not pleased me. Gifts or no gifts, I didn't want to think that in six months I would leave my father's house to marry Marcus.

I reached the bottom of the stairs and lifted my chin as I shuffled toward my father's workroom. I glanced at Darrah, but she stayed behind and motioned me forward. I knocked, a familiar shudder working through me.

"Come in," he called, and I opened the door.

Barukh was sitting at the table, scribbling something on parchment. My father looked up from a letter he was reading, and for a moment I wondered if he had forgotten why he called me. He set the letter on the table and walked toward me.

"Mary." He took my hand in his, and I looked at the dark hairs covering his fingers. "Come and sit." He guided me to a cushioned chair and released my hand. I sat on the edge, my heart pounding with sudden unexplainable fear.

"Yes, Abba?" I'd never seen such a look in his eyes. "Is something wrong?"

He shook his head. "Not wrong, exactly." He glanced behind

him at the table, then faced me again. "I've received word that one of my overseers has decided to move to the Decapolis, leaving me without a replacement. So I must travel to the cities of Galilee to find someone who is qualified to do the work. If I cannot find someone there, I will travel to Jericho or Jerusalem." Abba fidgeted with the coin purse at his belt. "I am leaving Barukh in charge, and Darrah will watch out for you. This comes at a bad time because the harvest is soon upon us." He scowled. I tried to tell myself he was scowling at the man who had quit, not at me, but the heat of his anger jarred me just the same.

"Is there no one in Magdala who can do the work?" I sat straighter, clasping my hands in my lap.

He shook his head. "No one I have interviewed is suitable."

He'd already interviewed replacements? How long had this gone on and he'd not told me?

"When are you going?" I swallowed hard. How did he expect me to inherit a business I did not understand?

"Tomorrow. Doron will also look out for you, and if anything were to happen, Marcus will take care of you." He spoke in such a way it made my insides churn.

"Happen?" The stories of thieves and scoundrels who sometimes waylaid travelers along the road were not a secret. "You are taking servants with you, aren't you? Perhaps several with weapons to protect you?"

Abba laughed. "You are so intense, little one. Of course I will take a servant, but there is no need to fear. I've made the trip through Galilee and Jericho to Jerusalem many times. I will be back in a few weeks."

I nodded. He was right. Hadn't he gone to Rome after my betrothal and returned without incident? The journey had kept him away for months. "You travel so much." My protest sounded shallow. "Might I go with you this time?" I brightened. "I wouldn't be any trouble."

My father considered my request for a moment, but when he frowned, I had my answer. "This is not work for you to trouble yourself about, my daughter. And I won't have time to watch over you while I'm busy interviewing men for this position."

I focused on my hands. On the ring catching the light coming through the windows. I would have loved time with him. I imagined the conversations we'd have if he allowed us to travel together. Nights alone around a campfire. Why did he never have time for me?

I looked up at his touch on my shoulder.

"I have work to return to, so run along now and mind Darrah. Practice your letters or visit Susanna, but be good while I am gone."

I stood and walked to the door. "I'm not a child, Father," I said under my breath as I slipped into the entry area. "I don't need to be treated like one." I glanced behind me, but he was already looking at the letter again and talking to Barukh.

"Come and eat, child." Darrah met me on the way to the dining area.

"I'm not a child," I snapped. "What good is it to be a woman betrothed if everyone still treats me like a child?"

Darrah took the tray of food from Chana and placed it before me. "You're right, Mary. It is too easy for us to still think of you as young, since we are old."

I looked at her. She did seem old to me, but I couldn't say so. Instead, I took the bread and cheese and ate in silence. It didn't matter that my father was leaving again. He was always traveling here or there. I didn't understand why he'd bothered to tell me this time. But I was glad he had. I would ask God to bring him home safely, and maybe when he returned, he would take me somewhere before I was whisked off to marry Marcus. He would miss me when I was no longer living here. Wouldn't he?

Morning dawned again, but this time when I arose, my father was already gone. How quiet the house was without his presence.

I broke my fast alone as usual, then took a handful of coins from a clay jar in my father's office and left for the market. I stopped to get Susanna to join me, but when I knocked on her door, her mother met me.

"Susanna is not here," Nira said, worry lines filling her brow. "She left two days ago and has not returned."

"Not here? Where would she go?" Susanna was always at home unless she was with me.

No. That wasn't true. Sometimes the spirits drove her away and no one could find her, and then she would suddenly appear again, clothes wet or mud-caked and hair a tangled mess.

Nira, my soon-to-be mother-in-law, twisted her hands at her waist. How frail she seemed. "She has these moments . . . you know how she gets. There is no stopping her when she wants to leave. It's like she's driven away from me."

Nira didn't know about the spirits. "Has Marcus looked for her?" My heart pounded with fear for Susanna.

Nira nodded. "He couldn't find her. He left again this morning to roam the hills for some sign."

I glanced behind me, anxious to leave. "Maybe I can help. I'm going to market. I'll look along the way." I hurried off before she could stop me, guilt weighting every step. I should have told Nira why Susanna left as she did. But Susanna had insisted I tell no one of her secret. Even when she came home battered and worn.

I half ran down Magdala's stone streets. Today should have been one of enjoyment, shopping for things for my upcoming wedding with my only friend. But Susanna was proving to be an untrustworthy friend at best. What would I do if something happened to her? She needed help.

I passed the market and made my way toward the Sea of Galilee. Perhaps I would find her walking along the shore or near the trees where she had found the idol she'd treasured so long ago.

Fishermen shouted to each other as they counted their catch from the night before and tossed the bad fish back into the sea. Water lapped the rocky shore, and I stepped with care along its banks, shading my eyes to look beyond Magdala toward Tiberias in one direction, then toward Capernaum in the other. So many people, mostly men, at work from their night of fishing. *Where are you, Susanna?*

I turned to walk toward Tiberias, where some Jews mingled with Gentiles in Herod's town. Idols were more likely there. Would Susanna's spirits have driven her so far?

I stayed near the shore, not wanting to draw near strangers, when I spotted a lone person sitting on a pier jutting into the sea. I squinted for a better look. Susanna? I crept closer.

She turned as if she'd heard me coming, jumped up, and flew toward me, arms raised to attack. High-pitched screaming came from this woman, this creature that I thought was Susanna.

I whirled about and ran, not caring that the stones along the shore snuck beneath my sandals, biting into my feet. She kept coming, screaming all the way. When I reached the safety of Magdala's crowded piers, I stopped and faced her, bracing myself.

"Stop! Susanna. Stop!" I flinched, but suddenly she quieted and sank onto the shore, sobbing.

Wary, I moved toward her and knelt at her side. "Susanna?" My breath still came in short bursts, and my heart beat like a wedding drum.

"Mary?" She lifted her filthy face and matted hair to meet my gaze.

I could barely speak. "What happened to you?" Would she attack me? Or had the spirits quieted at last?

"The spirits sent me away." Tears filled her eyes. "They told me to jump into the sea."

I swallowed hard. Susanna couldn't swim. Neither could I.

"How did you resist them?" Why did I care? I just wanted to take her home to her ima.

"We fought. If you hadn't come by when you did . . . I was going to jump, but they heard you." Her look held gratitude and pain.

"You need help, Susanna. Maybe we should go to a priest—"

"No!" She grabbed my arm. Her nails dug into my flesh. I hated the strength the spirits gave her, wishing that I was strong enough to easily fight her off.

"Stop it!" I jerked my arm back, surprised when she released me.

"Tell me you won't say that again. No priest." Was that hatred in her eyes?

I shivered. "All right. No priest." I rubbed the place where her nails had drawn blood. How did she live like this?

"The spirits aren't always like this," she said, slowly rising. "They protect me too."

It doesn't look like protection to me. I'd never seen the spirits do anything helpful, but then I wasn't always with her. Maybe they gave her power to fight off those who might hurt her, as had happened in her childhood.

"Let's take you home," I said.

She nodded. I walked with her back toward her house. How she would explain her appearance to Nira, I had no idea. But at that moment, all I could think of was getting away from her to the safety of my quiet home.

"Shouldn't your father be back by now?" Susanna asked on the morning of the beginning of his third week away. I had gathered the courage to visit her again after her servant told Darrah that Susanna was asking for me. She wasn't feeling well, the servant had said. I looked at her now from across her sitting room, questioning my good sense.

"You look fine to me. Your servant said you were ill." I glanced at the door to the room, making sure we were alone. "What's going on, Susanna?"

She picked up the spindle and distaff and gave me a disarming smile. "I wanted to see you. How else could I get you to come? Don't tell me I scared you away."

I glared at her. "I've been busy." The lie tasted gritty on my tongue. In truth, I'd been bored without her. She'd been teaching me to spin wool until I was finally able to turn the spindle and distaff without causing it to wobble or tangle the threads. I missed working with her.

"You're worried about your father," she said, arching a brow in a pointed look. "Jericho and Jerusalem aren't far to walk to. He should be back by now."

I shrugged. "Maybe he traveled to other towns as well, if he couldn't find someone in those first two places."

She stared at me for too long, her eyes turning from light to dark as if she were seeing something beyond the place we sat. "We should ask my father to send someone to look for him," she said in a voice not quite her own. "Something is wrong."

A moment passed in eerie silence as I processed the shock of her words. Nothing was wrong!

She shook herself. Her gaze cleared. "You should listen to them."

"No!" Why did I keep her as a friend? But now she was my sister, and I would never escape her spirits.

You should have your own. Then you could withstand her.

I whipped my head about, searching the room. Where had such thoughts come from?

"The spirits speak through me, Mary. They know what they're talking about, and we should pay attention."

I stared at her, unbelieving. "Stop with your spirits! They can't tell the future!" I looked away. "I don't believe them." I jumped to my feet. Her words made me cross, and I stomped out of the room and out of her house.

"Mary, wait!" Susanna ran after me and stopped me in her father's gardens. "Don't go."

I whirled to face her. "You shouldn't scare me like that. My father is late, but he's fine. He might be home right now." The thought made me determined to find out. "I'm going home."

I hurried to the gate, Susanna on my heels. "I'm sorry, Mary. Don't worry about what I said. But if he's not home by tomorrow, please let me tell Marcus."

"There is nothing to tell him. Your father is the one who is supposed to check on me." Never mind that Doron had not visited in over a week.

"Abba has been away too, Mary. That's why he hasn't been to visit."

I glared at her.

"Maybe Marcus can help." Susanna shrugged.

"I don't see how, and I don't think there's anything to worry about. Your spirits are becoming a problem, Susanna. Stop listening to them. All they do is lie to you." I turned about and ran home.

Was Susanna right? She was hard to trust. I worried for her. She tried to tell me the spirits weren't a problem, but where did those thoughts to have my own spirits come from? Did the spirits speak to my thoughts when she was near?

When I reached home and discovered my father was still not there, I paused. Had her spirits known the truth? Was something wrong? Should I do something to find out why Abba was delayed?

I would ask Darrah. If she was concerned, she would ask Barukh to send servants to find Abba. We didn't need Marcus to get involved. There was nothing to fear.

THREE

"Darrah, why isn't my father home yet?" I found her in the sitting room, mending a garment. I sank onto a cushion next to her. "He's been gone three weeks. I expected him home by now."

Darrah placed her needle into the fabric, then lifted her head to look at me. "Do not worry, chi—Mary. Before Doron left on his trip, he told Barukh to send servants to look for your father. We will be welcoming him home with a new overseer any moment now."

I noted the tight lines along her mouth as she spoke. "You're worried." My pulse jumped, and my palms grew sweaty.

Darrah shook her head. "Not worried. It's not like your father hasn't been gone for long periods of time before. We thought it wise to check if . . ." She looked beyond me. "He'll be home soon, dear one. Do not fret."

I didn't believe her. What was she hiding? "I'm going out." I hurried through the door, heart racing, before she could stop me. I was a woman now. I would do what I wanted, for who would stop me?

I ran to the edge of Magdala's border, though I had to force myself to stop there, for everything in me longed to run away from all that held me in this town's grip. To run from Susanna and her lying spirits. Why did I remain her friend? And why did her spirits intrigue me more than appall me? What was wrong with me?

Panic rushed through me as I passed the market. I pulled my headscarf up over my hair and cinched it against my neck. The Sea of Galilee rippled up ahead, but only a handful of fishing boats were visible in the distance. Most of them fished at night, and it was still late afternoon by the angle of the sun. I approached the water where black and gray stones dotted the shore. I slowed, catching my breath. When it was calm, the sea gave me peace. Something I desperately needed right now.

You know why the sea beckons you.

I whipped around. Had someone spoken? But there was no one in sight. Were my thoughts betraying me again?

A shiver worked through me. I walked along the shore to a small copse of palm trees waving their fronds in the breeze. The smell of fish and the tickle of the damp air caused gooseflesh to rise on my arms. I pulled my robe tighter.

I walked aimlessly, my thoughts whirling. What if something had happened to my father? He had to come home. I needed him. My throat clogged with unshed tears and my stomach clenched. I glanced up at the palm trees, a sudden memory hitting me hard.

This was where Susanna had found the idol when we were eight. I had avoided this part of the sea for years afterward, afraid the spirits lived in the trees or more idols were buried nearby. I didn't want to become like Susanna. Especially now. So why had I chosen this moment to come here?

Are you sure you don't want what she has, Mary? She isn't wrong about your father. We don't lie to her.

I nearly jumped out of my skin, spun about, and ran away from the trees. Why was I thinking those thoughts? Had the spirits spoken to me as they did to Susanna? But how? I hadn't invited them to talk to me.

In any case, they were wrong. My father was fine. He would be home when I returned, and Susanna and these voices would be proven wrong. I would not give in to fear that the worst had happened to him. *Please, God, don't let anything happen to Abba.*

Yes. I would pray. The rabbis prayed all the time, and the Pharisees prayed loudly on the street corners and in the marketplace every day. Maybe I should ask one of them to pray for Abba. Surely God listened to their many words.

I picked up my skirts and ran back toward the market, trying to muster courage I didn't have to approach one of the men. Would they speak to a mere girl, newly a woman, like me?

I had to try.

When I reached the market a moment later, I stopped near a Pharisee I had passed on my way to the sea. His eyes were closed, and he rocked back and forth as he spoke our Hebrew prayers over and over again.

"Sir," I said, trying to break in when he paused.

He continued praying as if he hadn't heard me.

My hands clenched the belt of my robe, twisting it, my nerves on edge. "Sir," I said again, louder this time.

He stopped. Opened his eyes and looked about. His gaze skipped off me, and his eyes shut again.

"Please, Rabbi." My desperation grew with my impatience.

He looked at me. "What is it?"

"I . . ." I swallowed past the lump in my throat.

"Well? If you're going to interrupt my prayers, speak up!" His angry tone made me want to crawl away and never see him again.

I drew a deep breath and shored up all my courage. "Would

you pray for my father? He has not come home for three weeks, and we fear something has happened to him." I held my breath, watching him.

He stared at me as if trying to process my question. "Have you kept the commandments, child?"

I nodded. I had, hadn't I? Why would he ask me such a thing?

"Has your father tithed as he should?" he asked.

Why should that matter? "I guess so." I could barely speak. "Will you—"

"Has he been to synagogue and kept the feasts?" he interrupted.

I had no idea what my father did, but in that moment, I realized this man did not care about praying for Abba. He asked too many questions.

"Never mind," I said, heart in my throat. I turned around and ran toward home. Behind me, his chanting began again. I doubted any of his prayers were for my father.

As I approached my father's house, male voices wafted to me from the courtyard. I slowed to a walk. Was Marcus among them? I paused to catch my breath and moved to the gate. Barukh and Marcus stood talking to Darrah and Elazar, the servant my father trusted with management of the household staff.

The gate squeaked as I pushed it open, causing the men to turn in my direction, halting their conversation. I moved closer, my legs weighted, dread pressing against my chest.

"Mary." Darrah hurried to me. She took my hands in hers. "Come, dear one. Sit." She pulled me toward one of the stone benches in the courtyard. I sank onto it as she released me. The men half circled me.

I dared a look at Barukh, then at Marcus. "What is it?"

My heart would stop beating if they said the words I dreaded most. "Tell me."

Marcus knelt at my side and took my hand.

"We have searched for your father," Barukh said. His Adam's apple bobbed in his thick neck.

"The servants have found no sign of him yet." Marcus looked haggard. "It is most unusual, but we are certain he must have decided to travel to another city."

I stared at my husband-to-be and searched for something to say. I pulled my hand from his. "Why would he do that? If he couldn't find someone, wouldn't he have come home first, or sent word? And what of the servant he took with him? Someone must have seen them."

Marcus held up a hand, then lowered it. "They were seen in Jericho. Jerusalem is a bigger city. We will keep searching." His voice trailed off.

"Who is searching?" I would have jumped up, but my knees were too weak. I looked from one man to the next, then searched Darrah's face.

"Elazar led men to look and left them in Jerusalem to continue the search." She glanced at Elazar.

"Why did you return without him?" I glared at Elazar. "You should have stayed until you found him!" My voice rose, and with it, my strength. I stood. Marcus stood beside me. "Take me with you. I will search with you until we return together." How commanding I sounded. But one look at these men who held my fate, and I saw how ridiculous they considered my suggestion to be.

"There is nothing more to do than send more men to look for him, Mary." Marcus looked as if he would do what he must to physically stop me from running off to Jerusalem on my own. Of course, I couldn't do such a thing.

"We have to do more," I insisted. Susanna's claims swam in my thoughts, and I couldn't bear what I was hearing. Then a new idea sprang to my mind. If her spirits told her unknowable things, they should be able to tell me where my father was. If he was dead, they would have found his body. Maybe if Susanna asked the spirits, she would be able to tell the men where to look one way or another.

I was certain my friend would be of more use than the Pharisee who would not lift his voice to pray for my need.

"We only came to tell you and Darrah what we've found," Marcus said.

"You mean what you haven't found." I pressed a hand to my middle, anxious and sick at heart. "What will you do now?" I tried to sound reasonable.

"I will leave again in the morning, mistress," Elazar said. "We will again check all of the cities along the way." He paused. "We'll check with the Roman garrisons. Perhaps he was detained."

"Detained?" I sank back onto the stone bench. The Romans controlled our land, and Abba had often complained about the taxes they exacted from us, but he also kept his distance from them.

"Perhaps your father was mistaken for someone else and questioned," Barukh said. "I don't think so, but it is wise for Elazar to look everywhere."

I stared at the scribe, dread coiling inside me like a living thing. The Romans were worse than Herod Antipas because they held more power. What if Abba had been arrested? But why would he be? My father was an honest man.

"You are welcome to come and stay with Susanna and our mother at our home if you prefer, Mary," Marcus said. "Darrah and the other servants will care for this house."

My thoughts spun faster than Darrah's spindle, and I wasn't sure what to do. But I did want to find out if Susanna's spirits had anything else to tell me. And a part of me wanted to ask them myself.

"I will come." I stood again.

"I'll gather some things for you to take." Darrah rushed into the house. When she returned with a basket holding my nightclothes and some of my ointments, she accompanied Marcus and me to his home, then left me there.

FOUR

Ask your spirits to tell me where my father is," I demanded of Susanna the moment we were alone in her room.

She sat on the bed beside me, tucking her legs beneath her. "I don't want to. You don't want to know."

"Yes, I do!" I was done playing this game. "Ask them!" I hissed. "If he is dead, where is his body?"

"He is in Machaerus, in Herod's prison." Her voice took on a strange sound, like that of an old woman.

"Am I speaking to Susanna or one of her spirits?" I asked, intrigued and anxious at the same time.

"I am the spirit of her grandmother Livia. What do you want me to tell you, child?"

How soothing she sounded. I found myself drawn to her.

"I want him back. How do I get my abba back safely?"

Susanna touched my shoulder as though her grandmother was comforting me. Was this why Susanna had invited the spirits in? Did they comfort her when she was afraid? Especially after she had been so badly hurt in childhood?

"You can't get him back," the spirit said.

I pulled away. "Yes, I can!" I jumped up and paced to the

other side of her room. "Don't tell me that!" I wanted to scream. And weep.

"It's understandable for you to feel this way," Susanna's grandmother said. Susanna walked across the room to meet me and pulled me into her arms. I sensed the warmth of an elderly woman coming through her, and her kindness brought tears to the surface.

She patted my back. "My dear, there is one thing you can do."

I pulled away, and she held me at arm's length. "What is it?"

"If you allow us to join you, we can help you find your father. We can help you break him out of Herod's prison."

I stood still, staring at the body of Susanna with the voice of someone else. "You can help me?"

I mulled over what she'd said. My powerlessness to help my father overwhelmed me. When he was home, Abba made my decisions, and now he was missing. Marcus was already telling me that I could not help as I wished. Once we wed . . . A woman had so little say in a marriage, and I would be living with Susanna's spirits in the next room. At her mercy.

"We can give you power even over Susanna." The voice sounded so assuring. "If you invite us in, you will be strong too."

"You would help me find my father?" The temptation to be equal to or stronger than Susanna grew. She wouldn't be able to hurt me, even unintentionally. But finding my father was what I really wanted.

Besides, Susanna was my friend. I didn't need to fear her. Maybe the idols and spirits weren't so bad after all. This one certainly seemed kinder than the Pharisee I'd met at the market. There was no anger in her tone, like that man had shown me.

"How do I invite you in?" I asked, still warring with the mixed desires. Hadn't I seen Susanna's recent struggles?

And yet, I wanted this. I wanted to help my father escape whatever mess he'd gotten into. I wanted people to take me seriously.

"Ask."

"Who do I ask?" I shivered at the thought of what I was about to do.

"Why not ask your savta Hedia to join you first? She can guide you from there." Susanna's body shook for a lengthy moment, and another voice replaced her grandmother's.

"It's like praying," the new voice said. "Say this: 'Savta Hedia, I want you to be with me always. I miss you. Please live within me so I don't have to be alone again.'"

I repeated the words, thinking how like a prayer they sounded, except they were personal. I was talking to my savta. Not reciting our Jewish prayers.

The moment the last word left my lips, something foreign stepped into my skin. I fell in a heap on Susanna's bedroom tiles, all my strength gone. Savta Hedia took over my body and lifted my spirits, making me light and giddy. I laughed like I had never laughed before, and Susanna joined me. We laughed until our sides ached and it was no longer funny.

And I wondered what I had done and if I would ever feel good again.

I woke the next morning in a strange room. I blinked several times to force my mind to remember, and in a rush the day before returned to me. My father was missing, supposedly in one of Herod's prisons, and I had changed.

What had I done? Had the spirit of Savta Hedia come to live

inside me? I swung my legs over the side of the bed and shook my head, trying to clear it. I didn't want to be like Susanna.

I stood, walked to the washbasin, and splashed water over my face. Light poured through the open window overlooking the gardens below. I went to look, breathing in the scents of lavender and rosemary, and the morning sun kissed my face. My sides ached, reminding me of my fit of laughter in Susanna's room the night before. I had never laughed so hard, and I didn't want to do so ever again.

I would tell the spirit of my savta to leave me. She would have to leave if I didn't want her, wouldn't she?

You don't want to send me away, do you, child? I loved you when I took care of you. I'm here to help you.

I gripped the end of the windowsill as my knees weakened. What was I supposed to say to her? Her quiet weeping filled me with confusion. Two different people warred within me. I couldn't bear to hurt her. But I desperately wanted her to leave.

My better self—was it that?—gave in.

Don't cry, Savta. I won't send you away.

Relief filled me when her weeping ceased.

I moved away from the window and walked cautiously, wary of my balance, to snatch my robe from a peg. I stuffed my nightclothes into the basket Darrah had given me and carried it to the dining area.

"Why are you packed as if you're leaving?" Susanna's mother asked as I took a seat on the cushion near Susanna, who eyed me with a suspicious look.

"I'm going home after we eat." I avoided Susanna's disapproving frown.

"So soon?" Nira placed bread and dates before me. "I had plans to meet with the cook today to go over the menu for your wedding. It's never too early to be prepared." She gave me a smile. I did not return it. Despite the ring on my finger reminding me of my future, marriage was the furthest thing from my mind.

"I . . . we need to find my father first." I broke the bread and took a bite. "We can't have the wedding without him." How on earth was I supposed to get to Herod's prison and break my father out when I didn't have any idea of where to go?

Nira sat beside me and placed a comforting hand over mine. "The men are doing all they can to find him, Mary. But . . . we have to prepare ourselves for the possibility they might not find him."

"He's in Herod's prison in Machaerus." I lifted my chin. "They need to look there."

Nira blanched and sat back, assessing me. "Child, how do you . . . You can't possibly . . ." She glanced at her daughter, then back at me. "Is Susanna telling you tales? No one knows where he is."

"God does." Susanna smirked.

As do the spirits, I almost blurted, but held my tongue.

"Well, certainly God knows everything, but He hasn't shown us what He knows. He doesn't concern Himself with our personal problems."

Why was Nira so certain? Was this why the Pharisee wouldn't pray for my abba?

Don't worry, child. We will help you. Savta Hedia's voice reassured me.

But how? I had no way even to travel to rescue him.

Wait. *We?* I had invited only Savta Hedia. *Who are "we"?* I asked her.

The distinct clearing of a throat came from inside me, and I clamped my mouth shut, fearing it would burst forth. I looked at Susanna, my eyes wide, panic crawling up my spine. I took another bite of bread as Nira and Susanna talked.

What do you mean, "we"? I asked again.

I brought a few others with me, Savta Hedia said. *You don't mind your ima, sabba, and a few other relatives, do you?*

I sat back, stunned. *I didn't ask for others.* I looked wildly about me, but the room clouded. The world was spinning out of control. *How many?*

Six. The voice was not of Savta Hedia but of Sabba Gidon, Hedia's husband when they had lived. I'd never met him, but somehow I believed it was him.

"No!" I cried aloud before I realized it. Nira and Susanna turned to look at me.

"Is something wrong, Mary?" Nira asked. "You don't look well."

"I need to go home." I had to figure out a way to get rid of the spirits before my father returned. What if he wasn't in prison but on his way to Magdala now and he found me like this? How would I explain myself to him?

"You can lie down here." Nira gave me a look of deep concern.

"No. I want to go home." I must get away from Susanna most of all. It was her fault I was in this situation. I glared at her.

"Let me have a servant take you," Nira insisted. "You look too weak to walk."

I shook my head. "I want to be alone." I stood, grabbed my basket, and hurried to the door. "Thank you for the food," I managed to remember to say before I ran off toward the gate.

I couldn't tell who I was fleeing. Susanna? Or myself? I longed to outrun my own thoughts and the spirits, who were one moment arguing, the next laughing, and the next begging me to be a good girl and let them stay.

I couldn't let them stay. The thought grew in force as I ran and finally reached my father's gate. But how could I get them to leave? Could I ask Darrah? Did I dare trust her?

FIVE

M ary, child, what happened? Why are you home so soon? Did you run the whole way?" Darrah's concern helped to calm my racing heart.

Tears sprang to my eyes, and in a spontaneous moment of emotion, I laid the basket on the table and threw my arms around her, sobbing.

"There, there. Mary. What is it?" She rubbed my back like she had when I was a child. "How can I help you?"

"I . . ."

Don't tell her! Are you crazy? She will think you mad and send you from the house. You will wander the wild places and have no food. Don't tell her about us!

The voices all shouted at once, forcing me to put my hands over my ears and try to blot them out.

"Mary! What is wrong? Does your head hurt?" Darrah sounded alarmed now. I had frightened her.

I nodded, unable to speak. She called to Chana for a cool cloth and led me to a cushion. "Sit," she commanded, then placed the cloth Chana gave her on my forehead as if I had a simple headache. "Rest now. Then I want you to tell me everything."

I nodded again, but the voices would not be silenced until I spoke to them. *All right! I won't tell her. But you have to leave me!*

Their arguing turned to wailing. My head pounded harder. I held it in my hands and rocked back and forth, begging God to make them stop. *Help me!* I prayed, but I did not hold out hope that He heard my prayers any more than He heard those of the Pharisee. I'd prayed as a young girl for Savta Hedia to live, and she'd died anyway. I'd prayed my father would be found, and still he had not returned. Maybe Nira was right. God didn't concern Himself with the personal affairs of people.

I moaned and Darrah looked on in silence, refreshing the cool cloths when they grew tepid. A knock sounded on the door. Chana hurried to answer it.

I heard footsteps on the entry tiles. A few moments later, Marcus stood over me. "What happened?" He looked at Darrah.

"I don't know." Darrah's voice sounded distant, overwhelmed by the louder voices in my head. "She came home and started weeping."

Marcus knelt at my side. "Mary." His voice soothed me, and the other voices quieted. "Are you ill?"

I shook my head. "Just a headache." I flinched at the pain that still beat against my forehead.

He studied me. "Susanna often gets those." His voice carried concern, so I looked up, hoping he didn't think me like his sister.

"Why are you here?"

"I have news." He stood. I couldn't make my legs work to join him.

"Tell me." *No, don't.*

Your father is dead. Sabba's voice was quiet, as though he was respecting my sorrow. Ha! The spirits respected nothing.

No, he's not. You told me he was in prison.

"Where is Abba?" I asked, weary.

"They found a body that might be your father's. He was badly beaten and left for dead beside the road from Jericho to Jerusalem." Marcus twisted his hands together. "Servants went to get my father to tell him, and he has gone to check."

I stared at him for a lengthy breath. "If he was so easy to find beside the road, why hadn't they found him before?"

"Our servants and Elazar found him in the brush, hidden by tree branches and scrub bushes," he said.

I swallowed the terror clawing at my throat. "And they are sure?"

Marcus shook his head. "The body had a robe like one your father wears, but . . . it is not fitting for me to describe what they found, Mary. My father will go, and then we will be certain. In the meantime, I'd like you to stay with us. Susanna said you ran off. Why did you come home?" He knelt beside me and placed a hand over mine.

I pulled back, fighting the urge to shake off his hand. I didn't want his help. "I want to stay here." The weight of what he'd said caused me to tremble from head to toe.

"We can help you, Mary. Ima wants you to stay." His look implored me.

We will help you, Mary. The voice claiming to be my sabba sounded so reassuring. But I didn't believe it.

You are a wealthy woman now, Mary. You don't need anything or anyone but us.

If my father was dead, I was now the owner of his estate. But what did I care about money? I wanted my father.

If he is dead, you can ask Marcus for a writ of divorce. You would be free, Mary.

The thought rocked me. Not marry Marcus? But divorce was wrong. I glanced at the ring on my finger. Marcus had done nothing to deserve me requesting such a thing.

He won't want you when he learns about us. The voice of the one claiming to be my ima laughed. It was not a kind sound.

I cringed and held a hand to my head again. I attempted to stand. Darrah's arm held me up.

"Tell me when your father returns," I managed to say, looking at Marcus. I was so tired. I had no desire to think his words were true.

"Are you sure you won't return with me?" He looked so lost that I almost took pity on him. But I couldn't bear being near Susanna again. Not after what she'd done to me. It was her fault I was helpless with no way out.

When he left, I excused myself to my room and lay down. Darrah fussed over me, but I sent her away.

Marcus was wrong about my father. He'd taken a servant for protection. If he was dead, where was the servant? But it made more sense that bandits had killed him than it did for him to be in Herod's prison far from Jerusalem. Why would they imprison him?

You don't believe us, Mary? Savta Hedia wailed in my ear. *We would never lie to you.*

I closed my eyes, refusing to argue with them. Susanna, when she'd been herself, had told me they'd lied to her and she never trusted them. And in the next breath, she wanted me to be just like her. One thing was sure. I almost hated Susanna for this.

If Marcus was right, his father would return with my father's body to bury. And I would be a wealthy orphan betrothed to a man I didn't want to marry. If he saw the truth about me, he wouldn't want me now, that was certain. But I couldn't tell him. Wouldn't tell him.

No. I would ignore the voices and try to expel the spirits and marry Marcus, and all would be well. Or Abba would return and I would still marry Marcus, and maybe Abba would find me a healer. If I dared to tell him.

A week later I kicked the stones along the shore of the sea, my body and mind weighted and numb. The sting of the stones against my bare toes did nothing to rouse me from the stupor. A week had passed since Doron traveled to Jericho in the hopes of identifying my father's body. A week of silence until Elazar had returned, bandaged and haggard, to my father's house.

Darrah had sat him down with a cool drink from the well as the servants and I gathered around him. Marcus joined us, looking worse than Elazar.

"It is bad news, mistress." Elazar glanced at me, then Marcus. "For both of you." He swallowed hard. "I accompanied Doron to check about your father. The body had been thrown into a cave and was so badly decomposed there was no way to tell if it was your father or not. An innkeeper along the road had a leather belt someone had used to pay for a room, and I recognized it as one your father used to wear." He pulled the belt from a pouch at his side.

I gasped, and an icy shiver worked through me, making even my teeth chatter uncontrollably. It couldn't be.

"Dissatisfied with this," Elazar continued, pointing to the belt, "Doron retraced the path from Jericho to Jerusalem. When we neared an outcropping of rocks, robbers came out of hiding, and though we were a sizable group of five men, they attacked us." He stopped again and looked at his hands.

I wanted to scream at him to keep going. Perhaps doing so would drown out the voices in my head.

"Doron and the other servants were killed. I barely escaped to tell you." He held up bloody hands.

Marcus slumped to the floor, head in his hands. I stood, shaking and numb inside. Both our fathers gone? Impossible.

Of course it isn't impossible, my dear, my savta's voice sneered in my ear, and the voice of my sabba cursed both men for their weakness.

Stop it! They weren't weak. Had the spirits killed our fathers? Was that even possible? But of course it was, if other spirits had inhabited the robbers. Many men and women in the land of Judea and Samaria were possessed by demons. They—we—were as unclean as lepers.

My shaking turned to trembling all over, and I could no longer stand. I sank to the floor and clutched my head. I was *not* one of them!

The memory haunted me now as I stepped to the water's edge and picked up a handful of stones to throw far into the sea. Anger grew to rage inside me, nearly blocking my vision of the fishing boats far out on the water. My breath still came fast after I'd run away from my house, leaving Marcus on the floor and Darrah tending to Elazar. They would miss me, but I didn't care.

We told you he was dead. And now you have no reason to marry Marcus. We will care for you at your estate. We are in control now, my dear.

I drew in a deep breath, pulled my arm back, and let a stone sail into the air toward the middle of the sea. Of course, it landed far short of the middle, but the plop still made a circle of ripples.

I would not let the spirits control me. I could not.

But my gut clenched painfully at the thought, and I doubled over and retched onto the shore.

You are ours now. The voice was deep, and I couldn't tell which "relative" had spoken but guessed this one was in charge. And he wasn't "kind" like the first one.

No, I cried. Weakly. *No.*

But they were right. I had lost everything. Probably even Marcus. And most definitely my sanity.

SIX

I opened the front door to the house and entered the cool interior. The sea breezes had been so inviting. I had almost walked into the water, robe and all, but I couldn't swim and didn't want to go too far. When the heat of the day began to blaze, it forced me to face a return home.

Marcus greeted me in the entryway, startling me.

"You're still here?" I looked at him, not knowing what else to say.

"We need to talk, Mary." His voice still held a trace of emotion. I couldn't blame him. I would welcome tears, but I was worn out from battling the arguing voices within me.

"I can't." I tried to sound compassionate. "I need to mourn my father." I walked toward the stairs, but he gripped my arm and turned me to face him.

"I can't leave you here, Mary. I am your husband, and with both of our fathers gone . . ." He looked beyond me. "I'm sending men to retrieve the bodies Elazar was not able to bring with him. We will have a proper burial, and then we will wed."

He just wants your money. He will try to take the estate and lands from you. Watch and see.

"Why do you want to marry me?" I asked, giving in to the voices, longing to prove them wrong.

He took a step back as though I'd struck him. "Don't you know?"

I shook my head, watching him.

"I've always cared for you, Mary. Since you were a child, you've been promised to me." His expression softened. "And I can't imagine anyone else I'd want to marry."

He wouldn't tell me he loved me. If love came at all, it came after years of marriage. Not before.

I nodded. "I suppose that's as good a reason as any." My tone came out flatter than I'd intended. "Are you sure it isn't because I've inherited my father's lands?"

He tilted his head and gave me a curious look. "I am already wealthy, Mary. My father's business dealings have made him well respected in Herod's household as the best jeweler in his circles." He paused. "*Had* made him . . . He was the best, Mary. I have no need of your father's money."

I considered his words, pleased to prove the spirits wrong. Then a new thought surfaced. "Do you think they killed your father for his jewels?"

Marcus shook his head. "He didn't have any jewels with him on this journey. He thought he was going to find your father, not sell his jewels."

I moved to a bench and sat. I wasn't going to escape this conversation, so I determined to get it over with. "Do you think they killed my father for his wealth? He wouldn't have been carrying anything of value on him to interview an overseer. Why would they attack him?" I accepted a cup of water Darrah brought me as Marcus took the seat beside me.

"Robbers hide in those hills all the time. God alone knows

why they attack those they do." He sipped his own water. "We're never going to find those responsible for this, Mary."

"Demoniacs killed them." The voice speaking through me was not mine. *No!*

"Mary? What's wrong with your voice?"

I swallowed, coughed, and put a hand to my throat. "I'm sorry. I had a tickle." I sighed, relieved at the sound of my own voice. Had I imagined one of the spirits spoke through me as Susanna's had?

Marcus regarded me for a lengthy breath. "We were supposed to wait six months until our wedding, but now . . ." He held my gaze. "A week is enough time, after the bodies are in the tomb. Agreed?"

The spirits began arguing. They would never agree. But I couldn't tell Marcus about them. I wanted him to care for me. The truth would ruin all possibility of marriage. "A week."

"Good." He stood, took my hand, and pulled me to my feet. He kissed my cheek.

Heat rushed to my face. Marcus had never done that before. The image of him as my brother faded. He released my hand and left the house, smiling.

I awoke the next day from a series of fitful nightmares. I stared at the ceiling in my room, too exhausted to rise.

A knock on the door jolted me. Darrah poked her head into the room.

An explosion of pain and anger rushed in on me as I flew out of bed toward her. "Did I ask you to come in here? LEAVE!"

Her shocked look at my shrieking should have troubled me, but she whirled about and slammed the door, stopping me from saying more. Her hurried footsteps receded, and I sank back onto the bed. Violent shaking overtook me, and my body convulsed, landing me on the hard tiles. My head banged against the floor, and words I did not understand came from my mouth.

She had no business coming into your private space. You were completely justified. Savta Hedia's high-pitched yelling blocked all other sounds.

"Stop!" I crawled on my knees to the door and held my aching head. Tears came in a flood.

I sobbed until it was hard to catch a breath. At last, the emotion spent, I leaned against the door, but a commotion in the courtyard drew my attention. I forced myself to stand, trembling, and stumbled to the window. Marcus stood talking to Darrah. Had he returned with the bodies already? What was Darrah telling him?

She's telling him all about you. Soon you will be completely alone. No one wants you. The voice claiming to be my sabba sounded so hateful.

I had invited Savta Hedia in, not the others. Why had they all come? Had I somehow allowed them all in without realizing it?

Trembling came again, from my chattering teeth to my cramping toes, and I could not stop the tears. I couldn't lose Marcus, but at the same time I didn't want him in my life. I didn't want him to see me like this. He wouldn't want the real me.

But who would I be without him? Since childhood I'd known myself as his future wife. I needed him to help me.

He isn't going to want you. Why would he help you?

I squeezed my eyes tight, trying to blot out the voice called ima.

She's right, a cousin said. And then they were all arguing again.

I leaned out the window, careful not to be seen, straining to hear.

"Mary is not well today, Marcus," Darrah said. "She's taking her father's death harder than we ever imagined. Might you return later in the week? She needs a week to rest and grieve."

"The funeral for my father will be today. We will honor hers, of course. She needs to be there." He crossed strong arms over his chest, his muscles visible with each movement.

Would Marcus be able to stop me when the spirits sent me into a rage? But maybe today's rage was not normal. Maybe I was just tired.

Darrah hesitated. "I will make sure she is ready."

"I'll be back before sundown." He turned and left.

I needed to dress and make Darrah believe I was fine. Instead, I returned to my bed after watching Marcus walk away. I was so weary. Weary of the voices. Weary of people telling me what to do. Weary of losing everything I loved.

Weary of life.

Had the spirits been with me for only a few days? I was certain I had lived with them for a lifetime.

If I didn't get help soon, perhaps from a priest or a healer, I had no doubt the spirits would overpower me. Susanna might hate the priests, and I did not blame her, but this could not go on for me. I couldn't become like Susanna because then everyone would know the truth, and I would be an outcast. I needed to be rid of the spirits.

You will not make that decision. Don't even try to go against our commands.

My hand moved of its own accord and slapped my cheek, hard. The other hand rose as well. *Slap. Slap. Slap. Slap.* All control left me, and I couldn't stop myself.

I cried out. "Stop! Please!"

But instead of leaving, they forced me to my feet, then threw me to the tiles. My whole body cramped, rigid. Foam came from my mouth, and a piercing wail filled the room.

Hours later, my body went limp. They'd gone silent at last.

Wary, I sat up, testing my limbs, tears streaming down my burning cheeks. Chastened as though I were a little child, beaten down by one of the town bullies and humiliated. And horrified that the spirits were so bold in such a short time.

I had been powerless to stop them. What would I do if they told me to kill someone? Or kill myself like they had told Susanna?

A cold shudder passed through me. Were my spirits stronger than hers?

Marcus was oblivious to all of this. Wasn't he?

Trembling and weak, I crawled to my bed, dragged myself onto it, and curled my body as small as I could make it. Death did seem better than life. Especially life like this. And yet . . . what happened after death? That thought alarmed me more than the spirits themselves.

I wanted to keep fighting them. But I would not say so aloud again. Never again.

SEVEN

After the funeral that night, which I managed to attend despite my exhausted state, I retreated to my room. Darrah tried to coax me to prepare for my wedding at the end of the week, but I had no strength.

I lost track of time. I couldn't eat, though Darrah left food outside my bedchamber twice a day. I did take sips of water, and I took turns pacing the room and attempting sleep.

The spirits had left me blessedly alone after the beating they'd given me the day of the funeral. But now I couldn't remember how many times the sun had risen and set since I'd left my room.

My clothes hung looser, and I cinched the belt tighter about my waist. I took time to clean up in the washroom my father had built for me, but one look in the silver mirror told me I was wan and weak.

At last I descended the stairs, ravenous. Darrah met me in the entryway.

"I need food. Now." I hurried to the eating area, and Darrah was right behind me. Chana placed food on the table before me, and I ate so fast I hardly chewed. When I finished, I asked for more until at last I leaned back, sick. I pressed a hand to my middle.

"Bring her some tea." Darrah gave me a compassionate look I didn't deserve.

I sipped the brew. The spirits laughed at my discomfort. It was their fault I hadn't eaten in days and now ate too much. Nausea overtook me. I jumped up and ran outside, losing the food I had so foolishly eaten in haste.

Darrah stood behind me and handed me a damp towel, saying nothing. I took it from her and wiped my mouth. There was no use trying to eat again.

"Has Marcus been by?" I straightened. "What day is this?"

Darrah shook her head. "I asked him to stay away. He should come today, I think."

Voices from the courtyard drew my attention. Marcus. But who was with him?

I went into the house to meet him and his companion at the door. "Marcus."

"Mary. You are looking well." He looked me up and down and smiled.

He's lying. You look terrible.

I ignored them. "Would you like to come in?"

He nodded, and I allowed both men entrance. As the second man entered, I sensed the spirits were not happy. But they did not speak. Were they afraid of this manservant?

"This is Clopas, my house manager. I'm not sure you've met him. He's come to help us." Marcus moved into the sitting room as though he were already in charge of the place. "Darrah, please call the other servants to join us."

I turned to face him. "What are you doing?"

He put his hand on my crossed arms, his gaze gentle. "Before I take you to my father's house, I need to set affairs for your father's house in order. Clopas will work with Barukh and begin today to go over your father's books and make sure his accounts are up-to-date and his taxes are paid. He will oversee your accounts from now on and keep me informed. I don't want your home to fall into disrepair or arrears."

I stared at him. "Barukh has served my father well, and this is still my home. We don't need another overseer." I stared at Clopas but couldn't hold his concerned gaze. "Besides, I want to stay here after we wed, so I can handle things myself."

Marcus tilted his head, confusion in his gaze. "You are betrothed to me. It is the custom to live with the groom's family."

"Which would have been fine before. But if only the servants are living here, what good is the house? Your mother and sister can have your father's house, and we can live here." I wanted to convince him. I took his hand and squeezed. "Please, Marcus. I'm safe here. And I don't want to move."

"You will be perfectly safe with my mother and sister. I thought you and Susanna were the best of friends. Besides, she will wed soon, and I can't leave my mother alone." He gave my hand a gentle squeeze. "Please, Mary. Try to understand."

I pulled away. I fought the urge to lash out. By now the voices should be screaming at me, but one glance at Clopas made me uncomfortable and kept them silent. I gave Marcus a curious look. "What happened to your father's household manager? Why not let me keep Barukh and you keep whoever you want? We don't need another." I saw the discomfort in Clopas's eyes as he shifted from foot to foot.

"My father's overseer is in need of rest. He is too old to handle such complicated affairs, so I recently hired Clopas. His wife is also named Mary. You will like her." Marcus's look wavered between pleading and controlling, as if he couldn't decide how to treat me or what to say. "Look, Mary, I've spent the week trying to settle things so you would be cared for. Barukh has indicated he would like to move on, and you can't live here alone with your father gone. The sooner you come to live with me, the better. You can give your opinion on what you would like to do with this estate if we have reason to consider selling it, but the day-to-day care would bore you. Let me help you. Then you can spend your days doing as you please. You'd like that, wouldn't you?"

I avoided his pleading gaze. I walked to the window and viewed the garden below. My father's gardens were twice as big as and more beautiful than the ones at Marcus's home. This house belonged to me. I had found rooms to hide in where no one could find me. Places that brought me peace as a child. I wondered if I would ever be at peace again.

But Marcus was probably right. I couldn't keep up this place on my own, and I shouldn't live alone and try to manage servants when I'd never done so before. In Marcus's home I would learn and one day return to take over the care of this place. I would have to convince him to keep it for our children to inherit one day.

Yes. That was what I would do.

I returned to where he stood watching me. The servants entered the room as I spoke. "All right. I will marry you tomorrow and live in your home. But we will never sell this house or the lands my father owned. They will be an inheritance for our children. They do belong to me, after all. They are what I'm bringing to our marriage, and I won't have you taking this from me."

Marcus held up his hands in a defensive gesture. "I have no intention of taking it from you, Mary. It is your inheritance. I only hope to manage it for you well. Will you let me?"

His question surprised me. Some men wouldn't have asked without my father near to defend me.

I expected the voices to say *they* would defend me, but they remained silent. I glanced again at Clopas. He was looking at me with a strange compassion, and I sensed light emanating from him. I took a step back, not sure I liked his presence.

"I will do as you ask. But I don't want to meet Mary Clopas, and I don't want him near me." I pointed at Clopas.

Clopas's eyes widened, and Marcus's brows drew down. "Mary, Clopas is good at what he does. I'm not going to look for another. But who you meet is up to you." He turned to the servants to make introductions to Clopas.

I backed away, increasingly uncomfortable in the room. I wanted to flee, but I didn't want Marcus to suspect my anxious thoughts. The spirits were afraid of Clopas, but I didn't understand why. I needed to get away from him, so I slipped out of the room and outside to the gardens. Tomorrow I would marry Marcus, and no doubt Clopas would be part of my life. I must find ways to avoid him because I could not tolerate the light coming from him.

"Do I look all right?" I faced Susanna, who stood examining my wedding clothes. My robes were woven in bright blues and reds with golden threads throughout. A jeweled headdress covered my hair, along with the veil that would hide my face once Marcus arrived and would not be lifted until he took me to the bridal chamber. My arms were laden with jeweled golden bracelets, and earrings of sapphire dangled from my pierced ears. Pearls intermingled with rubies draped my neck and matched those on the ring I studied on my finger.

The virgin maids from the village waited in the courtyard, but I was in no hurry to join them. Despite the rich clothing my mother had worn when she married my father, there were too many cuts and bruises on my body to hide. What would Marcus say when he saw them?

"You're beautiful." Susanna placed both hands on my arms. "Don't worry. It will be dark when you enter the room with

Marcus. He'll have had too much to drink and the lights will be low. He won't notice . . . anything."

"And do you think Tobias will notice your wounds when your turn comes? I can't believe both men don't realize what's happening to us. How have we been able to hide the spirits from them? Marcus lives with you, yet why doesn't he suspect? Does your mother?"

Susanna shook her head. "My spirits are secretive. They hide from Marcus and Ima. Maybe yours will too." Though she looked doubtful.

"Mine don't care so much." I chewed my lower lip. I still doubted the rightness of this marriage. I couldn't be a proper wife to Marcus. And what would happen the first time the spirits took control of my body and made me do things I didn't want to do? What if they drove me from the villages into the remote places, as they did to some so possessed? What if I couldn't stay "normal" forever? And if I was aware of other un-clean spirits, what would stop people from seeing them in me?

Like Clopas. Was he able to tell something was wrong with me, as I saw the light coming from him? I shivered. Would he ruin my wedding?

I followed Susanna down the steps to the courtyard, unable to get the man from my mind. "What do you think of Clopas?"

Susanna reached the bottom step. "I don't like him."

We walked to the door to the courtyard. "Have you met his wife?"

"Why are we talking about them on your wedding day?" Susanna's voice carried frustration. "Come."

I stepped into the courtyard and took my seat on a dais, irritated with Susanna. I'd asked a legitimate question about a man and his wife who would live on the same estate as me. Why should my question bother her?

The ten virgin maids Marcus had found to attend me drew my attention as they surrounded me and added flowers between the jewels of my bridal crown. They sang the traditional songs to the bride, and as dusk descended each one lit her lamp.

Time passed and the darkness deepened. I grew tired of waiting. Why was Marcus taking so long when he'd gone to so much trouble to hurry the wedding day?

Maybe he's not coming. The voice of Ima didn't carry its usual caustic tone. She sounded uncertain, so unlike herself. What if she was right?

I stood to pace the courtyard, impatience warring with anger inside me. If he didn't hurry, the spirits would say things to make my temper worse. I couldn't stay here. What if I lost control in front of the virgins? I walked from the gate to the door of the house.

"Where are you going?" Susanna intercepted me and gently gripped my arm.

I stopped. "He's not coming. I'm waiting for nothing."

"He's coming. He's waiting for the perfect time." She leaned closer. "Remember, the darkness is your friend."

My pulse jumped as I considered the cuts and bruises. "You're right." I returned to my seat as singing reached us.

"The groom is coming, Mary! At last he's here!" one of the virgins said, holding her lamp high.

As Marcus and his friends walked into the courtyard, the rest of the virgins also lifted their lamps in greeting. I pulled the veil over my face as Marcus approached, and my heart started pounding. He knelt before me, took my sweaty hand in his, and bid me to rise. The entire procession surrounded us, and we made our way through the streets with a crowd following, singing the praises of the bride and groom.

Practically the entire village was waiting to greet us when we entered Marcus's courtyard. How had he managed to convince so many to come in only a week? I shook aside my irritation, no thanks to the spirits' complaints in my head.

The rabbi waited as Marcus led me to stand beneath the huppa, the wedding canopy, in the courtyard. Seven blessings followed. The rabbi's words floated around me but did not penetrate the laughter and taunts in my head.

You're going to hate marriage, Savta Hedia said, snarling. *I certainly did.*

The comment started an argument with my sabba that went on until I wanted to scream. I dared not. I shut my eyes and swayed. Marcus steadied me with his hand on my elbow. The rabbi began the final blessing, and the spirits quieted.

"Blessed are You, Lord our God, Ruler of the Universe, who creates happiness and joy, groom and bride. Exultation, delight, amusement, and pleasure, love and brotherhood, peace and friendship. Soon, Lord our God, may the sound of happiness and the sound of joy and the voice of the groom and the voice of the bride be heard in the cities of Judah and the streets of Jerusalem—the rejoicing of grooms from their huppahs and youths from their singing banquets. Blessed are You, Lord, who makes the groom rejoice with the bride."

Marcus and I shared a cup of wine after this final blessing. I smiled at him, but I was drowning inside. Marcus would never rejoice with me.

Marcus put the corner of his robe over me, oblivious to my misery. He led us into the house, where we would receive guests, drink wine, and wait until he took me to his room to consummate our vows.

I should be excited and nervous. But I was dead inside.

EIGHT

"I have to go to Caesarea." Marcus took a bite of flatbread and goat cheese to break his morning fast. "I'll leave tomorrow morning. I'm not sure when I'll return." He smiled at me, then his gaze skittered to his mother, who served him.

"Again?" I regretted the word the moment I'd spoken it. Marcus often traveled. He supplied Herod's household with the jewels he'd learned to craft from watching his father. "Can I go with you?" I asked, tempering my tone.

Marcus's brow lifted. "It's business, Mary. You would have nothing to do." He scratched his bearded chin. "Though . . . I suppose if you came, Chuza's wife Joanna might enjoy the company while Chuza and I conduct business."

He stood, and I rose with him and followed him to the door, hoping Nira wouldn't follow. Too often she came between Marcus and me, and I didn't want to deal with her. I'd grown up without a mother and didn't need one now.

"I would like to come." I touched his arm as he grasped the handle.

I couldn't bear another day alone with his mother. Another

day of trying to hide the spirits from her and pretend all was well. With Darrah, I didn't care what she knew. She was a servant, after all. But Nira was so devout in attending synagogue and had been oblivious to Susanna's spirits. Yet Susanna's spirits wanted to remain hidden. Mine were unpredictable. And since Susanna had married a month ago, she wasn't here to distract Nira. If I went with Marcus, perhaps the spirits would behave while I was busy exploring a new location.

Marcus looked at my hand on his arm and met my gaze, his own still uncertain. "All right." He walked out without another word.

I sensed Nira beside me, watching. Always watching. "I should go and pack so I'm ready in the morning." I hurried off, but her words stopped me.

"Be careful, Mary. Marcus doesn't like company."

"I'm his wife, not company," I shot back. I ran to the room I had been given when I didn't share Marcus's and shut the door, breathing heavily.

You should have told her to be careful herself of what you could do to her. Such impertinence!

Or to her son. Laughter followed the remark.

"She wasn't impertinent. She was concerned," I said aloud.

Child, you have no idea how controlling Nira can be, Savta Hedia said.

Your savta is right. I never liked her.

Ima's words surprised me. Had she and Nira known each other long before Ima died?

Your father liked her too much.

Sabba's words sent me reeling. I stumbled toward the bed and sat on the edge. Why were they telling me this?

"What do you mean?" I whispered.

He means that Nira and your father were more than "friends."

I never liked her. Ima spat a string of curses at Nira and Marcus's family. *I told you, you should not have married him.*

"No, you didn't! I had no choice. Abba made the arrangements."

The voices did not respond to my outburst. Completely irritated with them, I walked to the chest, where I pulled out an extra robe, tunic, sandals, and jewelry for the trip. I hoped I was taking the right things and not too much. How long would we be there? Where would we go? I needed details.

Don't trust Marcus's business partners. The voice of a spirit claiming to be Aunt Hagit, my mother's sister, broke through the sudden buzzing of the others in my ears.

"Why not?" I hated encouraging them but couldn't help myself. Perhaps knowing was better than not knowing.

You're aware of the company he keeps. Look at Clopas! Chuza can't be better.

I ignored them. They were being petty, but I didn't want to anger them so I remained silent. I closed the chest and left the room, hoping to find something to keep me occupied and avoid the people who made the spirits crazy.

The trip to Caesarea by horse-drawn carriage took more time than I expected. "What will we be doing there?" Talking to Marcus wasn't my favorite thing to do, but I was bored.

"I've already told you." He gave me a strange look. What was wrong with him?

"Tell me more." I tamped down my anger, though the spirits started telling me how awful he was to ignore my question.

"You'll stay with Joanna while I do business with Chuza. I have no idea what you two will do." He pulled the curtain aside and looked at the passing landscape.

I closed my eyes. How frustrating it was when he was silent. Why couldn't we have a discussion? But I'd never been good at talking with anyone, so why should I expect my marriage to be different?

Marcus doesn't care about you. That's why he's silent. A spirit claiming to be a cousin I'd never met spoke. Had she read my thoughts?

When he's not looking, you should do something to make him regret it.

I searched my memories for my real savta having such a cruel streak but couldn't find any. My stomach churned at the thought that these spirits were not the spirits of my dead relatives but something more sinister. What were their real names?

We passed a field of white mustard. The sweet honey-like smell made me cringe. The spirits did not like sweets.

I held my breath, but when I tried to breathe again, I couldn't. Were they going to choke me to death? I clutched my neck and tried to cough.

"Are you all right?" Marcus was suddenly attentive. "Mary!" He turned me around to pound on my back.

The spirits released me, but not until the mustard field had passed. I gasped, violently coughing. Marcus pulled a skin of water from beneath the bench and handed it to me.

I drank greedily and took several deep breaths. *Why did you do that?* I seethed in silence as I handed the flask back to Marcus, who eyed me with worry.

"What happened?" He took my hand in his.

I fought the urge to yank my hand away, noticing the sleeve of my robe had exposed the edge of one of my many cuts. I gently pulled back. "The flowers, I think. They made it hard for me to breathe."

Don't do that again, I told the spirits, hoping they'd listen.

Are you telling us what to do? The menacing voice of Sabba, the strongest one, sent a shiver through me.

No. I'm sorry. I dared not cause them to control my body again. Not here. My ability to convince anyone I was normal was entirely dependent on these spirits.

One of them cleared their throat. Did they have throats? A guttural sound escaped mine. *Please, no. Don't say anything.* For one awful moment, I thought it was going to speak through me. If it did, would my husband throw me out of the carriage?

The spirit quieted, surprising me. I released a deep sigh.

"We will have to pass here again on the way home," Marcus said, "but I'll have the carriage covered better so you don't smell them."

"Thank you," I whispered, not trusting my voice.

When at last we arrived in Caesarea, Marcus had the driver take us to Chuza's home. The carriage stopped in front of a large estate, which I later learned belonged to Herod. His stewards used it while they stayed there.

We climbed large steps to the wide porch and knocked on the carved double doors. A servant opened them to us, and a moment later, Chuza appeared.

"Marcus! You made it. Wonderful!" He glanced at me. "And who is this with you?"

"My wife Mary." Marcus looked my way. "She wanted some excitement outside our home, so I suggested she come with me."

I ignored his lie and smiled at Chuza. "Thank you for having us."

"Come," Chuza said. "My wife Joanna is in the sitting room. She will be happy to meet you." He lowered his voice as we walked in that direction. "Joanna is lame from a childhood accident, so it is hard for her to walk."

I nodded, surprised. Why had Marcus not told me about this?

We entered the sitting room, where an elegant young woman about my age smiled at us. "Welcome!"

"This is Marcus and his wife Mary." Chuza addressed Joanna but pointed in our direction.

"Welcome," Joanna said again. "Won't you please sit?" she said to me.

"Let's let the women talk." Chuza motioned Marcus to follow him to another room.

I studied Marcus's back as he left. Uneasy, I sat on the edge of a chair, my emotions swirling, uncertain what to say to this stranger. The spirits were not happy I had come. They were making me fight the urge to twitch. The last thing I needed was to lose control of my body now. What had made me think coming here would be a good thing? Would the spirits keep quiet for once? What a fool I was.

"Mary, is it?" Joanna swiveled to face me. "It's a beautiful name."

"It's a common one among our people."

"Yes." Joanna's gaze grew thoughtful. "Is this your first time in Caesarea?"

"Yes." I searched for words to show more interest in her and our surroundings.

Joanna looked beyond me toward wide windows facing the Mediterranean Sea. "It is beautiful here, but I daresay Herod has made it more pagan than honoring to our God."

The spirits started complaining at Joanna's mention of God. They should be used to hearing of Him. It wasn't like they left me when we went to synagogue most weeks. Marcus, like his father before him, did not take much interest in synagogue, though his mother did. I stayed out of their arguments.

"Herod has chariot races nearby, and there is an amphitheater where one can enjoy all kinds of entertainment. He has spared no expense to make the port of Caesarea grand, but . . ." Joanna paused, looking at me strangely.

"But what?" I tried to ignore the voices in my head.

"Chuza and some of the other men like to gamble on the horses." She glanced at her hands folded in her lap.

"Gamble?" I hated my own ignorance. Did Marcus gamble?

"They place bets of money on the racers. The winner wins a generous sum. But the losers can lose more than they bet. Chuza thinks it's an enjoyable distraction." She glanced at the hall the men had taken to another room.

"You don't agree?"

"Some men have lost homes and families, for they have no way to support them. It is heartbreaking to watch." Joanna's gaze met mine, but I couldn't hold it. What would I do if Marcus bet my inheritance and lost it? He couldn't!

"Has Chuza lost a lot of money?" I whispered.

What do you care?

"Not a lot," Joanna admitted. "He knows we need the money to pay for doctors for me." She pointed to her lame leg. A beautifully carved walking stick rested against her chair. "I fell down the stairs from our roof when I was a child. I've never walked right again. Chuza doesn't mind. He'd like to find a doctor who can help me, but so far, his connections through Herod's household have yielded nothing. Though . . . there is talk of a preacher who heals."

"A preacher who heals?"

We can help Joanna. The male voice stopped me cold. *Tell her about us. If she invites us in, we will heal her.*

I cringed at the thought. I would not subject another living person to these unclean spirits that constantly tormented me.

If you can heal her, why haven't you healed me?

They didn't respond. They didn't think me "ill" but considered their hold on me something good. No, that wasn't true. They didn't understand the meaning of good.

"Are you all right, Mary?" Joanna gave me a curious look. "Can I have a servant bring tea for us?"

Deep within me, a female spirit growled. I clamped my mouth tight, begging her to calm. A moment passed. "Yes. Thank you."

Joanna called for a servant, who brought out a tray of cups with ginger tea and sweet pistachio cakes. Sweet again. A spirit gagged, but I took a bite and tried to listen amid the clamoring in my head to Joanna telling me about Caesarea and the play we would see at the amphitheater that evening.

At least the entertainment might distract the spirits.

Torchlights and colorful flags waved in the breeze as Chuza led us to enclosed seating covered by an awning, unlike the other seats in the amphitheater.

"As Herod's steward I'm allowed use of the better seats," Chuza said as he helped Joanna into hers. "Tonight we will be treated to a pantomimus by some of Rome's leading dancers." He smiled at us. "I hope you enjoy it."

"I'm sure we will." Marcus allowed me to sit next to Joanna. He moved to sit beside Chuza.

I glanced about and saw a man staring at me, his gaze intense. I shivered at the presence coming from him, though he sat some distance away. Our spirits were familiar to each other.

Would he expose me? I cinched my cloak tighter and looked away.

Joanna met my gaze. "Are you all right? If you're cold, Chuza can provide a blanket for you." She touched my arm where I had lifted it to hold the cloak. The sleeve had slipped down, exposing the cuts.

I snatched the sleeve and pulled it into place.

"Mary?" Joanna's voice was quiet, compassionate. "What happened?"

"Nothing. It was an accident." I fixed my gaze on the center of the theater where the players were setting up.

"How did it happen?" Joanna's question sounded innocent enough, but no curiosity was innocent. She would use the truth against me.

"I tripped and fell." I faced Joanna. "Please don't say anything. I feel like a fool for being so clumsy."

"Of course not. I do things like that too." Joanna lowered her gaze, and heat warmed my cheeks. If Joanna fell, she would have no one to help her up.

"I'm sorry you're hurt." I tried to sound sympathetic, though I didn't feel it. The spirits had stolen my compassion for anyone.

Could Joanna see the truth?

Of course she can. You cannot keep us from the world. One day everyone will know you because of us. Marcus will have the whole story.

I blinked away the sting and rage of unshed tears. I clenched my hands, trying to keep control. Oh, for a moment's peace!

The music started, and lamps lit the theater floor as the dusk deepened. The smell from so many oil lamps upset my stomach, but I fought the urge to be sick and swallowed the bile rising in my throat. I focused on the masked dancers and their strange body movements in their attempt to tell a story. They changed from one person to another, playing many personalities, all while not making a sound.

The music grew louder, and by the second act the heavy smell of the lamps overpowered me. I shifted in my seat and caught sight of the demoniac several rows below, still staring at me.

I needed to leave. But how?

I held my breath against the smell and leaned close to Joanna. "I have to go. I'm going to be sick."

Joanna turned to Marcus, touched his arm, and whispered in his ear, but I couldn't wait for his permission or approval. I hurried out of my seat and down the stairs, not knowing where to turn or where I was going.

Footsteps sounded behind me. *Faster. Faster.* I ran into the shadows near the theater's entrance.

"Mary!" *Marcus.* Relieved, I turned. But it wasn't Marcus. It was the man who'd been staring at me the entire night.

Heart pounding, I picked up my skirts and ran faster, chest heaving as I raced toward the area where the carriages were kept. If I found our carriage, perhaps our driver would take me back to Joanna's house.

Frantic, I searched, glancing behind me every few moments, but he gained on me. Crying out, at last I found the carriage and scrambled into it, hoping he hadn't seen, then swung through to the other side.

"Mary!" The voice sounded like Marcus. But it wasn't Marcus. It couldn't be. I'd seen the other man.

Out of breath, I leaned against the covered carriage, my stomach churning and my legs trembling.

"Mary!" The voice was behind me now, and my stomach heaved. A hand touched my shoulder. I screamed, bent over double, and retched.

NINE

I awoke in a strange room, the light of dawn well past. Had I slept the day away? Where was I? I sat up too quickly. Dizzy, I lowered one leg at a time to the ground. The room was decorated with wall tapestries and a thick wool rug on the mosaic tile floor. Flowers adorned a carved cedar wood table beside the bed, and unlit sconces were perched on either side of the door.

I searched for memories, but they came in spurts. We were in Caesarea. This must be the home where Chuza and Joanna stayed when they were here, though was this their house?

I stood on shaky legs. Somehow my discarded robe had been placed on a hook on the wall near the bed. I took it down and covered my tunic, wrapping it and tying the belt. Stomach growling, I found my sandals, tied them on, and opened the door into a large hall.

A servant met me as I headed to the stairs. "There you are, mistress. Let me take you to the dining room and bring you something to eat."

I nodded, not trusting my voice. Where was everybody? I followed the servant and found Joanna sitting at a low table as if waiting for me.

"You're awake at last." Joanna made an attempt to stand, but I bid her to stay.

"Don't exert yourself for me." I sat across from her, and the servant placed a plate of food before me. "I'm sorry I was not up earlier. I never sleep long. What happened to me?" My memory blurred, and the voices were silent, telling me nothing.

"You were frightened by something at the theater last night and ran off. Marcus had a hard time catching up to you. You were sick, so he brought you back here, and when I arrived I gave you something to help you sleep. Some chamomile." Joanna smiled. "I'm glad you slept. I trust you are better today?"

I picked up the flatbread and spread it with cucumber dip from a dish beside my plate. "I think so." I took a bite, ignoring my unsettled stomach. The food seemed to help.

"Marcus left early with Chuza. I'm afraid they wanted to attend the chariot races before Marcus takes you home. I don't enjoy them, so I said I would wait for you to awaken." She folded her hands in her lap. "We can walk in the gardens or I can get one of the servants to take us to market. What would you like to do, Mary?"

"I would like to visit the markets." Looking at the imported wares would be better than sitting and waiting for Marcus.

"Then that's what we will do." Joanna pushed to her feet with her walking stick and left the room to summon a driver.

I finished the flatbread and cheese and followed Joanna to the main room. "I'm ready."

We mounted a carriage and soon found ourselves in the center of a bustling marketplace. Joanna's servants walked behind us to offer both protection and help in carrying whatever we might purchase.

You hardly need their protection. Sabba scoffed. *With us you are stronger than anyone who might try to harm you.*

Where were you last night when I feared for my life? A long pause followed my question.

His spirits are stronger than we are, Ima's voice whispered, as though she was ashamed to admit such a thing. Did the spirits have different strengths?

If you invited more of us in, we would have overpowered him. He had many within him, Savta Hedia said with confidence.

No! The last thing I needed was more spirits causing me misery.

As I walked along the paved roads and followed Joanna into the shops, I couldn't force myself to find interest in any of it. My body had little strength, and the memory of that man made me helpless all over again.

When at last we returned to the house and Marcus said we would go home, relief filled me. I needed the safety and comfort of home.

We bid Chuza and Joanna goodbye and climbed into the carriage. I stole a glance at Marcus as we went along the same bumpy roads. Though he remembered to cover the carriage with an extra curtain, the same foul-smelling flowers penetrated it, causing me to be sick again.

"I should never have brought you with me," Marcus said after I threw up beside the road. The carriage started up again. "What is wrong with you?"

I looked away, unable to answer him. Were the spirits causing this? Or was something else going on?

"Well, don't ask to come with me again. I don't appreciate having to cut my business short because you get nervous or queasy." He wouldn't look at me, but his words stung.

A sudden overpowering urge to attack him rocked me. I fought it, but I couldn't stop myself from seeing me, in my mind's eye, pouncing on him, scratching and clawing and shoving him from the carriage.

No! My silent scream did little, but the urge lessened. If I hurt Marcus—or worse, killed him—they would stone me in the streets. *I don't want to die.*

A series of quiet grunts followed my declaration. At last the urge subsided. I looked at Marcus, my heart pounding with my silent victory. "I'm sorry, Marcus. Perhaps another time things will be better. I hope you will give me another chance." Better to placate him, even if I didn't care if I ever traveled with him again.

He regarded me, then shrugged. "I don't understand you, Mary. One moment you are sweet and lovely, and the next you are absorbed in your own thoughts and make no sense. You and Susanna are too much alike. I had hoped you were different, but I should have realized her best friend would be like her."

"Are you saying you wished you had married someone else?" What if he decided to divorce me before the five years my father had made him promise? Divorce happened too often in Israel. And if he discovered the spirits, he would have just cause.

He shook his head. "No." His gaze softened. "I only wish you were happy, Mary. I thought marrying me would make you happy, but you seem so . . . lost."

"I'm not always able to control the moods that come over me." I hoped he didn't ask more, but I wanted to give him a reason.

"Perhaps you need a doctor. They have herbs to help with such things, don't they?" He frowned and looked as though he was thinking of a way to help. But there was no cure for this.

"I don't think a doctor can help me."

"A priest? Surely something can be done."

I shook my head, adamant. The spirits would expose me to the priests, who would throw me out of the synagogue. Marcus would divorce me, and I would roam the hills with the worst of those possessed. I couldn't.

"What's wrong with seeing a priest? They are meant to help, Mary." Marcus's confusion fueled my frustration.

"I'll be fine, Marcus. I don't need help." This conversation needed to end.

"You and Susanna both need help," he said under his breath, though his words were clear. "Susanna takes idols and spirits too seriously. Is that the problem with you too?"

Startled, I met his gaze. "Why would you think that?"

He sat up straighter as we passed over smoother ground. "When we were young, I teased her about idols and spirits and told her they were real. It was all in fun, but maybe she didn't realize I didn't mean anything by it."

I twisted the belt of my robe. "She didn't."

Marcus stared at me, leaned forward, and tipped my chin up so I met his gaze. "You did too, didn't you?"

"Did what?"

"Took the spirits seriously."

I pulled out of his hold and shook my head. "No." Not then.

He leaned against the bench, studying me. "I don't believe you."

The spirits nearly blinded me with their rage. Sabba rose to the surface and took over my voice. "Believe her or not," he said, "she doesn't care what you think because we won't let her."

Marcus's eyes widened and his face blanched.

"We control her as your sister's spirits control her. Do not try to use or abuse her or tell her what she can or cannot do. We will oppose you."

"You protect her? How do you protect her from herself?" Anger laced his voice, but the spirits would not let me speak to reassure him.

"We control her," Sabba said again. "We can make her powerful. Be careful, Marcus."

As quickly as he'd taken over my body, the spirit of Sabba drew back. My eyes cleared, and the moment I found my voice, I wept. How could they do this to me? There was no hiding from Marcus now. I would lose him.

"I'm sorry, Marcus. He should not have spoken."

Marcus leaned away from me as though he wanted to climb out of the carriage or send me from it. I was at his mercy now.

"Don't leave me, Marcus. Please." I reached for his hand, but he would not take mine.

"You are possessed," he ground out through gritted teeth. "You should have told me."

"I couldn't." Tears coursed down my flushed cheeks.

"Or wouldn't." He stared at me. "I wouldn't have married you." He scooted to the door and looked through the curtain. The sun was descending, and Magdala was in sight. "When we get home, you will stay in the house of your father as you wished. I don't want to come near you again, Mary."

"No . . . Please, Marcus. Live with me as Tobias lives with Susanna."

"I should warn him against her."

"She will kill me for telling you."

He looked askance at me. "Never."

"She could."

He considered my words. "Both of you are dangerous. I will think on what to do with you both, but you cannot stay near my mother . . . or me."

He folded his arms over his chest and sat in silence the rest of the way while I quietly wept.

TEN

I t is late." The carriage pulled through the gate of Marcus's estate. "I will not take you to your father's house tonight." He looked at me, wary. "I don't trust you, though."

"You shouldn't." I studied my upturned hands. "Nor should you trust Susanna." She and I should both leave the city and live in the hill country away from people. But how would we survive?

Why do you want to survive? Your time on earth is so short. I hate you! I was so tired of their lies. But were they lying?

"For now, I will ask you to sleep in another room. I will speak to Susanna." Marcus jumped out of the carriage, refusing me his help to dismount. Silent, I walked behind him into the house.

"You're home! And sooner than I expected." Nira greeted each of us with a kiss as we entered the sitting room. "Look who has come. Susanna is staying with us for a few nights."

"You don't look well." Susanna peered at me beneath her own hooded gaze.

"She's not." Marcus took my elbow. "She needs to lie down."

"Let her eat first." Nira touched Marcus's arm. "You both must be hungry."

Marcus released his hold and nodded.

"I'm not hungry." The voices were arguing again, giving me a headache.

Nira's brows knit in concern. She drew me into an embrace, which I silently endured. "Let's get you upstairs. Marcus, have the servant bring her some tea."

I didn't want tea. I didn't want Nira or Marcus or Susanna or anyone. But after the outburst in the carriage, I begged the spirits to behave, ignoring their laughter at my request.

"Let me help her, Ima." Susanna came alongside me and took my arm. "We haven't had a chance to talk in ages." She dragged me up the stairs, leaving Nira behind with Marcus.

Susanna shut the door. "What happened to you? Did the spirits cause a problem, or are you ill?" She pulled me onto the side of the bed with her.

I couldn't stay seated.

"Tell me, Mary."

I paced the room. When I stilled, my vision clouded, and in an instant, the voice of Ima spoke through me. "You only think you understand what it's like for her. Your spirits know nothing. They are worthless and useless to you. They have no power over us."

Susanna's voice changed just as suddenly, and she jumped up, her stance combative. "We are more than you are. She only has six of you, and one is an infant in comparison to us. We can destroy you."

"But you won't because then Marcus would realize how evil you are." Maniacal laughter came from my mouth. I should have been appalled, but I didn't care.

As Susanna stepped forward, hands raised as if to attack, I braced myself. The door burst open.

"What's going on in here?" Marcus's booming voice caught us both off guard. The spirits disappeared into the background.

"Nothing." Susanna turned to give him a sweet smile. "We were laughing at Mary's ridiculous flight from the theater. She had you panicked, Brother."

I stared at Susanna. How did she know this? Did the spirits communicate with each other without our knowledge?

Marcus gave me a dark look. "I did not find it humorous at all."

"Nor did I at the time. I was afraid, Marcus. Please believe me." Why had Susanna twisted my words?

Marcus looked between us and backed out of the room without another word.

Susanna stared after him. "He's afraid of us."

"Yes." I stepped back, wary. "He wants me to move back to my father's estate."

Susanna sat on the bed again. "People will think he wants a divorce."

"He should. I am no good to him."

"You can't let him treat you that way."

"He knows about you too. He threatened to warn Tobias about you. They could send us to the wilderness or stone us." My heart beat faster. The spirits wanted to kill me. To join them. I shivered.

"Marcus won't say a thing. I will make sure of it." Susanna stood, confident like she'd always been. "He isn't as strong as he thinks he is."

"He's stronger than you know." Why did I think that?

You need to let us bring another spirit in to help you, Mary.

"You should go," I told Susanna, ignoring the voice.

She stood and walked to the door, looking back at me. "Ima has invited Mary Clopas here tomorrow. You won't be able to avoid meeting her. Be warned."

"Perhaps his wife is not like him."

"I've met her. She's more like him than he is like him." Susanna laughed. "She will trouble you more than he did. Beware."

She left, and the uneasiness within me grew. I would not sleep this night.

I stayed in my room until I finally forced myself to go down the stairs and join Nira and Susanna for the morning meal.

"I was beginning to wonder if we should send someone to get you." Nira set a plate before me and poured me a cup of tea. Was the cook at the market that Nira should serve me herself? "Mary Clopas will be here soon," she said. "Hurry and eat something so we can welcome her. Gilah is already preparing food for later. And Marcus left before sunup and took his fastest horse."

My heart skipped a beat at the mention of Clopas's wife. I had yet to meet her and didn't want to. But there was no getting out of this, so I nibbled my flatbread and exchanged glances with Susanna. She was not happy with her mother's comments either, no doubt.

I forced myself to concentrate on the food. "Where did Marcus go so early?" Would he expose me to the priests or elders of the town? If he did, he'd have to expose Susanna too. But no. His pride would keep him from showing how ignorant he had been of what went on inside his own household.

"He said he was riding to Jerusalem to visit Chuza." Nira shrugged, then left to speak with the servant.

"We just left Chuza and Joanna," I said to Susanna. "Why would Chuza return to Jerusalem so soon, and why would Marcus need to visit him again?" It made no sense.

She also shrugged. "He might have said he was going to

Jerusalem but is going somewhere else. It's hard to say with him." She took a piece of bread, broke it, and ate. "You should eat more."

"I'm never hungry."

"Are you with child?"

The question startled me. Impossible. Though . . . before our trip we had lived as husband and wife. "I don't think so."

"I hope not." Susanna gave me a pointed look. "You don't want to bring a child into this life."

No, I didn't. The spirits would probably kill the child when I wasn't looking or use me to harm it.

"Did he really go to Jerusalem?" He should have told me. Though I wouldn't fault Marcus for never speaking to me again. Silence was nothing worse than I deserved.

"Yes." Susanna popped one last piece of bread into her mouth. "My spirits told me so."

I wanted more, but a knock sounded at the door and Susanna stood. "We best get this done," she said.

As I set aside the food I couldn't eat, Nira hurried past me and welcomed Mary Clopas into the house. "Mary. Come in." Nira led her to the sitting room. "You must meet my daughter-in-law. She is also named Mary."

Mary Clopas stood a head shorter than Susanna and me, who were similar in height and size. Her thick black hair had tinges of gray and was tied behind a headscarf, accentuating her petite features. "How nice to meet you," she said, smiling.

I looked her up and down and took a step back. "Yes. You as well."

I sat where Nira directed but couldn't concentrate on the conversation other than catching that Mary was the mother of two sons, James and Joses. They had both left Magdala years before to apprentice under a stonemason in Capernaum. She rattled on about how well she liked the apartment that her family was allowed to use on the property of Marcus's estate and how the servants were treating her. I didn't care. I wanted to leave.

She is trying to be nice to her husband's employer's mother. She doesn't mean a word she says. She doesn't like any of you. Savta Hedia's voice held a nasty tone.

Liar! You all lie to me. Why should I believe you?

Silence followed, and I released a quiet sigh. If I was this uneasy around Clopas and his wife, the spirits must not like them. Or they feared them. I should feel safer around these people, but I didn't.

They think they're better than us.

"Clopas loves to study Torah, and he shares what he learns with me," Mary Clopas said, her face glowing. "He thinks Messiah is coming soon. All the signs point to it."

Gooseflesh prickled my arms, and my heart skipped a beat.

"Our people have thought that for generations." Susanna scoffed. "What makes him think it might be soon?"

"There is a man in the wilderness preaching about his coming. They call him the Baptizer. He showed up a few months ago. He's telling people to repent and be baptized. Clopas is convinced the kingdom of God is coming. Perhaps the Baptizer is our Messiah. Clopas wants to go see him and ask." Mary Clopas clasped her hands around the cup of tea a servant had set before her. "I want to go with him, and he said I could come."

"Will Marcus go with you too?" Why would I ask such a thing? What did I care what Marcus did?

Mary Clopas shook her head. "Marcus isn't interested in Torah the way Clopas is. He thinks it's nonsense."

Her words didn't surprise me. Marcus had shown his love of entertainment and even gambling with Chuza when we were in

Caesarea. He'd obviously resented having me ruin his fun when I ran off to escape the demoniac. Why would he care about our Jewish hope of a Messiah?

But a part of me wished I had what Mary Clopas had. Joy. And peace. Something I had never known and never would.

ELEVEN

True to his word, Marcus found an excuse to send me back to my father's estate, where I wandered the grounds, aimless. Hopeless. To his credit, he said nothing about a divorce or taking me to the priests. He thought time alone would help me.

He stopped in to check on me now and then and told me when he would be traveling. How long would it be until he figured out he didn't want me because I couldn't be helped? He should have a wife who loved him and would give him children.

Darrah tried to meet my needs, though at times she wisely kept her distance. Most of the servants were afraid of me. And no one visited. I was so lonely I might have even welcomed Mary Clopas, but I think Marcus told everyone to leave me be. Sometimes I left my father's grounds and wandered into the open spaces outside Magdala.

Today the gardens drew me. I pulled my robe about my neck and over my nose to keep from smelling the flowers' sweet scents. The gardens popped with vibrant colors of every kind, but the pink anemones, purple hyacinth, and red buttercups were my favorites. Yet the sight of too many weeds and the neglected foliage only fueled my restlessness. Marcus should be taking care of these things. Clopas handled the finances and made sure the servants were paid. I'd been given nothing to do, as though no one trusted me to do things right. I was as useless as a child.

Frustrated, I walked to the back of the estate where trees grew near the wall. Memories surfaced of my Torah studies, which my father, peace be upon him, had made me learn. Absalom had gotten stuck in a tree much like the large terebinth that stood before me. Would he have died there if Joab had not killed him? I had no one to pierce me with daggers.

But you could climb to the highest branch and jump over the wall.

My stomach clenched at the thought. A deep ravine ran along the back of the wall at this part of my father's land. The wall had protected me as a child from falling into it. To land on the rocks below might break my bones. There was no guarantee a fall would kill me.

You could hang yourself from the branches.

I whirled about at Sabba's hateful words and ran toward the house. When I neared the gardens, I sank onto a bench, trembling. The suggestion to hang myself repeated in my head, the spirits shouting it back and forth.

Come on, Mary. Just get a length of rope from the gardener's building and tie it to a branch. Your misery will end if you do. You know you want to. No one will miss you.

I fisted my hands, wanting to punch the spirit who suggested I end my life. If I died, where would the spirits go? Would I really be free of them? Would they inhabit another unsuspecting woman or child and ruin their life after I was gone?

The thought made me ill.

I drew in a breath and stood, walked into the house, and

sought something to eat. Darrah emerged from her room near the cooking area.

"Can I help you, dear one?" She straightened her brown striped robe and searched my face.

"I'm hungry." I wasn't really, but I needed to distract myself.

"Let me make you some tea, and we'll have some nuts and cheese." She hurried to the area where the cook had prepared bigger meals when my father lived. He would entertain business acquaintances and friends, as we had no real family to speak of.

"Do you know where Marcus went?" I searched my mind, trying to remember where he said he'd gone the last time he had visited. Back to Caesarea? Jerusalem? Was it a feast day?

"He went to Jerusalem." Darrah brought the food and tea to the table where we reclined. "The Feasts of Passover and Unleavened Bread are upon us."

"And he was required to go but didn't want to take me with him." To please his mother, he obeyed the requirement to attend the feasts, though I had never been with him. It was just as well. I hated crowds, and what if I'd met someone like the man who had frightened me in Caesarea? I nibbled an almond. "How long will he be gone?"

The sound of Susanna's frantic voice prevented Darrah's reply. "Mary! Mary, you must come!"

Darrah and I hurried to the courtyard. Terror filled the air around us.

"I'm here. What's wrong?" My heart raced like wild horses.

"You must come home with me." Susanna gripped my arm. "Ima needs you."

"Why? Marcus doesn't want me there." I pulled out of her grip and folded my arms over my chest, unmoving.

Susanna's body jerked and her face contorted. A deep voice

spoke in place of hers. "Marcus is dead." The spirit threw Susanna into a fit on the stone tiles.

I looked on, horrified. My spirits would do the same to me in a breath, not caring if I smacked my head on the stones and spilled my blood.

Susanna's spirits continued to toss her body back and forth. I was powerless to help her.

I stepped back as my servants entered the courtyard. Numerous gasps escaped them, but no one attempted to draw close. A few ran back into the house.

At last Susanna stilled and pushed herself up from the ground. Her body trembled, and she rubbed her hands on her robe in an apparent attempt to look less disheveled.

Is Marcus dead? My own spirits would tell me, wouldn't they? But my question was met with silence.

Susanna looked herself over. "What did my spirits say to you?"

I gave her a curious look. "You don't know?"

She shook her head. "Not this time. I was only told to come and get you."

I shivered. "They said Marcus is dead. Is he?"

Her eyes grew wide. "If they said so, he must be."

"But they are liars."

"Sometimes they tell the truth." She looked shaken. "Come to Ima's house with me so we can find out together."

"Marcus doesn't want me there," I repeated. Had she not heard me the first time?

"But Ima will if anything has happened to him. We need to find out for sure." Susanna reached for my hand. "Please, Mary."

Darrah approached us. "Is there anything I can do for you, mistress? Would you like me to come with you both?"

I looked at the other servants. They knew I was like Susanna. And yet they stayed. Why were they faithful to me?

"I need you to stay here and run the house." I looked into Darrah's concerned face. She was not a young woman, but since my father died, she had aged. Perhaps we all had. I felt far older than my fifteen years. "And find out why the gardener has not been keeping up with his work. I hate weeds."

Darrah gave me a curious look. "I'm sorry, mistress. Marcus let him go when you returned."

"He did what?" Anger rushed through me. How abrupt my emotions were, yet I found no way to control the changes.

Why would Marcus dismiss the man when he knew I loved the gardens? Was he punishing me? Did he want my heritage to crumble about me?

"Mary, we must go." Susanna pulled me forward, and this time I didn't resist.

I shook off her hand and followed, fuming. *I hope he is dead.* No, I didn't!

Yes, you do.

No! I hurried after Susanna, battling the thoughts in my head. We wove our way through the streets and came to Marcus's home. Susanna led us through the gate and into the house that should also be mine.

Nira met us in the entry, weeping.

"What's wrong, Ima?" Susanna asked.

"Clopas brought me the news." She crumpled into a heap on the ground. "Marcus . . ." Great sobs shook her. I stood helplessly.

Clopas emerged from a back room and knelt at Nira's side. "We will have a bier built before the sun reaches its midpoint. My Mary will be here soon. Come and sit, mistress."

He helped Nira to her feet while Susanna and I stepped back, uncomfortable as usual in his presence. He settled Nira on a cushioned chair and called a servant to attend her, then approached us. I should be grieving, shouldn't I? But as always, I was dead inside.

Clopas spoke with kindness in his tone. "Marcus was on his way home early this morning when he was met by a demoniac along a lonely path. The man overpowered the horse and killed Marcus. One of the servants with him escaped and brought his body home. If you want to see him," he said, looking at me, "I can take you to him."

A demoniac had killed Marcus? A shiver worked down my spine, and I began to tremble. Someone like me. Like Susanna. *Oh, God, help me!*

The spirits squirmed within me, unhappy with my prayer. Was God listening? Would He deliver me?

The strongest spirit rose in my throat, causing me to choke. I coughed hard for too long. *All right!* I cried.

Don't ever think such things again, he warned.

"Mary? Are you all right?" Clopas drew nearer.

I backed away. "I'm fine. Just a tickle." I swallowed.

"Do you want to see Marcus's body?" he asked.

No. I didn't care if I ever saw him again. But I couldn't say such a thing with his mother sitting there weeping.

The spirits grew silent again in Clopas's presence. What was it about him?

Suddenly I knew. Clopas was a holy man. Not like the Pharisee I'd encountered in Magdala's market but a true believer in Elohim. The spirits were not of God.

I waited for a lengthy breath. Would they harm me for thinking these things?

The thought that they would not bother me if Clopas was with me gave me a hint of boldness. "Where have you lain him?" I had to face this.

"In his bedchamber. The servants are preparing his body." His look held compassion. "Would you like me to go with you?"

"You can go with me to the door." I did not want anyone with me in the room, not even Susanna. I kept space between us, relieved when he did not attempt to close the gap I had made.

Susanna hurried after us. I sighed. I would not be able to escape her. "The spirits were right," she whispered so Clopas wouldn't hear.

She took my arm, and I let her. Clopas opened the door for us, and I stood back, allowing Susanna to enter before me.

As I crossed the threshold, I glanced about this room I had shared so briefly with him during our first few months of marriage, before the spirits had ruined everything. Before Marcus had ruined my life by sending me away and leaving me alone with the voices. If he'd cared about me, he would have tried to find someone to help me. But he hadn't cared, like everyone else who wanted to be rid of me.

I was glad he was dead. Now my decisions were my own. I didn't have to listen to anyone. I owned two estates, didn't I? Susanna belonged to Tobias's family, and Marcus had no brothers. I would have to ask Clopas, though the thought made my stomach hurt. I caught a glimpse of him outside in the hall. I recoiled at his nearness and yet rejoiced that the spirits were mostly silent in his presence.

You aren't yet powerful enough to control these things, Mary. You need to invite one more to join us. Their persistence at things I did not want tempted me to fly into a rage.

Biting my tongue, I took one last look at Marcus's body while the servants waited along the wall and Susanna wept at her brother's side. I turned and left, passing Clopas on the way. Let Nira and Susanna weep and Clopas care for his burial affairs. I had no tears for Marcus. He had never loved me.

The only emotion roiling through me now was anger. I stomped down the stairs and fled the house to pace the gardens. I couldn't take any more loss. Was everyone destined to leave me? I had no one from my family of birth, and I didn't want Nira or Susanna. I blamed Susanna for the state of my life. I tolerated her because I had no other friends. But she was not there for me. I was alone now.

We aren't leaving, Mary. You've got us. Ima sounded so comforting. But I didn't want their comfort.

You are better off with us. Let us bring in one more, Mary.

I pondered the thought. My head spun with all that had happened. I had invited only one spirit the first time and six came. Now they wanted a seventh?

Seven is the perfect number.

Was that my thought or one of theirs? I couldn't think straight as I paced the garden paths. Abba had taught me that seven was God's number because He had created the world in six days but made the seventh holy.

The spirits didn't want me to be holy. I held my head between my hands and wanted to scream. I did *not* need one more spirit.

Yes, you do, Mary. Seven isn't God's number. It's perfect because it holds the most power. You want to be strong, don't you, Mary? Sabba's soothing voice only confused me more.

I had no need to be strong. I needed to be free of them!

But if you have the power of seven, you will be free, Mary. We will set you free. But you have to ask. Just one more.

You all lie to me. Why should I trust you? I walked to the end of the path where the sweet-smelling almond trees were in bloom. Like with the white mustard, the spirits hated anything sweet-smelling. My throat grew tight, and I feared it would close, choking me again.

I ran away from the smell, but I fell face down on the dirt

path and scraped my palms on the small stones. Angry tears spilled from my eyes, and I hated everything about my life. I would never be rid of the spirits. So why should I try?

We only want to help you, Mary. Don't you trust us?

I laughed outright. Hurt murmurs filled my head. *All right! All right! One more. No more than that.*

You won't be sorry, my child. You will be pleased.

I didn't care. But when all the voices called Marcus's name, I couldn't move. *What are you doing? I don't want him here!*

But he is the strong one, child. He has always loved you, and now that he has joined us, he only wants what's best for you. He will give you everything you ever wanted, and you won't have to worry about anything again. He will take care of you.

His voice spoke outside me. I turned, but no one stood there. "Marcus?"

Yes, Mary. It's me. May I join you?

He sounded so loving. He hadn't spoken kindly to me in months. I hadn't seen him in weeks.

Please, Mary.

I envisioned him speaking kindly to me, holding my hand, when my father died. He had been kinder then. Would he be kind to me now?

I nodded.

You have to say it, Mary.

I hesitated. The others said nothing. What would it hurt?

Yes. As the word left my thoughts, my body was tossed in a whirlwind, and I clung to a nearby bench, panicked that I would be swept away.

You are mine now, little one. You will bow to me alone. You will do whatever I ask. The others cannot help you. They obey me as well. Your grandfather did well to bring me on, for we have declared you ours since your childhood.

My body convulsed. When at last I stopped moving, I trembled so hard my teeth chattered and I had no strength to rise. Did Marcus hate me so much? Or was I dealing with something different? Were the spirits really the spirits of my departed relatives? I had often wondered. If not, who were they? What were their real names?

At that thought, the shaking began again, worse than before, until I thought my head would explode. *Please stop!* But they wouldn't stop until I was more beaten, battered, and bloody than I ever had been. I wanted to die.

TWELVE

—————— AD 31, Three Years Later ——————

I kicked the pebbles on the path outside Magdala near the Sea of Galilee, dusty and sweaty and in dire need of bathing. In the years since Marcus's death, the surrounding mountains and caves had become too familiar to me. I couldn't function in normal society. The spirits, particularly Marcus's, had driven me from my father's estate.

My clothes hung in tatters on a body I no longer recognized for its thinness. Food had little taste, and when I did attempt to return home and Darrah saw to it I was fed, I ate little and didn't stay long. I couldn't stand the sight of my house and the memories of happier times when my father was alive.

Nothing was as it used to be or should be.

Susanna's marriage to Tobias was not going well, from what Darrah had told me the last time I'd seen her. No doubt Susanna's spirits drove Tobias mad, though I had heard no talk of divorce.

Spirits indwelling humans had become so commonplace in Magdala and surrounding cities that most people tried to avoid us or placate us to keep the peace. Some of us were worse than others. Like the one who'd killed Marcus.

Like me.

No one wanted to be near me. They feared the spirits within me, and how could I blame them? I never knew when they would throw me to the ground or toward a fire or send me into convulsions or attack someone.

So I wandered the outskirts of Magdala, only returning home when I could no longer tolerate the solitude. I was always amazed to find the servants still there. And faithful Darrah still managing things under Clopas's watchfulness and guidance.

I reached the market, where the scent of salted fish greeted me. My stomach growled at the familiar staple I'd grown up eating in my father's house. I searched the pockets of my filthy robe for a coin, and finding none, I stopped. Glancing about, I sidled near the barrels, snatched a few small fish in my palm, and added them to the breadcrumbs already lining my pockets.

I hurried away, listening for the merchant to shout after me, but no one called my name and no one ran to catch me. They were afraid of me.

The thought should have brought relief, but it only added to my despair. I scurried down a lane near my home, eating the fish. How long had it been since I'd eaten?

I kicked aside a stone in the path and stumbled along like a drunken man toward what used to feel like home. The breeze lifted the hair from my face, and my scarf, disheveled as it was, came untucked, blowing behind me. I stayed to the shadows along the deserted street.

I needed help. Real help. But every time I'd thought to find someone who might understand, the spirits drove me to my knees or threw me into a convulsion or stole my vision or made my head ache so bad I could barely breathe. There was no help for me.

Tears no longer came. What did it matter anyway? One day

someone would put me out of my misery, or I would die by the spirits' power, but I would not live this way forever. I couldn't bear it.

I approached the gate cautiously and looked at my house. No servants milled about, and I saw no movement behind the windows. The sound of whistling came from the cooking area to the right, and I followed the sound.

"Mary?"

I whirled about to find Mary Clopas, basket in hand, walking toward me.

"I haven't seen you in so long. We've missed you." She searched my face but said nothing about my disheveled appearance.

I hugged my arms to my chest.

Mary Clopas lifted the cloth from the basket and pulled a round loaf of dark bread from within. She offered it to me. "I hope you'll take this. I bought too much at the market."

A lie, no doubt, but I reached for it, tore off a piece, and stuffed it into my mouth. The cook might have food for me, but I had no way of knowing.

"I was wondering." Mary Clopas stepped slightly closer. "Clopas and I have been to see the Baptizer, and he pointed out a new preacher who has been living part of the time in Capernaum and is coming to Magdala this Shabbat. I thought perhaps you and Susanna might like to come."

I didn't want to speak to her. Couldn't she see that? I looked at my house, then decided that if I was going to get rid of her, I should respond. "I haven't spoken to Susanna since Marcus died." Not often, at least. "I can't speak for her. If you want her, you'll have to find her yourself."

Mary Clopas shifted from foot to foot. "But will you come?" She gave me such a pleading, compassionate look that something moved in my spirit. My numb spirit. "I'm anxious to hear him," she said. "They say he heals people. Clopas saw him heal a blind woman, but I wasn't with him. I'm hoping to see him heal here." She looked beyond me, her gaze far off. "Some say he has healed on Shabbat and upset some of our leaders for doing so."

"For healing on Shabbat? He sounds like a rogue. Why would the synagogue rulers allow him to speak if he breaks Shabbat?" A rebel teacher? I had to admit the thought intrigued me. But a healer?

You don't want to go.

The spirit called Marcus forced me backward, and I barely caught myself. I refused to respond to him lest he turn against me. But I found I *did* want to go to hear this teacher if for no other reason than curiosity. And to silence the spirits, if that was possible.

I looked at my robe, aware of my dirty skin and matted hair beneath a scarf that never managed to stay in place. I had once prided myself on my beauty, and Susanna had been jealous of my thick dark locks compared to her finer lighter brown curls.

"They say he speaks as someone with authority, not like the scribes," Mary Clopas said, interrupting my thoughts. "And he heals all kinds of diseases, even leprosy!" She gave me a smile, but I did not return it.

Don't pity me, I wanted to shout at her, for I saw the pity in her eyes.

She thinks you're sick, but you aren't, the spirit whom I'd thought to be my savta shouted in my ear.

"I don't go to synagogue anymore," I said to Mary Clopas, ignoring Savta. "The people don't want me there."

She touched my arm. I did not pull away. "Of course you're wanted, Mary. Clopas and I want you, and you can sit with me."

"You should ask Susanna. She needs you more." How bitter I sounded!

"I will visit her to ask." She paused. "You suffer, Mary. What if this teacher can help you? Wouldn't it be worth a visit?"

I pulled away from her and shook my head. "No. I don't think so." But I wasn't convincing her or myself.

"Think about it." She took a step toward the gate. "I will stop by in the morning before synagogue so you can go with me if you like. If you don't want to go, I won't argue with you."

She moved to the gate, and I dragged my feet toward the house. I needed to bathe and change and eat and sleep. I would decide what to do on Shabbat.

I arose from a fitful sleep exhausted and battered, but not from the spirits tormenting me. I blinked hard, remembering the dream. Had it been a dream? I never dreamed. But I remembered a man walking toward me with kindness in his gaze, offering me his hand to pull me out of a deep pit. The memory would not leave me. How had I ended up in the pit in the first place? The dream did not tell me.

I sensed I had seen the man before but did not know where. For a heady moment somewhere toward morning, I'd experienced such calm and peace I didn't want it to end.

Light streamed from the window now, and the household was awakening, hurrying to dress for synagogue. Would Mary Clopas come for me as she'd said she would?

If she comes, you can refuse her. Don't go. My grandmother's voice, usually so commanding, held a pleading tone. *You're too weary, child. Rest.*

I ignored the comment, amazed when she did not continue

108

trying to persuade me. Were the spirits afraid of synagogue? What would I find if I went?

I dressed in a fresh, clean tunic and robe, tightened the belt, and met Darrah at the door.

"Are you going to eat, mistress? There is some flatbread and your favorite date spread in the cooking room."

"I'm not hungry." My stomach growled, protesting my comment. "Let's go."

When we reached the courtyard, Mary Clopas and Clopas were waiting for us. "I'm so glad you're coming," Mary said.

I nodded. Intense longing to run back to my room or return to the fields and caves fought with the equal desire—no, need—to meet this man, the healer.

We walked together toward the main part of the village, where the synagogue stood.

"I wonder if Susanna will come today." Darrah adjusted the scarf over her head. "She hasn't been to synagogue in months."

"I visited her yesterday," Mary Clopas said. "She and Tobias will be there."

We turned onto the main thoroughfare and joined the other women walking behind the men to the large building not far down the path. I searched for Susanna and spotted her walking toward us. She did not look happy.

She reached us, and I looked her up and down. She was haggard and thin and pale. "I didn't think you'd come," I said.

"Tobias said we must. He is hoping the healer can help me." She laughed as though the thought was not only humorous but ludicrous.

"He may not heal now, considering this is Shabbat." Mary Clopas led us into the synagogue to sit on the stone benches on the left side of the open-columned building. She lowered her voice and leaned toward us. "But after the sun goes down, I think many are hoping to bring their sick to him."

Don't go in, Mary. He will make you worse off than you are now. He wants to kill you!

I don't care, I shouted at them in my thoughts. They already wanted me dead, so what did it matter if this man Mary Clopas spoke of wanted the same?

I took my place beside Susanna. I searched the crowd, and my gaze settled on those seated near the synagogue ruler and the rabbi. And then I saw him! The man in my dreams was sitting near the leaders. It couldn't be. But I would know his face anywhere.

He glanced my way. I gasped, and my heart started pounding as I recognized the kindness in his gaze. Exactly as I had seen in my dream.

He stood as the crowd quieted, went to the podium, unrolled the scroll of Isaiah, and began to read. My whole body burned with fire as I watched him, and his words seared into my mind.

"'The Spirit of the Lord is on me,'" he read, "'because he has anointed me to proclaim good news to the poor. He has sent me to proclaim freedom for the prisoners and recovery of sight for the blind, to set the oppressed free, to proclaim the year of the Lord's favor.'" He rolled up the scroll, gave it back to the attendant, and sat down in the seat of Moses, where the rabbis sat when they taught.

I drew in a sharp breath as he talked. *Set the oppressed free?* Was that possible? Could I be free of the oppressing spirits? I glanced about. Everyone was looking at the teacher, even those I recognized who also had unclean spirits.

"Today this Scripture is fulfilled in your hearing," the man said.

Soft murmurs filtered through the crowd, but no one spoke

aloud. My heart nearly burst in my chest. I stared at him, longing for him to look my way again.

He's going to hurt you, Marcus's spirit shouted at me, drowning out the rest of what the man was saying. *You need to leave now, Mary. He will destroy you!*

No, he won't. He is kind. Unlike you!

My body jerked, and a swift sense of terror that I would fall to the floor, out of control again, washed over me. I looked for a way out of the synagogue as the spirits tugged me toward the door, but a crowd of women blocked my path.

A guttural, booming voice filled the room. "Go away! What do you want with us, Jesus of Nazareth? Have you come to destroy us? I know who you are—the Holy One of God!"

I looked in the direction of the shrieking voice. A possessed man of Magdala, one I'd seen and kept my distance from, stood in the center of the men, flailing his arms.

"Be quiet!" The man he'd called Jesus spoke in a commanding voice. "Come out of him!"

The crowd gave a collective gasp as the demon or demons threw the man to his knees in the middle of the room. The possessed man stilled, but a moment later, Jesus stood, gripped the man's hand, and helped him to his feet.

The demoniac's eyes were clear and the demons had not hurt him, despite the violence with which they had thrown him down.

The man fell to his knees before Jesus. "Thank you. Oh, thank you!" He wept, and Jesus touched his shoulder and whispered in his ear. The man returned to where the other men stood as if waiting for Jesus to continue speaking. But the crowd wasn't listening.

"What words these are!" one man shouted.

"Look!" Another pointed to the man who was free of the

spirits I only dreamed of being freed from. "With authority and power, he gives orders to impure spirits and they come out!"

The words were repeated by others in the crowd, and by their excitement I knew they wanted more, but the synagogue ruler told them to be quiet.

"Please, let the rabbi Jesus finish speaking," he said. "Come after Shabbat to be healed. While we appreciate knowing this man will not interrupt us again, healing on Shabbat is work that should wait until the sun goes down. Wouldn't you agree?" The ruler looked at Jesus as if expecting affirmation.

Jesus shook his head. "If a boy can be circumcised on Shabbat so the law of Moses may not be broken, wouldn't God be pleased with the healing of a man's whole body on Shabbat?"

The ruler appeared to be about to answer, then closed his mouth, apparently having no good response.

The spirits in me pushed their way to the surface. I laughed outright, horrified at my inability to stop myself. Hysteria overtook me, and all seven of my spirits came out, laughing in different tones.

Please stop! But I was powerless. Marcus's spirit forced me to my knees, and the women all drew back from me.

Jesus walked toward the women. More gasps came from the men and they rose as one, but no one spoke.

I covered my mouth, but the laughter still broke through. "What have you to do with us, Jesus, Son of the Most High God? We don't want you here. *She* doesn't want you here."

Susanna joined my laughter, and she flew toward Jesus, arms outstretched to attack.

"Out of them!" Jesus' commanding voice thundered above every other sound.

The room grew utterly still. I lay in a heap on the mosaic tiles, too aware of my surroundings. Cheeks burning with the spectacle I'd made, I wanted to disappear and never be seen again.

And then he touched me. A rush of joy filled me. He took my hand as if to lift me up, but I clung to his feet, weeping. The voices were gone. The spirits had left at his command.

"Mary," he said, taking my arms and lifting me to my feet. "Rabboni." Tears streamed down my face, and when he opened his arms, I fell into his embrace. He held me as a father would a child, his pure love emanating to me.

At last, still brushing tears from my face, he set me beside him and bent to help Susanna to her feet. "Susanna," he said in the same kind, comforting voice he'd used with me.

"Teacher." Susanna wept as he embraced her in that fatherly way he had. Had my own father ever held me with such compassion and comfort?

"Please. Everyone listen." The synagogue ruler interrupted them. "Come to be healed *after* Shabbat. I think we've seen enough for today." He dismissed the crowd before Jesus could say more.

"Rabbi." A man approached Jesus. "Where would you have us go?"

"Come to my home," I said, hoping Darrah had prepared enough food. "Please. We have plenty of room." I looked into Jesus' dark, penetrating gaze. "Please."

His smile melted my heart. "We will follow Mary of Magdala to her home and stay with her for Shabbat," he said to the man. He turned to Susanna. "You and Tobias will also join us."

Susanna nodded, overcome. She looked about, but Tobias already stood at her side.

"Thank you for healing my wife, Rabbi. We've tried to help her. And Mary." Tobias looked from me to Susanna and pulled her into his arms. "We are most grateful."

The crowd pushed in as Jesus walked toward the synagogue door. A group of men followed him.

I sought Darrah. "I've invited these men to share the Shabbat meal with us. Is there enough food?" I whispered. Worry filled me. "Have I spoken too soon to them?"

Darrah put her arm around my shoulder, startling me. This servant had not touched me in a long time. "There is plenty," she said, smiling. "And if there is any lack, we will make it stretch."

Relieved, I patted her hand, then hurried after the men. Freedom coursed through me. This man, Jesus—I didn't know who he was or where he came from, but one thing was certain. No one had ever helped me like he had. I never wanted to leave his side.

THIRTEEN

As dusk descended, Jesus and his followers, along with Susanna, Tobias, Mary Clopas and Clopas, Nira, and several neighbors, gathered in my sitting room. I glanced toward the window revealing the courtyard. People from the village approached, some limping, others led by the hand, and children carried in the arms of worried-looking parents.

I stood, causing Jesus to stop speaking. He looked at me. "Is something wrong, Mary?"

I looked into his eyes, still so full of kindness despite the fact that he'd been teaching us all afternoon. "There is a crowd forming in the courtyard, bringing their sick with them. I'm sure they are looking for you." I clasped my hands, not sure what to do with them. "Do you want me to have the servants send them away?"

Jesus stood and his followers with him—Simon, James, John, Andrew, Philip, and Nathanael. "I will go to them." Jesus walked to the door.

I stepped back, allowing the men to pass.

Susanna and Mary Clopas came up behind me. "Can you believe what has happened to us?" Susanna's face glowed. I had never seen her smile so full of joy. "The spirits are gone, Mary!

Gone! I never thought they would actually leave even though I saw them leave that man."

I longed to do a little dance to match the joy in my spirit. I clutched Susanna's arm in a gentle embrace. "I keep listening, wondering, but they are not just silent. They've left. All seven of them."

Mary Clopas faced us. "You had seven spirits, Mary? How hard for you."

I nodded. "Susanna had six. They've been with her since childhood. With me a little later."

Mary Clopas's eyes widened. "So many and for so long. I'm glad the teacher has such power."

The noise from the crowd drew my attention as the men and women and children filled my courtyard and beyond. "I think all of Magdala has come." I walked with Susanna and Mary Clopas to the door of the house to get a better view of Jesus. "I never want to leave him," I whispered to both women. "I've never met anyone who was so kind, so giving, so loving."

"Nor I," Susanna said. "Tobias is kind, and Marcus tried to understand me, but he was nothing like Jesus."

"Would he allow women to follow him?" Mary Clopas adjusted her scarf, which the breeze had blown behind her. "Clopas and I want to support him, and Clopas would not mind if I traveled with him throughout Galilee since James and Joses no longer live with us, but I would not go unless other women were with me." She looked from me to Susanna. "Would Tobias let you go?"

Susanna rubbed her chin with her forefinger and looked beyond us to where Tobias stood near Jesus' followers. "I will have to ask him. He will understand my desire. And we have no children, so I hope so."

"I have no one to stop me from following him, so I will join you," I said, freer and lighter than I had been my entire life. "And I can help support them as they travel. I have money from the lands my father owned. The estate employs many people, and now that I can think clearly—" I paused. "How wonderful it is to say so!" I laughed, joy bursting inside me. "If Clopas can help me, I think together we can manage the estate and provide for the rabbi."

I jumped as the sudden shriek of one possessed filled the courtyard. Again Jesus commanded the demons to leave the person at once. I looked toward the sound and saw a child lying on the stone pavement.

"Is she dead?" The mother cried out and knelt at her child's side.

Jesus bent down, took the child by the hand, and raised her up, giving her to her mother. The woman wept, clinging to the little girl, while the crowd stood in awe, praising God.

I shared a look with Susanna.

"Life would have been so different if we had met him sooner." Susanna took my hand. "Should we go to them? Perhaps offer some water?"

I nodded. "Why didn't I think of it? Let me find Darrah." I hurried away to find my servant and asked for trays of water and pistachios to be brought for those who had been healed.

I returned to find Susanna talking to the mother and Mary Clopas mingling with the crowd, particularly the women and children. The men with Jesus had also dispersed among the people to keep things in order. Was this how to help him? If I were to become one of his followers—if he would allow women into his group—how could I help? Money alone didn't seem like enough. I had a deep, urgent need to do more. To help him like the men did. But women were not typically students of a rabbi. What did I have to offer him?

I looked at my hands, turning them this way and that. I didn't know how to weave or spin or cook well. I could read and write, as my father had insisted I learn, but I had no useful skill. The servants had done things for me all my life.

Discouraged, I studied him. *Adonai* . . . I could not remember ever praying or calling on the name of the Lord, but suddenly I needed to. *Please allow me to help him, and if he will allow it, show me what I can do.*

Mingling emotions of hope and unworthiness washed over me. Who was I to pray such a prayer? Why should I be allowed to follow such a rabbi? He was not like other rabbis I'd ever met either in my father's company or at synagogue or seen in the marketplace. He was unlike any other man.

And yet he'd healed me. He'd healed *me*! Love for him and for God, who was certainly part of this man's work, filled me. Was this what the Scriptures meant when they said, "Love the Lord your God with all your heart and with all your soul and with all your strength"? My heart lifted, and if it wouldn't have distracted from Jesus' work, I would have sung one of our psalms of praise.

He turned, glanced at me, and smiled. Did he know what I was thinking or what I prayed? But what man could do such a thing?

The crowd grew, with the men making sure they did not press in on Jesus too much, and he healed the people one at a time until they needed lanterns to walk home as dusk turned to night.

Servants lit lamps in the courtyard, and Darrah approached me. "Will you invite the men to stay with us tonight? I can have the servants make up beds in the extra rooms."

I saw the eagerness in her eyes. She was as taken with Jesus as I was. "Yes. Yes. If they are willing. But we will offer."

Mary Clopas and Susanna approached as the last of the people left. "Some of the men can stay at the other estate with Ima," Susanna said. "Tobias and I will stay with her."

"Clopas and I will do anything you need," Mary Clopas added.

"Let's see if they are willing." I smoothed my sweaty palms on my robe as Jesus walked over to me.

"You must join us, Mary. You and Susanna and Mary Clopas and the others who are to come."

My heart leapt at his invitation. "I will be happy to."

"We will ask our husbands," Susanna said.

"Your husbands are also welcome," Jesus said.

"For tonight, we have plenty of room for you and your followers." I feared he would say he must leave, but his smile told me otherwise.

"Thank you," he said. "If you are certain you have the room."

"There are two estates—my father's and my late husband's—so there are more than enough rooms for everyone."

It sounded strange to say so, but perhaps I had more to offer him than I'd thought. I had wealth and could purchase what my hands could not make, and in time I would learn to do all the things I should already know how to do. And help him I would.

PART TWO

After this, Jesus traveled about from one town and village to another, proclaiming the good news of the kingdom of God. The Twelve were with him, and also some women who had been cured of evil spirits and diseases: Mary (called Magdalene) from whom seven demons had come out; Joanna the wife of Chuza, the manager of Herod's household; Susanna; and many others. These women were helping to support them out of their own means.

Luke 8:1–3

FOURTEEN

The summer heat caused beads of sweat to trickle down my spine as I walked with Susanna and Mary Clopas toward Capernaum. We'd been up and down the towns along the Sea of Galilee in order for Jesus to preach in the synagogues of each and were now returning to his home base.

"Simon is smiling. No doubt he is anxious to see his wife Adi." Susanna came alongside me. "I look forward to meeting her."

"And the parents of James and John. They also live in Capernaum," Mary Clopas said.

"Yes, but Simon and Adi are the ones who have to host us all. She has her hands full with so many of us." I glanced at the strong fisherman, the one so capable and able to lead.

In the weeks I'd been with them I had learned of Jesus' calling of Simon and the sons of Zebedee, James and John. Andrew had met Jesus first when he'd been with John the Baptizer, who had pointed out Jesus as the Lamb of God who takes away the sin of the world. But what did that mean? I had pondered it from the time Andrew mentioned it but did not have the courage to ask Jesus to explain.

Pushing the thought aside, I drew nearer to Mary Clopas. "Do you think Clopas would come to Capernaum with some money for us to give Adi? They can't afford to feed so many, not since Simon gave up fishing to follow Jesus." I glanced ahead at the men. "I will go back to Magdala myself if I need to, but . . . I'd rather not leave him." The truth was, I couldn't leave Jesus. He had sent the spirits to the abyss and freed me. But what if they returned when he was not nearby?

"I'm sure Clopas will come. I will send one of the young men of the village to fetch him. He will want to see us regardless. Though I rather think he will prefer to see Jesus." Mary Clopas laughed, her joy contagious. "I'm so grateful he does not mind if we follow the rabbi when he cannot."

"May God reward him for his kindness to us," Susanna whispered. She looked ahead at the men's backs, gratitude in her gaze. "I'm also grateful Tobias does not miss me too much, though I will have to return home soon." She met my gaze.

"Not too soon, I hope. I don't want to be the only woman in the group. It would be unseemly." I was the only one without a husband and free to do as I wished. But I couldn't expect my friends to stay away from their homes forever. Mary Clopas's boys had visited, and I had seen in their eyes the desire to follow Jesus too. How long until the whole nation walked in the dust of the rabbi?

The village of Capernaum with its black basalt buildings came into view, and in the distance, the waters of the Sea of Galilee lapped against the shore. As we entered its streets, the sounds of merchants bartering and the scents of olive oil from the nearby presses and fish from the recent catches filled my senses. Like Magdala. But so much better because of Jesus' presence.

Simon bounded ahead of the group as we neared his home. "Adi!" he called. "We're back."

A petite woman with fine, gentle features emerged from the house, her expression a mixture of joy, relief, and worry.

"Something is wrong," I whispered to Susanna. "She looks anxious. Perhaps we can help. She has to be overwhelmed by so many of us."

"Welcome," Adi said, her smile fixed on Jesus. Her arm moved in an arc from the courtyard to the house. "Sit. Rest. You are weary from your journey." She turned slightly, but Simon took her hand. He spoke to her, their conversation muffled.

"You're back!"

James and John turned as an older couple, undoubtedly their parents, hurried toward them, arms open wide.

"Ima! Abba!" The young men embraced their parents, and a twinge of nostalgia came over me. What would it have been like to grow up with a father and mother who loved me?

I shook the feelings aside. It was wrong to feel thus. I was free of my misery now, and nothing else mattered except Jesus.

"They're going into the house," Mary Clopas said, drawing my attention back to Jesus. "Should we follow?"

"I think so. Adi said to go where we wished." I followed Jesus and the others inside but found the main room empty. I caught sight of Jesus, Simon, and Adi entering a sleeping room to the right.

The others entered the house behind us, and the mother of James and John approached. "I'm Salome," she said. "I'm so pleased you're traveling with the men. They may need looking after." She laughed lightly. "Though I suppose the rabbi can take care of them without our help."

I nodded. "I think we need him far more than he needs us."

I clasped my hands in front of me, longing for something to do. "I wonder what they're doing."

"Adi's mother has been ill while you were away. I assume they told Jesus when you arrived." Salome glanced at the room where Adi's mother must be staying. "Adi has been so worried. None of our herbal remedies help."

I looked up at the sound of hurrying feet. An older woman emerged from the sleeping room, Jesus, Adi, and Simon following.

"Come," she said, looking at the women. "Adi, help me. These men need to be fed. We have a meal to prepare."

Adi put her hands to her face and laughed amid her tears. "Thank you," she said to Jesus.

He touched her shoulder and nodded, moved to the sitting area, and sank onto one of the cushions surrounding a large table. Simon and the other men joined him. I longed to sit with him and listen to their conversation, but I turned instead to help the women prepare the food. I had to learn how to cook sometime.

As I chopped onions for a bread dip, I glanced about the spacious house. Simon must have done well to own such a large home in Capernaum. Not unlike my father's estate in Magdala, only closer to the sea and in the center of the village, not far from the synagogue.

"Can you add the honey to the onions and spread it over the pieces of flatbread?" Adi handed me a jar of date honey she kept on a shelf in a corner.

"Of course. Where is the flatbread?" I looked about.

"I'm taking it out of the oven now." Adi did so while the men spoke across the room.

I strained to listen to them, hoping to catch something Jesus said, but the women were making too much noise. I released a soft sigh. Once the men were fed, we would join them. I hated the waiting. I was always so hungry for his teaching. Delightful-smelling food could not match his words, which fed my soul.

I awoke to the sound of a rooster the next morning. The covered portion of the roof of Simon's house had proven more comfortable for Susanna, Mary Clopas, and me to sleep on than I'd expected. I rose from the mat Adi had given to me. The gray light of predawn gave way to the most colorful shades of pink I had ever seen.

"I thank You, living and enduring King, for You have graciously returned my soul within me. Great is Your faithfulness." My heart soared with praise to Adonai, with joy that surprised me every time I remembered to pray. Though my father had been a man of faith, I had never embraced the prayers as he did. Now I *wanted* to pray, a desire that was still strange and new.

I smiled, smoothed my tunic, and put on my robe, which I'd used as a covering, then tied it about me. Anticipation of a new day with Jesus made me long to run down the steps and into the house to find him. But it was more prudent I wait for my friends, who still lay on their mats.

I walked to the parapet and looked out over the city. Behind me, Susanna yawned and groaned. I turned to find Mary Clopas rolling over and placing an arm over her head as if trying to block out the morn.

I laughed. "You two will have to get up sooner than later. There is no use in fighting it." I walked back to where they still lay, picked up my mat, and rolled it up. "I'm going to see if Adi is up. I'll tell her you're coming."

I laughed again at the face Susanna gave me. She'd never been one to rise early. Neither of us had slept well—the spirits wouldn't let us—but I found I now loved the dawn as much as I had once loved the night. Perhaps more.

I slipped past the two drowsy women and took the stairs to the main floor. The smooth roof made a great extra area for working or sitting in the cool of the evenings, much like that of my home in Magdala. Though I'd rarely spent time on the roof. It had been my father's domain.

Why did I think of my father so often of late? He would have followed Jesus, wouldn't he? Or would he have sided with the rabbis who weren't happy when Jesus healed on Shabbat?

Adi and her mother Hava were already in the preparation area mixing flour and oil for flatbread when I approached. The men must not have emerged from the rooms yet, as I saw no sign of them.

"Susanna and Mary Clopas will be down soon." I took a stack of clay plates to set on the low table in the sitting room. "I assume the men are still sleeping?" I kept my voice low, not wanting to wake them.

Adi nodded. "Simon is still abed, but I think the rabbi left the house before dawn. At least, when I passed his room he was not there, so that's what I assume."

Disappointment curled inside me. "Will he be back soon?"

Adi shrugged. "Since Jesus came to live in Capernaum with us, we never know when he will come or go."

"But Simon and the others are his followers. Wouldn't he want to be with them, to teach them?" I set the plates down. There was no sense in setting them out if the men were not ready and Jesus was not here.

"He will be back," Adi said, offering me a comforting smile. "He often goes away early to pray. Or he stays out late to do the same."

I twisted the belt at my waist. "I should have thought of

that possibility. When we were on the road those few weeks, he often went off to pray."

"When he returns this time, I want to have the food ready." Hava handed me a sack of grain. "If you take this to the mill-stone in the courtyard, it won't be as noisy, though the men will be up soon regardless."

"Of course." I took the sack from her, slipped into the court-yard, and sat before the grinding wheel. I would have to get used to Jesus' absences.

The men should have risen with the rooster's crowing, but I did not have long to wait before the house held the sounds of them talking. Susanna and Mary Clopas joined me, taking the flour to add to the oil and bake. We would need many loaves, so I took turns with Susanna grinding the grain.

I looked up at the sight of James and John entering the courtyard, having spent the night in their father's house. "Good morning, Mary, Susanna, Mary," John said, and James inclined his head toward us in greeting. They entered the house to join the others while we continued to work.

When the last of the loaves was made, Susanna and I re-turned to the house. The men settled about the table while the women served them.

Simon raised the bread before partaking. "Blessed are You, Lord our God, King of the Universe, who brings forth bread from the earth."

As he finished praying, the door opened and Jesus came and sat at the table. Joy and peace filled me.

"Where were you, Rabbi?" John asked as they ate the bread, cheeses, olives, and dates set before them.

"Where I always go, John. Away. To pray to my Father." Jesus took a loaf of the flatbread.

"You go away often," Simon said around a bite of bread.

"And I will continue to do so, Simon. I need the fellowship with my Father." Jesus took a bite of the bread he had spread with the honey and onion mixture.

I considered his words. Why did he need to pray so often?

The sound of voices outside the house filtered through the window.

Simon stood. "We have company." He looked to Jesus. "Should I send them away, Master?"

Jesus shook his head. "See who has come first."

Simon walked to the door and opened it. Adi and I followed, peering around him. The courtyard was filled with men and women, scribes and Pharisees, some leading those who were ill, others curious onlookers. My heartbeat quickened. Couldn't they have waited for us to finish the morning meal? Selfishly, I wanted to keep our group small so I could listen more easily and ask questions. A crowd, which now stretched beyond the courtyard, made listening much harder.

"So many." Adi drew in a long breath and released it. She touched Simon's shoulder. "What will we do?" she whispered.

Simon closed the door and returned to the sitting room. "Rabbi, there are too many, and the religious leaders are among them. They didn't like the Baptizer's message, and we know they don't like it when you heal on Shabbat. But how can we allow the others to stay and send only the leaders away? We'd be thrown out of the synagogue."

Jesus stood and the others with him. "Do not worry, Simon. Welcome them in. Invite some of the leaders and some of the villagers into your home. The others can stay in the courtyard. They have come for my teaching, and some have come for healing, so let us give them what they desire, shall we?"

Simon gave Jesus a skeptical look, and I agreed. Shouldn't we be cautious with the crowds? What if they trapped Jesus in something he said? Would he stop being invited to teach in the synagogues? How would he preach as he had been if he couldn't meet with the people in the place where the Scriptures were taught?

Memories of the crowds that had met him as we walked along the outskirts of the towns surfaced. Perhaps I was worrying for nothing.

I joined the women as Simon opened the door and invited some of the people into his home. Several religious leaders dressed in their robes and phylacteries took the seats closest to Jesus, while men and women of the town sat on the floor or stood along the wall until the house could hold no more.

Jesus sat near the window. His voice would carry from the house into the courtyard from that vantage point.

I stayed with the women, leaning against the worktable, watching for trouble, though there would be nothing we could do if there was any. I shut my eyes, silently praying there wouldn't be. I didn't like the skeptical looks on the faces of the leaders. Why had they come?

Jesus' words pulled my attention away from my worries. "No one lights a lamp and hides it in a clay jar or puts it under a bed. Instead, they put it on a stand, so that those who come in can see the light." He motioned to a lamp Adi had placed in the center of the table. "For there is nothing hidden that will not be disclosed, and nothing concealed that will not be known or brought out into the open. Therefore, consider carefully how you listen. Whoever has will be given more. Whoever does not have, even what they think they have will be taken from them."

"That's rather unfair," one of the leaders said. "Why should those who have be given more? And what do you mean whoever does not have will lose what they think they have? What are they supposed to have?"

"I'm more concerned about hidden things being made known," one of the villagers said. "Can we have no secrets? Not even from the tax collectors?"

Laughter followed his remark, but Jesus looked at both men with compassion. "God knows all things," he said. "There is nothing you can hide from Him. To those who know Him, more knowledge of Him will be given. To those who don't know Him, they will lose even what they think they have."

"How can you say 'to those who know Him'? We are Abraham's children. We have no need of anything." The scribe who spoke straightened, his chest puffed out as though proud of what he'd said.

A commotion came from the roof above, and dust rained down on the table where the men usually ate. Those sitting there looked up but did not move.

Jesus moved away from the table, and Simon with him. Simon looked at Andrew. "Can you get up there and see what's going on?"

Andrew shook his head. "I couldn't get to the door or the stairs if I tried. Too many people, Brother."

Someone peeled the ceiling tiles from above, causing the people sitting around the table to jump up and back.

"What are you doing to our roof?" Simon shouted. "Stop now!"

Jesus touched Simon's arm. "It's all right, Simon."

I glanced at Adi.

"What are they doing?" she whispered, clearly agitated.

The open sky appeared through the hole in the ceiling, and my heart skipped a beat as four men lowered another by ropes to the room below.

A collective gasp came from those around me as Jesus stepped forward and knelt in front of the paralyzed man. Jesus glanced up at the men peering down at him, then looked intensely into the paralytic's eyes. "Friend," he said, "your sins are forgiven."

The Pharisees and teachers of the law squirmed, shifting in their seats. One of them stood, his stance almost combative, scowling at Jesus.

Jesus stood and faced the leaders. "Why are you thinking these things in your hearts? Which is easier: to say, 'Your sins are forgiven,' or to say, 'Get up and walk'? But I want you to know that the Son of Man has authority on earth to forgive sins."

He turned again and touched the paralyzed man. Jesus' expression, so filled with kindness and compassion, moved me. Even in the midst of opposition, he never lost his kindness. But my heart skipped a beat as the Pharisees stood, arms crossed. I couldn't tell if they were ready to fight or flee. Why had Jesus told the paralytic his sins were forgiven? Why say something to anger these men who might do him harm?

"I tell you," Jesus said to the paralyzed man, interrupting my thoughts, "get up, take your mat, and go home."

The man scooted to the end of the table and stood without hesitation. He danced a little despite the crowded space, laughing and crying all at once. "Thank you! Thank you! Thank you!" he exclaimed. "Thank you."

Jesus touched his shoulder. "Go in peace," he said.

The man held Jesus' gaze, turned to pick up his mat, and made his way toward the door. He did not seem to want to leave, but with the Pharisees now seething so close to him, he no doubt sensed the need to do as Jesus said.

"Praise Adonai in the highest heaven," he shouted as he walked away. In the distance, his voice lifted in one of the songs of praise from David's psalms. "It is good to praise the Lord and make music to Your name, O Most High, proclaiming Your love in the morning and Your faithfulness at night, to the music of the ten-stringed lyre and the melody of the harp. For You make me glad by Your deeds, Lord. I sing for joy at what Your hands have done. How great are Your works, Lord, how profound Your thoughts!"

The crowd picked up the Shabbat song and filled the courtyard and Simon's house with praise. The religious leaders pushed their way through the crowd, grumbling.

As the rest of the people dispersed, realizing the meeting was over, someone said, "We have seen remarkable things today."

Indeed, we had.

FIFTEEN

I t's hard to believe we've been with you a week." I scooped grain from the jar in Adi's cooking area and poured it into the stone bowl to carry to the mill in the courtyard. "I'm afraid I've stayed too long." Susanna and Mary Clopas had returned home for the week, but I'd had no desire to leave. I glanced at Adi, who stood chopping onions for the stew.

Adi set her knife down and touched my arm. "Don't ever think that, Mary. I'm glad to have other women here when we keep adding men to the rabbi's group." She looked behind her at the large sitting area where the men would gather in a few hours. "I hope Susanna and Mary Clopas return soon. Their help would be most useful."

Relief filled me. "I had thought to go home to Magdala with them, but I'm glad you wanted me to stay. They'll return in a day or so, I think, with supplies for the rabbi . . . for all of us."

"I'm happy you are here. Ima and I and Salome, when she joins us, find it hard to feed so many, especially when the teacher invites more than we expected. More and more people are following him. We can't possibly sustain them all if this continues." Adi set the chopped onions aside for the barley stew brewing in the courtyard.

I took the grain and headed toward the millstone to grind. I met Simon and Andrew as I opened the door. Simon acknowledged me with a nod, and Andrew smiled as they moved to the cooking area. Simon kissed Adi's cheek while Andrew snatched a sliced cucumber from the board where Adi had been chopping them.

"Where are the others?" Adi gave Simon a loving look.

Sudden memories of Marcus surfaced as I considered their interaction. I had never enjoyed such a connection with him. The spirits had never allowed me to enjoy any part of my life. How different things were now.

"Jesus is bringing a new follower. He told us to go ahead. James and John stopped home. Zebedee and Salome are joining us too." He turned at the sound of more people entering the courtyard and went to meet them.

Adi sighed.

"It will all work out," I said as I hurried to the courtyard to grind the grain. I should have done this sooner, but we hadn't expected them to return yet. Salome would bring food and help with ours. But until Mary Clopas returned with funds from Clopas, we would struggle.

I sent a silent prayer of gratitude to the Lord for giving me wealth. I hadn't expected it but was relieved there was a way for me to help. Only God knew how long we would stay in Capernaum or need funds to purchase food and lodging during our travels.

Adi followed me through the door, and we both stopped as Jesus came along the walk to Simon's house. He was leading three more men, but one stood out by his ornate robe, adorned not with the long prayer shawls of the Pharisees but with a band of red bordering the edges. A tax collector's colors to match the Roman soldiers who oppressed us.

Adi touched my arm. "What is *he* doing here?" she whispered. Simon stopped walking toward Jesus and stared.

"Is that a tax collector?" I spoke too loudly and everyone looked at me. I flushed, certain my face showed my embarrassment at my outburst.

Simon's hands clenched. The entire courtyard fell silent as all of us looked to Jesus.

At last Simon stepped forward. "Master."

"Yes, Simon?"

"What is he"—he pointed at the tax collector—"doing here?"

Jesus looked at Simon, then at each one of his followers. He placed a hand on the man's shoulder. "This is Matthew. I have asked him to follow me." Jesus faced Simon again. "Do you have some objection?"

Simon's expression held a mixture of disbelief and anger. "I don't eat with tax collectors and sinners. Especially not this one." He pointed at Matthew again.

Was this man Capernaum's tax collector? If so, Simon's reaction made sense. I had never dealt with tax collectors, as my father and now Clopas handled those things and the tax collector in Magdala was a different man. I had never seen this man.

I sought Jesus' face, yearning to understand what he wanted us to learn from this. Was I any worse than a tax collector? I was a sinner, had been filled with unclean spirits for years, and yet Jesus had called me. Healed me. I studied Matthew, whose face held a kind of embarrassed misery, and understood his gratitude. To realize Jesus accepted the worst members of society comforted me in a way I could not explain.

Simon's mouth was clamped shut in a grim line, and his eyes were not accepting. Jesus lifted his gaze to heaven and sighed.

He looked about at the group again. "Do not be like the religious leaders, who would think themselves too righteous to eat with those they see as outcasts. You are going to have to accept the fact that I came to seek and save those who know they are lost. Matthew knows what he has done. But who he was is not who he is now. I daresay, Simon, you must realize that you are not better than anyone else in this house."

Simon glanced at Matthew, and a look passed between them. What had Simon been like before he met Jesus?

"I didn't come to call the righteous, Simon, but sinners to repentance," Jesus said.

"Understood, Rabbi. So, he will be joining us now?" Andrew asked.

The question brought uncomfortable scowls from the other men.

"Yes." Jesus moved to enter the house and called the men to join him. "We also have Thaddaeus joining us." He pointed to the man who had entered the house behind Matthew.

I sat at the millstone and ground the grain, pondering Jesus' choice. Salome sat beside me, mixed the flour with oil, and began making flatbread. Adi returned to the house, then rejoined us and finished the stew.

Salome flipped the fourth round of bread and set it on a plate. "Simon is going to have a hard time accepting Matthew," she said, looking at Adi.

Adi nodded. "He doesn't talk about it much, but he has complained about our tax debts. If Matthew is our tax collector, I can see why his presence disturbs Simon."

I looked from one woman to the other. "I understand that Matthew sided with Rome and likely stole from our people and has been an outcast. But I was no better. When Jesus healed me of the demons' control over my life, he made me brand-new. I think that has to be true for all of us. Like Jesus said, Matthew won't be the man he used to be."

"I only hope the men, particularly Simon, can accept him," Adi said.

"Don't be surprised if Jesus adds more outcasts to our number." Salome glanced at the house, where the men waited for the food. "I have a feeling he is not one to respect a person's standing in the community or how important they are."

"Or think they are," I added.

"That too." Salome moved toward the door. "I'd best set these before the men. Is the stew ready?"

"Yes." Adi lifted it off the fire, and the three of us headed into the house.

I glanced at Matthew as I served him, seeing wariness and longing in his gaze. He wanted to belong, but they would not accept him easily. I would. Given the chance, I would do my best to make him feel accepted. And I prayed that at least one other follower would accept him too.

Shabbat began with an air of excitement as I rose from the mat in the home of one of Jesus' newest followers—a man named James, son of Alphaeus. The home actually belonged to Alphaeus, a well-to-do merchant in Chorazin. He had welcomed Jesus and his followers because of James. I did not see much interest in the eyes of his parents. Only common hospitality.

Susanna and Mary Clopas had joined us again, for which I was grateful. Adi and Salome had stayed behind in Capernaum. The women with Jesus had all shared a small room, and we now dressed and folded our mats before leaving.

"I wonder if they will ask Jesus to teach in the synagogue

today," Susanna said as we descended the stairs to the sitting area. "I haven't been to Chorazin in ages. They have a beautiful synagogue."

"I've never seen it," I admitted. How much I had missed in the years before I met Jesus. "When were you here?"

"My father brought me once when I was a girl. He had a meeting with some Pharisees here. I don't know why, considering he cared little for the ways of the Jewish people." Susanna straightened her headscarf when we reached the bottom of the stairs.

"Why didn't your father care for the teaching of our people?" Mary Clopas asked.

"He was Greek. My mother is Jewish. He came to synagogue when it was prudent for him or his business. He didn't believe in our God." A shadow of sadness crossed her face. I understood. I never knew whether Marcus believed in Adonai either.

"I'm sorry, Susanna. Mixed marriages are difficult. I'm grateful Clopas and I share the same faith." Mary Clopas looked over the large sitting area, keeping her voice low. Most of the men had already gathered for the morning Shabbat meal, which had been prepared the night before. "It was good of James's father to allow all of us to stay with them. Did Jesus say how long we will be here?"

"If he did, I did not hear him." I took a seat at the end of the table, accepted the food placed before me, and ate, listening to the men talk.

Thomas had joined us after Matthew, and now the other James had, along with Joseph Justus, Matthias, and a few other faces I did not recognize. Friends of James Alphaeus, no doubt.

The morning light broke through the windows as we finished eating. "Let us be going," Jesus said, leading the way from the house after thanking Alphaeus for his hospitality.

I kept pace with Susanna and Mary Clopas but at the same time urged them to keep up with the long strides of the men. Alphaeus's home was on a hill behind the synagogue, which was in the center of town. The synagogue doors opened to a large room with benches along three sides of the basalt-stone walls. In front of the wall facing Jerusalem stood a seven-branched menorah near a reading desk on a raised dais.

My sandals brushed the mosaic tiles ahead of Susanna and Mary Clopas, and I led them toward one of the benches. The men sat opposite us on another wall. The synagogue filled with men, women, and children, including scribes and Pharisees.

An elder of the town climbed the steps to the dais and called the congregation to pray. "Blessed are You, eternal and almighty God, who has established His covenant with Abraham, Isaac, and Jacob and who would bring a redeemer and grant peace to His people, Israel."

Shouts of "Amen" shook the room. When they died down, men and women raised their voices. "Hear, O Israel: The Lord our God, the Lord is one."

The official hazzan in charge of the synagogue brought a wooden chest, opened it, and withdrew a scroll swathed in fine linen. He removed the linen and unrolled the staves, held up the scroll for all to see, then laid it on the reading desk. "Blessed are You, Lord our God, King of the Universe, who chose us from all the peoples and gave to us His Torah. Blessed are You, Lord, giver of the Torah." After repeating the prayer, the man called on a visiting Pharisee to read.

The Pharisee stood, head held high, a wide phylactery covering most of his forehead and another wrapped the length of his arm. He climbed the steps to the podium.

Why hadn't they asked Jesus to speak? I glanced at Jesus, who was listening respectfully. I tried to do the same, but I couldn't keep my mind on the words. I turned back to the speaker, but out of the corner of my eye I saw Jesus looking at a man near him with a shriveled, useless hand. Scribes and Pharisees sat near the man, watching Jesus.

The Pharisee at the podium stopped mid-sentence, and I glanced at him. He was scowling. When his fellow leaders looked his way again, he cleared his throat and continued reading. Why had he stopped? Was he unhappy with Jesus? My heart skipped a beat, thoughts whirling. Would Jesus heal the man's hand? In the synagogue? On Shabbat? Like he had me?

When the reading ended, the Pharisee handed the scroll back to the hazzan, walked down the steps, and sat in the seat of Moses. I prepared to listen to the man's comments on what he had read, again wondering why the leader had not asked Jesus to speak. The religious leaders were still watching him. Frowning.

A familiar dread curled in my middle, along with a fierce sense of unexpected protectiveness, even though Jesus could take care of himself.

The Pharisee began to teach, but I paid little attention to his words for the pounding of my heart. I sensed evil was present. The religious leaders weren't evil, of course. But was another man or woman possessed of demons in the synagogue?

I shifted, uneasy, until at last the hazzan stopped talking and moved to the side of the room where the other scribes and Pharisees sat.

Jesus stood, looked intently at the man with the withered hand, and said, "Come and stand here."

The man glanced about, uncertain. But he met Jesus in the center of the room. The lights from the menorah flickered behind Jesus, as though they too waited with anxious breath for him to speak.

Jesus gazed at the man before him, then searched the room. "I ask you, which one of you who has a sheep, if it falls into a pit on Shabbat, will not take hold of it and lift it out? Of how much more value is a man than a sheep! So, is it lawful on Shabbat to do good or to do harm, to save life or to destroy it?"

His expression held a mixture of anger and grief. My heart raced, and I couldn't take my eyes off him. Did he realize what they might do to him? If he crossed them, the families of some of his followers could be cast from the synagogue. The synagogue was their livelihood, their connection to everything in the village.

The room held its collective breath as Jesus turned again to the man. "Stretch out your hand," Jesus said.

The man did not hesitate. The leaders had the authority to excommunicate him too, but he obviously didn't care. As he stretched out his hand, I saw the shriveled limb was like new, as one young and healthy. Gasps escaped those looking on, while the man leapt and danced in the center of the synagogue. My heart leapt with him, and I had to force my tapping feet to still. What marvelous power Jesus had! The demons fled, the lame were restored, the blind could see. Was anything too hard for him?

A commotion in the room made me shift in my seat. The Pharisees stood one by one, brushed off their robes, and walked out of the building, heads high. Seething. Their anger permeated the air, as though it carried a scent all its own.

This was not good.

Sweat trickled down my back. Why had Jesus healed that man in the middle of the synagogue? Was he trying to anger the Pharisees? Why would he want to give them cause to hate him more? They were already threatened by his popularity, as evidenced by the crowd surging toward him and the healed man.

I wanted to go to him, to ask him why.

I studied him in the middle of the crowd. The people loved him. But the religious leaders had power to do him harm. What would I do if they did?

SIXTEEN

The crowd pressed in on Jesus as he left the synagogue, but as he led us toward the outskirts of town, the people stopped following. A Sabbath day's walk restricted us from going farther without breaking the laws pressed upon us by the religious leaders. And yet, Jesus did not stop walking. "Let us go on from here," he said.

We followed him to a plain outside the city.

"Master, we will go where you lead, but shouldn't we have stayed in Chorazin one more night?" Simon, always the one to speak first, asked the question I was certain everyone was thinking. "Aren't we breaking Shabbat by walking so far?"

Jesus looked at Simon, then at the rest of us. "We will camp in that field tonight." He pointed a little farther beyond us and continued walking.

We followed in silence behind Jesus, picking up our pace to keep up with him. He seemed anxious to be far from Chorazin. We appeared to be headed toward Bethsaida, but we would have to cross the Jordan to get there.

We'd brought nothing with us to camp in the field other than the clothes on our backs. Most of us had thought we would return to Capernaum after our visit to Chorazin. By the looks on Susanna's and Mary Clopas's faces, they were as puzzled as I.

We entered a field of grain, and the men began picking the heads and eating, violating another of the laws, this one against harvesting. I locked gazes with Susanna as my stomach rumbled.

She simply shrugged and began to pick the grain as well. I wanted to do so, but I needed confirmation. Was picking the grain breaking Shabbat? I did not want God's anger coming down on me. If Jesus was who I believed him to be, why was he allowing this? Wouldn't it be better to fast until sundown so as not to break the Sabbath?

I made my way closer to Jesus. He had stopped walking to allow us to eat, though he did not do the same.

"Rabbi?" My heart beat faster as I approached.

"Yes, Mary," he said, turning to me. "How can I help you?"

I glanced at the men still picking some of the heads of grain. "I don't understand," I said, twisting my hands together in front of me. "The law of Moses tells us not to work on Shabbat. Aren't they working?"

He regarded me, but before he spoke, the sound of voices shouting in the distance drew our attention. My eyes widened at the sight of several Pharisees hurrying toward us. Weren't they breaking Shabbat by traveling to meet us? Or had I been mistaken, and our location was within a Sabbath day's walk?

Confusion filled me, and my stomach knotted at the angry looks on the men's faces as they approached Jesus. The evil I'd sensed in the synagogue floated in the air around us.

"Why are you doing what is unlawful on the Sabbath?" One of the Pharisees stared at Jesus, arms crossed, indignant.

I shifted my gaze from the man to Jesus. What did it mean to keep Shabbat holy? I waited for Jesus' answer. He studied the men whose hatred was palpable. I shivered, remembering the hatred the spirits had possessed when they lived in me.

"Have you never read what David did when he and his companions were hungry?" Jesus said, his tone kind yet challenging. "He entered the house of God, and taking the consecrated bread, he ate what is lawful only for priests to eat. And he also gave some to his companions. Or haven't you read in the law that the priests on Shabbat duty in the temple desecrate Shabbat and yet are innocent? I tell you that something greater than the temple is here. If you had known what these words mean, 'I desire mercy, not sacrifice,' you would not have condemned the innocent. For the Son of Man is Lord of the Sabbath."

The Pharisee who had spoken to Jesus flushed crimson, and I thought a blood vessel might burst in his neck. I moved behind Jesus, my heart burning with the truth of his words. Mercy over sacrifice. How grateful I was to have received his mercy in my life. Without him, I would still be under the control of the spirits, miserable. Or dead. Oh, the great kindness of the Lord!

The Pharisees drew closer, and on instinct I wanted to stand between them and Jesus. I caught myself. How strange it was to feel so protective of him, especially since I had never felt this way toward anyone in my life.

"You would dare call *yourself* the Son of Man? Do you think you are God that you can do and say what you want on Shabbat, the holiest of days? You speak idle words and work against the law and accuse us of having no mercy? We are trying to keep the people from breaking God's laws and suffering His wrath! We are showing them mercy by watching over them, and *you* are encouraging the people to sin!"

The men glared at Jesus. I didn't think they noticed the compassion and sadness reflected in his gaze, for they turned about and walked away, muttering, "Son of Man? Who does he think he is?" The evil I'd sensed in the synagogue and at their approach left with them.

I released a sigh and looked at Jesus, noting the rest of the men and women had gathered around him as the Pharisees disappeared over a hill back toward Chorazin.

"They wanted to trap you, Master," Simon said, frowning. "Why did you break their tradition and let them? We could have stayed in Chorazin and eaten the Shabbat meal at the home of Alphaeus and waited to travel."

"They do not care about keeping the law of Moses, Simon. They care about their own sense of righteousness. They add to the law with their rules of how to keep that law. Rather than trying to understand what the Father means when He says to keep Shabbat holy because He is holy, to rest so that we can come to know Him better by listening to Torah and worshiping Him, they reduce Shabbat to a list of things we can and cannot do. They miss my Father's intention and the spirit of the law in order to make sure everyone keeps it to the letter. But no one ever could." He looked at each of us. "That's why the sacrifices are necessary until the new covenant comes."

"New covenant?" John asked. "What will that be? When will that be?"

Jesus touched John's shoulder. "Soon."

Soon. How soon? What did *soon* mean? But I dared not ask more. If Jesus was going to anger the religious leaders because he broke their traditions, he must have had a reason. All I knew was I wanted to be near him. To do what he said and to listen to everything he had to say.

The following day, after sleeping on hard ground with only my robe for a covering, I tended the fire that had died down during the night. The men had slept around us, allowing Susanna, Mary Clopas, and me to sleep near the fire. They were a wall of protection to us, which I appreciated.

I was used to nights like this, for the spirits had often led me away from home after Marcus's death. When I did sleep, it was with my back to the ground and my face to the stars. Was this how traveling with Jesus would be from now on?

Susanna and Mary Clopas joined me at the fire, warming their hands. The men were rising, but as I looked toward where each one had slept, I saw no sign of Jesus. He wouldn't have left us, would he?

John approached and squatted before the fire. "Did you sleep well?"

I shrugged. "As well as one can without a tent on hard ground." I chuckled and those near me did the same. "But where is Jesus?"

John stood and looked about, concern etching his brow. "I will find out." He walked toward Simon, Andrew, and his brother James.

I noted how young John was in comparison to the others. He was probably the youngest in the group, closer to my age, I supposed, though I felt many years older than my eighteen years. The spirits and my short marriage to Marcus had aged me. I had lived many lifetimes in my struggle to survive them.

I stood and walked to a low rise to peer out toward the Sea of Galilee. We were headed in the direction of Bethsaida. Why had Jesus stopped us here?

"Do you find the rabbi difficult to understand sometimes?" Susanna asked, joining me. "I mean, why would we camp here where there is no food when we could have gone across the water to Bethsaida and been supplied?"

I shrugged. "Bethsaida might not be his next stop."

Susanna tucked a loose strand of hair behind her headscarf.

"We would have to turn around and head back to Chorazin if it's not."

I glanced in the direction John had gone, wishing Jesus would appear and explain. Did he realize how unprepared we were for camping in a field? He knew the thoughts of people, so he must.

"I wonder where he went," Mary Clopas said when she reached us. "John and the others have no idea how long he will be gone."

"We should talk to the men." I made my way back down the rise, the others following. I approached Simon. "If we don't know when Jesus will return, should some of us cross the Jordan and see if we can buy bread in Bethsaida?" I looked from one man to another. "If some of you men would accompany us, I have coins to pay for it. Perhaps there is a boat we can use to get across."

"There are boats for rent, but it's still a distance to walk. You stay here," John said, then looked at his brother. "Andrew, Joseph Justus, and Matthias can help. I think the five of us can manage."

I pulled out the pouch tucked inside my robe and handed it to John.

"Let's go." James motioned to John, then looked at Simon. "Are you coming too?"

"I'll stay here and wait for the rabbi." Simon began to pace. "Maybe I'll go look for him."

"I'm sure he'll return." Andrew touched his arm. "He always does."

"You're right. But go," Simon said. "Go while the markets are still open. Buy what you can before they've sold it all."

I turned to watch the men move toward the inlet of the sea to cross to Bethsaida, catching Joseph Justus's glance my way. He smiled, then turned to follow the others. My cheeks warmed.

A moment later, I spotted a lone figure coming toward us from the hills nearby. "Is that the rabbi?"

Simon turned to look, and the five men reversed their course and ran toward him.

"I guess we will wait to eat." I went to find twigs and dried dung from passing animals to add to the fire. Susanna and Mary Clopas joined me. We returned as Jesus came and sat on a stone near the fire.

The rest of the men who had followed him from Chorazin sat in a circle near him. We women stayed to the back of the group.

"I have spent the night praying to my Father," Jesus said, searching each upturned face before him. "I sought His will regarding the ones I'm going to choose to be my apostles."

"Have you chosen then?" Simon asked, his expression anxious as he shifted in his seat.

Jesus met his gaze. "Yes, Simon, I have." He looked at our group, which numbered about thirty men and the three of us women. Anxious faces turned to him. It was obvious they all wanted to be part of Jesus' inner circle, but he couldn't possibly choose them all. How many would he call?

My stomach rumbled, but the men were too focused on Jesus to pay me any mind. Grateful to be ignored, I glanced at Susanna, then back at Jesus.

"These are the twelve I have chosen," Jesus said, clasping his hands around his knee. "Simon. Andrew. James. John. Philip. Nathanael. Thaddaeus. Matthew. Thomas. James Alphaeus. Simon the Zealot. And Judas Iscariot."

As Jesus called each name, the men stood. Excitement came from those who'd been called, but those who had not been—

Joseph Justus and Matthias among them—appeared to withdraw into themselves, gazing into the fire. Would they leave and stop following Jesus altogether now? And how well would a tax collector and a Zealot fare in the same elite group?

"We will be heading toward the sea to the plain of Bethsaida. There I will teach you what my Father wants you to know." Jesus stood, as though ready to begin the trek down the hill.

"But Master," Simon said, "shouldn't we find food first? We brought nothing with us." A natural leader, he stood beside the rabbi.

Jesus met each person's gaze. "I suppose we should remedy that. What did you have in mind?"

"John, James, Andrew, Joseph Justus, and Matthias were about to buy bread in Bethsaida."

"Very well. Simon the Zealot and Matthew, you also go with them." Jesus sat down again, and I saw a bewildered look cross Simon's face. "Simon," Jesus said, and both the Zealot and Simon looked at him. "To avoid confusion, Simon the Zealot will be called Simon Z. Agreed?"

"Yes, Master," they said in unison.

Simon Z stepped close to Jesus, sharing Simon's bewildered look. "But Rabbi . . ." He looked at Matthew.

"It will be all right, Simon. I trust you can all work together. You are only buying bread, after all."

Jesus smiled, and warmth filled me. I might not understand him, but he knew what he was doing.

SEVENTEEN

I tucked the last of the cheese the men had purchased safely away and covered it with linen. The sound of voices in the distance drew my attention. I looked toward Chorazin and the plain below us. People were coming, crowds of them, all walking in our direction.

"Come!" Jesus called to us and began moving down the incline to a wider plain below, nearer the Sea of Galilee. "Follow me."

I hurried after the men who were already at his heels, Susanna and Mary Clopas behind me.

"The crowds are growing." Susanna fell into step with me. "Did you imagine such a thing would happen in Israel? Do you think he's the Messiah?" she whispered.

I glanced at her, then kept my eyes down lest I stumble over uneven ground. "I don't know. He is from God, though. How else could he have cast out our demons?"

"He might be Elijah or one of the prophets returned to life. If that's possible." Susanna pointed to the crowds up ahead. "They're coming from every direction. I wonder what the teacher is going to do when we reach them."

"Heal them? Teach them? I've never seen him do anything

else in a crowd, have you?" I searched for Jesus and picked up my pace. I could not lose sight of him, not with the throngs closing in on us.

"No. Never. But we haven't been with him long."

Susanna and Mary Clopas stopped with me as we came to the plain, where Jesus and the men greeted those who approached.

I moved closer to John. "What can we do to help?"

He looked from me to the other women. "Jesus told us to have the people sit so he can teach them. You can help us do that or find a place to sit near him." He smiled, then hurried off.

"Let us help," I said to Susanna and Mary Clopas.

They agreed, and we moved to a group of women and children and instructed them where to sit. When the crowd had all found seats in the grass, we settled near Jesus.

Jesus stood, looked at his disciples and the additional men who still followed him, then glanced at me and the other women. Joy filled me. He was including all of us, though we were not part of his elite twelve. My gratitude overflowed. I longed to walk with him forever, but I would accept whatever role he was willing to give me.

As he began to speak, his voice carried easily, magnified by the Sea of Galilee, whose waters lapped the shore and stretched to the far horizon. I listened, drinking in every word.

"Blessed are you who are poor, for yours is the kingdom of God. Blessed are you who are hungry now, for you shall be satisfied. Blessed are you who weep now, for you shall laugh. Blessed are you when people hate you and when they exclude you and revile you and spurn your name as evil, on account of the Son of Man! Rejoice in that day, and leap for joy, for behold, your reward is great in heaven. For so their fathers did to the prophets."

He continued on, but I couldn't get past what he'd said about weeping and laughter. I had wept often, not only during the years the spirits had controlled me but throughout childhood when I longed to feel wanted. But laugh? I had laughed a little since Jesus healed me, but I longed for the joy to outweigh the sorrow.

Will this laughter ever be mine for always?

He glanced at me and smiled, paused a moment, then continued. A tingling of pleasure lifted my spirit. I would laugh often one day, and it would be the laughter of unspeakable joy even greater than I felt now.

"But I say to you who hear," Jesus continued, catching my attention again, "love your enemies, do good to those who hate you, bless those who curse you, pray for those who abuse you. Give to everyone who begs from you, and from one who takes away your goods do not demand them back. And as you wish that others would do to you, do so to them."

Love your enemies? Impossible! My father had taught me the opposite all my life. This went against what the rabbis taught when they said, "Love your friends but hate your enemies."

And the psalmists had wished vengeance on their enemies. Was Jesus telling us not to listen to King David and others when they cried out for God to avenge them?

And what about blessings and curses in the law? We couldn't ignore those, could we?

Confusion filled me, as it did so often of late. First Jesus ignored the traditions of the elders regarding working on Shabbat, and now he was telling us to love those who didn't deserve it?

I longed to ask him how to do what he asked. How did one love those who hated them? Forgive those who purposely hurt them? To forgive in such a way was beyond human ability.

I listened to the rest of his teaching, but every time he said something new—don't judge others, produce good fruit, don't give in to anger or lust, don't seek divorce—everything was backward from all I'd been taught. Many in the crowd looked as perplexed as I felt.

But the Pharisees among the crowd did not appear confused at all. Scowls furrowed their heavy brows, and they stood with arms crossed, keeping his words at bay.

Why did everything Jesus say anger the religious leaders?

A shiver worked through me.

At last Jesus finished speaking and sat down. No one moved. It was as if his words had paralyzed them. Did Jesus really expect people to do all the things he had taught them?

I looked at him, but his eyes were closed.

When it was evident he would not stand to speak again, the crowd stood and the disciples and other followers with them. A line formed. Those who were ill or demon possessed waited nearby.

We walked along the line of men, women, and children, keeping clear of those who were possessed of unclean spirits. I wanted to see them freed, but I didn't want the reminder of who I'd been.

Love your enemies.

The words convicted me. Did I think of those possessed as enemies now? I shouldn't, but still, I kept my distance.

I glanced behind me. Jesus was now walking to meet the people waiting for him.

"You are the Son of God!" one of the demon-possessed men shouted before he reached the head of the line.

"Silence! Come out of him," Jesus commanded.

Susanna's question about who Jesus was surfaced as she stood beside me. "The spirits sometimes lie," she said, echoing my thoughts. "Are they telling the truth?"

The religious leaders moved toward Jesus, frowning.

"The leaders believe the spirits," I said, looking from them to Susanna. "At least, they are not happy about something."

"Are they ever happy?" We both laughed softly.

"Maybe the spirits are unable to lie in the presence of Jesus," I said. Did they know something about him we didn't?

The Son of God? They'd said so before. I searched his face as he continued to heal, pondering the demons' claims.

The day wore on. I rubbed the small of my back, longing to go off with some of Jesus' followers who had taken a break. To sit down and rub my feet. But those who were ill kept coming. Had every sick person in Galilee heard of him?

A sigh escaped and hunger gnawed at me again. The sun was taking its path to the west. How long would the people stay? They needed to return home for the night. But no one left.

The more people who accepted his ministry, the better for him. I didn't know how he would rescue us from the Roman occupation, or if that was his mission, but wasn't it a good thing for the crowds to want to follow him?

I spotted Susanna several rows over, talking with a group of women and children. Mary Clopas was not within my line of vision, so I returned to the row of people waiting for Jesus to reach them. I walked past each one, encouraging them to be patient. "He will see you soon," I repeated again and again.

When I neared the end of the first line, I stopped short. "Joanna?"

Joanna and Chuza, faces from a past life, smiled at me.

"Mary! Shalom! How good it is to see you here!" Joanna said.

I returned her smile. "Shalom to you as well. So much has changed since we first met."

Joanna gave me a puzzled look.

"Of course, you didn't realize it then, but I was possessed of six demons. I hid them well when I was with Marcus, peace be upon him." I straightened my robe, hoping I didn't look disheveled. We'd been working since dawn, and I'd not had a moment to myself. "The rabbi healed me."

"I'm sorry about Marcus, Mary," Joanna said. "So the teacher was able to heal you?" Eagerness filled her gaze, and I recognized the walking stick and remembered her childhood injury. I'd paid so little attention back when the spirits held me hostage.

"Yes. He healed Marcus's sister Susanna as well." Another smile came, and I laughed, surprised the joy had returned with the memory of that wonderful day. Worry, fear of the Pharisees, and confusion had driven it from me for too long. How good it was to laugh again!

"Surely he will be able to heal me." Joanna looked away. "I wondered if I shouldn't have come to burden him with my troubles. It's not as if I cannot live with this." She touched her leg and leaned more heavily on her walking stick.

"If you ask him and believe, why wouldn't he heal you? I've never seen him turn anyone away." I wanted to encourage her, but I couldn't promise something I didn't know for sure. Had Jesus ever refused to heal someone who asked?

"Did your heart burn within you at his words today?" Joanna asked as we took a few steps forward.

"I only fear his words are all we will take home with us. If he doesn't heal you . . ." Chuza let the thought die away.

"I don't think you should worry." I touched Joanna's arm. "Believe."

Joanna nodded. "If he doesn't heal me, I will still be glad we came. But oh, what joy it would be to run and jump like a girl again. To walk without this." She pointed to the cane.

Chuza patted her arm and tucked it against his. "Let us hope he's willing. I think . . . yes, I do think he can if he is willing."

We came to a stop behind a young couple with a girl of about six years old who clung to her mother's hand. Ahead of them, an older boy fell into a seizure where he stood. His worried father looked on helplessly but did not attempt to move toward him until the seizure stopped. He glanced around. "He's been like this since he was a young child."

Compassion for those still ahead of Joanna filled me, and again I glimpsed the little girl in front of us, who was blind. Had she been born that way? But I couldn't ask.

Farther up the line, several demon-possessed men shouted, "You are the Son of God," but the teacher silenced them and cast the demons from them.

As the men walked away with clear eyes, leaping for joy, I grew impatient for Joanna. I wanted to rush her and Chuza to the front of the line so she would finally be able to leap and jump too. But Jesus would want them to be patient.

"Do you follow him?" Joanna kept her voice low. "He allows women in his company?"

I nodded. "Since Marcus died and we had no children, I'm free to follow him. Also, I and some of the women"—I looked toward the crowd—"help support him from our means."

Joanna looked at Chuza. "We could do that with the money I earn. Herod pays you enough that we don't need my portion."

"Let's see if he heals you first." Chuza's expression held a mixture of hope and worry.

Joanna's turn finally came, and I stepped back as she stood

in front of Jesus. His look held such great compassion I wanted to weep for her. I knew that compassion.

"What would you like me to do for you?" he asked.

"Lord," she said, "I want to walk freely again."

"Without the walking stick," Chuza added. Nervous laughter escaped him, and a moment later, he fell to his knees. "Please, if you are willing, heal my wife."

Jesus touched Chuza's shoulder and bid him to rise, then took Joanna's hands in his. "I am willing. Your faith has made you whole."

When he released her hands, she tested her leg, then twirled in a circle and did a little dance, laughing.

Chuza's relieved laughter joined hers, and when she met Jesus' gaze, I saw he was pleased. "Thank you," she said. "I can never thank you enough."

"You already have. Go in peace."

Joanna hesitated. "Must we go, Rabbi? May we follow you as these others have done?" She pointed to me.

Jesus glanced at me, then at Chuza. "You are both welcome to follow me. Though I suspect Herod will want you to return to his employ."

Chuza raised his brows, clearly surprised Jesus knew he worked for Herod. "My wife would like to join the women following you. But you are right. As Herod's steward, I cannot often get away."

"She is welcome if you agree. Come and join her whenever you can."

They thanked him again and moved on to allow Jesus to talk to the next person waiting. I joined them. "I do hope you will come with us, Joanna. We are few compared to the men, but he welcomes all of us. Some stay for a time and return home. I only return home if I need funds to help in the support or to check on my father's estate."

"I will be happy to join you as soon as Chuza and I set things in order. Where can I find you?"

"I don't know where he will lead us next. We simply follow," I said. "Perhaps I can send word to you. Tell me where you will be staying."

"We have an apartment on the grounds of Herod's palace in Jerusalem. Anyone asking for Chuza will be able to get a message to us." Joanna's smile grew wider. "He healed me!"

She did another little dance, and I joined her. There would be joy in the camp tonight and in their home once they returned. Then again, how could anyone experience Jesus' touch and not come away rejoicing?

EIGHTEEN

Dusk deepened and at last the lines ended. Jesus dismissed the crowd, though many lingered, making it hard for us to separate from them. A sense of irritation tickled the edge of my thoughts, but I quashed the feeling. I understood the desire to be with him. These people were hungry for more from him. More of his teaching, his understanding.

I slipped away after bidding Joanna goodbye and found Susanna and Mary Clopas near John and his brother James.

"Good, you're here." John bid us to sit in a secluded spot beneath a copse of oak and willow trees. We had hung the baskets with the food from the morning on some of the low branches. "We are waiting for the others." He looked at his brother. "The teacher wants us to leave the area tonight."

"Tonight?" I began to rise, but John stayed me with his hand.

"Rest a bit. Jesus will explain once he joins us. Simon went to round up the others." He turned. "We're going to help him."

"Shouldn't we help too?" Though walking around the area in the dark was not on my list of things I wanted to do.

John shook his head. "You're here now. We will tell the others to find you."

162

I nodded and sighed. "Good," I said to Susanna and Mary Clopas. "I'm tired."

"My feet hurt," Mary Clopas admitted.

"I'm hungry and miss my bed." Susanna rubbed the small of her back. "I didn't know following the teacher would be like this."

"I didn't know what to expect," I said. "But to leave here tonight before we've eaten? In the dark? Is that his plan?"

Susanna shrugged, and we turned at the sound of the other men coming up the rise to our hidden spot among the trees. I recognized Thaddaeus, Nathanael, Joseph Justus, Matthew, and Simon Z. Jesus trailed behind them.

"Are we all here?" Jesus asked as the men gathered around us.

I again attempted to stand, but when the men sat, I stayed where I was.

Jesus looked about the group. "The crowd has not completely left, but that is all right. Not all of them want to travel in the dark."

"But we are, Master?" Simon asked.

Jesus nodded. He looked at me. "Do we have any food left over from this morning?"

Susanna and I went to get the baskets. I lifted the linen cloth on each one. "Yes, Rabbi. There is enough for each of us to have a little." I wished there was more, but the men had purchased all there was. Next time we would plan better.

"Good," he said, sitting in the midst of the group.

Susanna and I passed the baskets around, and each person took some bread and cheese and a few of the leftover almonds.

Jesus held up the bread and lifted his gaze heavenward. "Blessed are You, Lord our God, King of the Universe, who brings forth bread from the earth." He broke the bread, and we each did the same.

In the distance, the voices from some of those who had re-mained behind drifted to us. Fires dotted the hillside, and I felt the dampness in the breeze coming from the sea. The waters of the Sea of Galilee had kicked up and churned below us.

I breathed deeply, taking in the scents of poppies and ground-sel that blanketed the hill. Sleeping here would be so pleasant after such a day.

"I know we are all weary after today," Jesus said, as if read-ing my thoughts. "I had intended to travel back to Capernaum before dusk, but the people had many needs, and my Father wanted me to meet them." He lowered his shoulders as if releas-ing tension. "Rather than stumble in the dark, for we wouldn't be able to see well were each of us to carry a torch, let us sleep here now. Before dawn, we will rise and go."

We went around Chorazin without entering the town, so we weren't able to purchase food for the morning meal, but Capernaum was not far off. Simon's wife Adi and Salome would feed us, though the group had grown since we'd left the last time.

As we stepped into the town, I wanted to make a quick trip to the market, but before I could tell Jesus where I was going, some of the town's elders walked toward us. I glanced at Susanna and Mary Clopas, then joined the men. What did they want now? Hadn't the Pharisees caused us enough trouble inside and outside Chorazin?

"Teacher," one of the elders said as we stopped before we reached the center of the market. The scent of salted fish wafted to me, and I longed to fill one of the baskets with them for the men, but I didn't want to miss hearing what the leaders wanted.

"Yes?" Jesus waited, his expression curious.

"Teacher, we know you are able to heal those who are sick. You have healed many people in our town," the man said, his tone earnest. The others with him nodded. "There is a centurion stationed here whose servant is sick to the point of death, and he sent us to ask you to come and heal him."

"He is worthy to have you do this for him," another of the elders said, "for he loves our nation, and he is the one who built us our synagogue."

I looked at Jesus. Would he heal a Gentile, one of the despised Romans?

The earnestness in the expressions of the elders surprised me. For a Jew to say anything kind about a Roman was unusual. These men clearly held this man in high regard.

"All right," Jesus said, motioning for them to lead him.

I fell into step with our group again as we walked through the town toward the outskirts where the Roman lived. When we were still some distance away, another group of men approached. Jesus stopped.

"We come from the centurion's house," one of the men said. "We are friends of his with a message for you, Teacher."

"I'm listening," Jesus said. I moved closer to Joseph Justus and Matthias.

"The centurion told us to say this to you," the man said. "'Lord, do not trouble yourself, for I am not worthy to have you come under my roof. Therefore, I did not presume to come to you. But say the word, and let my servant be healed. For I too am a man set under authority, with soldiers under me. I say to one, "Go," and he goes. To another, "Come," and he comes. And to my servant, "Do this," and he does it.'"

The men waited, as did our group of followers, holding our collective breath.

Jesus looked at the men in wonder. "I tell you, not even in Israel have I found such faith. Go," he said. "I have done as he asked."

The men turned as one and left, as did the elders who had accompanied us.

"How will we know if the servant is healed?" Susanna whispered in my ear. "I'd hoped to see him heal . . . and I wouldn't have minded seeing the Roman's home."

I chuckled. "Of course the servant is healed. Jesus said as much. And in any case, we don't need to see how the Romans live. I'd rather stay as far from them as we can."

"This one must have been a good man, though," Susanna insisted as we followed the men back toward Simon's house, where we would gather.

"I doubt anyone is good in God's eyes, but I think Jesus was more impressed with the fact of the man's faith. How many of us here in Israel can say the same?" I said.

It was true. There weren't many who believed without seeing a miracle, and there were those who didn't believe even when they saw one, especially the religious leaders when Jesus performed those miracles on Shabbat. Did I have faith as strong as the centurion's?

We spent the next few days in Capernaum, some of us staying with Zebedee and Salome and the others staying with Simon and Adi. Susanna and I stayed with Adi while Mary Clopas stayed with Salome. I think the two of them had more in common since they were both mothers of boys.

I took my place in the courtyard grinding grain and saw Jesus coming toward me. I was used to hearing he had risen before dawn to seek solitude to pray. I stopped grinding to greet him.

"Shalom," he said before I could speak.

"Shalom." I looked into his clear dark eyes and smiled.

He sat on the stone bench near me. "We are leaving after we break our fast," he said. "It is time to move on, to preach the good news of the kingdom to the cities of Judea."

I nodded. I wouldn't have minded a few more days in Capernaum, but I did not say so. "I will be ready," I said instead. "Where will we stop next?"

"We're headed toward Nain, though first I have a stop to make in my hometown." He drew a hand down his beard.

"Nazareth?" I had never been there and was curious to see where Jesus had grown up.

"Yes. To visit my mother and brothers and sisters." His look held a hint of sorrow. "My brothers and sisters don't believe in me."

"You have brothers and sisters? I don't think I knew that." Had anyone mentioned them?

"You will like my mother, and I suspect she may join us now and then. My brothers—I have four of them—are James, Joseph, Simon, and Judas, though he likes to be called Jude. They are my half brothers, and I have three half sisters."

Jesus' comment surprised me. "Why don't they believe in you?" I couldn't help but ask.

"They grew up with me. I am too familiar to them." He looked beyond me and stood. "One day they will believe. But not yet."

"I'm sorry, Rabbi." I knew what it was like to feel unaccepted. I had never expected that he might feel the same. It was hard enough to be rejected by the people of the land, but by your own family . . . My heart ached with the thought. Was anything harder to bear?

He smiled. "It will be all right." He turned and went into the house.

I continued grinding. Now that he was back, the men would want to eat soon. And if we were leaving, I must gather my things, along with the coins. I would be prepared this time to care for the needs of us all, whatever that proved to be.

NINETEEN

We left soon after dawn, and this time Adi joined us, leaving her mother, Hava, to manage the house. The trip took four days, but we'd come prepared with mats for the hard ground and a tent for the women. The men didn't mind sleeping around the fire, though Jesus often spent the night in the surrounding hills. He always rejoined us before dawn, and we continued climbing southwest. Nazareth was at a higher elevation than Capernaum, so the walk was mostly uphill.

"I will never complain about flat ground again," Susanna said on the fourth day as we neared Nazareth. "Walking uphill is not easy."

I laughed at the face she made. "We're young enough yet. The journey is not so hard."

Adi laughed with me. "I can see you have not often made the trip to Jerusalem." She smiled at Susanna, who shook her head.

"I'm afraid my past kept me in Galilee," Susanna said. "The spirits didn't like Jerusalem on feast days, and my father, being Greek, only attended a few of them. Tobias wants us to go this year, perhaps with the rabbi, if we can."

"I'm sure he will go to the prescribed feasts," I said. I glanced at Adi for confirmation.

She nodded. She stood a head shorter than me, and it struck me how different she and Simon were in size and demeanor. Adi was gentle and petite, while Simon was much louder and burly. She smoothed Simon's rougher edges. "Jesus talked about it in the past. He goes to every commanded feast and sometimes others. He told us a tale of when he was a boy and stayed behind in Jerusalem. His mother and father were frantic trying to find him." She chuckled again.

"Perhaps his mother will tell us the story when we meet her."

What was his mother like? That we shared the same name made me already feel a kind of kinship to her. Funny, I didn't feel the same toward Mary Clopas, but perhaps it had something to do with the way we'd met before Jesus healed me. And besides, this Mary was his mother. That fact endeared her to me before I even set foot in Nazareth.

"There's the town," Adi said, pointing.

The men walked before and behind us, and Simon came up beside Adi. "We're here!" He touched Adi's arm as he passed by to walk with Jesus.

"He's excited," Susanna said. "You'd think it was *his* mother we were coming to meet."

Adi's easy laugh rang out again. "Simon has always been . . . exuberant. He's anxious to follow the teacher wherever he leads."

We entered the small town. Jesus waved to a few of the merchants as we passed the market, and we followed him to the outskirts of the town, where he entered the courtyard of a home built to connect to an adjoining cave.

"Jesus?" A younger man came from the cave and approached. A small woman emerged from the house. "Jesus!" She ran toward him, and he scooped her into his embrace as one might lift a child.

"Ima," he said, setting her back on her feet. They shared a look before she noticed us standing beside and behind him.

"You've brought guests." She smiled at us and motioned with her hand. "Come in. Come in."

"They are my followers, Ima," he said, his voice low and quiet.

I stepped ahead of the other women but refrained from pushing ahead of the men. Anxious to meet his mother, I waited impatiently for Jesus to introduce us to her.

Three other men entered the main part of the house from a room at the back, but I did not see the sisters he had spoken of. No doubt they had already wed and lived in the home of their husbands. But what of Jesus' father? So many questions filled me.

Jesus stepped forward to embrace each of his brothers, then turned to us. "These are my followers and the women who so graciously support our ministry—Mary of Magdala, Mary who is Clopas's wife, Susanna, and Simon's wife Adi. There are others, but not all of them could join us this time."

Jesus' mother met my gaze and came forward. "Mary! How good it is to meet you." She took my hands in hers and squeezed. "I am happy to know Jesus has some women along to make sure he eats." She chuckled and we joined her. She looked from one woman to another. "It is a pleasure to meet all of you."

She spoke to Susanna next, then Mary Clopas and Adi, while I glanced about the room. It was not a large house, but adequate. I imagined how crowded it must have been when Jesus was young and they were all together. But where were his brothers' wives? Had the men not married yet?

"Come now." Jesus' mother pointed to the cushions on the ground. "You must rest while I bring you something to eat."

I and the other women hurried to help her while Jesus' brothers sat with his disciples. Would their presence here make any difference in how his brothers felt about him?

Mary handed us vegetables to chop and gathered nuts and a great round of cheese to cut. There wasn't time to bake bread in the usual way, but she poured some ground flour, mixed it with oil, and made flatbread, a staple we'd grown quite used to.

Susanna and Adi brought the food to the men, and Mary Clopas took over in making the flatbread. I approached Jesus' mother to help chop herbs for a dill sauce.

"Jesus said he also has sisters," I said, still trying to accept that this man who had healed me came from a family like any other in Israel.

Mary nodded. "Yes. Three. They are all married and in Nazareth, so perhaps they will come by before Jesus decides to leave again. Did he say how long you will be here?" She glanced behind me, longing in her gaze. What thoughts went through her mind? If Jesus was our Promised One, the Messiah, had she always known he would be? Surely she'd heard of the miracles. How did they make her feel?

"You miss him," I said.

"Yes." She met my gaze. "But he is doing his Father's will, what he was born to do, so I could not be happier."

"His father?" I looked about. "Is he here?"

She stopped chopping, and by the look on her face, I was glad I'd spoken softly.

"Joseph, Jesus' adoptive father, is no longer with us." A nostalgic look crossed her wrinkled brow. "But Jesus' Father in heaven is the one who guides him now. He always has, I suppose."

I longed to step into the place where memory took her but knew it was better not to press for more details. She spoke of God, I knew. Was God in heaven Jesus' literal father?

A virgin shall conceive and bear a son. The words were a distant memory from long-ago teaching by my tutors, but the words came to me with such force now that I stared at her in awe.

"You are the virgin who conceived," I whispered, and she looked deeply into my eyes and nodded.

I said no more as the men's words drifted to me.

"Why do you think it necessary to travel so much?" One of Jesus' brothers spoke. "You should be here, caring for Ima."

"Ima has the four of you to help her." Jesus looked from one brother to another. "I was sent to preach the good news of the kingdom to our people."

"Then preach here among the people who know you best. Perform some of your miracles so we can all believe in you." Sarcasm laced the man's tone.

"James!" Mary's voice carried across the room, and everyone shifted to face her. "Jesus heals when God tells him to heal. He is only doing what he is called to do."

James crossed his arms in front of his chest and looked at Jesus. "You can't expect us to believe you have some great calling if you refuse to heal in your own town. Why didn't you stop Abba from dying if you're so powerful?"

The room grew silent at James's outburst, and a look of horror crossed his mother's face. But she didn't call his name again or reprimand him. Did she wonder the same thing?

"My time had not yet come," Jesus said quietly. He chewed a piece of flatbread, the silence growing heavier with every breath.

"And now it has?" James jumped up, followed by the other

three brothers. "I refuse to accept that answer. If you have the power to heal, you should have healed Abba for Ima's sake, if not ours." They left the room by a corridor leading into the cave, probably where they kept their shop or rooms for sleeping.

The awkwardness in the air about us lingered with their departure. Mary did not move or speak, her hand pressed to her middle. I wanted to embrace her, but I did not know her well enough.

Jesus stood, and the rest of the men stood with him. He approached his mother. "Ima." He pulled her into his embrace, and I was glad he did. They held each other in silence. "Forgive my brothers, Ima." He searched her gaze. "I hope you know why I could not heal my father back then."

She nodded. "I know," she said at last. "It was not your heavenly Father's will or His time for you to act. But I wish Joseph could have been here." She searched his face and touched his cheek. "He would have been so proud of you. He would have set your brothers straight. They would have listened to him."

Jesus smiled, though I could see his sadness lingered. "They would have. But it was not the path God had for him or for them. Do not worry, Ima. He is with the Father and we will see him again one day."

"And your brothers?" Worry lines appeared on her brow. What was it like to feel thus about a child? I would likely never know.

"Do not worry about them either. In time, they will understand." He motioned to the rest of us. "But we should go. We are on our way to Nain. Since it is so close by, I wanted to see you and to have you meet my friends."

"Can you not stay the night? We would make room, and your sisters have room if we need more space." She appeared anxious to hold on to him, as though releasing him meant something to her I could not understand.

He shook his head. "I do not want to bring tension to your home, Ima. I will come again another time." He kissed her cheeks and led us out of the house to the courtyard.

His mother followed. "Will you say goodbye to them?" I knew she meant James and the others.

"I think that's already understood," he said.

"I suppose it is." She stayed at the gate to the courtyard as we quietly followed Jesus, bid her farewell, and said it was so nice to meet her.

I longed to stay and ply her with questions about his childhood, his father, and meet his sisters. What was it like knowing she had carried the Promised One? But I hurried after Jesus, pondering the knowledge she had already given me. I hoped we would meet again soon.

The walk to Nain did not take long, despite the climb. Some from Nazareth had seen Jesus and followed us, and people from the direction of Capernaum joined them. They'd probably been following since we left the plains near Chorazin.

Susanna walked in step with me ahead of Mary Clopas and Adi. She glanced behind her, then looked at me. "Will there always be such large crowds following him?"

I shrugged. "I suppose there must be if he is the one we think he is." Large crowds were a good thing, weren't they?

"I guess so." She released a deep sigh. "But I prefer when he is more open with us without the crowds."

"He explains things to us later, though. When he does something we don't understand."

"True." Susanna tucked her hands in the pockets of her robe.

A large crowd emerged from Nain, causing Jesus to stop walking. Four men carried a bier, heading toward a cave in the nearby hills. Women wept and wailed, and a small group of them surrounded another woman bent with grief.

I moved to get a better glimpse of her. Black scarves draped her hair and wrapped around her, as though shrouding her as the white linens shrouded the person on the bier.

The procession slowed as our two groups met. Jesus looked at the bier and approached the woman, walking beside her. "Is this your son?" he asked.

"Yes," the woman whispered in a hoarse voice.

"She is a widow, and this was her only son," one of the other women beside her said, placing an arm about her friend.

The woman wept, and tears slipped from my own eyes. She covered her face with her hands. "I have nothing left. No one to care for or to care for me."

"Do not weep," Jesus said. Tears filled his eyes. He walked over to the bier and touched it, causing those bearing it to stand still. "Young man, I say to you, arise."

Shocked and in complete awe, I stared as the dead man sat up. When the initial shock drained away, my heart pounded. What was this? *Who* was this man that he could raise the dead? I looked from Jesus to the young man, whose friends were disentangling the graveclothes.

"Where am I?" the young man said.

Dazed, he shook loose the last of his graveclothes and, wearing only a loincloth, swung his legs from the bier and hopped to the ground. His mother rushed forward, and the man began to weep as he lifted her into his arms. Someone from the crowd removed their robe, hurried forward, and placed it around his shoulders.

"My son!" his mother said, laughing and crying at once.

My heart still raced as I tried to make sense of what I saw. Casting out demons had been miracle enough for me, and seeing Joanna and Susanna and so many others healed of blindness, lameness, and all sorts of other maladies . . . But this!

I searched the faces in the groups that had accompanied the widow and of those who had joined us from Nazareth and Capernaum. Wide-eyed and open-mouthed, men and women looked from one another to Jesus, disbelieving yet unable to deny what stood before them. I sensed fear and awe in their gazes, matching the feeling in my pounding heart.

Only God held the power of life and death. Only He could do this. Had God come to walk among His people?

When I looked into the face of Jesus, was I seeing the face of God?

"A great prophet has arisen among us!" a voice from the crowd shouted.

"God has visited His people!" came another.

A chorus of repeated praise filled the area where we stood until all of Nain was aware. As people hurried away, surprising me that they didn't stay, I wondered how long it would be until everyone followed Jesus.

News like this could not stay hidden. Soon all Israel would know God walked with us.

TWENTY

———— AD 32 ————

I rose from the ground, hurting in places I didn't know could ache. Despite the tent, mat, and grassy knoll, sleeping outside was nothing like sleeping in the spacious room of my childhood.

But it was worth it for him. Anything was worth it to be with Jesus.

I emerged from the tent to find Susanna already tending the fire. I pulled a sack of nuts from the basket I carried with me. Footsteps crunching the grasses drew my attention. Joseph Justus approached with Thaddaeus, each carrying handfuls of figs, which they handed to me and Susanna.

"We're heading to Cana," Joseph Justus said, biting into a fig. "We're leaving as soon as we eat. Do you need help taking down your tent?"

"I think we can manage." I blushed at his nearness. What was it about him that caused my heart to skip a beat? "Thank you, though."

"You're welcome," he said in the rich deep voice he had. He was pleasant to look upon, but I was not interested in any man. I would not marry again. It would hinder me from following

Jesus, and I knew I needed to stay near him to keep evil at bay. I did not need the complications marriage brought to a life.

I glanced at Joseph Justus as he walked away. Susanna and the other women joined me in taking the tent down, rolling it up, and fitting it into the sack to be carried. We were on the road headed toward Cana before the sun was partway to the middle of the sky.

"Why are we returning to Cana, Master?" John asked.

I'd been told of the miracle at the wedding in Cana when Jesus had turned water to wine.

"To preach the good news of the kingdom, John," he said. "The last time we were there was to celebrate a wedding, not to preach. But I came to preach and to spread the good news to the house of Israel, and that means visiting all of the towns, often many times."

"And to heal?" I asked, striding alongside the men.

He glanced at me and smiled. "My desire is always to do the will of my Father, and many times healing is part of His will, yes. But blessed are those who believe without signs and wonders. Those who believe the words I speak and see that I am the one Moses and the Prophets spoke of in the Scriptures. Abraham believed God and God counted him righteous. Faith is what I am looking for most of all."

"Thank you, Teacher," I said, grateful for his lengthy answer.

He nodded, and I drifted back a step, pondering his words. I could never have had such faith if he had not healed me. Was I less blessed because of the miracle than one who believed without such a sign? I searched my heart and my memory. I couldn't think of anyone who had believed in him without healing, with the exception of his mother. And yet, even she'd had the miracle of a virgin birth to tell her he was who he said he was.

Adi joined me after we had traveled a lengthy distance. We could see Cana looming closer. "You're terribly quiet," she said.

I shifted the basket from one shoulder to the other. "I'm thinking of what Jesus said. How many people believe in him without miracles? I never thought of faith in that way."

Adi tilted her head as if thinking. "I don't know of anyone who has. I mean, Simon and his partners saw Jesus multiply fish until their nets were breaking. He called them to follow him after the miracle. Zebedee told Salome of the catch, and some of the disciples saw him turn water to wine. I don't think any of them believed before they saw the signs. How could they?"

"Jesus is looking for a deeper faith . . . or a different kind, I think," I said. "He wants faith that believes his words more than the miracles."

We walked in silence. My mind struggled to grasp Jesus' meaning, but now Cana was upon us, and the moment we entered, people flocked to his side.

"Teacher, my daughter is deaf and cannot speak. If you are willing, please heal her," called a woman leading a young girl forward.

"Teacher," another called, "can you come to my house to dine tonight?"

Still another cried from the outskirts of the crowd, "Son of David, have mercy on me!"

I craned my neck, trying to look above the heads of those blocking my view, but I could not see who had called to him. Did the people of Cana believe Jesus was the Promised One?

A little shiver ran through me as Jesus made his way to the square near the synagogue, which was in the center of town. Men and women, many bringing children, formed a circle about him. The disciples attempted to get them to form a line so they wouldn't crowd each other, but they didn't listen.

"I wonder if anyone will ask Jesus to turn their water into wine," I said to Adi. We both laughed.

The humor of the thought lingered, but as the people waited to see him, I saw weariness cross Jesus' brow. That new-to-me feeling of protectiveness washed over me, and I wished I could find a way to help him.

"My desire is always to do the will of my Father."

Of course it was. I had just never considered what it would cost him.

The people waited, anxiety pulsating in the air. Jesus spoke with the disciples a short distance away. He had yet to lay his hands on anyone for healing. Did he plan to preach before he healed?

A commotion rippled through the crowd as a small royal entourage approached Jesus. I tensed, wondering what was next, when an official, undoubtedly from the court of King Herod Antipas, broke through the crowd of people and made his way to Jesus. Again, protective fear for his safety rushed upon me. What would an official of Herod want with Jesus?

Besides, these people had been waiting. Why should this official, just because he was wealthy, be able to see him first? My righteous indignation festered a moment, then disappeared as the man fell to his knees before Jesus.

"Please, sir, come with me to Capernaum and heal my son. He is near death." The official clasped his hands in supplication, and I noticed moisture in his eyes. Clearly, he loved his son.

"Unless you people see signs and wonders," Jesus said, "you will never believe."

The man's face contorted, his eyes wide. "Please, sir, come down before my child dies."

My breath caught as I waited, watching Jesus. Would he get

up and leave all these people to accompany this wealthy man all the way back to Capernaum?

"Go," Jesus said. "Your son will live."

I released a relieved sigh as the man turned about and, followed by a contingent of men I hadn't noticed before, hurried away.

Jesus turned his attention back to the people of Cana and began healing them, but I watched the official as he and his men mounted horses and galloped out of town. Jesus had healed from a distance before, but never from so far. What else could he do that I had yet to see?

The crowd finally died down as the sun began to set. The family in the house where the wedding had taken place invited us to stay with them. They didn't have a large house, but the men camped in their inner courtyard while the women shared a guest room. I was relieved to sleep on a mat indoors.

At morning meal the next day, our host, Chesed, supplied us with a simple fare of bread and cheese. "How long do you plan to stay?" he asked Jesus.

"Until after Shabbat tomorrow. Then we will return to Capernaum," he said.

"We will never forget what you did for us the last time you were here," Chesed said. "It's been the talk of the town ever since. If you went about doing that for everyone, you wouldn't be able to enter a town." He chuckled and Jesus joined him.

"It is already becoming difficult to enter the towns of Galilee for the crowds. We do not want to become a burden to those of you who live here," Jesus said.

The door opened, and John poked his head in. "Master, the people have returned with more of their sick."

Jesus stood. "I'm coming." He looked at Chesed. "Thank you for allowing us to stay with you. We always appreciate having a place to lay our heads other than a rock for a pillow and grass for a mat."

He turned to enter the courtyard. People clamored to touch him. Would they crush him against the wall in their attempt to be healed?

"Can we help you clear the food away or prepare for this evening?" I asked Chesed's wife Devora, trying to ignore the crowd noises outside.

She shook her head. "No, no. There is no need. If you want to return later, you can help me."

"We will be here." I walked to the door, and the other women followed.

We entered the outer courtyard, but there was little room to move. Jesus sat on one of the circular benches placed at intervals about the court, and this time the disciples convinced the people to line up and wait patiently.

Jesus healed throughout the day with only a little water to sustain him. It was time for us to return to the house when another commotion drew my gaze toward the street. The small royal entourage that interrupted Jesus yesterday had returned. Why? But this time, they waited.

The line continued, and Jesus, compassionate as always, listened to the people's requests and granted their desires for healing. The sounds of praise and echoes of David's psalms filled the air as each one left to return to their homes.

I lifted my gaze heavenward. *Blessed are You, Lord our God, King of the Universe, for giving us the Promised One to deliver us from our oppressors.* When Jesus was off praying, the disciples talked impatiently of him delivering us from the oppression of Rome. But I had already been delivered from the oppression of the evil one and his demons. I had no concerns about any other kind of deliverance. At least not yet.

At last the royal official stood before Jesus. I moved closer to Adi and strained to listen to their exchange.

"Teacher." The man knelt and bowed his head. "Yesterday as I returned to Capernaum, my servants met me on the road with the news that my son was alive and well. I asked them what time the fever had left him. They said at one in the afternoon, the very time you told me, 'Your son will live.'" He paused, swallowed, and fought emotion. "I wanted to thank you. And to tell you that my whole household believes in you."

"I thank you for telling me." Jesus touched the man's shoulder. "Go in peace."

The official stood, thanked Jesus again, and left.

"Did you hear what he said?" Adi whispered to me. "The exact moment Jesus spoke, the boy was healed!"

I nodded, overcome by awe and holy fear. The demons had obeyed Jesus in an instant. The fever had left the boy in an instant. Everything Jesus commanded happened immediately, even as he spoke the words. I didn't know what to do with this realization. How little I understood.

TWENTY-ONE

The day after Shabbat, we left Cana for Capernaum at dawn, on the heels of more complaints from the Pharisees. I'd seen Simon's troubled gaze, and the men continually talked about Jesus' safety. Many of them wanted to protect him, much as I did. Was Jesus oblivious to the anger he caused? To what the religious authorities might do to him? But he did not appear to care what the leaders thought.

As the sun set and we gathered in Simon's home, Jesus looked from one man to another, his brow furrowed. Had he overheard them talking on the road?

"Be on your guard against the yeast of the Pharisees, which is hypocrisy," Jesus said. "I tell you, my friends, do not be afraid of those who kill the body and after that can do no more. But I will show you whom you should fear. Fear Him who, after your body has been killed, has authority to throw you into hell. Yes, I tell you, fear Him."

The silence in the room grew palpable. I had never thought about hell in a serious way, though the spirits within me had often spoken of the abyss, where they dreaded to go and wanted to take me. I had not felt such terror since Jesus healed me. But now I looked about, noting worry lines along the brows of most of the men and women.

"Master?" John asked at last. "What do you mean? Are we in danger of hell—we who believe in you?"

The look Jesus gave John and then extended to the rest of us calmed me. "You are worried because of what I said, and many should be, for they do not believe in me, and by their unbelief they put their souls in danger. But not with you who are mine. Those who put their faith in me will never perish," he said. "Are not five sparrows sold for two pennies? Yet not one of them is forgotten by God. Indeed, the very hairs of your head are all numbered. Don't be afraid. You are worth more than many sparrows."

"Master," Simon said, "we know we must keep God's name holy and we should not be afraid of those who can kill us, but shouldn't we be a little concerned about the religious leaders, not to mention the Romans, who might see you as a threat to them? You've seen the way they act, heard the things they say. They could cause you a lot of trouble. Shouldn't we also fear them? Or at least be ready to defend you against them?"

Jesus smiled, meeting Simon's gaze. "When you are brought before synagogues, rulers, and authorities, do not worry about how you will defend yourselves or what you will say, for the Holy Spirit will teach you at that time what you should say."

Puzzled looks passed among the disciples, and confusion filled me as well. What was he talking about? Isaiah's readings mentioned the Holy Spirit, but none of us really understood who he was.

"Do not worry about the Pharisees or the Romans, Simon," Jesus added. No doubt he sensed our lack of understanding. "Fear God and keep His commandments. Acknowledge me. Believe in me and you will have no need to be anxious about defending yourself before others. God the Holy Spirit will give you the words you need when you need them. And do not feel the need to defend me. My Father in heaven is the one who defends and protects me."

He stood, and I knew his teaching was at an end. But at least his last comment helped me to grasp better what he'd said. The Holy Spirit was God's Spirit. He would teach us all things. But wasn't that what Jesus was doing?

"Let's get some sleep now," he said. "Tomorrow is a big day."

It was? We were home now and it wasn't Shabbat, so what was so important about tomorrow?

I rose early and stepped out of the tent on Simon's roof. In the gray haze of predawn light, I glimpsed Jesus leaving the courtyard and moving away from the house.

The rest of the household was still, the only sounds that of Susanna's light snoring and the occasional snort from Mary Clopas. The birds had not begun their morning twitters and chirps from their perches in the nearby trees and on rooftops.

I walked to the edge of the parapet, yawning, and watched Jesus' form disappear into the shadows. What did he say to his Father, and why did he feel the need to pray so often? I searched my heart and memory. Had he ever explained that to us? Should we pray as often?

The truth was, I wasn't sure I understood how to pray. It wasn't like I had ever prayed before I met him. Before he healed me. Of course, I knew the prayers of our people—most of them—but they were memorized words, not anything from my heart. Could someone like me talk to the Father as though He truly was *my* Father?

Longing filled me, and I lifted my gaze toward the east. The sky slowly changed. Dawn was still perhaps an hour away. I couldn't begin the morning meal. It would awaken the household. I could return to my pallet, but I was up now.

I returned to the tent, retrieved my robe and sandals, and dressed, then descended the stairs on tiptoe and moved to the courtyard. I considered a walk in the streets, but I didn't have the confidence I once had on my own. When the spirits controlled me, they had made me strong. Powerful. No one could hurt me. Walking in lonely places was something I'd been used to.

Now I had no desire to be alone. And I couldn't chase Jesus everywhere he went. So I gathered sticks and dried dung from a pile beside the house and added them to the smoldering fire. I could cook the barley from the sack of grain Adi had sitting inside the door. I checked the door, grateful it was unlocked, and retrieved the pot and sack. I strained water from the cistern beside the house and poured it with the barley into the pot over the fire, then sat on the bench to watch the flames. Restlessness filled me. Anxious for Jesus to return, I wanted to see this day start and worried about it at the same time. What big thing did Jesus expect today?

I didn't have to wait long to find out as the household sprang to life. The women joined me, adding food to go along with the porridge, and Jesus returned as the men sat to eat.

"We will spend the day in the streets of Capernaum." He broke a piece of flatbread Adi had made.

"Doing what?" James, John's brother, asked around a mouthful of porridge. "Walking about to see who recognizes you? Wouldn't you prefer to take a break from the crowds, Rabbi?"

Jesus gave him a look of gentle censure. "I have come to do the will of my Father, James. It is my Father's will that I preach the good news of the kingdom to the people." He popped a bite of bread into his mouth.

"But don't you already do that at synagogue on Shabbat?" Simon dipped his bread into the porridge.

"Yes," Jesus said, "but the message of the kingdom is not only for those in attendance at synagogue. It is for all people everywhere. For our people first, then the others."

"Others, Master?" John asked, clearly puzzled. "Gentiles? You don't mean Gentiles?"

"I have come into the world to save it, John. Including the Gentiles. But first I am here to speak to the house of Israel." He looked about at the group. "Don't be so surprised, my friends. Did not Isaiah prophesy of me when he said, 'I will also make you a light for the Gentiles, that my salvation may reach to the ends of the earth'?"

"Yes, but . . ." John's expression held both confusion and a hint of misery. None of us could imagine the Gentiles sharing in our nation's history or our Messiah.

"All people," Jesus repeated. He stood. "Now let us be going. I have people to see in the city. One who needs me." He glanced at me.

One who was like the woman I used to be? His slight nod gave the answer without me voicing the question. Apparently he knew my thoughts.

We filed out of Simon's house and entered the streets of Capernaum, heading toward the marketplace, where most people gathered. The merchants and townspeople coming to market recognized Jesus almost immediately, and they quickly drew near.

Susanna and I walked together behind the men. "I think he's looking for a demoniac," I whispered, meeting my friend's gaze.

She stiffened. "What makes you think so?"

"The way he looked at me before we left," I said. "I want him to heal those who suffer as we did, but sometimes . . ." I looked away, swallowing hard.

"You fear they will return," Susanna said, finishing my thought.

"Yes."

It helped to have each other, knowing where we had come from and how much better life was now.

A commotion, louder than the clamor of the crowd, drew our attention. A man led by two others was brought to stand in front of Jesus.

Mary. The sinister tone flew toward me from the demoniac. I could not tear my gaze from the wild look in the man's eyes.

Mary. We know who you are! Don't think you are free now. You will never be free of us.

Bile rose in the back of my throat, and tears stung my eyes. *No!* I was spurred by an intense need to run, but my feet could not move.

A moment later, as a small group of Pharisees joined the crowd, Jesus spoke. "Out of him!" he shouted. "Do not return."

Jesus glanced at me, and all my tension seeped away in that instant.

"My brother has been unable to speak for years," a middle-aged man said to Jesus as I attempted to process what had just happened. "No doctor has been able to help him. Thank you!"

The demoniac's face, once twisted with rage, had softened and his eyes were clear. "Thank you!" he cried. "Thank you!"

"Go and sin no more," Jesus warned him, surprising me. "Lest something worse happen to you."

The man nodded vigorously, repeatedly thanking Jesus, as his brother and a younger man led him away. The Pharisees, whose presence carried a spirit I did not like, frowned at both Jesus and the man. But the spirits within them, whatever they were, did not call my name. Perhaps they had a different kind of spirit.

I drew in a deep breath and released it. I looked at Jesus again, who had turned to help another, then at Susanna. "Why didn't he tell us to go and sin no more?" I asked her. "We are all sinners. What was so different about this man than what we experienced?"

She shrugged. "I don't know." She faced me, and uncertainty filled her expression. "Did the demoniac call your name?" she whispered.

I nodded. "Yes."

She wiped a hand over her face. "His voice reminded me of everything I was. I feared . . ."

"I did too," I said, touching her arm. "But it's over now. I think Jesus knew what the demons were doing, so he stopped them."

She released a breath. "I am so relieved."

I nodded, saying nothing more. What else could we say? We were free, and Jesus was not going to let the demons torment us again. As long as we stayed near him, we were safe. But what would happen if we were parted?

My heart thumped hard at that thought.

"Even the demons obey him," someone from the crowd exclaimed, drawing my attention away from my fear. Other voices began to praise Jesus.

"He casts out demons by Beelzebub, the prince of demons," one of the nearby Pharisees said. I felt the venom in his tone and shuddered.

"If you are really the one we are waiting for, show us a sign from heaven." This from another Pharisee.

"What's wrong with them?" I leaned closer to Susanna. "Did they not see what he just did?"

I wanted to push the Pharisees away, to make them leave. But they would laugh at anything a woman might say or do to them. And I no longer had the power of evil to do them harm. That was a good thing, I told myself, even as I shivered at the looks of hatred in their eyes.

As I watched Jesus look over the crowd, his gaze resting on the religious leaders, I held my breath.

"Every kingdom divided against itself is laid waste, and a divided household falls," he said. "And if Satan also is divided against himself, how will his kingdom stand? For you say that I cast out demons by Beelzebub. And if I cast out demons by Beelzebub, by whom do your sons cast them out? Therefore, they will be your judges. But if it is by the finger of God that I cast out demons, then the kingdom of God has come upon you."

Jesus turned away from them and looked my way again, holding my gaze and Susanna's. "When the unclean spirit has gone out of a person, it passes through waterless places seeking rest, and finding none it says, 'I will return to my house from which I came.' And when it comes, it finds the house swept and put in order. Then it goes and brings seven other spirits more evil than itself, and they enter and dwell there. And the last state of that person is worse than the first."

He turned to the crowd and dismissed them, then led us back to Simon's house. But my mind whirled and my stomach churned with his words. The peace I'd had for a moment disappeared, replaced with dread. What if the demons that had left me returned with more? Was that what Jesus was saying? He wouldn't let that happen to us, would he? I couldn't live that way again!

But how could I stop them?

I would never invite them in again, but what if they came anyway? Was I strong enough to keep them out?

I shivered, hurrying after Jesus, hearing the religious leaders grumbling behind me. I needed answers and silently prayed Jesus would explain more when we were home again.

TWENTY-TWO

The door shut to Simon's home, and relief filled me that I was free of the religious leaders' condemning words and any more men or women who might approach Jesus with unclean spirits. My stomach knotted at the memory of Jesus' comment about demons returning. Why had he looked at me when he said those things?

The men took their places on the cushions in the sitting room, though it was not time for a meal. Every one of us was hungry for more of Jesus' teaching.

"Mary of Magdala," Jesus said when we joined the men. My face grew warm at being singled out, but his look of compassion made my embarrassment abate. "Did you understand what I said about demons returning to the house they have left?"

I shook my head. "I . . . I thought I understood." I quietly studied my hands.

"I didn't understand either, Rabbi," Susanna said, touching my hand.

"When a person is freed from a malady, whether it is an illness or demon possession, they have a choice," Jesus said. "They wanted freedom from the misery of their malady, but if that misery does not lead them to faith in me, all they have is a body with less suffering." He looked about at each one listening.

I pressed my hands to my knees, leaning forward, anxious for him to continue.

"But in this life, they will one day suffer again because the body will break down until death claims it. It is not the body you are to be concerned with, for which of you by worrying can add a single hour to his life? True healing comes when a person gains the salvation of his soul. If the demoniac is set free of the demons but does not believe in me in order to be saved, his soul—his house—remains empty. He has nothing beyond earthly things with which to fill his life. Do you understand what I'm saying?"

I waited for someone else to speak but sensed he wanted my response. Every eye was looking in my direction. "I think so," I said. What did I know of these things? I didn't understand salvation and faith. Not really.

"Do you believe in me, Mary?" Jesus asked.

My heart skipped a beat. "Yes, Rabbi. I believe you are the Promised One who was foretold to us by the prophets. I believe you have come from God."

"And do you trust me with your life, with every part of you?" His persistence caused me to think deeper.

"Yes," I said after a slight pause. "I believe you are our Redeemer. I trust you with my life."

"And so you need not fear ending up like the person who has his or her house swept clean but does not fill it with faith in me. If that man I healed today returns to the life he lived when the demons came and does not repent of his sins and seek the salvation the Father offers through me, the demons will return, and he will be worse off than he was at the start."

"Why will he be worse off, Rabbi?" Simon asked. "Won't he simply be the same as he was before you healed him?"

Several people nodded. We all shared the same curiosity.

"No, Simon," Jesus said, "he will not be as he was. He will be worse because he was given the chance to know the truth and be set free and he chose to remain in bondage. His chances of believing the truth after rejecting it are much worse than they were before he was first set free."

"But it's hard to stay true to faith, Rabbi," Philip said. "I mean, we believe you, but sometimes you say such hard things that confuse us. Does that mean we are rejecting the truth because we don't understand?"

"It is not wrong to have doubts and confusion, Philip." Jesus accepted a cup of water Adi placed before him and sipped it. "It is what you do with your doubts and confusion that matters. Do they lead you to me, to faith and to seeking the Father, or do they push you to go your own way?"

"I would seek to understand you," Philip said.

"That is what the Father and I are looking for. People who will seek and find us when they seek us with all their hearts. Don't give up the search because you don't understand. And don't walk away because you don't like our words. Many do."

I clasped my hands in my lap, twisting them together. When I looked up, I met Jesus' smile and felt my whole body relax. I understood him now. I need not worry about ending up in a worse state. I needed to trust him, no matter what I faced in my life.

"Tomorrow the women will stay in Capernaum while we take the boat and sail to the Gadarenes. There is another man living in the tombs who needs to be set free," Jesus said.

John shifted to face Jesus better. "But Rabbi, they have mostly Gentiles in that area. Did you not come first for the people of Israel?"

"Yes, John, I did. But there are Jews living in that area as well, and this man is a descendant of Abraham. He may be living among mostly Gentiles, and our message will also reach to them, but he is not one of them."

"How long will you be gone?" Adi asked.

"Not long," Jesus said, rising. "I am going out for a little while."

Simon and several of the others jumped up. "Shall we go with you?"

Jesus stayed them with a hand. "I will be back soon."

He left, and the men continued to sit about discussing things he'd said until some of them left to attend to things in the city.

I stood and looked about the room. It was time to start the evening meal, but I felt restless. I didn't want to be left behind, but there were going to be times like this. Perhaps I should go home to Magdala. It might do me good, and I could gather more funds to help support the teacher.

"Are you coming, Mary?" Susanna headed toward the courtyard to prepare the bread.

"Yes." I walked toward her. "I think I might go home tomorrow to check on things."

"I'll go with you," Mary Clopas said, and Susanna nodded. "We should also go home while the men are gone. And I will admit, I miss Clopas." She smiled.

"I miss Tobias too. And Ima," Susanna said.

I nodded my understanding, though I had only my servants to miss. I would miss Jesus most of all. But there was nothing I could do about that.

The next morning, some of the men who were not among Jesus' twelve chosen ones left to do whatever they needed to do.

They did not tell us what that was, though I overheard Joseph Justus and Matthias talk about returning to their hometown of Gennesaret, which was a farther walk than Magdala.

We left after the men headed for the boat to take them to the Gadarenes. "We won't be gone long," I told Adi as we bid her and Hava and Salome farewell.

The walk to Magdala took us until the sun was halfway to the midpoint of the sky. We arrived as the heat was beginning to rise, and I parted from Mary Clopas and Susanna and entered my father's courtyard.

Darrah met me at the door and pulled me into her arms. "Mary! You look well!" She held me at arm's length.

I hugged her in return. "I missed you. I don't tell you often enough."

She looked embarrassed at my words but couldn't hide her smile. "Well, now you are home. How long will you be with us? What can I get you? You must be hungry."

"Very!" I said, laughing. My stomach growled at that moment. "I came to see how things are going while Jesus and the disciples take a trip across the sea. I need to meet with Clopas tomorrow to check on the harvests and take some funds to help the teacher."

Darrah led me to the eating area and ordered Chana to provide me with some food. "Clopas comes every other day to meet here with the overseers of your father's property. He is a fine man, and I believe he takes good care of things. The servants are pleased with him and are well paid as you instructed." She busied herself getting me some tea while Chana set a plate of bread and nuts and cheese before me.

"The stew is almost ready," Chana said.

I nodded, grateful for what was here. I lifted the bread heavenward and prayed, "Blessed are You, Lord our God, King of the Universe, who brings forth bread from the earth." As Darrah placed the clay cup of tea before me, I said, "Come, sit with me, Darrah. Have a cup for yourself."

She looked skeptical. Servants did not eat with their employers.

"I have been serving the rabbi and his followers for months," I said. "I no longer consider a distinction between us. You have been like a mother to me, so sit, please."

She complied, cupping her hands around her mug.

"Tell me how you've been. Are all of the servants well? Is the gardener keeping the gardens tended?" I looked into her dark eyes, noting new lines at the corners. Darrah was not young, but seeing her continue to age with every visit worried me. I couldn't lose her too.

"Yes, yes." She nodded and searched my face. "You are so different. I'm so glad you are healed."

I blushed, embarrassed at the praise. "I'm glad as well. I wish you could be with us as we walk with the rabbi."

"I'm content to serve you here, mistress. I'm afraid I am too old to travel as you're doing, up and down Galilee," she said, chuckling. "Many have left their shops and nets to join the crowds following him. I don't think there is a sick person left in Magdala." Darrah took a sip from her cup. "Though the synagogue rulers and the visiting Pharisees often complain about Jesus in the marketplace, the people love him. The rulers warn the people during Shabbat services not to follow him, but no one pays attention to them after Shabbat is over."

"Don't they fear being put out of the synagogue?"

"They just don't tell the leaders. Most of them make sure they are back in time for Shabbat so they are not missed."

"The crowds are large. Sometimes I worry that they will wear Jesus out. The lines of people who want healing can grow long." I broke off a bite of cheese and popped it into my mouth. I hadn't had cheese this good in a long time. Chana made the best in Magdala. "Do we have a good store of grain and oil that we can part with?" I glanced about, but Chana kept the extra jars of food in a storage building just outside the house.

"We have plenty from the good harvest God gave us last year," Darrah said. "Though this is a Year of Jubilee, a time for the fields to rest, there is still more than we will need. Shall I have the servants transfer the grain from the stone jars to sacks so you can take them with you? The oil can be poured into flasks, unless you want to take the larger stone jars?"

"I will take one of the large jars, and if we put them on a cart, the jars of grain can also go with us," I said. "I will leave them with Adi. We meet most often at Simon's home in Capernaum, and they could use the extra food. Especially as our number grows."

"I can have Elazar travel with you. He can drive the cart and return it." Darrah beamed, happy to help me. Or perhaps helping Jesus caused her as much joy as it did me.

"That sounds good," I said, relieved that her enthusiasm made her seem young again. Perhaps her aged appearance was only caused by too much time in the sun. I stood, satisfied.

"There will be stew a little later," she reminded me.

"Perhaps Susanna and Mary Clopas and their families can join us," I said. "Do we have enough?" I looked at Chana.

"I can add more barley, mistress. We will make it stretch."

"Good. Send Elazar to invite them. And include Nira. It's been too long since we were all together, and we have much to celebrate now that Jesus has entered our lives." I smiled at them and excused myself, knowing they would do what I asked.

Tonight the house would be full, and I would invite the servants to join us. Perhaps, if I had the courage, I would tell them what Jesus had done for me. Isn't that what he commanded his followers to do? We were to spread the message of the kingdom wherever we went, and if I didn't start with those in my own household, I would never forgive myself. Those I loved most needed his salvation too.

TWENTY-THREE

Two days later, I joined Susanna and we walked toward Capernaum with Elazar, who led a cart loaded with more food than I had seen in months. This, added to what Susanna's servant led on another cart, could feed the entire town.

"Mary Clopas isn't joining us?" I asked as we followed the carts, each carrying our own sacks of personal belongings.

"Her sons, James and Joses, wanted to come with her, so she is coming later." Susanna brushed the hair from her forehead and tucked it beneath her veil. "They were able to come home for a time, so I think she wanted to stay with her family a little longer."

"I don't blame her. Won't you miss Tobias?" I gave her a curious look.

She shrugged. "He is traveling again this month, but he is planning to join us soon." She smiled. "I told him he'd better! I don't want to be accused of abandoning our marriage."

I laughed. "You never were one to stay at home, were you? I'm surprised he doesn't mind your absence. I often wonder what my life would look like if Marcus had lived. Would he have allowed me to follow Jesus? Would he have wanted to follow him as well? I'll never know." I stopped walking to adjust my sandal.

Susanna touched my arm. "He would have been happy you are healed, Mary. I know my brother. He may not have loved you, just as I don't yet love Tobias, but he was a good man. He wanted to care for us both. He just didn't know how."

We began walking again and picked up our pace to catch up to the carts.

"You are free to do as you please now, Mary. Marcus wouldn't fault you for wanting to be with the teacher."

I nodded. "In any case, I don't feel entirely free. I'm able to come and go as I please, I suppose, but I feel bound to do what God would have me do. I can never be free of that desire, so I wonder how free we really are."

"Jesus could tell you," she said, swinging her basket as she walked. "He set us free from the demons. He'll tell us how to live now that we have a different purpose."

"I've missed him and the men, haven't you?" My heart did a little flip as I saw Capernaum come into view. "I hope they're back."

"If not, I'm sure Adi will be glad to see us."

As we neared the town, we saw a growing crowd in the streets. I glanced at Susanna. "Jesus must be back."

She nodded. "We need to take the back road to Simon's house or the carts won't get through."

I hurried to tell Elazar, while Susanna did the same with her servant. We made it to a lane that led toward Simon's house. I desperately wanted to wade through the crowd to see what was happening, but I needed to explain to Adi the food we had brought and find out where to put it.

When Simon's home came into view, I rushed ahead and entered the courtyard. "Adi?" I knocked on the door, smiling when she opened it.

"Mary!" She glanced behind me. "Susanna! Welcome home!"

She laughed. "But what is all of this?" She pointed to the carts overflowing with jars of grain and oil and the wine I'd added at the last moment.

"We both brought these from our storehouses. You can't continue to feed all of us without help. So we brought help." I looked about, relieved to be back. How was it that Simon's house felt more like home to me than the estate where I'd grown up? Surely it was because of Jesus and the people who loved him. "Where are the men?"

"Jesus has returned and a crowd formed outside the house almost as soon as he arrived, so they've all gone to the town square. I suspect he is healing and teaching there," Adi said. "I would have gone, but I wanted to begin the bread baking."

I had to fight my longing to leave the women and join the crowd. I couldn't just leave Adi with the food and not help. "Where do you want our servants to put all of this? Do you have a storage area that can hold it?" I'd seen most of Simon's house, though not all.

Adi stepped into the courtyard and approached the carts parked in the street in front of her house. "Some of this will fit in our back room, but some will have to go to Salome and Zebedee's house. Come," she said, motioning to the men.

Susanna and I joined them, and together we carted load after load to a room where Adi dried herbs and waited for the wine she'd made to ferment. The rest we took to Salome's home, where we found places to store what we could.

"Thank you for bringing so much," Adi said as we made our way back to her house. We came upon the crowd, and I spotted Jesus in the middle, attempting to walk toward the synagogue.

"Is he going to preach at the synagogue when it is not Shabbat?" I glanced at my friends.

Adi shrugged. "Let's get closer if we can."

My heart lifted with the relief of knowing Adi agreed that seeing Jesus was more important, or perhaps simply more edifying, than baking bread. We wove our way between the people until we could see the disciples.

A man dressed in the garb of a synagogue ruler approached Jesus. To my utter shock, he knelt at Jesus' feet. Had the rulers changed their opinion of Jesus in the short time we were away? I leaned in, straining to hear over the press of the crowd.

"My daughter is dying," the ruler said. "She is only twelve years old." He choked on a sob, his gaze imploring. "But please, come and put your hand on her, and she will live."

"I will come," Jesus said, touching the man's shoulder. "What is your name?"

"Jairus, my lord."

Jesus glanced at the disciples, then followed Jairus toward his home. I hurried to keep up, but the crowd fought me, and I kept feeling as though I took one step forward and two backward. Jesus would never get there in time to heal this man's daughter if the people did not let him go!

The ruler's face was a mask of anxiety, but he could not move faster because of the crowd.

Abruptly, Jesus stopped walking, bringing everything to a halt. "Who touched me?" he asked, looking in all directions.

Murmurs of denial came from those on the outskirts of the crowd. "It's impossible to get close enough to touch him," said someone at a distance.

"It wasn't me," another closer voice declared.

"Master, the crowds surround you and are pressing in on you!" Simon said.

My thoughts exactly. Why would Jesus ask such a question with everyone touching him?

"Someone touched me," Jesus insisted, "for I perceive that power has gone out from me."

I searched the area nearest him, and then I saw her. A small woman, perhaps thirty years of age, approached him. She trembled and fell to her knees at his feet. "It was me." Slowly lifting her head to meet his gaze, she said, "I've bled for twelve years, and no one has been able to help me. I've spent all of my money on doctors, but they only made it worse. I thought . . . I thought, 'If I could just touch his cloak, I will be healed.'" She paused. "And I was." Amazement filled her gaze.

Jesus reached for her hand and lifted her. "Take heart, daughter," he said. "Your faith has made you well. Go in peace."

I caught the look of pure joy in her eyes. I wanted to laugh and cry with her, for I understood how she felt. When Jesus healed me, hadn't I experienced unbelievable joy?

A commotion coming from the direction of the synagogue drew my attention, keeping me from my desire to reach the woman and offer her what I could. Bleeding like that would have made her as much of an outcast as I had been. I must see her. But a man dressed like a servant pushed his way toward Jairus, and Jesus turned to him.

"Your daughter is dead," the servant said to Jairus. "Do not trouble the teacher anymore."

Jesus looked into Jairus's eyes. My heart quickened. I had seen Jesus bring the boy in Nain to life again and return him to his mother. Would he give this young girl back to her parents in front of this crowd? Nain and Capernaum were very different cities. I always sensed more hostility here than in some of the smaller towns in Galilee where we had traveled.

"Do not fear," Jesus said, causing me to focus directly on him. "Only believe, and she will be well."

He pushed ahead, and we followed in relative silence except

for the occasional question or comment. We passed the synagogue and came to the ruler's house, and another crowd met us, noisy and mourning the dead.

I desperately wanted to be with the disciples and enter Jairus's house. Perhaps I could comfort his wife. Do something. But Jesus told the mourners to leave. Though they mocked him, he took only Simon, James, and John along with Jairus into the house.

Susanna and Adi pressed against me. "Do you think we should return home and prepare the evening meal?" Adi asked. "We don't know how long Jesus will be detained, and he might disperse the crowd after this."

"If the girl is dead, Jesus could still heal her," I whispered, drawing them slightly away from the larger crowd. We were near the courtyard of the house opposite Jairus's. "He raised a boy in Nain from the dead."

"Simon told me of that," Adi whispered. "But what will happen to him if he does so here?"

"Wouldn't that be a good thing?" Susanna asked, clearly puzzled.

"Can you imagine what the crowd would do to him? Everyone who's had a loved one die would want him to bring them back." Adi looked toward the house.

"Or the leaders who hate him will use it against him somehow," I said. I could never quite shake the worry of what they might do to Jesus one day. Why did I fear this? "Raising the dead proves his power over anything we've ever seen before. That alone might make them see him as a bigger threat to their own power."

Susanna and Adi nodded, and Susanna held a finger to her lips. The door to Jairus's house opened, and Jesus emerged with the three disciples. As we suspected, he dismissed the crowd. There was no sign of Jairus.

"Let's go home," Adi said. This time I didn't disagree.

That night, no word was said about what Jesus did in Jairus's home. But over the next few days, Jairus's daughter was seen in the courtyard grinding grain, and the rumors began.

Before we got ready to move on to another town, news came to us that Jesus had indeed raised the child from the dead and the news had spread far beyond Capernaum. What did it all mean?

About a week after the incident with Jairus's daughter, Susanna and I rose before dawn to reach the well outside Capernaum before the other women of the town awoke. A donkey accompanied us this time, its back draped in goatskin sacks. I lowered the bucket to draw the water while Susanna helped me fill the sacks one at a time.

"I suppose we're worrying too much about water," I said, glancing at her as I poured it to fill the next sack. "But this will save time if each man carries his own."

"It would have been easier if we'd all come here together and let the men help," Susanna said, straining as she took a turn to lift the heavy bucket.

I laughed. "Yes, it would have. But it's nice to help Jesus in this way, don't you think? I don't want to be the one to slow him down."

She looked at me as if I had lost my mind. "I think if they were here to help, this would have gone faster, Mary, not slower."

I shrugged. I felt useful when my hands were busy. I would never be in Jesus' inner circle or see what the twelve did, but I would do what was set before me.

"In any case, we're done now," I said, placing the last sack over the donkey's back. "I hope we haven't weighed him down too much." I patted the animal's side as Susanna took his reins and led him back to Simon's house.

Within a few hours, we said our goodbyes to Adi and Salome and walked with the men as we headed toward Gennesaret. The air carried little breeze, but we soon found a crowd from Capernaum and probably other nearby towns following us.

Joseph Justus came alongside Susanna and me as we walked the dirt path, the dust coating our sandals. "Why don't the two of you move up ahead? With the crowd closing in, it's safer if you are nearer the men."

Were we in danger with Jesus nearby? I looked at Joseph. He was a head taller than I was and had a bigger build than Marcus. His brown beard hid an angular jaw, and he pushed his smooth dark hair out of his eyes. I had to admit, I appreciated his protectiveness.

"Thank you," Susanna said before I could speak. "The crowds grow every time we set out. I can't blame people for wanting to be near Jesus, though."

At that moment, Andrew and Thomas joined Joseph. "Mary, Susanna," Andrew said, smiling. Where Simon was strong-willed and outspoken, Andrew was one of the quiet ones among the group. I'd liked him the first time I'd met him.

"Andrew," I said, returning his smile. "Does Jesus have anything special planned for Gennesaret?" I had missed the discussion when Jesus laid out today's plans.

"We're going to spend a day there. Matthias has invited us to stay at his parents' house," Andrew said. He uncorked the skin of water he was holding and took a sip. "Thank you for this." He held it up, then capped it again.

In the distance, the noise of the crowd grew.

"Have mercy on us, Son of David!" The voice sounded distant but distinct.

I turned to glance behind me but could not see who had spoken.

"Come with me," Joseph said, directing a look toward Susanna and me. We followed him until we were walking between the men, Thaddaeus and Matthew ahead of us, Philip and Nathanael behind. Joseph fell back with them.

"Well, I feel safer, I suppose," I whispered to Susanna, "though I didn't feel *unsafe* before."

"I think Joseph likes you," she whispered back. She gave me a knowing look.

I felt my cheeks heat in that telltale blush. "He's a brother to me. You're imagining things."

She winked at me. "Maybe."

"Have mercy on us, Son of David!" The voice was louder now as we passed lush grapevines bordering the town.

"Who is calling to him?" I stood off to the side and craned my neck to look behind me, but I couldn't tell who had spoken.

I turned again to follow Jesus, not surprised when the crowd continued, overwhelming the small town. The disciples and the other men who followed Jesus ushered all of us into the house of Matthias's parents. But the calling did not stop after the door shut behind us.

A knock sounded on the door a few moments later. Simon, always the leader, approached Jesus. "Master, shall I send whoever it is away?"

Jesus regarded him. "I did not come here to escape the people, Simon. We are here to minister to them." He looked at Matthias's father. "Thank you for your willingness to accept all of us into your home. I know it is a sacrifice."

"It is no trouble at all," Matthias's father said. He carried a proud-of-his-son look as he glanced from Jesus to Matthias. "We are honored to help you in any way we can."

"Thank you," Jesus said again as he walked with Simon to the door.

I moved to a place in the house that had a view of the window and the courtyard. The crowd filled the court and beyond. I was thankful to be inside as the noise from the people clamoring to see Jesus grew.

Simon opened the door, and at the front of the crowd stood two men whose eyes were clouded and unfocused.

"They're blind," I said to Susanna.

"Greetings, friends," Jesus said as the men fell to their knees.

"Son of David, have mercy on us," they said in unison.

"What do you want me to do for you?" Jesus asked, his voice rich and kind. How I loved the sound of it.

"We want to see, Lord," each man said in turn.

"Do you believe that I am able to do this?" Jesus asked them.

"Yes, Lord," they replied.

Jesus touched first one, then the other. "According to your faith, let it be done to you."

A shout erupted from each one. "I can see!"

My heart lifted with their praise, but Jesus' words stopped them. "See that no one knows about this."

I noted their confusion and felt the same.

"Thank you, Lord," they said, then hurried away, still shouting and whooping. They had no intention of keeping quiet.

The rest of the crowd pushed toward the door, and that old protectiveness washed over me. The disciples stood between the crowd and Jesus and commanded the people to give Jesus room. He stepped into the space they'd made for him. I motioned for Susanna to join me at the door.

"The kingdom of heaven is like treasure hidden in a field," Jesus said, lifting his arms toward the crowd. "When a man found it, he hid it again, and then in his joy went and sold all

211

he had and bought that field. Again, the kingdom of heaven is like a merchant looking for fine pearls. When he found one of great value, he went away and sold everything he had and bought it."

Men and women in the crowd asked a question here and there, but my mind wandered, trying to imagine the kingdom of heaven Jesus spoke of. He often said, "Repent, for the kingdom of heaven is at hand." People had spoken of a kingdom when my father was alive, and Jesus often mentioned it to the disciples, but I still didn't understand.

"What does he mean by 'the kingdom of heaven'?" Susanna asked before I could voice my questions.

"I'm trying to understand that myself." I studied the faces of the people caught up in his words. "The rabbis teach that the Messiah will be of the line of David, a warrior to overthrow our oppressors and set up a kingdom of people. But if Jesus is the Son of David, our Messiah, where is the army to overthrow the Romans or conquer the world to rule over it? How can he say the kingdom of heaven is at hand?"

Susanna shook her head. "I don't know."

We looked at each other. "I think Jesus wants us to know that the kingdom is important. Valuable. A treasure," I said. "But I want to know more."

I glanced toward the courtyard. The sun angled toward the west, yet the people stayed. Hopefully Jesus would dismiss them soon. Then the men would join us again, and perhaps Jesus would explain to us what he did not say to the people.

TWENTY-FOUR

The opportunity to ask Jesus more about the kingdom of heaven did not come that evening as I'd hoped. After the men had eaten, Jesus left us alone with Matthias's family. Susanna and I were sent to sleep on the roof, while the men slept in the courtyard or wherever they could find space.

I lay on the mat I had brought with me but could not sleep. After listening too long to Susanna's light snoring, I arose and walked to the parapet. A few lights shone from the windows of the homes that spread throughout Gennesaret's streets. Had Jesus returned yet? Or would he spend the night in the hills praying as usual?

Memories of the nights I had spent roaming the hills around Magdala surfaced. I had never really minded being alone. I had experienced little else all my life. It was when the spirits invaded my life and drove me to the wilderness that I began to fear the dark and hate the solitude.

I'm free of all that, I told myself.

The full moon rose and illumined the inner courtyard below. In the moon's glow, I could see Andrew, Philip, Matthew, Thaddaeus, Judas, and Nathanael. How peaceful they looked. If only I felt the same.

Restless, I moved to the part of the roof that overlooked the outer courtyard where the others slept, including Joseph Justus and Matthias. Why wouldn't Matthias sleep in his own bed?

I'd always wanted brothers and sisters, but though we could be called an unusual sort of family, these men were not my brothers and the women were just acquaintances. Susanna was the closest thing I had to a friend, so why did I feel left out even with her?

I searched the hills and what I could see of the streets but saw only the occasional lone lurker walking in and out of the shadows. There was no sign of Jesus.

The cool breeze raised gooseflesh on my arms, and I cinched my robe about me. I made my way back to the tented enclosure where Susanna slept. Mary Clopas should be joining us soon, and I thought briefly of Joanna, wondering if she would find us as she'd hoped.

Perhaps that was what we needed. A larger group of women to follow the rabbi. Women to talk to when the men went off without us. Perhaps adding more women would settle my restless heart.

But the truth was, I needed his peace. I needed Jesus to keep my worries at bay, because though he had assured me the demons would not return, I still feared something nameless. Trusting him was going to take time.

Before I knew it, dawn had come rushing in with pink skies and birdsong and the rooster's crow. I rose, noting that Susanna had already left the roof. Why hadn't she wakened me?

I rolled up the mat to take with me and donned my robe, tying the belt. By the time I entered the house, the men had finished eating and were making plans for the day.

"Why didn't you wake me?" I whispered to Susanna.

"You looked so peaceful. I thought you needed to rest." She looked at me with an understanding smile. "I know you don't always sleep well, Mary. It's all right to rest sometimes."

"I don't need to rest," I said, surprised at the anger I felt. "Are we leaving?"

Susanna nodded as she handed me a loaf of flatbread. "Eat." She pointed toward the sitting room, where the men were rising and bidding Matthias's father farewell.

"Do we have everything packed? You should have wakened me." My heart beat too fast. I moved toward the door to check on the donkey and the saddlebags, but Susanna stopped me.

"It's all set, Mary. Jesus told the men we would stop at the well to refill the skins on our way out of town. There is nothing more to do but follow him." Susanna tilted her head. "Is everything all right?"

I looked away for a moment. "Yes." I faced her, aware of my clenched hands. "Let's go." I walked out the door, stopping to thank our hosts, then fell into step with Susanna between the men.

"Are you sure all is well?" Susanna asked as we took the road toward Magdala.

I drew in a breath and released it. Why did I feel so cross? So I had overslept. It wasn't like I had sinned. But the whole morning had put me in a bad frame of mind, and I struggled to change my feelings.

"Mary?" Susanna touched my arm. "I'm sorry I didn't wake you. You're not upset about that, are you?"

"Of course not!" I fairly snapped. "Of course not," I said again gently and smiled. "I'm fine." I wasn't fine, but I didn't know why.

I looked at the men walking ahead of us, toward Jesus. Normally, I wanted to be as close to him as I could get, but today my mind whirled with too many confusing thoughts, and I couldn't define what I feared. I shouldn't have slept late and been left out of knowing Jesus' plans.

As I pondered my frustrated thoughts, aware of Susanna's concern, Judas left Philip's side to join us. I didn't know this disciple well, but he seemed an intelligent, passionate man. Like so many of the others, he was anxious for Jesus to amass a large following. While they loved the crowds, I cringed around too many people. But I shoved aside my thoughts and smiled at him.

"Shalom, Judas," I said. I had not given him a good look in the past, as I was always so focused on Jesus. Judas was a handsome man of medium build and had the darkest eyes I had ever seen.

"Shalom, Mary, Susanna. I hope you don't mind if I join you." He kept an easy pace behind Simon, James, and John, who walked in sync with Jesus.

"Not at all." I glanced at him and caught the smile on his face. I didn't know what else to say, so I looked ahead as we walked in silence.

"Did you hear the teacher as he spoke to the crowd yesterday?" Judas asked. "I wish he would have said more about the kingdom. I'll admit, I grow impatient for him to bring that kingdom to our land and begin to rule." He kicked a stone off to the side and looked at us. Why did he care what we thought? We were women, after all. But he continued to direct his attention to us, so I nodded.

"Yes. We heard him while we prepared food," I said. "I'll admit, my mind wandered once he explained the kingdom as something to treasure. I don't understand it all."

"Nor do I," Susanna said, wiping sweat from her brow. The

sun grew warmer as Magdala came into view, and I hoped we would stop there before heading to Tiberias. I wanted to welcome all of them to my home again—another frustration that I had missed the opportunity to ask at the morning meal.

"I think he's healing to gather the crowds to him in order to overthrow Rome, and from there, the rest of the world," Judas said, lowering his voice.

My eyes widened. "He hasn't said that, has he?" I had heard no talk from Jesus about overthrowing Rome, though I knew that was what the people wanted from the Messiah when he came.

"He hasn't said so outright yet. But I can sense it. Why else would he want to welcome the size of the crowds we have? Why heal so many if not to gain their acceptance?" Judas's earnest tone stirred me, though his drop in volume intrigued me more.

"The others don't share your speculations, do they?" I wasn't a very good judge of a person's character, but I liked Judas. I had just never heard anyone say such things, and I wasn't sure what to make of his words. I glanced ahead to where Jesus and Simon, James, and John stood some distance ahead.

"Not yet," he said, shrugging. "I'm not wrong." He offered us a reassuring smile. "But I don't think the teacher wants to share his full intentions just yet. He is careful, measuring his words, and wants to be sure we are all on board, ready to fight when the time comes."

A shiver worked through me. "Why would he invite women to join him if he is building an army?" I asked, confused. "We could all be killed if we attempt to rise against Rome."

"How do we know that the kingdom of heaven is also a kingdom of earth?" Susanna asked Judas.

"What are you all talking about?" Joseph Justus asked, coming alongside Susanna.

Magdala was not far off now, and I didn't want to have this discussion with anyone. I wanted to ask Jesus if we would stop at my home before heading to Tiberias.

"The kingdom the rabbi is building," Judas said, stepping back to walk beside Joseph. "Don't you agree that he is welcoming the crowds in order to prepare them for bigger things? To rule the world?"

"I don't know," Joseph said. "I'm not sure that the kingdom he speaks of is like any kingdom we've ever imagined. He has not been clear enough for me to speculate."

"His words and actions are pretty clear to me. We need to help him spread his message to the ends of the earth. That will be far easier once he rules as king over all." Judas sounded so earnest, but I found myself torn between the two men's varying opinions. "I wonder who will be greatest in the coming kingdom," he added.

At that point, I shook my head and picked up my pace. Men! Was that all they thought about? Did the others feel and think the same?

Susanna hurried to catch up to me, but before I could reach Jesus, a crowd from Magdala came toward us. The disciples circled us as Jesus stepped forward to meet them.

"Rabbi." A man I recognized as the bread merchant led another man toward Jesus—one I'd seen when I wandered the hills during the days the spirits controlled me.

I instinctively drew back. My breath caught in my chest as the demon-possessed man looked my way. I listened, but this time I did not hear my name. My heart skipped a beat, and I prayed the man did not remember me.

"Rabbi," the bread merchant said again, gripping the other man's arm. "My brother has not been able to speak for years, not since the demons possessed him." The merchant struggled as his brother tried to wriggle free. The demons were stronger than this man, but one look at Jesus and I understood why they did not wrench him free of his brother's hold. "Please, if you are willing, help him!"

"Out of him!" Jesus commanded, looking directly into the glazed eyes of the mute man. And then he touched the man, who promptly fell to his knees.

"Thank you! Thank you!" He gripped Jesus' feet, weeping. "Thank you."

The merchant's eyes filled, and I looked beyond him to others from Magdala whom I'd known all my life.

"Nothing like this has ever been seen in Israel," said one of the men in the crowd.

At that moment, a Pharisee approached. My heart skipped another beat. I knew this man. Or rather, I remembered him well. He was the Pharisee I had asked to pray for my father years before. I would never forget him, though I had hoped to never see him again.

But here he stood facing Jesus, arms crossed over his chest, his wide phylactery moving beneath his furrowed brow. "It is by the prince of demons that he drives out demons," he said, venom in his tone.

I could not suppress a gasp. Though it was not the first time Jesus had been thus accused, how dare he say such a thing!

The Pharisee whirled about and pushed back through the crowd before Jesus could respond. The crowd parted for him. Whispers began. Some men nodded in apparent agreement with the Pharisee, others shook their heads in vehement disagreement.

Jesus headed around Magdala toward Tiberias. I glanced at my hometown, saddened that we would not be spending the day and night there. But one look at Jesus told me his sorrow was far greater. He'd again been accused of being demon possessed, something I knew was entirely impossible for him. I recognized those who possessed unclean spirits, and one thing I knew for certain. Jesus was not like them and never could be.

That Pharisee, though . . . I wondered.

TWENTY-FIVE

By the time we neared Tiberias, the breeze had cooled and the sun had dropped to the edge of the horizon. We entered the gates only moments before they were closed.

"Are we going to spend the night in the town square?" I asked Susanna.

She looked about, her eyes wide. "I hope not. I would have rather spent the night in the fields."

"I would have rather we stayed at my home in Magdala," I said under my breath, still frustrated with my inability to convince or ask Jesus to do as I'd hoped. I released a pent-up breath. "Did Jesus mention a house where we would stay?"

The men gathered around Jesus while we stood just outside their circle. What had happened to their protectiveness of us?

At that moment, a man approached Jesus, wearing the typical garb of a shepherd. "Greetings, Rabbi," he said, bowing slightly. "Welcome to our town."

"Greetings," Jesus responded.

I shifted my basket and felt Susanna touching my side.

"I am Yitzhak," the man said. "I am a shepherd of Tiberias."

He glanced at the group of us. "You are welcome to stay with me tonight. Do you plan to stay long in Tiberias?"

"Not long," Jesus said. "Just through Shabbat. We have many places yet to travel after this."

Yitzhak looked at us again. "I have room for all of you, though the women will have to sleep in the room where we store the wine. The men can sleep on the roof."

"Thank you for your hospitality," Jesus said.

Yitzhak led the way through the streets, carrying a torch to his home on a hill overlooking the city. For a shepherd, he had done well. Perhaps he owned many flocks like Abraham, Isaac, and Jacob of old.

We settled into the man's home and into the roles we had now grown used to. I was so tired that the thought of helping the women prepare food for our men did not please me. How I longed to simply crawl onto a mat and sleep. Would this day never end?

I forced my hands to chop the herbs as Susanna talked with Yitzhak's wife. I tuned out their conversation, trying instead to listen to Jesus, but the men were all talking at once, making meaningful conversation impossible to follow.

About an hour later, Yitzhak broke bread and passed the basket to the men. Susanna and I finally took a seat at the back of the room to eat with them.

"Teacher?" Yitzhak asked as he dipped his bread into a barley stew.

"Yes, Yitzhak?" Jesus held the bread in his hand but did not eat.

"I have a question."

"I'm listening." Jesus waited, and I found myself unable to eat, my mind focused on a hunger for his words. He was the only person who had ever brought peace to my jumbled thoughts, and I desperately needed him today.

"Lord, are only a few people going to be saved?" Yitzhak asked.

This was not the question I'd expected. A hush fell over the room. My pulse quickened, anxiety washing over me. How did this man know of Jesus well enough to recognize who he was? But he could have been among any of the crowds during our travels. Perhaps the people of Tiberias had already heard of Jesus' message and ministry.

"Make every effort to enter through the narrow door," Jesus said, "because many, I tell you, will try to enter and will not be able to. Once the owner of the house gets up and closes the door, you will stand outside knocking and pleading, 'Sir, open the door for us.' But he will answer, 'I don't know you or where you come from.' Then you will say, 'We ate and drank with you, and you taught in our streets.' But he will reply, 'I don't know you or where you come from. Away from me, all you evildoers!'"

Jesus paused and looked about the group. What of Judas's claims that Jesus wanted the crowds in order to begin the kingdom and overthrow Rome and rule the world? How could Jesus say that many would not be able to enter?

"But Master," Simon said, "who then can be saved?"

Jesus looked at Simon, then at the rest of us, though I couldn't make eye contact with him from where I was sitting.

"With man this is impossible, but with God all things are possible."

"We have left everything to follow you!" Simon said. "What then will there be for us?"

That Simon would ask such a thing in a stranger's home made me squirm, but Jesus' look held compassion, as it always did. Apparently he didn't mind the question or where it was asked. "Truly I tell you," he said, "at the renewal of all things, when the Son of Man sits on his glorious throne, you who have followed me will also sit on twelve thrones, judging the twelve tribes of Israel. And everyone who has left houses or brothers or sisters or father or mother or wife or children or fields for my sake will receive a hundred times as much and will inherit eternal life. But many who are first will be last, and many who are last will be first."

The rhythm of my heart slowed with his words, and I looked about the room, wondering what our host thought. I could read nothing in the man's expression, unlike the Pharisees, who openly showed their displeasure with Jesus.

But Jesus' words went against Judas's question about who would be greatest in the kingdom, didn't it? Or did Jesus actually answer it when he said that the twelve would sit on thrones judging the twelve tribes of Israel?

My head began to pound with confusion. Why had Jesus only mentioned the twelve in a stranger's home? And what of me, Susanna, Mary Clopas, Joanna, Adi, and Salome? Were we included in the few he spoke of? Was I among the first or the last, and what did that mean?

Where did I fit into all this? I longed for an acceptance I'd never had. But as the questions from the men and our host filled the room, I felt more left out than ever.

I slept fitfully again that night, wishing I could free myself of the questions. This time I rose with the dawn, determined not to repeat the way I'd felt the day before. After the morning meal, Jesus left with the men to heal and preach in the marketplace. Susanna and I joined them after we had helped prepare food for the evening meal.

As we rounded the bend to the street that bordered the market, we found reaching Jesus almost impossible because of the crowds. The clamor of voices asking for healing and the shrieks of those possessed before he silenced them filled the air.

How I wished possession by evil spirits had not been my past, but there was no changing what was.

We squeezed between the people to get closer to Jesus. When we were within earshot, his voice came to us clearly, like a gentle breeze.

"If anyone would come after me," he said, his tone urgent, laced with what sounded like longing, "let him deny himself and take up his cross daily and follow me. For whoever would save his life will lose it, but whoever loses his life for my sake will save it. For what does it profit a man if he gains the whole world and loses or forfeits himself?"

He looked about and lifted his arm, encompassing all, passion in his eyes. *Take up his cross?* What did that mean?

"For whoever is ashamed of me and of my words," Jesus said, pulling my thoughts back to him, "of him will the Son of Man be ashamed when he comes in his glory and the glory of the Father and of the holy angels. But I tell you truly, there are some standing here who will not taste death until they see the kingdom of God."

The sun was past the midpoint in the sky, and its warmth heated my skin as Jesus' words heated my soul.

As he dismissed the people to their homes, promising to speak again the next day on Shabbat in their synagogue, I walked with the disciples back toward Yitzhak's home.

"He says a lot of hard things," Susanna said, falling into step with me. "Did you understand any of what he said? Take up your cross? Some of us won't die until we see the kingdom?"

I shook my head. "I don't get it either, but it's exciting, isn't it? Are we among those who won't taste death until we see the kingdom of God? Wouldn't that make what Judas suggested true? Maybe Jesus is going to bring the kingdom to the land soon and the disciples will sit on twelve thrones, and we will live without Rome's rule. Everyone will embrace him and know the Lord." My heart lifted at the thought. Maybe I did understand. Much of what Jesus said pointed to him bringing about the fulfillment of everything we had been taught all our lives. The Messiah had come, and I was part of it.

"I wonder what our roles in the kingdom will be," Susanna said, interrupting my thoughts. "I mean, we won't sit on thrones like the men will, so what about the rest of us? What of the women?"

"I don't know," I said. "Jesus will probably explain it to us as soon as he can. I want to know when he's going to show us the kingdom. I mean, we could live a long time before we die, and he is not old. Might the kingdom wait for years before it comes? How long does it take to win a war against Rome? Or will he fight at all? Maybe they will just fall at his feet like we have."

The scent of baking bread wafted to us as we neared Yitzhak's home, reminding me that we should be helping with the meal. Talk of the kingdom would have to wait. The practical needs of our current life came first.

Shabbat's dawn brought a sense of excitement. The night before, after Jesus left the house to go to the surrounding hills to pray, the men had talked of the kingdom. Yitzhak and his wife allowed us the main room as they went to bed, but the men were too excited to rest.

"Who do you think will be greatest in the kingdom?" The question began with Judas but spread to the rest of the twelve and some of the others.

Susanna looked at me with a raised brow. I shrugged, and when the men began to quietly argue, we'd left them for the night.

Now, as we sat in the women's section of the synagogue, I wondered if the men had ever decided on an answer to their question. It was foolish to me, but Marcus had shown me how competitive men could be when it came to showing their strength or power.

I shifted in my seat to better see Jesus as he stood to read the Scriptures. He gave a traditional reading and spoke about the meaning behind the words, but before he could finish, a commotion in the women's section caught his attention. A woman, who at first appeared to be sitting with her head bent in her lap, shuffled forward to the center of the synagogue. My senses were alerted as she brushed past me.

"A spirit controls her," I whispered to Susanna. She nodded.

Jesus rose from Moses's seat and approached the woman. "Come forward," he said as she struggled to put one foot in front of the other. When at last she stood before him, his gaze fixed on her, he said, "Woman, you are set free from your infirmity." He touched her shoulders.

She straightened so quickly, I thought she would need steadying. But she did not waver. Instead, she lifted her hands and voice toward heaven. "Then they cried to the Lord in their trouble, and He saved them from their distress. He sent out His word and healed them. Blessed are You, Lord our God, Maker of the Universe."

Murmurs of praise broke out among the men and women alike. I laughed for joy. Another woman set free from bondage. How long had the spirit crippled her in that way? I shuddered. How had she survived?

"Men of Israel!" The voice of the synagogue leader rose

above the sounds of praise to Adonai. "There are six days for work. So come and be healed on those days, not on Shabbat."

How often would I hear that same refrain?

The crowd immediately quieted, and I caught the self-conscious looks and wariness on the faces of those who belonged to this synagogue.

But Jesus turned to look at the synagogue ruler. "You hypocrites!" he said. "Doesn't each of you on Shabbat untie your ox or donkey from the stall and lead it out to give it water? Then should not this woman, a daughter of Abraham whom Satan has kept bound for eighteen long years, be set free on the Sabbath day from what bound her?"

The ruler's face reddened, and scowls from the other leaders dampened the joy that had been present moments before.

Jesus turned to walk out of the synagogue. We followed him in silence, but I did not miss the delight in the eyes of the people we passed. The leaders might hate Jesus, but the people didn't. That was good for the kingdom, wasn't it?

TWENTY-SIX

———— **Ten Months Later** ————

The Sea of Galilee gently rocked the boat we were in as we followed Jesus and the twelve toward the region of Caesarea Philippi, the pagan city of the god Pan. I shuddered at the thought and could not understand why Jesus would bring his followers to a place where no self-respecting Jew would go. Yet the men followed Jesus' lead.

I felt the spray of the sea as Joseph Justus, Matthias, and a few other men rowed our boat to Bethsaida, where we would disembark and walk to that forbidden place. Susanna, Joanna, Mary Clopas, Salome, Adi, and I had joined the men, despite our misgivings. We'd been traveling for months throughout Galilee, down to Jerusalem for Passover, and back toward Judea. At one point we went to the Decapolis and as far north as Syria for a brief time.

I relished this respite from all the walking, though it would be short-lived. I did not look forward to entering a city that reminded me of the demons. No doubt this town was filled with them and the worship of them.

We reached the other side of the lake and headed north. A

hint of dread filled me as we gathered around Jesus. Our group had dwindled because of one of Jesus' difficult teachings, not long after Jesus had performed one of his greatest miracles and fed more people at one time than I could count. The disciples claimed the number at five thousand men, but so many women and children were left uncounted that the number could have easily been triple that amount.

I looked up at the sound of Jesus' voice. He had moved some distance from the shore and was headed toward the city. I hurried to keep up and was soon walking only a few paces behind him.

The city loomed in the distance, and Jesus turned to us. "Who do people say the Son of Man is?" he asked.

"Some say John the Baptist," John said, speaking of the prophet who had paved the way for Jesus.

"That's ridiculous," Andrew said. "I was John's disciple and saw him baptize you, Rabbi. Anyone who knows John would know better."

The Baptizer had met a tragic end at the hand of Herod Antipas, but Andrew was right. John and Jesus had lived at the same time. Where did people get such ideas?

"Others say Elijah," Matthew said.

I glanced his way, surprised at the wonder and doubt that flickered in his gaze. Did he think Jesus was Elijah come to life again? Scripture taught that Elijah had not died but was taken in a whirlwind to heaven.

"Still others say Jeremiah or one of the prophets," Judas said, shaking his head. "I don't understand how they can think such things."

Neither did I, but I merely listened and studied the expressions on Jesus' face. Did he honestly care what we thought of him? Couldn't he tell how much we loved and adored him?

"But what about you?" Jesus asked. "Who do you say I am?"

"You are the Messiah, the Son of the living God," Simon said.

Yes. I knew it was true beyond doubt. We had believed for well over a year that Jesus was the Son of Man spoken of by the prophet Daniel, and the Son of God, our Messiah. Hadn't I thought so from the very beginning of knowing him? Yet I think it had taken me until this moment, at Simon's declaration, to feel it so strongly in my heart.

"Blessed are you, Simon son of Jonah, for this was not revealed to you by flesh and blood, but by my Father in heaven," Jesus said, looking directly at Simon. "And I tell you that you are Peter, and on this rock I will build my church, and the gates of hell will not overcome it. I will give you the keys of the kingdom of heaven. Whatever you bind on earth will be bound in heaven, and whatever you loose on earth will be loosed in heaven."

The pronouncement caused a hush to fall over the group. A little gasp escaped Adi. She looked from Jesus to Simon—now Peter—to me. The people of Caesarea Philippi believed that the gates of hell, or the entrance to the underworld of the dead, were located in the deepest depths of the caves at the mouth of the Temple of Pan and the Dancing Goats. Was Jesus saying the church, whatever that was, would defeat the beliefs, the gods of this area? Or all false gods, like those that inhabited the demon possessed who came to him for healing?

"What does he mean by 'church'?" Susanna whispered in my ear.

"I don't know. Something new?" I whispered back. "But why is he giving the keys of the kingdom to Simon—to Peter?"

She shook her head. I looked at Jesus, hoping he would explain himself.

"None of you are to tell anyone that I am the Messiah. Do you understand?" Jesus said instead of explaining.

"Yes, Master," Simon Peter said, and many of the men nodded. "But why not?" he added. "The Pharisees already suspect that this is your claim. You call yourself the Son of Man."

A soft sigh escaped Jesus' lips. "They are not interested in hearing the truth. By their unbelief, they have already rejected me." He turned at the sound of voices coming toward us from the city. At the same time, more boats landed on the shore near ours, bringing more people to see him.

The men spread out to help secure order among the throngs of people coming toward Jesus, bringing family and friends who suffered from many different maladies.

I pulled the women aside. "Let's do as the men are doing and mingle with the crowd to assure them that they will be seen. I'm going to try to avoid the demon possessed," I added, glancing at Susanna. "Perhaps Mary Clopas, Joanna, Adi, and Salome can help with them, if they are needed?"

"Of course," Salome said. "We understand, Mary."

She didn't, but I thanked her as I walked toward the crowd. How could I explain the pain in my middle that would not leave every time I drew near those possessed? Every time I feared they would call my name? I didn't understand it myself.

"What did you think of the reception Jesus received in Caesarea Philippi?" Mary Clopas asked as we passed the red-rock bluffs and forests near the base of Mount Hermon the following day.

"The city is so influenced by Rome that I was surprised anyone would come for his message. There is so much worship of false gods," I said. "They don't mind it when he is healing, though." In truth, I had felt unsettled in the city with its temples to Augustus and Zeus and a shrine to Pan. Gods that were just as evil as those spirits that had lived within me. "I wasn't comfortable there," I admitted as we came to a spot at the base of the mountain near a flowing spring, where the grass was lush.

"I wonder why we came here at all," Mary Clopas said, glancing ahead to where her sons James and Joses walked with the other men.

"I don't know."

We settled near the spring, though the twelve stood apart from us. A few moments passed, then Jesus led Peter, James, and John, his intimate three, up the mountain. The rest of the disciples joined us.

"Why are they climbing the mountain?" Joseph Justus asked Andrew.

"Jesus has something to show them. We are to wait here." Andrew sank onto the grass, and we followed his example.

"Did he say why they were going? They could be gone for days. That mountain is higher than any other in Israel," Matthias said.

Andrew shook his head. "Jesus just said to wait for them, and if anyone comes out to us from the city, we are to help them as we did when he sent us out two by two." He stretched out on the grass and put his hands behind his head. "I think this is a perfect time to rest."

"But what of all he said to Peter?" Judas asked. "He said he would build his church and the gates of hell would not prevail against it. We are right here in the city of the god Pan and the gates of hell. Why did he say such a thing?"

I looked at Judas, not surprised by his question. "It is a curious thing, isn't it? I mean, what is a church? I thought Jesus came to bring the kingdom of heaven to earth. Did I misunderstand something?"

Andrew came to sit cross-legged on the ground near me. "I don't think any of us can answer that, Mary," he said, tenting his hands. "This whole trip away from the cities of Judea and Galilee is not normal. It's like something has changed with him."

Silence followed Andrew's comment, but a moment later, the men started talking all at once.

"I'm not sure if the kingdom is now or later," Philip admitted. "He talked like it's near when he first called us. But now he's different."

"Yes," Matthew said. "He used to preach that the kingdom of heaven was near, but now he tells stories of what the kingdom of heaven is like. Do the stories mean it is no longer near?"

"But he told Peter that he was being given the keys to the kingdom of heaven. Does that mean Peter is going to be our leader now?" Simon Z rarely spoke, but I never missed the intensity in his gaze.

"Something does seem different," Andrew admitted. "Jesus combined 'church' and 'the kingdom' in the same comment to Simon—er, Peter."

The men continued to discuss and argue, as was their habit, when the sound of other voices drew nearer. We stood and looked toward the city. A crowd emerged from the gates, walking toward us. How did they know where we had gone?

The women moved behind the men, allowing them to address the crowd. A man with a young boy pushed his way to the front and fell at the disciples' feet. "Please," he begged, "heal my son."

At that moment, the boy fell to the ground in a convulsion, foaming at the mouth.

The all-too-familiar dread crawled up my spine. I'd seen plenty of people with demons, but somehow this boy was different. There were more demons in him, stronger than the seven that had lived in me. A strongman controlled him, and though I tried to ignore the feelings, I sensed the head demon calling to me.

Mary. I remember you, Mary.

Panic rushed to the surface, and I could barely breathe. I backed away, then turned toward a cascade of water that fell over rocks not far from us.

"Please, can you cast out the demon?" Desperation filled the father's voice, but I could not stay to comfort him. I picked up my skirts and rushed toward the water.

In the distance, I heard Andrew and Philip attempting to do as the father asked. But when I glanced back, the demons threw the boy toward the firepit. Three disciples grabbed him before he could be burned.

I whirled around and ran faster toward the waterfall, my heart pounding. Tears filled my eyes. Why did Jesus have to be gone when this happened? I stopped near the base of the falls and looked up at the cascading rainbow coming from the light bouncing off the rushing water. The spray dampened my face, mingling with my tears.

"Mary?"

I jumped and turned about. Susanna and Joseph Justus stood breathless behind me.

"What's wrong?" Joseph asked.

"It was the boy, wasn't it?" Susanna said, granting me a knowing look.

I wrapped my arms about myself to still the sudden chill and trembling. I nodded. "I wish we had not come," I whispered.

Susanna embraced me, and I let her hold me, feeling a small

sense of relief at her touch. "It will be all right," she said. "You know it will."

"Will it?" I asked. "This one spoke my name, Susanna! And worse than the last one. It's a strong one and it knows me, and they always make me afraid. I can't let them in again. Why did they have to bring the boy when Jesus wasn't here?" I shuddered.

"Andrew and Philip are trying to rid the boy of the demon," Joseph said as Susanna released me.

"A very strong demon," I corrected. "That boy can't speak, he gnashes his teeth, and the demon sends him into convulsions. He acts like there are more than one, but I don't know that for sure."

Joseph's eyes widened.

"I had seven of them living in me, Joseph. That boy is in agony." I was pushing Joseph away. He deserved a wife, a friend, who didn't have such a past. I'd sensed his interest in me, and I could not subject him to my fears.

"We all have a past, Mary," he said softly. "Everyone needs Jesus to forgive them of something. If we were all holy as God is holy, we wouldn't need him." His reassuring gaze gave me a welcome sense of relief.

"Do you want to stay here for a while?" Susanna asked. She glanced at the falls. "It is peaceful here. There is no need to return to the group until tonight."

I looked from one to the other. Suddenly, I was not sure if I wanted to stay here by myself. "If you'll stay with me, I'd like to rest for a while."

Joseph smiled. "They don't need my help with the crowd," he said. He sank onto the ground near the water's edge and dangled his legs.

Silence settled between us as I moved to sit near him, with Susanna on my other side.

"I had a sister," Joseph said, his voice low.

I leaned toward him. "Had?"

He nodded. "Before I met Jesus. She was the youngest of us." He looked at me. "I also have three brothers. But Hannah was the pride of my father and joy of my mother."

I followed his gaze toward the falls, noting his deep sigh and pensive expression.

"I don't know if she was possessed like that boy, but she did have seizures. They came on her at unexpected times, causing her to fall to the ground and her body to jerk uncontrollably. The last time, she hit her head on a rock, splitting it open. She never recovered."

His admission filled my heart with empathy and a desire to comfort him. I reached for his arm and touched it briefly. "I'm sorry. I know what it feels like to have no control of your body." I glanced at Susanna. "We both do. But that doesn't mean she had a demon. There are other maladies that cause things the demons mimic."

"She was too young for us to know, and I doubt she knew anything about demons," he said, studying his hands. "I . . . The loss of her devastated my parents. I think I left to follow Jesus because I could not bear their sorrow any longer. I only wish we had met him before she died. He might have healed her."

"I think he would have," I said. "But he didn't heal his own father before his ministry began because it was not his time to heal and it was his father's time to go to heaven. The same might have been true for your sister."

He nodded, and the tension and worry left me with not only the roar of the falls, which drowned out all other sounds, but also the need to help this friend.

Friend? Yes. I could see him as a friend. I felt a kinship to him now for his having shared his experience. How hard life could be. How awful for his parents to lose a child. Worse than me losing my father or Marcus.

The shrieking demon-possessed boy in the distance quieted as we sat watching the beauty around us God had created. For the first time away from Jesus, I felt peace.

TWENTY-SEVEN

The sun sank in the west in a glorious display of oranges and pinks and golds, and still Jesus and the three had not come down from the mountain. We returned to the group as men and women filled the plain, bringing their sick to be healed. The demon-possessed boy still foamed at the mouth and was thrown to the ground, raised up, and sent into a violent convulsion again and again. Then he went completely rigid.

My heart ached for him, though I wanted nothing more than to go back to that place of peace near the waterfall. But one look at the frazzled and overwhelmed disciples, and I fought my fears and decided to stay, if at a distance. The women and some of the men, Joseph Justus among them, set up camp at the mountain's base, but we kept the rest of the disciples within sight.

Having Joseph near bolstered my spirits, and as the women gathered around a small fire to sleep, he called us to recite one of David's psalms.

"Keep me safe, my God, for in You I take refuge," he quoted, and we repeated his words phrase by phrase. "I say to the Lord, 'You are my Lord. Apart from You I have no good thing.' I say of the holy people who are in the land, 'They are the noble ones in whom is all my delight.' I will praise the Lord, who counsels me. Even at night my heart instructs me. I keep my eyes always on the Lord. You make known to me the path of life. You will fill me with joy in Your presence, with eternal pleasures at Your right hand."

The words fell like balm over my soul. "What a perfect psalm," I said, giving him a look of gratitude. "We are in the middle of other gods at the very gates of death and the underworld, and Jesus is not here." That thought deeply troubled me. "But we have the words of David, who surely suffered as much."

"Perhaps more," Salome said, stirring the fire before settling back again. "I think I can rest easier now."

"Yes," I said. "Thank you, Joseph."

He nodded and gave me an embarrassed smile, as if the praise made him uncomfortable. He was a humble man, of that I had no doubt. Far kinder than Marcus had been, peace be upon him.

"Let's try to sleep. I can't promise that the people will rest with the demon possessed still among them," Joseph said. "But let's try. Hopefully Jesus will return tomorrow and set all these things right."

"Yes. I hope so," I said.

Rustling in the grass drew my attention. The remaining disciples joined us.

"We need to keep our distance from the crowd," Andrew said to Joseph in a low voice. "We'll stay here tonight and return to them in the morning. I don't know why the demons won't leave. They did before when Jesus sent us out in pairs. Why not now?"

"I don't understand it either," Philip said, and Matthew nodded his agreement. "Perhaps Jesus will sort it all out."

"If he returns soon. I hope he hasn't disappeared like Moses did for forty days. We won't survive that long."

"Why do you think that?" Susanna asked.

"We don't have God raining manna down from heaven, and we don't have enough money to purchase food from the city and villages for that long. And I don't want to leave when he said to stay," Andrew said. He pulled the turban from his head and ran a hand through his hair, then sank to the ground.

I lay down next to Susanna, grateful for the men surrounding us. But I did not like Andrew's comment or the anxiety it evoked. How long would we have to stay near these demons and this demonic city? I wished in that moment I had not come on this trip. The roof of Peter's house or my own home in Magdala seemed much safer about now.

I awoke the following day, rubbing the kinks from my back. I looked about me, saw the dead campfire, and stood. Some of the men still slept, but the other women were up. I could see them in the fields gathering sticks for the fire or searching for food among the nearby flowers and trees.

One glance in the direction of Mount Hermon told me nothing. There was no sign of the four men who had ascended the day before. I walked toward the edge of our camp and peered into the morning mist. The crowd had lingered overnight. No doubt the father and demoniac son were among them.

Compassion for the child filled me again. I walked to a nearby brook for a drink of water and washed the sleep from my eyes, pondering the boy's plight. Susanna had embraced the goddess at an early age, so I knew it was possible for demons to enter a child. But she had never been this bad. Not even when we grew older. How helpless the father must feel.

And where was Jesus? We needed him.

I returned to camp to find the rest of them had risen and were talking among themselves. Wild emmer wheat grew nearby, and the men had gathered some for us to eat.

"Are you going to try again with the boy?" I asked, fixing my eyes on Andrew before glancing at the others.

"I don't know what more we can do. The demon won't listen to us, not even when we invoke Jesus' name." He wrung his hands as though the whole thing troubled him far more than his expression revealed.

"Perhaps Jesus will return today. Then we can take the boy to him," Susanna said, looking toward the distant crowd. "They are going to grow restless if he does not return soon."

How well I understood. Thankfully, we did not have to wait more than half the day. Matthew spotted them first. "They're back!" He ran toward the mountain, Andrew and Philip close behind.

The women followed, and we all met Jesus, Peter, James, and John at the mountain's base. One look at the three disciples made my heart skip a beat. They looked dazed and bewildered, as if they had seen a ghost.

"Teacher, we have a situation," Andrew said, approaching Jesus.

"Yes, Andrew. What is it?" Jesus followed Andrew toward the crowd, who had no doubt heard Matthew's exclamation and were headed our way.

"This boy," Andrew said, pointing at the father who was attempting to direct his son toward Jesus.

"Teacher," the man cried, clinging to his son with both hands. "I beg you to look at my son, for he is my only child. A spirit seizes him, and he cries out. It convulses him so that he foams at the mouth, and shatters him, and will hardly leave him. I begged your disciples to cast it out, but they could not."

Jesus released a heavy sigh. "You unbelieving generation.

How long shall I stay with you? How long shall I put up with you? Bring the boy to me."

Andrew and Philip hurried over to help the father bring the boy to Jesus, but at that moment, the demon threw him to the ground, sending him into a convulsion again.

"How long has he been like this?" Jesus asked the father.

"From childhood," he said. "It has often thrown him into fire or water to kill him. But if you can do anything, take pity on us and help us."

"'If you can'?" Jesus looked intently at the man. "Everything is possible for one who believes."

"I do believe," the father cried out. "Help me overcome my unbelief!"

Jesus glanced at the crowd now running toward us. "You deaf and mute spirit," he said, "I command you, come out of him and never enter him again."

I wrapped my arms about myself as the spirit shrieked, violently convulsed the child, and at last came out of him.

"Is he dead?" asked one of the people who had just approached us.

"He looks dead," said another.

Jesus bent down, took the child by the hand, and lifted him up. I knew by the clarity in the boy's eyes and the wide grin across his face that he was healed. Jesus released him to his father's open arms.

"My son!" The father's tears matched my own, for I could imagine the joy he felt at last.

"Abba!" The child clung to his father, also weeping.

The father lifted his head, tears still streaming down his face. "Thank you," he whispered. "Thank you."

Jesus nodded. "Go in peace." He turned and left the crowd, surprising me.

Why did he not stay to heal more? But he walked away and the disciples followed, so the women did as well.

"Why couldn't we drive it out?" Andrew asked, the roar of the falls nearly drowning out his voice.

"This kind can come out only by prayer," Jesus said.

No one asked him another thing, and in fact, as we headed back toward the area of Capernaum, we walked on for miles in silence. The crowd did not follow, which I found strange.

Something had changed since Jesus came down from the mountain, something different from what the disciples had previously noticed—something I could not define. There was a certain quality about him, and a steadfast expression that told me he was headed toward a mission that was not what it had been. It was as though he had a new purpose and was determined to fulfill it. I could not imagine what that could be.

The walk from Caesarea Philippi back to Galilee took days, but Jesus managed to avoid the crowds by staying far from the cities and villages. I didn't think it was possible, but it was clear that his intentions held a single focus.

As we skirted Chorazin and headed toward Capernaum, my heart lifted. I longed to be back in a home, behind closed doors.

"We're almost there," Adi said on our final day of travel. The outline of the city was visible in the distance. "I long for my bed."

"I long for your roof . . . and my own home," I said, realizing that I missed Darrah and should probably talk to Clopas about how things were going. Besides, I could use more funds from my investments and food from our stores if they could be spared.

"You will stay with us for a while, though, won't you?" Adi asked, her dark eyes hopeful.

I nodded. "Yes. I am not yet ready to make the trip back to Magdala. I want to see where Jesus plans to go next."

Jesus stopped walking and the men gathered about him. I quickened my pace to hear what he would say.

"The Son of Man is going to be delivered into the hands of men," he said, looking from one to the next. My heartbeat quickened with every dreaded word. "They will kill him," he continued, "and after three days he will rise."

He was going to die? But I thought the Messiah couldn't die. Confusion washed over me as Jesus turned and strode ahead of the disciples, who hung back, seemingly just as bewildered.

"Who do you think will be greatest in his coming kingdom?" Judas asked, directing his question to the three who had ascended the mountain with Jesus. "Did he tell you anything about it?"

"He gave you the keys to the kingdom, Peter," Matthew said. "Does that make you the greatest?"

"What about us?" John said, glancing at his brother. "Jesus called us up the mountain too."

"Does that make you greater than us? He said we'd all sit on thrones judging the twelve tribes." Andrew sounded slightly annoyed.

"I don't think it's up to us to decide who will be greatest," Thaddaeus said, glancing at James Alphaeus. "Won't he keep us equal? He didn't say one tribe would be better than another."

"Judah was picked to be the line of kings," Nathanael pointed out.

"But Jesus is in the line of Judah. Will one of us judge his tribe?" Simon Z said.

"The greatest ought to sit on his right and left," John said, again looking at his brother. Did they have such a desire?

"Well, we know it won't be us," Susanna said.

I looked at her, appalled, but her comment caused the men to laugh, which eased some of the tension. Why were they arguing about who was greatest when Jesus had just told us he was going to die?

But I didn't have the courage to bring up the subject. I couldn't wrap my mind around the idea that the Messiah could die. The thought was impossible to me, and the men felt the same or they wouldn't be having this argument.

Their words quieted as we neared Capernaum. Excitement to return to Peter's home filled me. I slipped my arm through Susanna's and fairly skipped the rest of the way.

Hava, along with a young family I didn't recognize, welcomed us as we entered the house.

"Ima!" Adi rushed into her mother's embrace, then greeted the others. Peter also greeted them, kissed the man on both cheeks, and welcomed him to join them in the sitting room of the house.

"Mary, Susanna, Joanna, Mary Clopas," Adi said, pointing to each one of us. "This is my brother Ronen's wife Sera and their son Chaim. They have come to meet Jesus. They live in Jericho and came to visit."

"How nice it is to meet you," I said, smiling at Sera. I stooped to greet the child, a boy of about three, who stared at me with his fingers in his mouth as though drawing comfort from them. "Welcome, Chaim." I smiled, but he only stared at me. I stood and took a step back, chuckling. "He's probably not used to people he doesn't know." I looked at his mother, who nodded.

"Chaim is a quiet one," Sera said, taking the child in her arms.

Adi touched the boy's head and kissed his forehead. "One day I hope he has a cousin to play with when he visits."

I studied Adi a moment as the men gathered around Jesus in

Peter's sitting room. She was a young woman, but old enough to have been married for a few years. Much like myself, I supposed. She wanted a family, but what would that look like with Peter in Jesus' inner circle and holding the keys to the kingdom, and Jesus predicting he was going to die?

I shuddered and quietly moved toward the men, wanting a moment to listen to Jesus. I knew one thing for certain. I would not want to bring children into such an uncertain world. What would happen to us if Jesus was right and the Messiah could die? Would he have said so if it wasn't true? A deep sigh escaped me as I sank onto a cushion in the corner, catching my breath after such a long day.

"What were you arguing about on the road?" Jesus asked as the twelve sat near him. Had he heard their arguing? He'd been so far ahead of us. "Anyone who wants to be first must be the very last, and the servant of all," he said, as if reading their thoughts.

The looks on the men's faces showed their embarrassment. I was very glad that I did not care about such things as greatness or sitting on a throne. Men!

Jesus looked toward the cooking area, where the other women still stood. "Sera," he said, "please bring Chaim here."

Adi's sister-in-law looked startled. Jesus had not yet met her, but he knew her name and that of her son. Why did it surprise me when he knew things that no one else could?

Sera brought Chaim to the sitting room, and Jesus lifted his arms to take him from his mother. He held the child on his lap, then set him in the middle of the room, still resting his hand on Chaim's shoulder. "Whoever welcomes one of these little children in my name welcomes me, and whoever welcomes me does not welcome me but the one who sent me. Truly I tell you, unless you change and become like little children, you will never enter the kingdom of heaven. Therefore, whoever takes the lowly position of this child is the greatest in the kingdom of heaven."

Jesus hugged Chaim and gave him back to his mother, then continued teaching the men. I wanted to listen, to absorb all I could of his words, but I was still pondering his compassion for a child. Children were a blessing from the Lord, a proverb we were taught in synagogue, but in practice, they were often ignored by the adults in society. Certainly no one had ever suggested that children would be in the kingdom of heaven!

I looked at the men, wondering if any of them thought Jesus' example of the child was important teaching. Or had they shrugged it off like they had his words about dying?

How I wish I understood him! I wanted to be in the kingdom with him. I never wanted to be without him. So how could I become like a child again in order to attain access?

I glanced at Chaim, who clung now to his mother's skirts. I would be humble like he was. Not be proud or argue like the men about who would be greatest. I could do that. But how would I know whether my lowly choices were low enough?

PART THREE

When they came back from the tomb, they told all these things to the Eleven and to all the others. It was Mary Magdalene, Joanna, Mary the mother of James, and the others with them who told this to the apostles. But they did not believe the women, because their words seemed to them like nonsense.

Luke 24:9–11

TWENTY-EIGHT

—— AD 33 ——

The calming scent of lavender wafted through the window in the cooking area. I'd been home for two months, while Jesus had gone back to Nazareth and other places with only the twelve accompanying him. I ached to be with him again.

I felt my pulse quicken at the sight of Susanna hurrying up the walk from the gate to my courtyard. I rushed outside to meet her. "What have you heard?" I asked, hugging her.

"Tobias has learned that Jesus is back in Capernaum and is planning to attend the feast. If we leave today, we can be there and go with him." She giggled, and I joined her for the joy filling me.

Sukkot, one of our people's favorite holy days, would start soon and last a week. Each day was significant, and the men were required to be there but the women did not have to attend. We just wanted to be wherever Jesus allowed us to be.

"Tobias was in Capernaum when Jesus returned from seeing his brothers," Susanna continued. "They gave him a hard time about the feast, so he let them go on without him. He came home to go with his disciples and followers. Tobias is planning to join us."

"How soon can we leave?" I glanced back at the house. "I just have to tell Darrah I'm leaving and gather a few things."

A few moments later, after hugging Darrah goodbye, I joined Susanna and Tobias and we kept a quick pace on our way to Capernaum. My heart soared as we entered Peter's home in time to join Jesus and the other disciples, including the women I'd missed—Salome and Adi. Joanna had returned to Chuza in Jerusalem, so I didn't know if we would meet her there or not, given the crowds. Mary and Clopas had left for the feast two days earlier, but I had waited, hoping Jesus would include us.

The trip to Jerusalem took five days, much longer than the walk from Magdala to Capernaum. We arrived late and stopped outside Jerusalem in Bethany at the home of Lazarus, who lived with his sisters, Martha and Mary.

Susanna glanced at me as we entered the large courtyard and looked at the two-story home. "Lazarus appears to be a wealthy man," I said, mentally comparing it to my father's estate.

She nodded. "Let's see if his sisters need some help." She looked behind us at Salome and Adi, who hurried to join us.

"Yes, let's," I agreed, though I wondered, given the size of the home, whether we would be able to hear Jesus teaching the men if we were in a different area preparing food. In Peter's home, the work area was right next to the sitting area, so it was easy to listen to most of their conversations as we sought to feed them.

We stepped through the door. Lazarus greeted Jesus as though they'd been friends for a long time.

"Shalom," an older woman said, stepping up to us. "I'm Martha, and this is my sister Mary."

"Shalom," I said, and the others said the same. "Thank you for having us."

"Of course," Martha said, motioning for us to enter the

large food preparation area. We set our baskets on a wooden table and rolled up our sleeves.

"How can we help?" I asked, looking about the room. Drying herbs hung from an overhead beam, while another table held onions, leeks, cucumbers, and an assortment of other vegetables. Through a wide opening, I saw a long, low table with cushions surrounding it, where empty plates and baskets and clay cups sat waiting for their guests.

"If I counted correctly, there are twenty men and six women, including us," Martha said, lifting a knife from where it lay beside a large slab of smooth wood. "I think a stew and flatbread with pistachio cakes and several different sauces should suffice. What do you think?" She looked from one of us to another.

"It sounds good," I said, not sure what else to say. This would be a feast compared to our normal traveling fare.

The rest of us followed Martha's lead, and soon the sound of chopping vegetables drowned out the conversation coming from the adjacent room.

I glanced up from the onions I chopped, trying to keep my eyes from watering. Where was Martha's younger sister? How odd that she would not help her sister prepare such an elaborate meal. But there was no sign of Mary. Had she stayed with the men?

The thought caused my own heart's longing to rise. I much preferred sitting at Jesus' feet, taking in his every word, but someone had to prepare the food. It was a woman's job to do so, and I didn't really mind. I would have time to listen to Jesus later, though I was not much consoled by the thought of waiting.

A few moments later Martha came in from the courtyard, where the stew hung over the fire. "Has my sister not joined us?" Her brows scrunched, showing fine lines, and her mouth tipped down in a frown.

I shook my head. "I haven't seen her since you introduced us."

Martha set the spoon on the table, squared her shoulders, and left us in the cooking area while she stomped to the visiting area. I looked at Susanna, then followed Martha at a discreet distance, curious.

Jesus was in the middle of speaking when Martha burst into the room. "Lord," she said, interrupting him. "Don't you care that my sister has left me to do the work by myself? Tell her to help me!"

I hung back, shocked by Martha's outburst. I could never have done such a thing. Besides, she wasn't working alone. We were helping her. And yet, why did Mary think it fair for her to stay with the men and sit near Jesus, her attention fully focused on him, while the rest of us worked away from him?

"Martha, Martha," Jesus said, his gaze fixed on her, "you are worried and upset about many things, but few things are needed—or indeed only one. Mary has chosen what is better, and it will not be taken away from her."

Martha visibly blanched, and I also felt the sting of the rebuke. I stepped backward, not wanting to be seen by either the men or Martha. I would have comforted her, but then she would know I had listened to the conversation.

Besides that, Jesus' words to her had pierced my heart. I was jealous of Mary's ability to ignore her sister and the rest of us to sit at Jesus' feet. I wanted to do the same. But I didn't feel I could just leave the rest of the women to follow what my heart desired. Wasn't it selfish somehow? Exactly how I suspected Martha felt. And yet, Jesus had not considered Mary selfish. He had rebuked Martha, not Mary.

Was I worried and troubled about many things that deserved his rebuke too? Chagrined, I returned to the cooking area to help the women. Next time I would sit at his feet.

The next day we traveled with Lazarus and his sisters to the Feast of Sukkot in Jerusalem. The feast was at the halfway point, with three days of celebration left before the day of solemn assembly. People lined the road to Jerusalem waving branches of palm, myrtle, willow, and citron. Here and there voices rose singing the traditional Hallel psalms, but the biggest thing I noticed were the many booths built in the fields and on the roofs of homes.

Magdala could not compare to the excitement of Jerusalem for this feast. A surge of joy filled me as the words of David and Asaph filled the air along the stone streets.

"Where do you think he's leading us?" Adi asked as she and Salome joined Susanna and me. "Simon thinks he will teach in the temple. But I wonder, where will we build our sukkah?"

I looked ahead, still overwhelmed by the sights and sounds of the bustling city. "I did not hear him say anything about that," I admitted, glancing at Mary, Martha's sister. "Perhaps she knows."

Mary and Martha walked ahead of us behind Tobias, Lazarus, Joseph Justus, and Matthias, who followed Jesus and the twelve. I moved ahead of my friends to join the sisters. "Do you know where Jesus intends for us to build our sukkah?" I asked, looking at Mary. "Did he mention it when you were listening to him?"

Mary of Bethany was a young woman and not yet married, though I wondered why Martha also had no husband. Was she a widow as I was?

Mary looked at me with her large dark eyes, so trusting, and nodded. "He said we would return to our home each night."

"Shouldn't we have built the booths before we left this morning?" Susanna asked, joining me. "We will need more than one with so many of us."

"The men built three of them yesterday, after the meal," Mary said, her expression so innocent she could not possibly have realized that we would have liked to help.

"Why were we not aware?" Adi asked. "Simon said nothing to me."

"I think Jesus had only a few of the men build the shelters in the inner courtyard. One for the women and two for all of the men." Mary shrugged. "I only know because Matthias mentioned it to me this morning." Her face flushed. Was she dealing with attraction to Matthias as I saw in Joseph Justus toward me?

"We are only here for the day," I said, picking up my pace to catch up to the men. "Let's keep up with them. I don't want to lose our way among these crowds."

Jesus reached the temple, walked to the Court of Women, and began to teach. Relieved that he had chosen this place where all of us could listen, I maneuvered through the crowd to better hear him.

Joseph Justus came alongside me. "If you want to be closer, follow me," he said, touching my elbow. I glanced at Susanna, but Tobias was already leading her to the place behind Jesus where Joseph pointed. Not far from the Nicanor Gate was an open court where the crowds did not press in.

"Thank you," I said. I smiled, and he returned the gesture.

"Do you mind if I stay with you?"

I chuckled. "Do I have a choice?"

"Not really. Consider me protection." He straightened, and

I had to admit I appreciated his concern, though I wasn't sure I needed protection. Jesus was the one the elders wanted to silence.

A priest emerged from the Court of the Priests and walked down the stairs through the Nicanor Gate, carrying a golden pitcher. The crowd's attention turned from Jesus' teaching to him. As he passed through the Court of Women, we stood to follow him from the temple to the Pool of Siloam. The crowd picked up palm fronds and other branches, waving them in the air as we walked. Blasts of the shofar accompanied us.

"Have you seen this before?" I asked Joseph as he walked with me behind Tobias and Susanna.

"Many times," he said, waving his own palm frond.

We reached the pool, where the priest filled the pitcher with water, then returned to the temple. People around us began to chant, "We will gather water from the wells of salvation" and "Hosanna, save us now."

The priest passed through the Court of Women and the Nicanor Gate, went up the stairs, and came to the altar. The men followed him into the Court of the Priests, but the women stopped on the stairs or looked down from the balcony. We were allowed no farther, but we could see the ceremony. The priest circled the altar once, then poured out the water and prayed that God would provide the salvation He alone could give.

My heart quickened with the significance of this ritual while I tried to grasp its meaning. Jesus was our Messiah, though not everyone believed that. He came to bring the salvation the priests prayed for during these holy days, but they couldn't see it in him.

Had he been unclear? Or did something more have to happen for them to see?

TWENTY-NINE

The light of dawn filtered through the branches that made the roof of our sukkah. I covered a yawn and stretched. We were anxious to enter Jerusalem to see what Jesus would do or say to the leaders and the people.

I rolled up my mat and carried it to the small room where things on the roof were stored, then took the stairs to the ground. Salome met me near the booth in the courtyard.

"Are you as excited as I am?" She looked toward the house. "Do you think Jesus will set up his kingdom soon? There are a lot of people singing his praises in Jerusalem."

I caught sight of her sons, James and John, called Sons of Thunder by Jesus for their passion . . . and perhaps also for their quick tempers. They had mellowed in the past year, but it was clear that Salome took great pride in them. How could I blame her? I would love to have had sons called to follow the rabbi.

"I don't know," I said. "I mean, some love him, but I have heard others argue over him. I heard one man say, 'Have the authorities really concluded that he is the Messiah?' So I think they're divided about him."

"They're threatened by him," Salome said, walking with me

into the house to help Martha, Susanna, and Adi prepare the morning meal before we left for Jerusalem again. "The leaders want to keep their power, so they will do anything to silence him. If everyone follows Jesus, no one will follow them. From what Zebedee tells me, the religious leaders can't abide being overlooked or forgotten."

"Not even to welcome our Messiah? They could be leaders in his kingdom." I took flour, which we had ground the night before, mixed it with oil, and set it in the courtyard oven. "Then again, the twelve are supposed to be leaders with Jesus in the kingdom. I rather doubt he would choose the religious leaders. He hasn't been all that accepting of their ways."

"Tobias said he's called them hypocrites and whitewashed tombs," Susanna said, accepting a pomegranate from Martha.

"Are you talking about the kingdom?" Martha asked.

"We were wondering if Jesus might take advantage of the feast to bring it about," I said, mixing another loaf of flatbread.

Susanna took a knife and cut the top off the pomegranate, then scored the sides into four to peel it. "If he does, he could meet with a lot of opposition, considering what he said to the leaders."

"I'm sure 'hypocrites' and 'whitewashed tombs' didn't go over well," Adi said, helping Susanna peel more of the ripe seeded fruit.

"It didn't." Mary of Bethany entered from a side room. "I don't think Jesus is planning to begin the kingdom now anyway."

I looked about at the women, catching Salome's slight frown. Had she hoped to see her boys ruling in the kingdom soon? "Why do you say that?"

"Because he keeps talking about going away where we cannot come. He talks about suffering and death. Haven't you heard it too?" Mary looked about at us, her eyes wide with concern and wonder.

I placed a hand on my middle, the reminder of Jesus' words about dying making me feel nauseous. I had pushed those thoughts aside, caught up in the joy of this feast. Why did this woman have to bring them up again?

Susanna stepped closer and touched my shoulder, whispering, "Are you all right?"

I swallowed hard and straightened. "I don't like the direction of this discussion," I whispered back.

"He has mentioned dying," Adi said to the women, "but the men don't appear to understand him, so no one talks about it. I think they're afraid to ask him to explain."

"But it's so plain," young Mary insisted. "How could they not see it?"

"Perhaps because they have always looked for our Messiah to free us from our struggles here on earth," Salome said. "The Romans. Anyone who has oppressed us. Not something we can't see."

Mary shook her head. "But he has healed so many. Set the captives free. Isn't that what he came to do?"

"Yes, of course," Martha said, sounding a little piqued. "Talking of this is not helping get the food ready. How about we finish our work and then we can talk on the road to Jerusalem?"

She said the words to her sister, but every one of us fell silent at her rebuke. Perhaps Martha feared losing Jesus as much as I did.

I didn't want to keep rolling the discussion around in my mind, but it would not leave my thoughts throughout the meal and cleanup afterward, and along the road back to Jerusalem. We entered the temple courts to the heightened joy of the feast, and I forced myself to pay attention to what was happening.

The priest with the golden pitcher in his hands appeared again. As before, we followed him, along with the praising and worshiping crowd, to the Pool of Siloam, where he filled the pitcher. Excitement moved through the crowd as he climbed the steps to the inner court where the altar stood and circled it seven times. With each turn about the altar, the crowds cried louder, "Hosanna! Save us now! Hosanna! Save us now!"

As the priest poured out the water, before the cries of the people had died down, Jesus' voice, coming from the Court of Women, rose above the din. "Let anyone who is thirsty come to me and drink. Whoever believes in me, as Scripture has said, rivers of living water will flow from within them."

Swift silence fell. What did he mean?

"Surely this man is the Prophet," someone in the crowd said moments later.

"He is the Messiah," said a few others.

"How can the Messiah come from Galilee?" shouted another. "Does not Scripture say that the Messiah will come from David's descendants and from Bethlehem, the town where David lived?"

I searched for Jesus among the throng, but he had slipped away. Frantic to find him, for the disciples had also moved from my view, I found Susanna and the other women.

"Hurry," Susanna said, taking my hand. "Jesus is leaving for Bethany."

"Already? We only just arrived." I made my way through the court to the street below and soon caught up with our group.

Jesus turned to address us. "I have accomplished what I needed to today. Tomorrow we will return." He turned about and led us out of the city, down the now familiar stone streets, across the Kidron Valley, up the Mount of Olives, and into the town of Bethany.

"What does he mean?" Susanna asked as we tried to keep up with the men's hurried steps. "What did he accomplish?"

I looked at her, still struggling to understand. We came upon Martha and Mary. "Did you understand him?" I asked Mary, finally admitting that perhaps she knew more than I did.

She shook her head. "Not really. But there must be a connection between the priest pouring the water over the altar and Jesus declaring himself to have life-giving water. I wish he had said more."

"Maybe we aren't supposed to know more right now." I pushed the hair that had escaped my headscarf away from my eyes.

"Perhaps not," she said.

Obviously not. Unless Jesus explained it to us, how could we possibly figure out his words? Oh, but I wanted to know. I didn't want to be like those who were blind and deaf to his teachings. Was I no better than those who didn't believe because I couldn't understand?

On the eighth and last great day of the feast, we arrived at the temple earlier than normal and settled in the Court of Women, where four seventy-five-foot-high menorahs stood. Jesus settled himself, and the rest of us joined him opposite the treasury, where we observed the people putting their gifts into the offering box.

Men in flowing robes, Pharisees and Sadducees in their elaborate garments, and many other rich people carried leather pouches filled with coins. Others stood and measured out herbs like dill, mint, and cumin and placed them carefully into the treasury box.

One rich young man strode to the treasury, head held high,

and turned to his servant and said something I couldn't hear. Then he placed a heavy, intricately carved box beside the treasury box because it was too large to fit inside. What did it contain? This man must have a generous heart to give so much. But when I caught a glimpse of his expression, I wondered. He strode from the area with his servant behind him, a smug smile on his lips.

I looked at Jesus but could not read his thoughts. He revealed nothing to me and did not look at any of us. He simply continued to watch the people.

A Levite descended the steps of the Nicanor Gate from the Court of the Priests to collect what had been given, but before he reached the treasury box, an elderly woman, thin and bent, hobbled toward the box. The Levite stopped, allowing her to pass.

She moved slowly, determined. At last she stopped in front of the treasury and fumbled with a drawstring bag she carried, trying to open it with shaky, wrinkled hands. The urge to jump up and help her washed over me, but I stayed where I was, knowing that this was something she would want to do on her own.

The bag opened and she reached inside and pulled out something I could not see for its size. Probably copper coins rather than gold, considering her threadbare clothes and a body that looked like she had not eaten enough in weeks, months. She faced the treasury and dropped in first one coin, then another. I could hear the clink, soft as it was. Her face lit with the last coin drop. She pulled the strings of her bag, which looked completely limp, and straightened, her smile bright. Then she hobbled toward the place where the menorah stood.

"Come," Jesus said, turning to face the disciples and the rest of us.

I moved near the women as the men crowded around him.

"Truly, I say to you," he said, "this poor widow has put in more than all those who are contributing to the offering box. For they all contributed out of their abundance, but she out of her poverty has put in everything she had, all she had to live on."

All? How could she do that? How would she live? And yet, she'd walked away smiling. She had given all she had to God's temple and had nothing left. I marveled, considering the wealth I'd always had. Could I give all I had?

"She must believe that God will supply her needs," Adi whispered next to me. "Why else would she give up everything?"

I nodded. "Perhaps that's why Jesus pointed her out. She is an example to us of how we should approach God. With a heart that is willing to give Him all."

"Simon says that we've left all to follow him. What more can we give?" Adi asked as Jesus led us around to the area of the menorahs. Young Levites prepared to extinguish the lights that had shone all night, illuminating the city.

"I don't know," I said, watching the Levites climb the ladders to the tops of the menorahs. One by one, they snuffed out the lamps.

On this last holy day, we did not celebrate as in the first seven. This was to be a solemn day. One where we hoped the Messiah would come and be Israel's light so that his salvation would reach to the ends of the earth.

My heart pounded, knowing the Messiah stood among this throng of people, all waiting, hoping, that this would be the year God would finally fulfill His promise to us. Would Jesus use this moment to begin the kingdom?

I craned my neck to get a better glimpse of him. He stood near a now darkened menorah, and his voice rang throughout the Court of Women and beyond. "I am the light of the world. Whoever follows me will not walk in darkness but will have the light of life."

"You are bearing witness about yourself," a nearby Pharisee shouted. "Your testimony is not true."

"In your law it is written that the testimony of two people is true," Jesus said. "I am the one who bears witness about myself, and the Father who sent me bears witness about me."

"Where is your Father?" came the sneering voice of one of the priests.

"You know neither me nor my Father. If you knew me, you would know my Father also," Jesus said.

"They don't want to believe him," Susanna whispered, sidling up next to me.

"They hate him. He's claiming his father is God," I whispered back.

Jesus had often spoken of his Father during his teaching. A flash of memory crossed my mind of another feast when Jesus had claimed equality with God. The religious leaders had tried to stone him then.

My pulse quickened and my hands grew clammy with the memory. Would they do the same now? It was no secret that they wanted to silence him and might just use any means possible to do so. My only consolation was the crowd. The religious leaders feared the people. Perhaps Jesus was safe yet another day. But I did wish he would stop provoking them on purpose. Did he want to cause controversy? Why? How could controversy have anything to do with the kingdom? How could it bring about the things he claimed?

"I am going away," Jesus said, drawing my thoughts back to him, "and you will seek me, and you will die in your sin. Where I am going, you cannot come."

Cannot come? My heart ached with his words. The conversation about his dying filled my mind again, despite my efforts to keep it at bay. This was supposed to be a joyful occasion. Why did Jesus keep reminding us of things I didn't want to hear? He couldn't leave!

Murmurs of "Will he kill himself?" filtered through the court.

Kill himself? He would never!

"What a ridiculous thing to say," Susanna said, likely louder than she intended. "Of course he won't kill himself."

No, of course not.

"You are from below. I am from above," Jesus said, raising his voice for all to hear. "You are of this world. I am not of this world. I told you that you would die in your sins, for unless you believe that I am he, you will die in your sins."

"Who are you, that we should believe in you?" One of the leading Pharisees, though not the high priest, spoke for the others.

"Just what I have been telling you from the beginning. When you have lifted up the Son of Man, then you will know that I am he, and that I do nothing on my own authority but speak just as the Father taught me."

He turned then, and the disciples scrambled to their feet to follow him. I and the other women did the same. Heart pounding with Jesus' words, I glanced behind me as we were about to leave the Court of Women to see many of the people following Jesus. But the Pharisees and religious leaders huddled together, their expressions hateful.

THIRTY

Jesus kept a steady pace, neither hurrying nor slowing as we headed for the Eastern Gate to return to Bethany. His words to the Pharisees rang in my ears, and as I glanced at him, I could not shake the fear of losing him.

I pressed a hand to my heart, my breath coming fast as I hurried to keep up. The people in the marketplace filled the air with rapid speech, bartering for wares. The braying of a donkey came from behind me. I glanced toward the sound, seeing a female donkey with its foal tied to a post near a jeweler's shop. Circlets of gold, filagree earrings, and jewel-bedecked armbands were spread on purple cloth, expensive in its own right, behind a locked wooden cage. The owner, dressed in a colorful, flowing robe, called to the crowd, "Come and find the perfect jewels for your bride. Which of you doesn't deserve to wear the finest Israel has to offer?"

Susanna walked on one side of me, Salome on the other. "The only people who can afford his 'finest,'" Susanna said when we were out of earshot, "are the wealthy. Certainly not the pilgrims who are weighed down by Roman taxes. They struggle to afford an animal for sacrifice at these feasts."

"My Zebedee does well on the docks, but we would never spend money in such a frivolous way," Salome said.

I touched my robe, feeling the softness of the weave. My father had always supplied me with the highest quality goods, perhaps to make up for me having no mother. And Marcus's father had dealt in such jewels. But I agreed with Salome. I would never use the wealth God had entrusted to me on such frivolous things. I enjoyed using my funds to help Jesus' ministry. Nothing else seemed as important—certainly not earthly riches.

We turned at the next street and had left the city when the men ahead of us stopped abruptly. Jesus knelt beside a blind beggar not far from the gate.

"Rabbi, who sinned, this man or his parents, that he was born blind?" Peter asked as the men surrounded Jesus.

Joseph Justus hung back a little, allowing the women to see. Of all the men who followed Jesus, he was one of the few who always thought of us and included and encouraged us. I'd also noticed that Matthias treated Mary of Bethany in a similar way. Was Joseph kind only on my account? The thought warmed me, surprising me that I should feel thus.

"Neither this man nor his parents sinned," Jesus said, drawing my attention. "This happened so that the works of God might be displayed in him. As long as it is day, we must do the works of Him who sent me. Night is coming, when no one can work. While I am in the world, I am the light of the world."

His words echoed what he had just said in the temple courts, causing me concern and confusion, perhaps because I not only didn't understand but wasn't sure I wanted to. "While I am in the world" indicated a time when he wouldn't be.

I leaned closer for a better view. Jesus stepped to the side of the road, where the clay met the stone walk, and spit on the ground. He bent down, scooped the wet dirt in his hands, and worked it between his fingers until it turned to mud. He leaned forward and smeared the mud over the man's eyes. "Go," he told the man, "wash in the Pool of Siloam."

The man stood and, using his stick to guide him, walked past us to the Pool of Siloam, which was nearer to the temple. A small group of Pharisees stood near, frowning.

I looked at Joseph, who stood at my side. "He's making mud on Shabbat."

"Yes." Joseph's dark eyes were filled with concern. "They will use this against him."

"Yes," I said, watching the man walk away.

Jesus continued toward the Mount of Olives, back to Bethany. Relief filled me. I didn't want to admit it to myself, but I wanted to go home. To Bethany, yes, but also to the gardens of my home in Magdala, where the lavender bloomed and the almond trees budded with their sweet scents. Had I grown weary of following Jesus?

Impossible! I was only tired. Too many nights of sleeping in different places or not sleeping well at all were taking a toll. The urge to flee as I would have in the days when the spirits drove me churned my insides. Sweat dampened my tunic and ran down my back as I forced one foot in front of the other.

"Are you all right?" Joseph leaned over to look at me. "Your face is pale, Mary." He gripped my elbow, though I didn't need steadying.

I blinked, glanced at him, and shook my head.

He moved me away from the group a slight distance, and I saw confusion and curiosity cross Susanna's face. But she didn't follow, probably because Tobias walked with her.

"What's wrong?" Joseph's handsome face so full of concern for me gave me a small sense of calm.

"I'm fine," I assured him, though I felt no such thing in my churning belly. "But I do worry about what might happen to him." I pointed toward Jesus. "He is always healing on Shabbat, even on feast days, and those Pharisees are not going to keep quiet. What will they do when that man is healed?" A shudder worked through me.

"I don't know," Joseph said, clasping his hands in front of him as if he didn't know what else to do with them. "I fear for him too."

"Do you think he's planning to go somewhere else and leave Israel, like David did when he fled to the Philistines, running from Saul?" My father had made sure I knew the history of our people and understood God's holy words. But I didn't understand His holy Son. That was who Jesus claimed to be, wasn't it?

"I don't think he plans to leave Israel," Joseph said as Andrew drew up beside us.

"Leave Israel? Who's leaving Israel?" Andrew kicked a stone to the side of the path.

"No one," Joseph said. "We were just trying to understand why Jesus keeps saying that he's going away."

"Maybe he's going to sneak away for time to pray as he often does," Andrew said. I did not agree with his suggestion.

"I think he means more than that," Joseph countered, and though I wanted to continue to listen to what these two men thought, I really just wanted Jesus to reassure me that all would be well. That he wouldn't leave me.

Besides, where did he plan to go? Would he let me go with him?

I absolutely could not lose him!

The next morning in Bethany, when I stepped into Martha's cooking area, I learned that Jesus had left early that morning to return to the city. The worries I thought I had left in Jerusalem the day before rushed through me.

"Did he take no one with him? Someone should be there to protect him." I immediately wished the words back at the looks I received from the other women.

"You think Jesus needs our protection?" Salome picked up a leek that had come from the nearby garden and chopped it into fine bits. It should feel normal for the women to be preparing the food while Jesus went off alone, but nothing felt normal to me this morning, and I wasn't sure why.

"Simon—Peter, James, and John went with him," Adi said, giving Salome a look of gentle censure. "While I agree that Jesus does not need our protection, I think he enjoys the company when he is likely to encounter the religious leaders." She mixed starter with flour and kneaded as she spoke.

"I wonder why he wanted to go back." I busied myself with chopping dates, but I could not shake the unsettled feeling that had arisen when we were at the feast. So many questions swirled in my mind. If Jesus was the light of the world, why would he leave and take the light away? How long would we have him, and would he answer my questions if I found an opportunity to ask him? He was always so busy with the men, though he never shunned the women. I just felt so unworthy to ask.

Stomping feet filled the outer court, and moments later the men—minus Jesus, Peter, James, and John—filled Martha's eating area. Lazarus laughed at something Judas said, and the distinct voices of Nathanael and Philip mingled with Matthew's conversation with Joseph Justus, Matthias, and Tobias. I walked to the area and peeked around the corner, then returned to the women.

"They are all there waiting," I said to Martha, whose arms were covered in flour with some splattered on a covering she wore over her tunic.

"Well then, we'd better feed them," Martha said, brushing the flour from her hands.

We carried the bread, sauces, and fruit and set it before them, then retreated to the cooking area to eat. Susanna sat beside me, broke a piece of bread, and handed part of it to me.

"Talk to me," she said after swallowing a bite. "You're troubled. I can sense it."

I gave her a sharp look. "You sound as you did when the spirits controlled us. Don't talk like that!"

Susanna's eyes widened, taking me in. "Mary. You know that's not the way it is. We've been friends since childhood. I can tell when you're afraid. I read your feelings in your eyes."

I looked away, ashamed. "I shouldn't have said that." I chewed the tasteless bread. Why did everything feel wrong today? I drew in a shuddering breath. Lowering my voice, I looked about the room, then at Susanna. "He keeps talking about going away. I don't know where he is going, and I can't bear the thought."

Susanna studied me. "Perhaps he just means he will die like everyone else does one day. It could be years from now, Mary. We could die before he does."

I pushed my palms against the table. "Judas and the others say he can't die. So he can't mean that. Can he?"

Susanna shrugged. "Maybe the men are right. In any case, they don't seem concerned about his talk of going away."

"I don't think the men are paying attention." My stomach twisted as I remembered the bickering they so often engaged in about the kingdom and who would sit beside Jesus and when he would finally set it up. I could hear them arguing in the other room now. "They are no help."

"Then ask Jesus what he means." Susanna scooped dates mixed with pistachios into a bowl.

"I think he expects us to understand. And I'm afraid to ask." Sometimes fear of the unknown was easier to bear than the known.

"You make no sense, my friend. Do you want me to get Tobias to ask him? Or you could see if Joseph will question him for you. He likes you, you know."

"I know." I set what was left of my food aside, no longer hungry.

At that moment the door opened and Jesus with the three disciples entered the house, talking among themselves. I hurried to greet them and saw Mary of Bethany already waiting. Jesus smiled at her. I silently begged him to notice me, but he moved past me with the men. Could he not read my thoughts? I needed him. An overpowering urge to weep swept through me. Why did Mary of Bethany get to stay with the men while the rest of us worked? Martha's complaint came rushing back, and I couldn't have agreed more, but for Jesus' rebuke.

I sucked in a breath, forcing my emotions down, and walked to the edge of the room to listen.

"You should have heard Jesus talk to the Pharisees," John said, laughing. "After the man who was healed of blindness told Jesus they'd thrown him out of the synagogue, Jesus said to him, 'Do you believe in the Son of Man?'"

"And the man said, 'Who is he, sir? Tell me so that I may believe in him,'" Peter added.

James's words came out in a rush. "'You have now seen him. In fact, he is the one speaking with you,' Jesus told him. And the man believed and worshiped him!"

"Then some Pharisees showed up," John said, giving Peter and his brother a look, "though I don't know where they came from, and Jesus told them, 'For judgment I have come into this world, so that the blind will see and those who see will become blind.'"

"And the Pharisees, looking all indignant with their big phylacteries and extra-long tzitzit, said, 'What? Are we blind too?'" James said, laughing.

John crossed his arms over his chest, giving his brother his own indignant look. I nearly laughed aloud. Sometimes these men acted like children.

"What did you say, Master?" Andrew asked, chuckling at all of them.

Jesus looked about the group, and in that moment, he glanced at me, the familiar compassion in his gaze. "I told them, 'If you were blind, you would not be guilty of sin. But now that you claim you can see, your guilt remains.'"

"They did not like that!" Peter said, grabbing a loaf of bread from the low table.

"Not one bit," James agreed. "They walked off muttering, and if I didn't know better, I would have accused them of cursing, but of course, they would never do such a thing."

"No," I said, surprising myself that I could be so bold, yet at peace again in Jesus' presence, all of my anger gone. "They wouldn't curse the teacher. But they have no problem hating him."

"I think they would have stoned you if they could have, but there were no stones nearby," John said, suddenly sober, looking at Jesus.

"Yes, well, remember, hatred and murder are the same in the Father's eyes," Jesus said. "Those men are blind guides leading the blind. They sit in Moses's seat in the synagogue, so do what they tell you, but don't do as they do, for they live falsely, and I would have you live in love and truth." He took bread and blessed it, broke it, and shared it with the others.

When he handed a piece to me, I knew he understood me. Somehow, I think he knew of the fear that I could not tell him.

THIRTY-ONE

The women listening to Jesus stood reluctantly to put the food in a secure place, but before we reached the door, Jesus stopped us. "We are leaving for Galilee," he said.

I turned about, seeing the looks of surprise on the faces of Lazarus, Martha, and Mary. The rest of us were used to Jesus moving from one place to the other without much notice.

"Are you sure we can't coax you to stay another day?" Lazarus asked, extending his hands in supplication. "You know you are always welcome."

Jesus smiled, and they shared a familiar, understanding look.

"I know we are," Jesus said, rising. "But my message must reach more people. There is not much more time."

He moved toward the courtyard, and the men followed, Lazarus included. The women hurried to help Martha clean the cooking area, but she surprised us, shooing us toward the door. "Go, gather your things. Mary and I will clean up after you're gone. You don't want to keep the teacher waiting."

"Are you sure?" I asked her, glancing at the mess we'd left.

"I'm sure. Go!" She waved her hands, dismissing us.

I ran up the steps to the roof, gathered my basket, and returned to the courtyard, the other women behind me. "We're ready," I said to Andrew, who stood closest to me while Jesus spoke quietly to Lazarus.

"We're just waiting on him." Andrew picked at his tooth with a piece of straw from a nearby bale of hay kept for the animals. Martha kept a couple of goats and donkeys and a large garden. I wondered how she managed it all without servants. They obviously had wealth. Perhaps Martha was one of those people who preferred to do everything herself.

Jesus turned and motioned for us to follow him, bidding Lazarus goodbye. I fell into step with Susanna and Adi, with Mary Clopas and Salome behind us.

We walked the well-worn path from Bethany to Jericho, to homes where we had stayed before. But when the disciples checked with the homeowners, asking for lodging, they turned us away.

"Master," Peter said as we all gathered in Jericho's town square, "the homes where we stayed before have refused our request." He gave Jesus a concerned, quizzical look. "What do you want us to do?"

A deep sigh lifted Jesus' chest, his look resigned yet determined. "We will leave the city and sleep in the fields."

My heart sank. No warm bed tonight?

"But why are they unwelcoming?" Andrew asked.

"Do you want us to call down judgment on them from heaven?" James asked.

John nodded. "They should not be allowed to treat you like this!"

I looked at Jesus, catching the sorrow in his eyes. "Come," he said, turning to leave Jericho. He didn't even respond to the brothers' question.

When we had passed through the gates and walked some

distance to a field north of the city, Jesus faced us. "If you are going to follow me, you must get used to this type of rejection. From now on, we are not going to be as well received as we once were." He glanced about the group. "Build a fire and settle in. We leave at dawn."

We slept, though mine was fitful. Jesus was making it harder to follow him, even for his chosen disciples. He knew why the townspeople were keeping their distance from him. The crowds had thinned of late, but this was the first rejection I'd felt from the people who had once flocked to see him.

I was only too happy when we finally made it to Magdala, exhausted from the trip. We'd arrived the night before Shabbat, and I invited everyone to stay with me, thankful when they did.

Darrah filled the table with Magdala's famous salted fish and a loaf of the finest wheat bread for each person. I thanked her before crawling into my bed, worn and longing for sleep.

I woke early and found Jesus in the courtyard before dawn, coming from outside the gate. "Did you sleep?" I asked, pleased and surprised by this private moment with him.

"I spent the night with my Father," he said. "But I'm glad you are up and could join me."

"You are?" He wanted my company? "But what of the others?"

He smiled. "The others don't have the concerns you do, Mary. As you have rightly judged, they are not paying attention."

My eyes grew wide. I had sensed that he could read my thoughts, but to discover it was true jolted me. I swallowed hard. "You keep talking about going away."

He nodded. "Yes. When the time comes."

"But why? Everyone thinks you're here to set up your kingdom. Why would you go away then? Where will you go?" My heart pounded with each rushed breath.

"I am here to do my Father's will. My kingdom is not of this world, Mary. In time, you will understand, when I return to my Father. I cannot explain it to you now as you cannot yet bear to hear it." He held my gaze, and I wanted to weep.

"I want to come with you."

"Where I am going you cannot come. You will come later, but not now." He sat on the stone bench and motioned for me to sit near him.

"But I can't live without you," I said, gulping back a sob.

"You will have my Spirit, and he will never leave you."

I didn't understand, but I nodded regardless. "You aren't going yet, though, are you?" I asked after a lengthy pause.

"My time has not yet come. But it is coming." He looked at me again, and I felt his peace wash over me. "Don't be afraid, Mary. I will never leave you or forsake you. I know you have lost much in this life. Your mother and father and husband. But you will never lose me."

Relief filled me. "You will never leave me?"

"Never," he promised. "My Spirit will always be with you."

I longed to ask what he meant by his Spirit, but I couldn't bear to break this moment of reassurance. In time, he would tell me more. Hadn't he promised?

"Now I think it is time I prepare for Shabbat service," he said, standing.

I jumped up. "Yes. I will see if Darrah needs my help with the food."

The men would eat the food that Chana had cooked the night before or left on the fire—porridge perhaps. I hurried off to check, glancing back for one last look at Jesus.

He was looking heavenward, and the dawn cast a glow about his face, giving him a glory I had never seen before. He looked regal in that moment, and I simply stared, utterly amazed at his majesty.

$\backsim$

Several days after Shabbat, Joanna came to my courtyard from her home in Tiberias, where she and Chuza lived from time to time, two servants in tow.

"Joanna! It's been too long." I hugged her, pleased by this surprise. "Are you joining us again?"

She pulled her headscarf to the side of her face, its colorful hues enhancing her tan skin. The breeze that came down from Mount Arbel caught my scarf as well, and I tugged her inside, out of the wind.

She turned to her servants. "You may return to Chuza now and tell him that I have arrived safely."

They bowed, then turned and left the courtyard.

Joanna faced me. "Yes," she said, smiling and holding up a leather pouch. She shook it. Coins jingled inside. "Chuza sent me with this for the teacher. He said I am free to join him as long as other women are along. I assumed you would be with him?"

I nodded. "Yes. And I'm so glad you came. Susanna cannot accompany us this time, though Mary Clopas is coming. We are leaving soon for Capernaum." I pointed to the pile of belongings in the entryway that the disciples would be carrying with them. "We are getting used to sleeping outside as people are less welcoming to us than they once were."

She raised a brow. "Chuza also hears talk in Herod's household." She pulled me aside and glanced about the empty room. "Where are the men?"

"Out gathering supplies with the funds Susanna and I gave

them. We will stop in Capernaum for a few days, and then I don't know where. Why? You look worried." My own tendency to worry spiked at the way she gripped the money bag until her knuckles whitened.

"Ever since Herod had John the Baptizer killed, he has wanted an audience with Jesus. To do him harm, no doubt. He might not be as bad as his father, Herod the Great, but he is still bad. And it doesn't help that he wants to please the Romans more than he does our people. Jesus isn't making any of the leaders happy." She looked at the pouch and loosened her grip.

"Do you think Herod will send soldiers after him?" I swallowed the lump in my throat. "Should we tell him?"

Joanna's face held uncertainty. "I suppose so, though will it make any difference? He does what he wants to do, not what we tell him."

"He does his Father's will," I corrected, though I agreed with her.

"Of course," Joanna said, touching my arm. "That's what I meant."

The door opened, and Joseph Justus, Matthias, Judas, Andrew, Matthew, and Simon the Zealot entered, all talking at once.

"We're leaving," Joseph said, heading toward the pile of tents and sacks of grain and other food.

"I guess we're leaving," I said to Joanna, chuckling. "Let me get my things." I hurried to find Darrah, who supplied me with a large sack and made one up for Joanna as well.

"I assumed we would accept the hospitality of the townspeople," Joanna said, tucking the coins into her robe. "I should have brought more."

"Your contribution will allow us to buy more wherever we go." I smiled at her. There was nothing we could do about

Herod or the Romans, and I preferred to think about seeing Adi and Salome again rather than worrying about what I could not change. Jesus could do miracles, so he could surely handle the Pharisees, religious leaders, and Romans.

"Ready?" Joseph asked as we approached the door.

"Yes," I said, pushing my thoughts aside and avoiding his probing gaze.

He walked ahead of us, and I closed the door behind us. Jesus led us out of my courtyard, through Magdala's main street, and past the houses, fish-salting buildings, markets, and synagogues, toward Capernaum.

Outside Magdala, we came to an outcropping of rocks, and Jesus stopped. We gathered around as he sat on a rock and beckoned to us.

"We are going to Capernaum," he said, his dark eyes shining with light.

Why had I never noticed his clear gaze before now? As though there was no darkness in him at all. But of course there wouldn't be. Not if he was the light of the world, as he'd said.

"But soon," he continued, "we will return to Jerusalem for Passover." He paused.

Passover was still several months away. We had only finished the Festival of Sukkot. Why was he concerned with Passover?

"The Son of Man is going to be delivered into the hands of men," he said, his expression sad. "They will kill him, and on the third day he will be raised to life."

Silence followed his words. What did he say? I struggled to swallow. I looked from one man to another, then at Joanna and Mary Clopas. No one spoke.

Jesus stood and began walking again. No one questioned him, but I could see their reactions. The women were wide-eyed and pale. The men looked stricken, as though there had been a death in the family.

Grief overwhelmed me. Jesus had spoken of dying, just not like this. Not with such certainty. The realization that he meant this would happen soon struck me.

Sorrow pervaded the group as we trudged after Jesus. His words swirled in my mind. He couldn't die. Not now. It made no sense.

The farther we walked, the more the men murmured similar thoughts. The Messiah couldn't die. So why did Jesus say such things to confuse us all? I didn't understand, but I did know one thing with all my heart. He promised to never leave me. And if he didn't keep his promises, then no one could ever be trusted.

THIRTY-TWO

Winter rains chilled the air, and for a time, I thought Jesus would remain in Capernaum throughout the winter, but he did not change his plans. When the Festival of Dedication came, Jesus left with the men, but the women stayed behind in Capernaum.

"Why do you think he didn't want us with him this time?" I asked one day after the festival ended, as we anticipated the men's return. We worked in the sitting room, Adi and Salome using the spindle and distaff while Susanna and Mary Clopas wound yarn into separate colorful balls. I mended a garment and Joanna did the same. A sense of belonging filled me as I shared this moment with these women.

"It's a long walk in the winter," Adi said, working the spindle without looking at it. "Peter didn't want me to have to traipse through soggy areas or sleep on cold ground in those places where there is no town. Tents can be warm, but it's not the most pleasant journey."

"I'm just as glad to stay behind," Susanna said, tying off the end of the red yarns and picking up the yellow. "With all of the men required to appear at the temple in Jerusalem, I'm glad we can be together while we wait for them."

"Yes," I said, studying the garment to see where the needle must go next. In any other case, all these women would go to their homes with their husbands, but their husbands were with Jesus on the way home from Jerusalem. A pang of longing filled me as I realized not for the first time that I was the only one without a husband. Joseph Justus's image entered my mind.

"They've been gone two and a half weeks," Salome said, interrupting my thoughts. "If all went well, they should be home in a few days."

"Unless they are delayed for some reason or take longer to come home." Adi met my gaze. "Do you worry about Joseph?"

I flushed at her look. "I don't know what you mean." A moment later, I shook my head. "That's not true. I suppose I do think about him now and then." I glanced anxiously at the window that faced the courtyard.

Silence followed my remark.

"I did not mean to make you uncomfortable," Adi said after a moment. "We all have our own struggles."

"It's all right. I'm content being alone." I tied off a knot in the thread. Was that the truth? I chose not to continue to examine my feelings and studied the stitching instead.

The sound of children playing outside turned my attention again to the window. I stood and walked toward it, straining to see. A cool mist fell, and the children soon returned to their homes.

"What are you looking for?" Susanna asked from across the room. "The men aren't going to come any faster for you staring at the window, Mary." She laughed.

I glanced at her, then turned back at the distant sound of male voices. And suddenly they were there, earlier than anyone had expected. "They're back!"

The women stopped their work and tucked it away as the men burst through the door, talking and laughing. Every part of my being longed to rush into Jesus' arms—not in an inappropriate way, of course, but just to be held by the one who had healed me. The one who loved me despite my past.

But I could not make my feet move toward him, for the men surrounded him. A deep sigh escaped me. Adi's question made me see that perhaps I longed for more—to have what she had with Peter. To have what each of these women had. Even Jesus' mother had Jesus and could claim him like no other, not to mention her other sons and daughters.

I had no one. Memories of Marcus surfaced, but they flitted away. Marcus had been such a brief part of my life.

I glanced at Joseph Justus and saw him watching me. He smiled, and I suddenly felt shy. Embarrassed perhaps? What was this new feeling growing within me? Did I want Joseph to care for me in that way?

"Tell us what happened," Salome said, drawing me back to the group. She looked with pride at James and John as the women took a few moments to join Jesus and the men. We didn't need to serve them for at least an hour—a rare moment to just listen.

"Jesus didn't make the Pharisees very happy again," John said, looking at Jesus. "They tried to stone him."

I could not withhold a gasp. I knew they hated him. Had felt it in a single look from many of them. I easily recognized hatred, even from those who attempted to hide it. The religious leaders had many ways of disguising their intents and motives, but somehow I knew. Perhaps in my healing, Jesus had given me a spirit to discern.

"They asked Jesus if he was the Messiah," Peter said. "'Tell us plainly,' they said." He placed an arm around Adi, clearly happy to be home.

Again I felt that twinge of longing, but one look at Jesus and all I could think of was wanting to serve him. To please him. I needed his presence, not a husband's.

"Do you want to tell them, Master?" Peter asked, facing Jesus, who leaned against a cushion, looking weary.

"You can finish," Jesus said, closing his eyes. I never thought about how tired he might get. He'd always been so full of life.

Peter paused, then nodded to John. "You tell them."

John set his hands on the table, intertwining his fingers. "He said they didn't believe because they weren't his sheep. He said his sheep listen to him, he gives them eternal life, and they will never perish, and no one can take them out of his or the Father's hand." He paused. "But then he said, 'I and the Father are one,' and they grew livid. They picked up stones right then to stone him."

"They didn't believe him," Susanna said, leaning against Tobias.

"They tried to seize him, but he escaped their grasp," John said. "He was like oil slipping through a flask. We all fled and didn't stop until we crossed the Jordan."

"I'm glad you're safe," I said softly.

Jesus opened his eyes and gave me an appreciative nod. "It is not yet their hour," he said, closing his eyes again.

I pondered his words, longing to ask what he meant. Normally he talked about *his* hour not yet coming, but did everyone have an "hour" or a time when something momentous would happen?

And what was Jesus' hour? Was it when he would set up the kingdom at last and be crowned King and Messiah of Israel?

"The Son of Man is going to be delivered into the hands of men. They will kill him, and on the third day he will be raised to life." The words he'd spoken months ago filled my mind, along with the usual accompanying dread.

Is that what you mean by your hour? I searched his face, but Jesus did not meet my gaze this time.

Conversations swirled around me, and the women soon left to prepare food, but the memory of Jesus' words had shaken me. The Pharisees were growing bolder. What would they do when Passover came?

Several weeks passed while we remained in Capernaum. I woke early one morning and walked with Susanna and Joanna to the market to purchase spices that Adi had run out of—cinnamon and cumin and dill—hurrying to reach the merchants before they were overrun with other women.

"I'm not sure why we are heading up to Jerusalem with Passover still a few weeks away," Joanna said as the sun displayed its pinks and yellows against the backdrop of a bluer sky than I had seen all winter.

"I agree," Susanna said, voicing the confusion we'd all felt over Jesus' decision to leave Galilee.

"Won't Chuza want you to return home to Tiberias? Or is he heading back to Jerusalem?" I asked Joanna, knowing that Chuza moved from place to place in Herod's employ.

"Chuza doesn't care whether I'm with him or with Jesus. He knows how much it means to me to follow the teacher. But I also think he is torn between loyalty to Herod and following Jesus himself." A deep sigh escaped her. "He was so grateful when Jesus healed me, but now . . . I'm not sure he likes the cost of upsetting the Jews and Herod. Not to mention the Romans."

I looked at my friend and touched her arm. "I'm sorry, Joanna. So many people are torn in how they feel about Jesus. I never thought Chuza would struggle. I thought he believed."

"I think he does," Joanna said. "I hope he does."

Silence filled the space between the three of us as we considered her worry. She wanted her husband to believe that Jesus was the Messiah and worth following. But not many were willing to give up everything to follow him.

I picked through sticks of cinnamon and placed them in a pile for the merchant to package. "I don't know why Jesus wants to head to Jerusalem so soon, or where he is taking us on the way. I'm just glad to be with him."

"Even fewer crowds are following him now," Susanna said as we turned to head back to Peter's house. We would eat and pack and go with the men to head in the direction of Judea.

"Ever since he fed the multitudes, they haven't been happy that he won't commit to being our leader."

"They wanted to make him king," Joanna said.

We passed a row of smaller homes where grinding stones turned in the courtyards, drowning us out. We walked on in silence until we came to Peter's courtyard. Joseph and Judas met us as we entered, each carrying packs, which they set down.

"Ready so soon?" I asked, heading toward the door where more of the men were coming through. I stood back to let them pass.

"Jesus wants to leave as soon as we've eaten. Are you ready?" Joseph asked, striding up to me. "Are all of you coming?" He meant all the women, though his gaze held only mine.

"Yes. I think so." I slipped past him, disturbed at the flutter in my middle, and joined Susanna and Joanna before more men could stop us.

We hurried to prepare unleavened bread and pack food for the journey. Salome entered with Zebedee, and soon all of us were eating, some sitting, some standing, like the Israelites had done at the first Passover, packed and ready to go at a moment's notice.

I carried my pack like the rest of them out of Capernaum. We took the main highway along the Jordan into Judea. But we had not gone far from Capernaum when Jesus turned back and looked at the city.

"Woe to you, Chorazin! Woe to you, Bethsaida!" he said. "For if the miracles that were performed in you had been performed in Tyre and Sidon, they would have repented long ago in sackcloth and ashes. But I tell you, it will be more bearable for Tyre and Sidon on the day of judgment than for you. And you, Capernaum, will you be lifted to the heavens? No, you will go down to Hades. For if the miracles that were performed in you had been performed in Sodom, it would have remained to this day. But I tell you that it will be more bearable for Sodom on the day of judgment than for you."

He turned and walked ahead of the rest of us. No one attempted to catch up to him. Instead, I noticed the men breaking into groups, two here, three there, perhaps like they had done when Jesus sent them off to preach and heal.

I had the sudden uneasy feeling that we would not be returning to the cities that Jesus had just condemned. But if we didn't return, where would we go? Was Peter to never return to his home?

My feet hurt as the path crossed an area of broken stones and then turned to dirt. Jerusalem was about a five-day walk, and Jesus was in no hurry to get there. He stopped at last near an open grassy field, where we set up camp, and then he walked away into the nearby hills.

"He's distant," Judas said where he sat by a fire with some of the other men after we had settled. I stood nearby with Susanna. "I think we should do something about it," he said, looking at Andrew and Simon the Zealot, who sat nearest him. "I mean, we know who he is. Isn't it time that we help him fulfill his mission as Messiah?" Judas leaned forward, elbows on his knees, intensity in his tone.

"Isn't that what we're already doing?" Matthew said from where he sat beside Simon. In the beginning, I would never have thought a former violent Zealot who hated tax collectors would actually be friends with Matthew, a former tax collector. Jesus' choices never failed to surprise me.

"True," Simon agreed, glancing at Matthew.

"What's true?" Peter asked, coming from outside the group to place dried dung on the fire. "What are we talking about?"

"Judas thinks we need to do something to help Jesus fulfill his mission," Simon said, shrugging. "But we are already doing what he's asked of us. He isn't asking us to fight the Romans or to take the kingdom by force."

"Coming from a Zealot, you surprise me, Simon," Judas said. I didn't miss his slight frown.

"Former Zealot," Simon corrected. "Trust me, I'm ready in a moment to help him go after the Romans, though the religious leaders are the ones who hate him most."

"They are in alliance with Rome," Judas insisted. "The religious leaders need to be convinced of who he is so he can take his rightful place as Messiah."

"I think," I said, stepping into the conversation, wanted or not, "that if Jesus wanted to rule as king, he would already have done so. He's been walking about Judea and Galilee and Jerusalem for almost three years, and yet he's no closer to fighting the Romans or the Jews to claim any throne."

I looked at the astonished faces of the men. They didn't expect me to speak up, as I often kept my thoughts to myself or talked only among the women, but Judas was wrong and I couldn't keep silent. "Jesus isn't ready," I finished when no one else spoke.

"That's why we need to help him," Judas said. He stood to pace a short distance from the fire. "Don't you see?" He turned to look from one man to another. "He is the Messiah. Despite what he says, he can't die. God can't die, and he has told us he's equal with God. So what is stopping him? He keeps going off by himself for what? To plan strategies?"

"To talk with the Father," Peter said, calmer than I expected. He stood and faced Judas. "You are on the wrong track, friend."

Judas snorted, but he didn't say anything more. He walked off, and Peter returned to the fire.

"He's just anxious for Jesus to tell us what is next. When *is* the kingdom coming?" Simon leaned toward the fire, took a stalk of dried grass, and dipped the end in the fire. He held it up, looked at it, then tossed it into the flames. "I think we would all like to know Jesus' plans." He looked toward the hills where Jesus had gone, but there was no sign of him.

The men nodded here and there, but no one said what Jesus had already told us twice. We were going to Jerusalem and he was going to die. If he could not die because God could not die, then why would he say it? God could not lie either.

The familiar dread curled in my middle. The feeling I got every time I thought of losing Jesus in one way or another. The thought that he would leave me, despite his promise. Judas was wrong. But I desperately wished that were not so.

THIRTY-THREE

A few days later, the gates of Jericho loomed before us. Jesus had taken his time getting here. I was grateful for the slower pace and enjoyed time with our group, but the fact that he would enter a town that had turned us away the last time we passed this way surprised me.

As we neared the entry to pass the guards, I adjusted my headscarf. I had no desire to expose my hair and be thought of as an adulteress or otherwise promiscuous woman. I also hid my face, needing time to think. To watch.

Judas appeared to have let go of his desires to convince Jesus to act and take hold of the kingdom he preached. A good decision, in my opinion. But when Samaria refused us entry to pass through their country, I couldn't help the feeling that we were walking toward something from which we should run the other way. Something foreboding. The Samaritans had once welcomed Jesus at a time when I was not with the men. Why were so many hostile to him now?

Susanna and Joanna drew up beside me, freeing me of my desire to walk alone for a time. "Do you think we can convince some of the people to let us stay with them this time?" Susanna asked, completely unaware of my concerns. But then no one except Jesus could read my thoughts.

"I assume we are passing through, considering last time." I looked at her, then at the crowd that had emerged from the city before I could respond.

"Chuza has a friend here who is welcoming toward Jesus," Joanna said as we entered the city. "Come with me. Perhaps we can secure lodging for tonight." She glanced back at Jesus, who had stopped to heal a line of sick people waiting for him. "We may be here a while."

I nodded, then paused. "Shouldn't we ask Jesus first? What if he wants to move on tonight?"

Joanna gave me a look. "We can always tell them the teacher changed his mind. Or that we misunderstood him. Come." She moved through the growing mass of people and led Susanna and me to the wealthy section of town.

"Do you think the person you seek will be home? It looks like the whole town has come out to see Jesus." I glanced at the sprawling brick home where Joanna stopped.

"The servants will be here. I will at least leave word." She approached the door and knocked, not nearly as hesitant as I felt.

Moments later, after Joanna had done exactly as she'd said, we returned to find that Jesus had moved on from the town's entrance and made his way through the streets, not far from the very area from which we had just come. A row of trees lined the path, and we hurried to join our group.

Jesus stopped and looked up, as though searching for a bird among the branches. "Zacchaeus," he said, causing me to search the trees to find a man perched on a heavy branch. "Hurry and come down, for I must stay at your house today."

The man scrambled down from the tree. Murmurs from the crowd reached us.

"Why is he speaking to a tax collector?"

"He's going to stay at his house?"

"Blasphemer! He consorts with sinners!"

I looked at the man's wealthy clothing that marked him as a tax collector like the Romans. Like Matthew had been. Of course Jesus would eat with the man. He accepted anyone who willingly came to him.

Later that afternoon, we crowded into the spacious home of Zacchaeus. Matthew easily engaged him, more animated than I'd ever seen him. A warm feeling moved through me, and for the first time in days, I smiled. This meal might not be a taste of the kingdom Jesus preached about, but the love here was a wonderful reprieve from the hatred of the Jewish leaders. *Thank you for this.*

A throat cleared, and Zacchaeus, a small man who came to my shoulder, stood, smoothed his hands on his multicolored robe, and faced Jesus. "Behold, Lord," he said, eyes alight with the same joy I felt, "half of my goods I give to the poor. And if I have defrauded anyone of anything, I will restore it fourfold."

Matthew nodded, approval in his eyes.

"Today salvation has come to this house," Jesus said, "since he also is a son of Abraham. For the Son of Man came to seek and to save the lost."

That evening, the women moved to the house where Joanna's husband had connections, but Jesus and the men slept in Zacchaeus's home. We offered to help the servants with the meal, but our host refused. How strange it felt to be treated as I had been in my childhood. I should have missed that life, but I didn't. I enjoyed feeling useful. Helping Jesus.

The morning meal passed, and I chafed, longing to do something. "Should we go to Zacchaeus's house to see what Jesus wants to do next?" I finally asked when Susanna and I had a moment alone. Joanna was caught in conversation with our hostess, and the others had gone to the rooms they'd been assigned to gather their things, which I'd already done.

"That's prudent, if we can get away," Susanna whispered, angling her head toward Joanna, who did not seem able to break free.

I peered through a large window that faced the street, relief filling me. "We don't have to worry. They're coming to us."

I opened the door and hurried to meet them, Susanna behind me. "Are we leaving?" I asked.

"Soon," Jesus said. "We will preach and heal in this city, then head to the other side of the Jordan for a time."

The other women emerged from the house, and we bid our hostess farewell. We headed toward the marketplace, where the crowds grew the largest. Jericho was different from any other city, and I had always been intrigued by its history and thick, stout walls. Walls similar to the ones God had toppled in Joshua's day.

Jesus stood in the center of the town square and talked about a nobleman going to a far country to receive a kingdom and then return. I listened as he told about the nobleman giving his servants different amounts of money to invest while he was gone and what happened to those who were wise and the one who wasn't.

"He speaks in stories all of the time now," Mary Clopas said. The five of us women stood in a group, watching him. "What do you think he means by a nobleman going to a far country to receive a kingdom? Does he mean that the kingdom isn't coming yet? The men are not going to understand this."

"Probably not," I agreed. "They grow more excited about the coming kingdom the closer we get to Passover."

"Jesus doesn't appear to share their excitement," Mary Clopas said.

"No, he doesn't."

Jesus finished speaking to the crowd, then motioned for us to follow him. He led us through the gate and headed east toward the Jordan.

Relief filled me as we left the city and the crowd behind. I once thought the crowds indicated proof of his coming kingdom. We had hope in the future. Joy in knowing the Messiah had come. But Jesus didn't act like the Messiah the people expected, and I couldn't blame them for misunderstanding him. None of us knew what to expect from him.

Where were the laughter and joy that had first accompanied him? Though we were taking a sidetrack from Jerusalem, Jesus' countenance carried a heaviness, a weight I could not comprehend. Sorrow shrouded him, and I longed to ask why.

As we set up camp across the Jordan, Jesus again went off by himself, leaving us alone. The women prepared food for the men, then retreated to our tent while the men slept around the fire. I listened to their muffled voices, hearing the highs and lows of men arguing in whispers.

Sighing deeply, I prayed that Jesus would return and settle their problems. Even if he didn't need us as often as he did his Father, we still needed him. I hoped he realized that.

The following day, Jesus had joined us again, and the sun broke through the clouds like a kiss from heaven. My heart lifted, grateful for this moment, but my joy in being with our small group vanished a few moments later when a man came and knelt at Jesus' feet.

"Lord," the man said, lifting his head to meet Jesus' gaze, "Mary and Martha have sent me to tell you that the one you love is sick."

Murmurs I could not hear came from the men. "The one he loves? Jesus loves everyone," I said to Susanna and Mary Clopas. "They must be speaking of Lazarus, don't you agree?"

"I would assume so," Mary Clopas whispered.

"This sickness will not end in death," Jesus said.

Good. We were not being called away to something urgent.

"No, it is for God's glory so that God's Son may be glorified through it," he added.

How could an illness be for God's glory unless Jesus healed the man?

"Are you going to come, Lord?" the man asked, clearly anxious. "What should I tell the ones who sent me?"

"We will come," Jesus said.

So we would be leaving again after having just settled here? I stifled the desire to release a heavy sigh, accepting this as no different from any other time Jesus had bid us to go. And yet it felt different somehow.

His words satisfied the man, who turned and ran back toward the Jordan. He must have found out the direction we had gone from the people of Jericho.

I hesitated a moment, then called to the women to help me take the tent down.

"Not yet," Jesus said to my retreating back.

"We're not leaving?" I asked him. "But if Lazarus needs your healing . . . Bethany is another two-day walk."

"This sickness is to bring glory to my Father and to His Son," Jesus said.

I nodded, deciding not to question him further. Jesus could do anything, so I had no doubt that Lazarus might already be healed. If he was in no hurry, then I was happy to wait. Lazarus would be well.

Two days later, Jesus called us together after the morning meal. "Let us go back to Judea," he said.

"But Rabbi," Philip said, "a short while ago the Jews there tried to stone you, and yet you are going back?"

The "short while" had been a few months ago, and Philip knew we were headed to Jerusalem, so I didn't understand his question. But clearly that experience had worried the twelve. I glanced at Joseph Justus and Matthias and realized that they, too, were concerned.

I searched Jesus' face, fighting the sudden thudding of my heart.

"Our friend Lazarus has fallen asleep," Jesus said, drawing my gaze to his, "but I am going there to wake him up."

"Lord, if he sleeps, he will get better," Andrew said, clearly troubled. "I mean, I know you said we would go to Bethany, but it's so close to Jerusalem. And they hate you there. Can't you just heal him from here?"

All eyes focused on Jesus at Andrew's question. Lazarus had already been healed, hadn't he? If he was sleeping, that was a good thing.

"Lazarus is dead," Jesus said, jolting me. My heartbeat quickened, and I was certain I'd misheard him. Jesus looked from one of us to another. "And for your sake I am glad I was not there, so that you may believe. But let us go to him."

"Let us also go, that we may die with him," Thomas added, resigned.

"What does he mean?" Susanna asked me as we lifted our packs and trudged behind the men toward the Jordan. "Why would Thomas suggest we will die too? Lazarus is dead? I thought Jesus healed him from a distance."

We exchanged looks, my stomach dipping. "What if . . ." I swallowed hard. "What if we're wrong, Susanna? What if Jesus really meant it when he talked about dying? Nothing would make sense if he dies. He can't die!" I kept my voice low, afraid to be overheard. The men all talked in subdued tones among themselves while Jesus again walked alone ahead of us.

She shrugged, and I didn't know what to do with that response. She didn't know any more than I did, and that was no help to me. How could Lazarus be dead? Why would Jesus allow such a thing?

The other women clustered around me as we walked mostly in silence, each of us with our own troubled thoughts. I supposed I would have to wait until Jesus showed us his reasons, because right now he wasn't talking, and no one had the courage to question him.

THIRTY-FOUR

We stopped on the outskirts of Bethany two days later, as Jesus did not want to enter the city, though it was one of the few that was small and welcoming. I huddled together with the women while Jesus sent Andrew to Martha's home.

"Why can't we go to comfort her?" Susanna asked, her brows drawn low.

"He must have his reasons," I said, though none of us were happy with waiting when we could be sitting shiva and comforting Martha and Mary. Why had Jesus let Lazarus die? I couldn't process the thought.

We waited, watching the road where Andrew had gone, and moments later Martha rushed out to meet Jesus.

"Lord," she said, hands lifted in supplication, "if you had been here, my brother would not have died."

Her voice wavered and cracked, and I quietly wept with her. Jesus took her hand between both of his.

"But I know," she said, choking on a sob, "that even now God will give you whatever you ask."

Jesus focused his attention on her alone. I felt like an intruder watching this exchange, and yet I knew Jesus wanted us with him. "Your brother will rise again," he told her.

"I know he will rise again in the resurrection at the last day," Martha said, nodding, as though assuring him that she believed in him as the Messiah.

"I am the resurrection and the life. The one who believes in me will live, even though they die, and whoever lives by believing in me will never die. Do you believe this?"

"Yes, Lord," she said, and my heart soared in agreement. "I believe that you are the Messiah, the Son of God, who is to come into the world."

He smiled at her with that deep compassion I had never seen in anyone else. "Please, ask Mary to come to me," he said.

Martha picked up her skirts and hastened back the way she had come. Moments passed as we waited in silence. Jesus seemed wrapped up in something surreal, as though in that moment he was communing with heaven and we were simply spectators.

Footsteps drew my attention, and I looked to see Mary followed by prominent Jews who had come to comfort her.

Mary fell at Jesus' feet, her tears silent but unending. "Lord," she rasped, unable to keep the emotion from her voice, "if you had been here, my brother would not have died."

Her anguish pricked my heart, and I wished I had never been jealous of her relationship with Jesus. He loved each one of us and did not have favorites. Mary was such a young, sensitive soul. How could she bear such loss?

A deeply troubled look crossed Jesus' face. "Where have you laid him?" he asked.

"Come and see, Lord," the group with Mary answered.

We followed the Jews who led the way. Martha and Mary held back, staying beside Jesus, while he led the rest of us to where caves lined the low hills.

When we stopped at a tomb where a large stone covered the entrance, Jesus groaned. Martha and Mary and the Jews with them continued their wailing. My tears spilled as I looked at the sisters, who could barely stand. I sought Jesus, shocked at what I saw.

His face contorted, and a deep cry erupted from him as tears ran unchecked into his beard. He lifted his hands to his face, weeping like Martha and Mary, only his cries carried a different tone. Stronger? Angrier?

He looked at the tomb, and the expression on his face held . . . fury.

"See how he loved him!" one of the Jews said.

"Could not he who opened the eyes of the blind man have kept this man from dying?" said another.

Ignoring their comments, Jesus moved in front of the tomb. "Take away the stone," he commanded.

Take away the stone?

The twelve moved to do as Jesus said.

"But Lord," Martha objected, "by this time there is a bad odor, for he has been there four days."

I felt Jesus' compassion from where I stood. And yet, I sensed a deeper emotion in him, a mystery.

"Did I not tell you that if you believe, you will see the glory of God?" Jesus looked toward the skies, lifting his hands to the heavens. "Father," he said, loud enough for all of us to hear, "I thank You that You have heard me. I knew that You always hear me, but I said this for the benefit of the people standing here, that they may believe that You sent me."

A moment passed. Jesus looked again at the tomb. "Lazarus, come out!" he cried.

My breath caught in my throat. Time stilled. Then the sound of shuffling feet. The entrance filled with a sight I knew I would never see again. A body wrapped in strips of linen and with a cloth around his face stood before us.

A collective gasp spread through the crowd, and my heart pounded. I had seen Jesus raise the boy in Nain but never expected to see this. Not someone dead for four days.

"Take off the graveclothes and let him go," Jesus said, his voice triumphant.

Martha and Mary rushed forward and began to unwind the wrappings they no doubt had placed around Lazarus four days earlier.

Awe swept through the crowd. As I looked from one face to another, I saw some who believed but others who were skeptical. What would it take for these people to believe Jesus was who he claimed to be? He'd just raised a man from the dead! Was anything too hard for him?

Yet I sensed that bitter spirit, even hatred, that I so easily discerned in people who did not want Jesus in their lives or in our country.

Susanna and I and the other women joined Martha and Mary the moment Lazarus was free and held in Jesus' arms. We laughed and cried, and Martha carried the graveclothes with her to burn.

Some of the Jewish leaders slipped away. I told myself they left because there was nothing more they could do to comfort the sisters, but I knew in my heart that their reasons were greater than that. And I didn't like where my thoughts took me.

We stayed with Lazarus and his sisters for a few days, but on the third morning, as the dew kissed the earth and the sun brushed away the cool night air, word came from Jerusalem.

"The Jews want to kill you, Master," Peter said after speaking to a young man who had run the distance to Bethany. "Those who witnessed what you did"—he looked at Lazarus as he spoke—"reported everything to the Pharisees. Of course, they don't believe it."

Jesus' expression was resigned. I longed to comfort him. "They don't believe in me, Peter. They do believe the miracle took place. They have eyes to see but cannot see. Miracles to them merely threaten their power rather than cause them to glorify God." He stood then and we with him. "We bid you farewell, my friend," he said to Lazarus. They shared a look of understanding.

Lazarus had not spoken much about those four days he had spent in the tomb, almost as if he wished he had not returned. Though he did look with affection on his sisters and accepted that they still needed him.

I wanted to ask him what it was like there with the Father, but I was too uncertain. He was reticent to talk much at all except to Jesus. What was life like after the grave? Would Lazarus eagerly accept death when it came for him again?

I hugged Martha and Mary as the men gathered our things, and we followed Jesus out of Bethany toward a wilderness village of Ephraim. We reached the village at nightfall, but Jesus called us to set up camp outside in the wilderness rather than look for lodging in the town.

"Master," Judas said that night as we sat about the fire, the women sitting across from the men.

"Yes, Judas," Jesus said, looking wearier than I'd ever seen him. The threats were taking a toll on him. Was there not some way I could lift his burden?

"If you let us, we could appeal to some of the Jewish leaders who support you and try to get them to convince the others of your mission. Show them that you don't intend to take away their place or change the law of Moses, as they think you are." His earnest look caused me to glance about at the others to see if they agreed.

"What is he doing?" Susanna hissed next to my ear. "Why does he keep trying to push Jesus?"

"I have no idea," I whispered back.

"What makes you think that I don't intend to take away their place?" Jesus drew a hand along his jaw as though contemplating Judas's words.

Judas sputtered a moment before he found words. "They would make better allies than enemies, wouldn't they?" he asked at last.

Jesus said nothing for a lengthy breath. "I did not come to make friends with those who think they are righteous. I came to save those who know they are not," he said. "The leaders who want to kill me will not want to join me. I did not come for that purpose."

"Then why did you come?" Matthias asked. "I thought you came to set up your kingdom."

"My kingdom is not of this world," Jesus said, repeating what I'd heard him say many times before but never understood.

At that moment, Salome stood and motioned to James and John to join her. She approached Jesus and knelt before him. I looked at Susanna, but she appeared as puzzled as I was.

"What do you want?" Jesus asked her.

I tilted my head to better hear above the crackling embers of the fire.

"Say that these two sons of mine are to sit, one at your right hand and one at your left, in your kingdom," she said.

What? I knew Salome loved her sons and carried a sense of pride that they were in Jesus' inner circle, but to be so bold? I felt a shiver work through me, embarrassed for her and her request, which I could have never asked.

"You do not know what you are asking," Jesus said, looking at James and John. "Are you able to drink the cup that I am to drink?"

Salome took a step back, allowing her sons to approach Jesus.

"We are able," each one said in turn.

"You will drink my cup," Jesus said, his tone one of gentle rebuke, "but to sit at my right hand and at my left is not mine to grant. It is for those for whom it has been prepared by my Father."

By their silence, I wasn't sure whether they were happy or wished they had not asked.

The three of them returned to their seats, but the indignant voices around me caused the hair to rise on the back of my neck. Susanna and I exchanged troubled glances. Even Mary Clopas showed her irritation. Had she wanted the same for her two sons but not thought to ask? Why was everyone so caught up in the kingdom when the Jews wanted to kill our Messiah?

"Listen to me," Jesus said, and the ripples of unrest slowly ceased. "You know that the rulers of the Gentiles lord it over them, and their great ones exercise authority over them. It shall not be so among you. But whoever would be great among you must be your servant, and whoever would be first among you must be your slave, even as the Son of Man came not to be served but to serve, and to give his life as a ransom for many."

His gaze swept over us one at a time, and when it reached me, I felt as though he had pierced my soul. Ransom? But why?

A rustling caused me to see Salome shift uncomfortably in her seat, and well she should! Had her ambition for her sons caused Jesus to say such things? I ignored the niggling guilt accompanying that thought.

"Listen," Jesus said, leaning toward the fire, elbows on his knees. "We are going to stay here until Passover nears. Then we are going up to Jerusalem, and everything that is written by the prophets about the Son of Man will be fulfilled. He will be delivered over to the Gentiles. They will mock him, insult him, and spit on him. They will flog him and kill him. On the third day he will rise again."

Rise again? Like Lazarus?

He stood, excused himself, and walked off to be alone.

"Why does he keep saying he's going to die?" Judas asked when Jesus was out of earshot. "It is clear that he doesn't want to take our suggestions or our help. I don't know what more we can do." He stalked off.

The others broke into groups, and some left to get some sleep.

"I'm going to bed," I told the women, unable to look at Salome. I needed to think. Was I wrong to think her request had led Jesus to again tell us he was going to die? This was the third time he had spoken of this. Surely there was some truth to what he was saying. And what did he mean about fulfilling the words of the prophets? What words? I wished I'd paid more attention to my tutors or had the teaching the men received in Torah classes.

Susanna followed me, and we slipped into the women's tent. "Salome shouldn't have asked that," she said.

"No, she shouldn't have. She just made things worse." I didn't think I could be angry at one of these women, and the guilt I tried to suppress wasn't helping, but we'd had no idea Salome would ask such a thing.

"I suppose we have to forgive her, though." Susanna gave me a look as I lay on my mat.

"Not tonight," I said, turning to face the wall of the tent. I had too much to consider to forgive anyone right now.

THIRTY-FIVE

Five days before Passover came sooner than anyone wanted. We'd grown used to staying in our wilderness camp, where few outsiders came to see Jesus and he could teach us in peace. When he spoke on forgiveness and loving one another, I knew he was speaking to me and how I felt about Salome. I had held a grudge for days, but when Jesus spoke, such feelings became so meaningless.

Judas had stopped trying to convince Jesus to rise and take his place as our king, but I noticed he appeared the slightest bit sullen at times. I'd never seen him pout, but his mood had definitely darkened.

Joseph Justus had also kept his distance, though not from Jesus, more from me. It wasn't like I'd tried to engage him, but had I put him off too often? Susanna thought so, but I acted as though her comments meant nothing. I liked Joseph, perhaps more than I should. But I had too many worries to think about pleasing anyone other than Jesus.

These thoughts and more accompanied me as I followed Jesus on our climb toward Jerusalem. I wrapped my cloak tightly about me, though the spring air was warm. There was a chill deep inside me that I could not shake with every glance in Jesus' direction. He walked with purpose, unwavering, but he did not laugh as he once had.

As Bethany drew near, I looked forward to seeing the sisters again, but rather than dine at their home, we ate at the home of Simon the Leper, a man Jesus had healed early in his ministry. Though it was not her house, Martha served us all, refusing any help.

"It is my service to him," she said after I'd asked her for the second time. "Allow me to do this."

I nodded, wishing I had something more to give Jesus than I already had. What could I possibly give him to lift the burden he carried like an invisible weight about his neck?

The men talked and ate as I picked at the food set before me, watching him. I felt out of place here and wanted to steal away to be alone, but I could not leave him. Not now. He was facing something too important.

The conversation had turned to Rome and the occupation when Mary of Bethany rose from her seat, carrying an alabaster jar. She walked directly to Jesus, knelt before him, and poured the fragrant perfume over his feet, then undid her headscarf and wiped his feet with her hair. I could not stop a sharp intake of breath, not because she had poured the ointment on Jesus' feet but because she had undone her hair to wipe them. Why not bring a cloth?

The heady scent of the perfume permeated the room. Shock registered on the faces of the men. But Mary did not care what they thought of her. She cared only for Jesus, as I'd seen countless times before. It was her way of serving him. While Martha offered us food, Mary offered herself and all that she had.

A throat cleared, drawing my gaze from Mary.

"Why this waste?" Judas stood, his tone indignant. "Why wasn't this ointment sold for a hundred denarii and given to the poor?"

I searched his face. Anger simmered in his eyes.

"Why are you bothering this woman?" Jesus said, looking from one man to another. "She has done a beautiful thing to me. The poor you will always have with you, but you will not always have me. When she poured this perfume on my body, she did it to prepare me for burial. Truly I tell you, wherever this gospel is preached throughout the world, what she has done will also be told, in memory of her."

My heart skipped a beat. He'd promised he would never leave me. Why was he so contradictory?

Jesus' words silenced the men, and Judas sat, though he did not look happy. Was he worried about losing Jesus as I was? Were the men finally understanding what Jesus was telling us, or were they just frustrated?

Mary wrapped her hair again, as though she had unbound it for a bridegroom and was covering it again as a bride. But of course, she wasn't going to marry Jesus. He wasn't going to marry anyone. He was going to be our king.

And yet, as we left Simon's home to return to Martha's to spend the night, I could not get the image of Mary's sacrifice out of my mind. Why did Jesus say she had done it for his burial? He was still living. You couldn't anoint someone in advance of death unless you were anointing them to be priest or king.

The thoughts would not let me sleep. That feeling of dread I'd been able to shake off before would not leave me now. I did not want Passover to come. I didn't want to think about what would happen when it did.

The following day, I woke early as usual to help Martha and the other women with the food. A somber mood permeated the entire house. Mary's sacrifice of the costly ointment and the unbinding of her hair for our Lord would never be forgotten. *"You will not always have me,"* he'd said. I swallowed hard.

How I wished I could have stopped time and kept Jesus in Bethany until after Passover. If we could just make it through Passover without incident—without the Pharisees and teachers of the law trying to stone him, without trouble—I would finally breathe easier.

But as we placed the food before the men, Jesus' words only made my chest tighten, and I struggled to breathe.

"We are going into Jerusalem," he said after blessing the food and breaking the bread. "Be ready to leave as soon as you've broken your fast." He looked at the women. "All of you may come."

My heart lightened at that, but one look at Susanna only confirmed my earlier feelings. We both understood evil, could recognize it in an instant, and Jerusalem held evil men who wanted to hurt Jesus. What good could come from entering the city so soon before Passover?

I wanted to question Jesus but didn't. I simply fell into step with the women after Martha closed the house door, and we set out on the trek to the Mount of Olives and down the hill to Jerusalem.

When we reached the village of Bethphage, Jesus stopped and turned to Matthew and Simon Z. "Go to the village ahead of you, and at once you will find a donkey tied there, with her colt by her. Untie them and bring them to me. If anyone says anything to you, say that the Lord needs them, and he will send them right away."

The two men hurried toward Bethphage while the rest of us waited on the Mount of Olives. Disquiet filled me as I tried to make sense of this action.

Joseph Justus joined Susanna and me where we stood near

Jesus in anxious silence. His look held excitement, surprising me.

"He is fulfilling prophecy," Joseph said, his eyes alight and his smile wide in his handsome face. "Zechariah said, 'Say to Daughter Zion, See, your king comes to you, gentle and riding on a donkey, and on a colt, the foal of a donkey.'"

The dread I'd felt all morning melted at his words. "He is going to let them crown him king?" I whispered, not wanting to let the others hear, especially Jesus.

Joseph nodded. "It looks that way. I didn't think he was going to set up the kingdom now, but what else does this mean?" He glanced at Jesus' back. We couldn't read his expression, though this morning he had still carried a somber weight on his shoulders. What had changed?

Matthew and Simon Z soon returned, one leading the mother donkey, the other leading a colt too young to be separated from its mother. As they brought the colt to Jesus, they took off their cloaks and placed them on it. The other disciples and followers did the same, though the women did not. It would not have been seemly for us to disrobe in public even with our tunics to cover us.

"I think Joseph is right," Susanna said as the men began to sing.

Jesus rode slowly down the Mount of Olives, the mother of the colt walking beside her offspring, while we followed, rejoicing. The men led us in the Hallel hymns of praise. "Praise the Lord! Praise, O servants of the Lord, praise the name of the Lord! Blessed be the name of the Lord from this time forth and forevermore. From the rising of the sun to its setting, the name of the Lord is to be praised!"

Even Judas rejoiced, and I caught the gleam of triumph in his gaze. This was what he'd wanted all along. Now he would see the fulfillment of it from the Messiah.

Would Jesus set up his kingdom today? Would he crush the Romans right now? My questions kept time with my excited breaths, and I couldn't stop smiling. He wouldn't leave me now. He would reign forever as our prophets had long foretold!

As we neared the gates of Jerusalem, a crowd larger than I had ever seen spread their cloaks on the ground in front of Jesus. Others cut branches from nearby palm trees and placed them ahead of him on the road.

"Hosanna to the Son of David!" they shouted.

"Blessed is he who comes in the name of the Lord!"

"Hosanna in the highest heaven!"

My heart lifted with such joy that I wanted to weep. It was true. They were ready at last to make Jesus their king and recognize him as our Messiah! Susanna and I linked arms, skipping behind him.

The crowd ushered him toward the temple, continuing their songs of praise to the Son of David every step of the way.

"Blessed is the King who comes in the name of the Lord! Peace in heaven and glory in the highest!" the crowd cried, the sound of their rejoicing rocking the very stones of the pavement beneath our feet.

As we neared the Temple Mount, a group of Pharisees pushed their way up to him. "Teacher, rebuke your disciples," their spokesman said.

Faster than they had lifted in praise, my emotions crashed like a boulder hitting the ground. These men breathed hatred, and their gazes locked on Jesus with venom that took my breath. I recognized this evil, only it was worse than the last time I'd seen it. My anxious heart beat hard, and terror crashed in on me as it always did in the presence of this kind of evil. How could Jesus set up his kingdom if the leaders so harshly opposed him? Would he crush them too?

"I tell you," Jesus said, his intense gaze fixed on the men in their flowing robes with extra-long tzitzit, "if these were silent, the very stones would cry out."

The colt continued moving, the Pharisees silent.

A moment later, someone in the crowd called out, "Who is this?"

Someone yelled back, "This is Jesus, the prophet from Nazareth in Galilee."

With that, the praise continued until we stopped at the temple. Jesus climbed off the colt and instructed Matthew and Simon Z to return the donkeys to Bethphage, to their owner.

Matthew gave Jesus a look, and Simon Z opened his mouth but closed it again. Wasn't Jesus going to let the people make him king? These two disciples would not want to miss his coronation!

As the sun rose almost to the midpoint in the sky, Jesus turned about and walked back toward the Eastern Gate from which he'd entered the city. The crowd followed for a time, but their praises gradually ceased, and murmurs of confusion filled the air behind us as we followed Jesus up the Mount of Olives toward Bethany.

"I don't understand," I said as Joseph joined Susanna and me again. "I thought he was going to let them crown him king. Wasn't that what the prophecy said?"

Joseph shrugged, looking haggard in comparison to his joyful expression of only an hour or so ago. "Zechariah said, 'See, your king comes to you,' but he didn't say more than that. I don't understand any more than you do." He shook his dark head and rubbed a hand along his bearded jaw. "I'm sorry to have suggested something I don't fully comprehend."

"None of us do, Joseph," I said, lightly touching his arm in comfort, then pulling away. "Jesus had his reasons for entering the city that way four days before Passover. Perhaps he will explain himself when we return to Bethany."

"Four days," Joseph said, his dark brows drawn low as though he realized something he had missed. "Tonight we pick the lamb for Passover, four days before we kill it for the feast," he said.

"But what has that to do with Jesus?" Susanna asked.

Joseph shrugged again. "I don't know. Probably nothing."

That night at Lazarus's house, Jesus did not talk much. He did not explain his actions even when Lazarus chose the lamb that would live with us until Passover, causing me to believe those four days were not connected. But somehow it seemed like they were.

THIRTY-SIX

The next day, Jesus returned again to Jerusalem, but this time he took only the men. I chafed to be left behind with the women in Martha's home, but we couldn't very well go against Jesus' wishes.

The only comfort I had was that Joseph kept us informed on what Jesus did.

"He wept over Jerusalem," Joseph said the first night. The women sat with him, Matthias, Lazarus, Tobias, and the disciples Andrew, Matthew, Thaddaeus, and Simon Z around the fire in the courtyard. Jesus had gone to the hills again to pray, and the other disciples slept.

I'd seen Jesus weep over Lazarus's death, so I imagined his sorrow all too easily. "Did he say anything?"

The other women nodded, leaning forward, anxious to hear every detail.

"He said that Jerusalem would be surrounded by her enemies and destroyed," Andrew said with a worried frown. "Not one stone left upon another."

"Because they didn't recognize the time of their visitation," Simon Z added. "I didn't know whether to go into the city and destroy the rulers that had caused his weeping, or stay with him and wait to see what he did."

"Obviously, you waited," Susanna said, leaning her head against Tobias's shoulder.

"Later, he surprised us more," Joseph continued.

I straightened at the anxious look in his eyes.

"He went into the temple, made a cord of whips, and drove out the money changers in the Court of the Gentiles," Thaddaeus said. "He quoted Jeremiah, saying, 'It is written, "My house shall be a house of prayer," but you have made it a den of robbers.'" Thaddaeus looked about, his usually peaceful countenance clearly troubled.

"You can imagine how that went with the Pharisees and temple guards," Andrew said. "But no one touched him."

"Yes, at least they didn't try to stone him again," Matthew said, expelling a breath of relief. "But why does he continue to anger them?"

The men exchanged worried glances. "It's like he wants to turn them against him, which makes no sense," Simon Z said, clasping his hands in his lap. "Judas isn't happy with him," he added, his voice low.

"Judas hasn't been happy with him for a long time, has he?" I asked. "I mean, except for yesterday when Jesus rode the donkey into Jerusalem and we all thought they would proclaim him king. I haven't seen Judas smile since."

"I can't say that smiling is something any of us are doing right now," Andrew said, resting his elbows on his knees, staring into the fire.

I studied the men and then the flames licking the dry logs and dung, sending sparks upward. The sky, now littered with stars, offered no answers to our many questions, and my heart cried out, longing to understand. And to put a stop to whatever was coming that did not seem good to me at all.

How could the destruction of Jerusalem or Jesus' death be

good? One look at my companions, male and female, told me nothing. Even Mary of Bethany, who grasped Jesus' words better than I did, said nothing, her dark eyes large and solemn. Yet she was also unusually serene, as though she knew and accepted what was coming.

I dared not ask her what she knew, for if she said what I didn't want to hear, that Jesus was walking toward his death, I would not be able to bear it. And I would hate her for saying so. Some things were better left unsaid.

We remained in Bethany while Jesus left for Jerusalem each dawn with the men. "He's teaching the people," Joseph Justus told me, but the words did little to quell my anxious thoughts. I wanted to be there, to hear everything he had to say.

"He called the leaders hypocrites, blind guides, whitewashed tombs, and even snakes and vipers," Joseph said later that day.

Jesus had worried us all again at the evening meal when he said, "As you know, the Passover is two days away—and the Son of Man will be handed over to be crucified." Was this how he intended to be arrested and turned over to them?

"He's making it easier for them to hate him," I said after the meal. I sat across from Joseph and Andrew, with Tobias, Susanna, Joanna, and Mary of Bethany nearer to me. "It's like he's making sure his words come true." Despair filled me, and I heard it in my tone.

"He held nothing back, that is true," Andrew said, glancing up as Peter, Matthew, Simon Z, and Thaddaeus joined us.

"It's like he's inciting war, except that it's with our own people, not the Romans." Simon Z rubbed a hand along the back of his neck. "I have to admit, he is nothing like I imagined our Messiah to be. He shows no interest in engaging the Romans."

"They tried to trap him about paying taxes to Caesar," Peter said. "The Pharisees brought the Herodians with them when they asked, but he deflected their question and left them silent."

"They are doing everything they can to find cause to accuse him of something worthy of death," Simon Z said. "I can tell. I've seen plenty of Zealots in my life, and these leaders are more zealous to destroy Jesus than any of us were to destroy Rome."

I couldn't listen anymore, so I excused myself, unable to stop my fear.

Despite my worries, I joined the men the next evening as they continued to discuss the many things Jesus had taught the crowds, but my mind whirled with the question, *Why? Why* was Jesus thinking he had to die, was certain he was going to die? And by crucifixion? There was no death more gruesome. I pressed a hand to my churning stomach.

"But the Pharisees can't crucify anyone," John said, joining us and drawing my attention. "Only the Romans have such power. So how are the Pharisees going to accomplish what Jesus says will happen to him?"

"It makes no sense. Jews hate Rome," Matthew said. If anyone understood Rome, Matthew did.

"But the leaders of the Pharisees always try to appease Rome because they want to maintain their power," Simon Z said.

I wondered at how well he understood these powerful men. Zealots knew more than other citizens.

Silence followed Simon's remark, each one of us lost in our own grief-filled thoughts.

"I still don't understand how the Messiah can die. Do the prophets predict this?" I asked. The men knew the Scriptures better than I did.

"We were taught that the Messiah would be the descendant of David who would sit on David's throne. David was a mighty warrior, therefore, Messiah would be too," Andrew said. "The rabbis have long looked for a leader, a king, to free us from any oppression, like Moses led us out of Egypt and Joshua led us into the Promised Land."

"But after King Solomon, we couldn't keep the land because of our ancestors' disobedience to the Lord," Peter said. "Ever since, we've looked for the Messiah to lead us back to that glorious time when we were a united nation at peace."

"I don't think Jesus thinks the way the rabbis do," I said, still feeling slightly nauseous as my mind flashed with images of crucified men along the sides of roads we had passed in our travels. I never imagined such a thing could happen to Jesus.

We continued our discussion long into the night, and when we finally made our way to our mats, I could not shake my disturbing thoughts. What kind of king did Jesus intend to be? I knew he was our king. He just didn't act like one, and that made no sense to me.

After a restless night, I rose early. I left my sleeping area, hoping to catch a glimpse of Jesus before he went to the hills to pray or to Jerusalem to teach again.

But it wasn't Jesus I saw slipping out of the courtyard into the gray light of predawn. I squinted, trying to make out the features of the man hurrying from Martha's home. One of the disciples? He turned at the end of the lane and I saw his face. Judas. Why was he in such a hurry?

I frowned, watching him until he was no longer in sight. I'd never known any of the disciples to leave the group alone.

Perhaps Jesus had sent him on an errand? But what? The shops were not yet open. Where was he going?

I worked with the other women in Martha's spacious cooking area that morning in preparation for the feast we would share that evening, but I said nothing about Judas. Whatever his business, it had nothing to do with me. As we served the meal to Jesus and the men, no one else said anything about Judas's absence, so I decided they knew something I did not and weren't concerned.

I set a dish of salted fish on the low table as Jesus spoke.

"We will not be eating the Passover meal with you," Jesus said, looking at Lazarus. "I thank you, my friend, for your hospitality, but I plan to spend this Passover with the twelve in Jerusalem tonight. The rest of you will stay here." He looked about at us.

Passover was meant to be shared, and I had hoped . . . But clearly Jesus had something in mind for the twelve men he had chosen out of all the others. I glanced at Joseph Justus. He and Matthias were not invited this time.

"You will return for the rest of the feast?" Lazarus asked Jesus. "We will be happy to have everyone else stay with us for all of it."

"Yes, of course," Martha added. "All of you are welcome."

Jesus held Lazarus's gaze and shook his head. He would not be returning here? This couldn't be.

Jesus looked at Peter and John. "Go and make preparations for us to eat the Passover."

"Where do you want us to prepare for it?" John asked.

"As you enter the city, a man carrying a jar of water will meet you. Follow him to the house that he enters, and say to the owner of the house, 'The Teacher asks: Where is the guest room, where I may eat the Passover with my disciples?' He will show you a large room upstairs, all furnished. Make preparations there."

Peter and John immediately left the house. Jesus stood and walked to the door.

I hurried to his side. "Are you leaving too, Rabbi?"

"I am going to pray," he said, resting a hand on my shoulder. "Don't be afraid, Mary."

The look he gave me did not reassure me despite his words, and I wanted to cling to his arm, keep him from leaving. But he released his hold and left before I could protest.

He disappeared behind the house toward the nearby hills. Reluctantly, I edged my way back to the cooking area to help clean up the leftovers from the morning meal.

Whatever reason Jesus had for sharing the meal with only his disciples tonight, I couldn't know, but we still had much to prepare for our Passover meal. Lazarus must kill the lamb and Martha would want to baste it with her own spices.

But why this change in Jesus' plans? Why not eat with all of us?

Nothing made sense to me, and I grieved what I did not comprehend. With each hour that passed, I could not shake a horrible sense of dread. If this had been a normal week, I would not have felt this foreboding, but Jesus had made this week anything but normal. And I did not know what to do with these feelings.

After the sun set, Lazarus led us in the prescribed prayers and blessings as we partook of the Passover seder. Martha had also invited neighbors whose children asked the questions about each part of the ceremony. Memories surfaced of a time when I asked, "Why is this night different from all other nights?"

Lazarus answered the questions as we ate the bitter herbs and vegetables dipped in salt water, drank four cups of wine, and cracked the unleavened bread in two. Each part reminded me of the heritage I had forsaken when the demons lived within me but that Jesus had restored. Would he be the one to explain our history to his disciples and repeat the same blessings?

Of course he would. He hadn't come into the world to change our holy days or their meaning. Had he?

"I wonder what their meal is like right now," I said to Susanna as we sipped from the third cup of wine. "I do wish Jesus had spent it with us as well."

"I agree," she said, glancing across the table at Tobias, who sat near Lazarus and Joseph Justus. "It feels strange to have traveled with him all this time and miss this important night."

Perhaps that was why I also felt strange. Jesus had included us on many of his journeys and most of the feast days when it was a good time to travel. But to bring us all the way to Bethany and then leave us here when we were so close to Jerusalem . . . I shook my head.

As the meal came to an end, the men retreated to the courtyard to sit about the fire while the women put the remaining food away.

"You will have to give me your charoset recipe," I said, touching Martha's arm. "Yours tastes better than the one I grew up with." I would happily give Chana the new ingredient list, though I knew the recipes would not be much different as we all followed a similar formula for this meal.

"I add pears to it," she said, smiling. "Lazarus loves pears."

"As do I," Mary said. "Martha is kind to make our favorite."

Martha beamed at the praise, and I wondered at the differences in these two women. Sometimes they got along well. Other times they bickered, but I supposed that was true of all relationships.

Worry gnawed my middle, and a tear slipped down my cheek as I thought of the lamb that had given its life for mine to cover my sin. Why did we need the sacrifices? Why was the shedding of blood necessary for the forgiveness of our sins?

Troubled and equally sad, I moved to the courtyard and walked to the area just beyond the house. Stars glittered above, the air cool, and I pulled my cloak more tightly against my body, unable to stifle a shiver that came from a place deep within me. How long I walked before returning to find the men still sitting around a fire in the court, I did not know. There was no sign of the women, who had likely already taken to their mats.

Joseph beckoned me to join them. Reluctantly, I sat near him.

"What are you discussing?" I asked, folding my hands in my lap, hoping they didn't mind my presence.

"Just some of the things Jesus talked about in the temple these past few days," Joseph said. "Particularly the way he treated the religious leaders."

This again? Could they talk of nothing else?

"They were asking for his rebuke by trying to trap him in what he said," Matthias said.

"True." Joseph ran a hand along his jaw.

"Do you know why Judas left early this morning before most of us were up?" I asked, wanting to change the subject, and also to know whatever they did.

Joseph faced me, and by the expressions coming my way, I realized they had no idea what I was talking about. "Judas left the house?"

"Yes, before dawn. Didn't you notice he was missing at the

morning meal?" Sometimes I wondered if they ever paid attention to the smaller details that the women noticed.

"I have no idea where he went," Joseph said, looking about at the small group of men who had been left behind. "Perhaps to give money to the poor? He does handle the purse, so only he knows. Give to the poor or purchase supplies for their meal with the rabbi?"

I shrugged. "That would make sense, except that he left before any of the shops were open."

"Perhaps he was heading to Jerusalem to purchase them," Matthias said. The others nodded, and the subject was dropped as the men talked about other things.

I longed for my mat and was about to head to bed as the moon rose high in the sky, when we heard the sound of someone running, their sandals hitting the stones along the path before Lazarus's house.

Lazarus stood. "It sounds like a lone runner."

The others stood with him. Joseph looked at me. "Stay behind me," he said, his stance protective.

A moment passed and the runner's feet stopped, and a man turned onto the path leading to Lazarus's courtyard. He rushed up to Lazarus, dragging in air.

"Jesus has been arrested," he blurted, leaning forward and placing his hands on his knees.

Had he run the whole way from Jerusalem?

"How do you know this?" Joseph moved closer to him.

"I am Mark," he said, "son of the woman who owns the home where Jesus ate with his men tonight. When they sang the Hallel hymns and left, I followed."

"Why would you do that?" Lazarus asked.

"I was curious. I had heard rumors." He paused. "They say one of the disciples betrayed him to the religious leaders. Jesus took the disciples to Gethsemane, and so I went along to see. Sure enough, guards came with Judas to arrest Jesus."

A gasp came from each one of us, and I felt faint.

"The disciples fled from him, as did I," Mark continued, though I barely heard him. "They caught the linen garment covering me, and I had to go home for clothes before I came to tell you."

I glanced at him, seeing his embarrassment.

"Where is he now?" Lazarus crossed his arms over his chest as if to ward off a chill.

"They took him to the home of Annas, the high priest's father-in-law. I don't know anything more." Mark drew in a gulp of air, and I hurried to get him a drink of water.

My heart hammered so hard in my chest I thought it would burst. Arrested? *Oh, Adonai, help us!*

The men sat again around the fire, and I thought to wake the women, but what good would that do? I knew I would not sleep, so I stayed.

"We must go to Jerusalem," Joseph said, fists clenched as if he would fight every leader and Roman with his bare hands.

"There is nothing we can do," Mark said, both hands clutching the water skin. "If they are interrogating him at night, it can't be good. But none of us can get into the home of Annas, much less the high priest Caiaphas. We could be arrested as well."

"Mark's right," Lazarus said. "But we can pray. In the morning, we will go to Jerusalem to see what is happening. But to go tonight will not help him. We should try to sleep."

I looked up, noting how dark the sky had become, the stars now hidden behind clouds as though they refused to shine. Only the moon gave its intermittent light. Jesus had said they were going to arrest and crucify him. But Judas! How could he betray the Lord?

Nothing made sense. This could not be happening! My body trembled, and if I had tried to stand, I would surely have fallen.

As the men went to find places to sleep, Joseph turned to me and offered his hand. "Let me help you."

I nodded. I clenched my hands, wanting to fight every leader and Roman as Joseph seemed to want to do. I could *not* lose Jesus! I wanted to rush into the place where they held Jesus and demand they let him go. I would fight to my death to save him.

As I lay on my mat, unable to sleep, a deep sense of loss filled me. Who was I trying to fool? I had no power to save Jesus. He alone had power to save. I only hoped that he would use it to save himself.

THIRTY-SEVEN

V oices came from the sitting room the next morning, and soon the entire household had heard the news of Jesus' arrest. Before the sun moved any higher, all of us hurried out of Bethany, past Bethphage, down the Mount of Olives, and through the Eastern Gate of Jerusalem.

Worry curled inside me, making it hard to breathe. None of us spoke as we walked. How would we possibly help Jesus once we arrived? And how would we find him? If the men had been allowed weapons past the Roman guards, I suspected they would have armed themselves. But such a prospect was useless and too big a risk.

We slowed as we entered Jerusalem simply because the crowds blocked our way. What were so many people doing in the streets? But it was a high holy feast day and Jerusalem was overflowing. The people should not have surprised me. I was more annoyed that they were keeping us from getting to Jesus.

At last, as we came near the Antonia Fortress at the north-west corner of the Temple Mount, the crowd moved with us, and more people stood before the open space where the governor came to speak to the people.

"Why are they all here?" I drew beside Joseph, knowing he

would not mind my presence. This wasn't the place our people often came. No one liked to interact with the Romans, and this area was their domain.

Joseph looked at me, then back at the crowd that was as large as the ones that used to follow Jesus months before. He craned his neck to see above them, as did I, but we were too far back to see or hear. "I don't know," he said. "Let's try to get closer."

We huddled together, and Mark, who knew the city better than any of us, led us through a side alley to reach the Praetorium. As we neared the front of the crowd, the governor, Pilate, emerged with Jesus surrounded by soldiers. My knees buckled at the sight of him bloodied and bruised, his face marred with thorns crushed into his head. He wore a purple robe like a king's.

Joseph caught one of my arms, and Susanna held on to the other. *Oh, God! What have they done to him?*

"Look, I am bringing him out to you to let you know that I find no basis for a charge against him," Pilate said. "Here is the man!"

Voices somewhere near the front of the crowd reached me. "Crucify! Crucify!"

My heart threatened to stop beating, and I feared I would faint. *No! No! No!*

"You take him and crucify him," Pilate continued. "As for me, I find no basis for a charge against him." He sounded weak, as though the religious leaders and the crowd were wearing him down.

Don't listen to them! I wanted to scream the words, but my voice would not work for the tears clogging my throat. *Jesus!*

"We have a law," one of the leaders shouted, "and according to that law he must die, because he claimed to be the Son of God."

At that, the governor blanched. He returned to his palace, and Jesus was led there with him.

"What's going on?" Susanna asked as Tobias came and pulled her to him. "Why did he go back inside?" But of course, no one knew.

"Why is Jesus letting them do this to him?" I asked with a raspy voice, my heart pounding with a new kind of terror. He had said this would happen. But why? "The Messiah can't die," I whispered.

Joseph heard me and touched my arm. "That might not be true."

"But he's God," I said.

"And the Son of Man," Joseph reminded me.

At that moment, Pilate emerged again and argued with the religious leaders, trying to find a way to set Jesus free.

But for all his efforts, they shouted louder. "If you let this man go, you are no friend of Caesar. Anyone who claims to be a king opposes Caesar."

Our group huddled together but said nothing. When the crowds shouted "Crucify him!" again, I clung to Joseph's arm. Would the people notice that we were his followers and arrest us too?

"Are we in danger?" Mark asked the men.

Lazarus shrugged. I don't think death troubled him like it did Mark or the others.

Pilate had Jesus brought out again, then he sat down on the judge's seat known as the Stone Pavement. "Here is your king," he said, looking at the religious leaders. "I am innocent of this man's blood." He dipped his hands into a bowl of water and washed them before us all. "It is your responsibility!"

"His blood is on us and on our children!" This time the words came from most of the crowd, until the ground shook with their cries.

Tears streamed down my face, and I wanted to curl into a ball and weep.

"Take him away! Take him away! Crucify him!" The shouts grew so loud my head began to ache.

"Shall I crucify your king?" Pilate asked above the noise.

"We have no king but Caesar," yelled a man in rich robes who stood an arm's length from the Praetorium.

"He's one of the chief priests," Joseph said next to my ear. "Now we see how thoroughly they hate him."

Soldiers grabbed Jesus' arms and shoved him toward the steps to the street. He stumbled but righted himself.

I looked at the women. Susanna, Joanna, Mary Clopas, Mary and Martha, and Salome stood near. "Come," I said, suddenly so angry I was sure I could have pushed through the mob with the force I once had in those awful days of the demons.

Joseph touched my shoulder, stopping me. "Let's follow Mark again and go around the crowd to the road where they will take him," he said.

I followed, my heart pounding and my body numb, until we arrived at the paved road that led outside the city. Moments later, the soldiers flanking him again, Jesus came carrying a cross, the beams so thick and heavy he trembled as he put one foot in front of the other. When he stumbled, the soldiers grabbed a man from the crowd and forced him to carry Jesus' cross.

The whole crowd followed, but it was the women, including us, who were weeping.

"Daughters of Jerusalem," Jesus said, lifting his head, "do not weep for me. Weep for yourselves and for your children. For the time will come when you will say, 'Blessed are the childless women, the wombs that never bore and the breasts that never nursed!' Then they will say to the mountains, 'Fall on us!' and to the hills, 'Cover us!' For if people do these things when the tree is green, what will happen when it is dry?"

Blood dripped down his face into his eyes as he said the words. Words I did not understand.

He lifted a shaky hand to wipe away the blood, trudging ever forward with weak but weighted steps. I pushed away from Joseph to walk as close to him as possible. But his focus was on the stone pavement, slick in places with blood that oozed from his back and sides. How was he able to walk, let alone stand?

Every part of my being longed to rush to his side and help him, but the soldiers blocked anyone who might attempt such a thing.

The road led out of Jerusalem to Golgotha, the Place of the Skull. I climbed the hill where three crosses lay on the ground, and rough Roman hands shoved Jesus' bloody back onto the rugged beams. They forced his arms out wide and pounded nails through his feet and hands. I covered my mouth and backed away, unable to stop myself from releasing a strangled cry.

In the middle of it all, I heard Jesus say, "Father, forgive them, for they do not know what they are doing."

Forgive them? How could he say that after what they were doing to him?

When they lifted his cross to stand it in a hole in the earth, his whole body jerked until his very bones shifted and his face contorted in such obvious pain, I felt it in my very being.

"We should move away." Susanna touched my arm.

I looked about, my vision blurred, and realized that the men were nowhere in sight. But all the women who were part of our group had remained.

"Where are the men?" I asked.

Susanna shook her head. "Tobias and the others fled. They are more in danger of arrest than we are."

I had no idea how to respond to that, but I followed her a little distance from the three crosses that now stood on Golgotha. Two thieves, who cried out in agony, had been crucified on either side of Jesus.

The religious leaders and some of the crowd stayed to watch, mocking Jesus. As I glanced at them, I recognized two who loved him walking over to us. The disciple John and Jesus' mother, Mary. They joined us but said nothing.

I placed a hand on Mary's shoulder. I was not sure my heartache could ever match the look in her dark eyes. How did she bear watching her son die? And such a son as this? One whom she knew to be the Son of God, whom she had birthed and raised and loved all his life? I couldn't imagine. I had never loved anyone like that and suspected I never would.

Mary's anguish pulsated the very air around us, until I felt as though I breathed in her pain along with my own. Jesus looked in our direction, and I ached to tell him I would not leave him. I would die with him.

But he was looking at his mother, not me. "Woman," he said, looking from Mary to John, "here is your son." He looked again at John, then Mary, and said, "Here is your mother."

John placed his arm about Mary's shoulders and led her away from Golgotha.

Jesus apparently didn't want his mother to see his pain, and as her firstborn, he was providing for her, thinking of others even now. How was he able to think of anything but the intensity of his pain? I certainly couldn't think of much else. I wanted to take him down from the cross and put balm on his wounds. I wanted to tell him that everything would be all right.

In the middle of my muddled thoughts and constant tears, I was vaguely aware of soldiers casting lots for his clothes and offering him something to drink on a sponge. Time eked by.

Suddenly the sun darkened as though covered with a celestial hand. Darkness so thick I could almost touch it fell over us for hours, though without the sun, time was impossible to tell.

Then, just as suddenly, the light returned. The sun hung lower now, and I guessed about three hours had passed.

A hand on my arm assured me that I was not alone. I knew it was Susanna, and on the other side of me was Mary Clopas.

We clung to each other as Jesus cried out, "Eli, Eli, lema sabachthani?"

"He's calling for Elijah," someone said in the distance.

"Let's see if Elijah rescues him," said another.

But I knew from my childhood tutor that his cry was something far different, from David's psalms. *My God, my God, why have You forsaken me? Why are You so far from saving me, from the words of my groaning?*

Had his Father forsaken him in his most desperate hour of need? Why would God do that?

His cry of desperation rent my heart. The earth shook, causing us to cling more tightly to each other. Jesus' voice rose above the cries of the people trying to escape the shaking earth.

"Father, into Your hands I commit my spirit," Jesus said when the earth stilled.

I stared into his unrecognizable face, and saw his chest rise and fall and not rise again. I glanced at those with me.

"Is he dead?" Salome whispered, clasping my arm.

We waited for several more moments, but he had stopped pushing his body up with his legs to take a breath, as the two thieves on either side of him still did. His head hung to the side, and his eyes were closed, though I'd seen other dead bodies with their eyes open. A strange relief filled me that his were not.

"What do we do now?" Joanna asked from behind me. Many of our women had said little during the entire ordeal. Our only language had been our tears. "I mean, if he's gone, what do we do?"

"We wait to see where they bury him," I said, determined not to leave his side, dead or not.

"It might mean we wait a long time," Susanna said, glancing at the sky.

Sundown would be soon, and it was Preparation Day for a high holy Shabbat tomorrow. We were standing here watching our Messiah die during what should have been a weeklong Passover celebration. The realization, a kick to my gut, nearly knocked me over. Tears came again as I tried to make sense of everything.

"The religious leaders won't want him on the cross during Preparation Day," I said, surprised by my words. "It would bloody their hands even more." The very thought angered me, and I felt something in that moment that I had not felt since I'd met Jesus. Hatred. I positively hated the Jewish religious leaders who had led Jesus to his death. Who had plotted his death. Wanted his death.

Now they had succeeded. And I had lost the only person who had ever loved me. Who had promised to never leave or forsake me. Who had just broken that promise.

Angry tears replaced my grieving ones, and I longed to lash out at someone or something. Instead, I stood helplessly, watching the middle cross with the broken body of my Lord, surrounded by the women who had loved, supported, and followed him to this place.

I had never felt so utterly alone.

THIRTY-EIGHT

The sun angled farther west, and most of the people who had stood watching Jesus left after the earth quaked and he died. I stood unmoving, for I was too numb to do anything but stand and stare at the one who had delivered me from evil. Now evil had conquered him, and I did not know what to do.

An hour passed. The only noise came from the guards and the two thieves still suffering on their crosses.

The women with me slowly walked away. Susanna touched my arm. "Come on, Mary. There is nothing more we can do. I need to find Tobias." By her look I knew she didn't want to leave me. I didn't want her to go, but I couldn't leave him.

"I'll come later," I promised, though I wasn't sure I would ever be able to leave this place. Would someone come and bury him? Or would he be thrown into a pit or left to rot with other crucified bodies?

"I'll stay with you," Mary Clopas said, taking my hand.

Susanna looked at me, torn. "I need to find Tobias," she said again.

I nodded. "I will be fine. The others have already left. We will wait and tell you where they lay him." She hurried off, glancing back at me once, then disappeared over the hill.

"I will also stay," Salome said.

I looked at her, surprised. "John left with Jesus' mother. Why would you stay?" I asked.

Salome lifted her eyes to Jesus' body. "I want to help bury him. John thinks a few of the wealthy leaders were secret followers of Jesus. I want to see if they will honor him now."

"Which leaders?" I asked. "I didn't think any of them cared for him."

Salome shrugged. "Some time ago one of the Pharisees came to meet Jesus at night—Nicodemus, I think. There is another, but we will have to wait to see if John is right."

I nodded. "Then we will wait."

We didn't wait long. Salome's words proved true when Joseph of Arimathea and Nicodemus appeared with a linen cloth, and with the help of the soldiers they took Jesus' body down from the cross. First, though, the soldiers broke the legs of the other two men to hasten their deaths and then pierced Jesus' side. Could they do him any more harm? They had to pierce him too?

My anger flared, but relief followed as I watched the two followers tenderly anoint Jesus' bloodied, broken body with myrrh and aloes, then wrap it in pure white linen. The heady scents of the spices nearly overpowered me with their sheer amount. Clearly these men wanted to honor our Lord, and by all accounts they had done more than enough. But my heart still ached with each wafted scent of the spices, and though some would think my desire foolish, I knew I must do more. Double the amount of myrrh. Triple the amount of aloes. I would spend every shekel I had to honor him. Yet one glance at the setting sun told me there was nothing to do about it now.

The two men hurriedly carried Jesus' body on a bier to a garden not far from Golgotha. Mary Clopas, Salome, and I followed. If the men noticed us, they didn't seem to mind.

In the garden, a new tomb stood open as if waiting for Jesus. The men carried him inside, laid him on a stone bench, and rolled a large stone in front of the entrance.

We sat opposite the tomb, the finality of it all hitting me hard. He was really gone. His life had ended too soon, his talk of a coming kingdom lost.

"We should get home before the sun fully sets or we will violate Shabbat," Mary Clopas said. "We need to return to Bethany. We don't have anywhere else to stay."

"The others are probably already waiting there," Salome said. "At least we know where they laid him."

"We will come after Shabbat and redo the wrappings with more spices. I will spend every last coin to make sure his burial is what he deserves," I said, stiffening, my jaw clenching. "Even if no one else cares, I do."

"I will come with you," Mary Clopas said. "Now come!" She tugged my arm, and I glanced at the sun and realized we would have to run most of the way to make it home in time.

Home? Bethany wasn't home. Magdala wasn't home either, nor was Capernaum. Home had been where Jesus was. And he was no more.

Shabbat had never moved so painfully slow. The atmosphere in the house of Lazarus was like one where everyone was sitting shiva. No one spoke. The men sat about looking defeated, dejected. Hopelessness filled the house with a palpable beat, as though the feeling was a living, growing thing.

My life had known much pain, but not like this. This felt like

I had died with Jesus, and the only thing keeping me breathing was my desire to give him a burial fit for the king he was. After that, I would lie beside him in the tomb and wait for death to claim me as well.

The thought took hold in my heart, and for the first time since his arrest, I felt a strange calm wash over me. Many times, when the demons lived in me, I'd thought of death. They had urged me to take my life, but fear had stopped me.

The moment Jesus healed me, I had not worried about what came after death. I had only feared losing him. And now I had. There was nothing left to lose but my life, and what value was that to me now?

Resolve filled me. I would rise well before dawn, before the other women got up, and go to the tomb alone. I wouldn't be able to buy the spices that early, but I would just go and see. Perhaps there was a way into the tomb so I could lie beside him. My mind whirled with how I would get the stone aside. Should I ask Joseph Justus to come with me?

I shook myself as I paced the roof, where I'd found a little solitude. He would never understand my request. Perhaps God would make a way for me. Yes. I would ask Him. He would not deny me this small thing. He had to know that I was nothing without His Son.

"Do you want something to eat, Mary?" Susanna asked that evening when Shabbat finally came to an end. We were sitting with the others in the main room of the house. No one felt like eating, but the men had begun to talk quietly, as had the women.

"I'm not hungry," I said, feeling strangely calm. Tomorrow I would die with Jesus, or wait for death to come, and my pain would end.

"It's sad about Judas," Joanna said. "How desperate he must

have felt to hang himself." She shook her head, and I noted sadness as I looked from one woman to another.

"He had to have been desperate to betray Jesus," I said, unable to hold back my scorn.

"Still, I wonder if he regretted his choice when it was too late," Mary of Bethany said. I looked at her, surprised by her words.

"He was always so passionate about getting Jesus to set up his kingdom here on earth," Susanna added, leaning forward, elbows on her knees.

"He misunderstood Jesus' mission." Mary of Bethany returned my gaze, her expression sad but serene.

"I think we all did," I said, fighting anger and grief.

She nodded and said nothing more.

I excused myself as the sun finally set, then climbed to the roof to sleep instead of going to the room I normally occupied. I wanted to leave in the morning unnoticed, and the roof had outside stairs that would allow me to do just that.

The moon rose, shining on my mat. I stared at it, wondering. Did God live up there? Where was the kingdom of heaven Jesus had spoken of so often? Why had he said the kingdom of heaven was at hand? He was the one who was supposed to bring it about, wasn't he?

Maybe I had misunderstood him when he'd promised to be with me. Maybe he meant after death I would be with him, as he had promised the thief on the cross that he would be with him in paradise. Whatever that meant.

I closed my eyes against the moon's bright glare and turned onto my side. I must have slept, because when I opened my eyes, the light of the moon had waned and the dark gray that precedes the dawn filled the sky. Surely dawn would come soon, and I didn't want to miss my chance to get to the tomb before the others.

I pulled my robe tighter, slipped my sandals on my feet, and hurried down the steps. The house remained still with only a few oil lamps flickering inside. The sky offered little light to guide me, and I prayed I would not lose my way. Fierce determination spurred me on.

The walk felt longer alone, but soon I was past the Mount of Olives, entering the garden near Golgotha outside Jerusalem's walls. I walked toward the place where I remembered the tomb lay, praying for a way to somehow move the stone away. Darkness had lifted to its predawn pinks, and when I looked up, my heart stuttered.

The stone was not there! I whirled about. Did I have the right tomb? But I did not see another and was certain this was the place. Panic washed over me. On the ground not far from me, the bodies of men dressed as guards lay. Were they dead?

Heart pounding now, I turned around and ran all the way back to Bethany. Why was the tomb open? I should have looked inside.

I was almost to Lazarus's house now, all thoughts of dying with Jesus gone. I would tell the women. We would gather spices from the merchants as we had originally planned and return.

I slowed, telling my heart to calm. I must have had the wrong tomb. But what of those men on the ground?

I stopped in the courtyard, then looked into the cooking area, where I found Martha already working. I moved past her and found the other women.

Salome and Mary Clopas already knew our plans. Susanna was nowhere to be seen at that moment and I did not want to wait, so I told Joanna to join us as we grabbed baskets to fill with spices and hurried out of the house back toward Beth-phage. The markets were finally open when we arrived, and we purchased every spice they carried, then walked as quickly as our feet would carry us to the garden.

"Who will roll the stone away from the entrance of the tomb?" Joanna asked.

As we drew near, the early light confirmed I had been right the first time. The guards were not there, yet the tomb was still open. My whole body trembled. We looked at each other. I walked toward the tomb, the others following.

Suddenly, two men in clothes like a flash of lightning in a storm stood beside us. A cry escaped my throat. I fell to my knees and bowed my face to the ground, and sensed the others doing the same.

"Why do you look for the living among the dead?" one of them said. "He is not here. He has risen! Remember how he told you while he was still with you in Galilee: 'The Son of Man must be delivered over to the hands of sinners, be cruci-fied, and on the third day be raised again.' Do not be afraid, for I know that you are looking for Jesus, who was crucified. Come and see the place where he lay. Then go quickly and tell his disciples and Peter, 'He has risen from the dead and is going ahead of you into Galilee. There you will see him.' Now I have told you."

The men disappeared as fast as they had come. My heart raced. Trembling, we ran from the tomb. Exhaustion mingled with a sense of bewilderment in me as I ran for the second time back to Bethany. I'd had nothing to eat since the day Jesus was crucified and knew that the only thing keeping me going was sheer terror.

"We must tell the disciples and Peter," I said as we neared the house.

Mary Clopas shook her head. Salome and Joanna agreed with her. "They won't believe us," they said, slinking off to the cooking room as if nothing had happened. What was wrong with them?

I rushed into the main room, where most of the men were talking quietly and waiting for Martha and the others to serve the food.

Suddenly, I understood the women's fear. They were right. These men would not believe the testimony of women, even if they were used to our company.

I clamped my mouth shut as all eyes focused on me. I drew in a breath, willing my anxious heart to calm. "They have taken the Lord out of the tomb, and we don't know where they have put him!" I said, looking at Peter and then John.

Both men looked at each other, then at me.

"You're sure?" Peter asked.

I nodded.

They jumped up and ran out of the house, and I knew at least they would believe me enough to check.

But what of the message of the angels? Why not tell the others? Or had I imagined them? I was no stranger to the unseen realm. I knew what demons sounded like, though I'd never seen one. These men wouldn't have been demons, would they? No. Demons would not want Jesus to be alive.

And yet, I struggled.

I turned around and followed Peter and John back to the garden, slower this time. They were far ahead of me already, and apparently Joanna, Mary Clopas, and Salome were too shaken to return or speak about what we had seen.

Did no one care what had happened to our Lord but me?

If those guards or someone else had taken his body, I wanted to know. I needed to know. I needed to find him, anoint him, and care for him, then get someone to move the stone back into place.

Exhaustion weighted my steps, and I got a stone stuck under my sandal. I stopped, removed it, and stumbled on.

Oh, Lord, where have they put him? Help me!

I neared the garden in time to pass Peter and John, who barely glanced my way. They seemed shaken as they headed back up the Mount of Olives toward Bethany.

I pressed my hand hard against my middle, barely able to keep my balance as I entered the garden for the third time that morning. Tears came, filling my eyes, nearly choking me. Weeping, I dragged myself to the tomb, bent over, and looked through blurred vision into the tomb once more.

The angels—or different ones, I couldn't tell—sat in the place where his body had lain, one at the head, the other where his feet should be.

"Woman, why are you crying?" one asked me.

"They have taken my Lord away," I said, my voice rising with emotion. "And I don't know where they have put him."

I turned away from them and straightened. Why were angels in his tomb? I blinked several times and noticed a man standing nearby. Perhaps the gardener had come to tend to the plants. When he approached me, I took a step back.

"Woman, why are you crying? Who is it you are looking for?" the man said gently.

I lifted my hands in entreaty toward him. "Sir, if you have carried him away, tell me where you have put him, and I will get him." Someone had to know where he was. Had those guards carried him away? I knew the disciples would not have come to get him in the night. Until a few moments ago, none of them had left the house since his death.

I rubbed the tears from my face and looked away, praying this man would help me.

"Mary."

I would know his voice anywhere.

Shock rushed through me, making my heart skip several beats. Joy burst within me, too great to hold. I whirled about and fell at his feet, clinging to them. "Rabboni!" I cried.

"Do not hold on to me," Jesus said, "for I have not yet ascended to the Father. Go instead to my brothers and tell them, 'I am ascending to my Father and your Father, to my God and your God.'"

"I don't want to leave you," I said, releasing my hold. "I never want to leave you again."

"I will never leave you or forsake you," he promised. "Did you not remember what I told you? That I must die and rise again? For now, my mission on earth is finished, but yours is just beginning. You will always have my Spirit to guide you in it." His look, always so full of compassion, filled me with immense peace. "I keep my promises, Mary."

Joy rushed through me, the kind I thought I would never know again. And yet I did! I could not contain my smile, my laughter, and when he disappeared from my sight, I whirled about, a song of praise to God filling my heart. I sang the last Hallel song all the way to Bethany.

"Praise the Lord. Praise God in His sanctuary. Praise Him in His mighty heavens. Praise Him for His acts of power. Praise Him for His surpassing greatness. Praise Him with the sounding of the trumpet, praise Him with the harp and lyre, praise Him with timbrel and dancing, praise Him with the strings and pipe, praise Him with the clash of cymbals, praise Him with resounding cymbals. Let everything that has breath praise the Lord. Praise the Lord!"

I reached the house of Lazarus, out of breath, and rushed into the room where the men still sat talking, this time about Peter and John's experience at the tomb.

"I have seen the Lord!" I said, still laughing for joy.

They looked at me, and as the women joined them, I told them everything he had said to me and all I had seen.

THIRTY-NINE

Throughout the next forty days, we saw Jesus come and go among the group of us staying with Lazarus. Jesus' mother and eventually his brothers and his sisters and their husbands joined us. None of us wanted to leave, but when we heard reports of others who had come out of their tombs and walked about Jerusalem, some of the men went to investigate.

Two of those who had traveled often with us met Jesus on the road to Emmaus, and he also appeared to Peter, solidifying the faith of most of us. But the best time came when Jesus just appeared in the middle of the room where we sat to eat.

"Peace be with you," he said.

Some of the men and women cried out. "It's a ghost," Susanna whispered, and a few others said the same, but I knew they were wrong.

"No. It's Jesus," I whispered back. I had had my doubts about him in the beginning, but not anymore. My heart beat with love and gratitude with every look at him.

"Why are you troubled?" he asked, reassuring us all. "And why do doubts rise in your minds? Look at my hands and my feet. It is I myself! Touch me and see. A ghost does not have flesh and bones, as you see I have."

How well he knew our thoughts!

He held out his hands where the nail prints showed and lifted one foot, then another, the scars clearly visible. "Do you have anything here to eat?" he asked, while most of us looked on amazed and still not quite sure.

I hurried to the cooking room to get a piece of leftover broiled fish and brought it to him.

As we watched him eat the fish, he said, "This is what I told you while I was still with you. Everything must be fulfilled that is written about me in the law of Moses, the Prophets, and the Psalms."

Then he explained those very prophecies he had fulfilled so that each one of us understood, even the women. Most rabbis did not care if we understood, but Jesus wanted everyone to know him.

"This is what is written: The Messiah will suffer and rise from the dead on the third day, and repentance for the forgiveness of sins will be preached in his name to all nations, beginning at Jerusalem. You are witnesses of these things. I am going to send you what my Father has promised. But stay in the city until you have been clothed with power from on high."

He left us then, and we talked for days about all he had said. Yet Peter, James, John, Thomas, Nathanael, Joseph Justus, and Matthias seemed to struggle to process it all. They left us in Bethany and returned to Capernaum.

"Why are you going back to Galilee when Jesus said he had a new mission for us?" I had asked Joseph the night before they left.

His look held such kindness, and I felt my heart quicken as he took my hand. "Mary."

I swallowed. Would Jesus want us to begin our new mission together? Peter had Adi, after all, and some of the others would surely marry. Very few men and women remained alone.

"Peter wants to go fishing," Joseph said, still holding my hand in both of his. "He is struggling with the way he denied the Lord before his death. James and John and a few of the others agreed to go with him."

"And you also agreed." I looked at our hands, then into his probing dark eyes.

"Yes. I don't think we will stay long. At least, I think most of us are just going to try to convince him to return and do as Jesus has commanded us." He glanced about, but we were alone. He looked at me again. "He feels such guilt, Mary. I can't imagine how he feels."

I nodded, my face heating. I studied the hairs on the backs of his hands.

"When we return," he said, his voice soft and low in my ear, "I would like you to consider becoming my wife."

I drew in a quick breath and looked up. Become his wife?

He smiled. "If you'll have me."

Sudden shyness crept over me. I gently pulled my hand from his and hugged myself as I nodded.

I think he might have shouted for joy except for the fact that we were in Lazarus's home and he was about to leave me to follow Peter to Galilee.

I couldn't help smiling at the memory. Somehow Jesus' resurrection had not only set me free from the fear of losing him but also expanded my heart to include immense love for everyone. Love for each brother and sister, which was how each follower of Jesus felt to me, and for Joseph in a way I never expected to feel in my life. Even Marcus had not made me love him as Joseph had.

As Peter later told us when the men returned to Bethany, Jesus had met them as they fished in Galilee and restored Peter's love and confidence. The rest of the eleven had joined them, and Jesus had given them instructions.

"'All authority in heaven and on earth has been given to me,' Jesus told us," Peter said. "'Therefore, go and make disciples of all nations, baptizing them in the name of the Father and of the Son and of the Holy Spirit, and teaching them to obey everything I have commanded you. And surely I am with you always, to the very end of the age.'"

Just as he'd promised me. He would never leave me. He would be with all of us until the very end of the age.

What joy filled me! How had I ever doubted or worried? How fickle I was.

Please, Lord, don't ever let me doubt you again.

A few days after the men returned from Galilee, Jesus met us in Bethany and led us to the Mount of Olives. His ministry had begun here with a sermon I had not witnessed and would end here as well.

"The Lord bless you and keep you," he quoted from the priestly blessing we knew so well. "The Lord make His face shine on you and be gracious to you. The Lord turn His face toward you and give you peace."

As he finished speaking, his feet rose off the ground and his body lifted into the sky where the clouds enveloped him, and he disappeared from our sight.

We stood watching, unmoving, for no one seemed to know what to do next. Suddenly, two angels stood among us.

"Men of Galilee," they said, "why do you stand here looking into the sky? This same Jesus, who has been taken from you into heaven, will come back in the same way you have seen him go into heaven."

My heart fairly burst with the joy of such news. He would come again! In the same way he left us!

"Yes!" Peter and John said together. The others leapt and danced, and we praised God.

Peter led the way to the temple, where we worshiped until evening. As we returned to Bethany, I realized that I had come full circle. Once I was full of fear and overtaken by the evil one. But Jesus had changed everything. I no longer worried about the future. I had seen my Lord die and come to life again, then ascend to heaven with the promise to return. I had a commission to fulfill for however long my life lasted. And I had the promise of a godly man to walk with me through what was left of this life until I would be with Jesus forever.

Was anything better than that?

Note to the Reader

The story of the life of Mary Magdalene was a complicated one to both research and write. There is much written about her in history that does not fit with Scripture. There is no biblical evidence that she was a prostitute or married Jesus, nor is there truth to any other fantastical commentary that has been attached to her name through the centuries. I hope my account has given you a truer look at her life.

That said, as with all my books, please remember that they are fictional accounts of a historical biblical person. For instance, we know that Mary was delivered of seven demons, but we do not know how she came to be possessed in the first place. We do not know where she acquired her wealth, but Scripture tells us that she was one of several women who supported Jesus' ministry from her means.

Was she ever married? It would have been highly unlikely for a woman of her day to remain single, but it was possible, especially if she was a widow. Since there is no mention of a husband in Scripture, I chose to make her a young widow of means. Whether she married after Jesus' resurrection is also speculation. Joseph Justus, however, was a real disciple of Jesus who was one of two men considered to replace Judas after his betrayal of our Lord.

One other person who deserves greater mention is Salome. In the Bible, she was the wife of Zebedee and mother of James and John. There is speculation, however, that she was also the sister of Mary, the mother of Jesus. I chose not to pursue that possibility, for it would have changed the relationship of James and John to Jesus if they were His cousins. It might have put a very different spin on how we see the Gospels. It just didn't fit the scope of this book.

This book is my first biblical novel set in New Testament times, which meant a lot more research. I still struggle to fully understand the timing of Jesus' death and His last Passover meal with the twelve disciples. Because there is debate on this issue, I took creative license to make things work for the story.

We do not know definitively what year Jesus began His ministry or the timing between each event in His life. I chose to follow the Jewish calendar for dates and seasons and went with my best assumption for the rest.

I also took creative license when trying to mesh four Gospel accounts of Jesus' life into Mary's story. When I put words into Jesus' mouth, I did my best to use either direct quotes from the Gospel accounts or words that He might have said that did not contradict Scripture.

I hope you enjoyed Mary's story and that it gives you a better idea of what she suffered with demon possession and the joy she felt when Jesus set her free.

Free. I wonder how many of us feel that way.

And yet, by the grace of God, we can be. Jesus came to set each one of us free from the power of sin and death. He arose the victor over the grave, and if we know Him, we never have to fear losing Him or the promises He's given to us.

May you know Him and realize all that He came to do for you and for me.

In His Grace,
Jill Eileen Smith

Acknowledgments

When I considered making the switch from writing about women in the Old Testament to writing about those in the New, I never imagined how many questions I would need answers to from people far more knowledgeable than I.

Many thanks go to the following people for their help and insight:

Bill Myers—thank you for your invaluable help in understanding the realm of demon possession and for steering me to your book *Supernatural War* on the subject. Both are much appreciated.

Wayne Stiles of Walking the Bible Lands—thank you for your geographical help with regard to the Jordan River crossing near Bethsaida. I can picture it now.

Glenn Harris, rabbi at Shema Congregation Shema Yisrael—thank you for answering my questions about working on Shabbat.

Paul Mashni, a Jewish believer at my church, and Dennis Kananen, a fellow writer at my church—thank you for helping me understand the timing of the Passover and Jesus' sacrificial death for us.

Pastor Steve Baker of Community Bible Church for connecting me with three of these men—thank you for your support!

Arthur Klassen, one of our dearest friends—thank you for explaining the timing of the Last Supper and putting up with my right-brained struggles to put it all together in my mind!

Thanks again to my fabulous team at Revell. We've seen some changes with this book, but the quality of your help is always top notch! Thanks to Rachel McRae and Jessica English, editors extraordinaire. And to my marketing and publicity teams, particularly Karen Steele and Brianne Dekker, along with the cover design team and everyone else who works so hard to bring a book to life.

Thanks also to my agent and friend, Wendy Lawton, who has been with me from the beginning of my career. This year she, along with our agency president, Janet Grant, worked with a producer for film possibilities for one of my books. Thanks to both of you for always keeping your clients' best interests at heart.

I'm not sure I will ever feel confident in any of my books, and that is always true until my friends Hannah Alexander and Jill Stengl read the manuscript before my editor sees it. Your help and support through the years, not to mention your friendship, mean more than words can say.

Of course, writing would mean nothing without the love of my life, Randy—my husband of forty-seven years as of this writing. Family has always meant so much to me, and I thank God for our sons and their families as well. There is something wonderful about grandchildren.

Most of all, my love and gratitude go to Jesus, my Messiah, who healed Mary Magdalene of her demons. Who is still healing us today of whatever oppresses us. We desperately need a Savior. We need look no further than Jesus.

JILL EILEEN SMITH is the bestselling and award-winning author of the biblical fiction series The Wives of King David, Wives of the Patriarchs, and Daughters of the Promised Land, as well as *The Heart of a King, Star of Persia: Esther's Story, Miriam's Song, The Prince and the Prodigal, Daughter of Eden,* and *The Ark and the Dove: The Story of Noah's Wife*. She is also the author of the nonfiction books *When Life Doesn't Match Your Dreams* and *She Walked Before Us*. Jill lives with her family in southeast Michigan. Learn more at JillEileenSmith.com.

A Note from the Publisher

Dear Reader,

Thank you for selecting a Revell novel! We're so happy to be part of your reading life through this work. Our mission here at Revell is to publish stories that reach the heart. Through friendship, romance, suspense, or a travel back in time, we bring stories that will entertain, inspire, and encourage you. We believe in the power of stories to change our lives and are grateful for the privilege of sharing these stories with you.

We believe in building lasting relationships with readers, and we'd love to get to know you better. If you have any feedback, questions, or just want to chat about your experience reading this book, please email us directly at publisher@revellbooks.com. Your insights are incredibly important to us, and it would be our pleasure to hear how we can better serve you.

We look forward to hearing from you and having the chance to enhance your experience with Revell Books.

The Publishing Team at Revell Books
A Division of Baker Publishing Group
publisher@revellbooks.com

Revell

Meet

Jill Eileen Smith

at **www.JillEileenSmith.com** to learn
interesting facts and read her blog!

Connect with her on

f Jill Eileen Smith

X JillEileenSmith

◎ JillEileenSmith